RISING EMBER

THE EMBER CROWN
A YA DYSTOPIAN FANTASY SERIES

BOOK ONE

SARA WRIGHT

ISBN: 978-1-957947-18-1 (hardback)

ISBN: 978-1-957947-19-8 (paperback)

ISBN: 978-1-957947-13-6 (eBook)

ISBN: 978-1-957947-20-4 (deluxe edition)

1st edition 2025

www.sarawrightbooks.com

To everyone whose odds are not in their favor.

Note From the Author

THANK YOU, DEAR READER, for descending into this thrilling world with me.

I wanted to let you know I did not write this book with the use of A.I. programs. Don't get me wrong, I am all for advanced technology (I am a fan of Star Trek). It's a really great tool, but it lacks the human experience that I think we crave in stories.

To prove to you I am human, here are a few misspelled words. unbelievalble irideceant whielder

And if you didn't receive this book directly from my website, Bookfunnel, or an authorized bookstore, you likely downloaded an illegal copy. Please be a decent human being and inform me, then buy my books legally.

Can't afford to support my creative projects? Don't resort to piracy; join my review team instead.

Thank you for reading!

~Sara Wright

sarawrightbooks.com

Contents

"How do you rid the Earth of humans? Rid the humans of their humanity."

Rick Yancey, The 5th Wave

"Better never means better for everyone. It always means worse for some."

Margaret Atwood, The Handmaid's Tale

"Who controls the past controls the future. Who controls the present controls the past."

George Orwell, 1984

Chapter One
Tomorrow

DIFFERENT DAY, DIFFERENT CHORE, but it's always the same stupid music.

I don't know why my guardian blasts it on repeat in the receiving room every day, especially since it's an old cheerful tune from the time before the planet was decimated. To me, it seems in poor taste to have a fictional orphan girl singing of a better tomorrow in an orphanage located in a backward town in the middle of nowhere. There are no wealthy families coming for us to whisk us away to a better life. If we want out, we have to work for it ourselves.

In this tiny town, everyone seems to be solely focused on how they can exploit each other. Even Ms. Brown, my caretaker of sorts, will do just about anything to manipulate everyone around her, especially her foster kids. She says we owe her for all her past expenses caring for us, which is absurd given her government stipends. Add to that her extensive network within the black market and with wealthy landowners and she should have more than enough to take care of us, but according to her, it never is.

Plunging the brush into the sudsy brown water, I continue cleaning the dark wood floor. My arm, still sore from a fall weeks ago, aches as I scrub, removing the grime tracked in from the rain-soaked roads. Doing my chores is difficult with half my fortune hidden in my coat, but it's safer than locking it in a drawer around here. If I hurry and get this done, I might still have time to meet my friend Luna before I have to study.

The door opens on the other side of the ornate living room, drawing my attention. When I see the girl with pristine blond hair and fair skin stroll inside, my lips squeeze together as I fight to keep from rolling my eyes.

Abby shouldn't be back so early, but here she is giggling with her friends as they take off their rain-soaked cloaks. The last I heard, Ms. Brown has her aiming to swindle a lord, or possibly his son. She was supposed to be gone for an entire month, but it's only been a week. I could have done with a few more days without them around, but now I'll have to work a little harder to stay out of her way.

Before she sees me staring, I lower my gaze, concentrating on my task. Maybe, just maybe, I won't draw her attention today. Maybe I could become invisible to her icy gaze.

When the spiteful girl arrived at the orphanage at seven years old, she made it her mission to pour a bucket of misery all over my head, constantly getting me into trouble. Just a few weeks ago, she pushed me out of a window, furious that I had reached the safe and stolen the necklace before her. It didn't seem to matter that Ms. Brown gave me the thief's assignment and her the grifter one, or that I needed it to pay for my books. Thankfully, I heal fast, or I'd still be confined to my room instead of dealing with an achy arm.

I've never figured out why she hates me so much. Maybe she is just upset her parents died. But everyone who lives here has similar stories, and they don't act like her, bullying everyone around her. At least she knew who her parents were; I'd give just about anything to have that information. Since I was abandoned on the edge of town, the likelihood of me finding out is low. The only clue I have is the silver necklace looped around my neck.

No matter Abby's reasoning, with my future on the line, the last thing I need is another confrontation with her.

The clicking sound of boots approaches me, and I take a deep breath to quell the heat rolling inside me.

"You missed a spot, Clarissa. Or did falling out of the window make you blind?" Abby asks as her pair of mindless hens snickers.

Out of my peripheral vision, I see the mud tracks from their shoes leading from the back door toward me. They didn't clean the muck off like they were supposed to, but I'm not shocked.

Heat courses through my veins, and my hands clench around the brush as the girls file past me. All I want to do is throw it at them for making my job ten times worse, but I stop myself, remembering my agreement with Ms. Brown.

Healer school. Remember the academy. Ms. Brown won't let me go if something happens. Internally, I repeat words to douse the rising tension within me.

"I'll be sure to clean it up." I try to keep the irritation out of my voice while focusing on my task, but I'm not sure how successful I am. My annoyance levels are at their maximum right now. Between my studies and all the "errands" Ms. Brown gives me, I don't have time to clean this floor again.

Abby crouches, her plain pink dress fanning out on the wet floor as she grabs my hand. "Clarissa, I really want to be friends with you, but you're doing it wrong."

The next thing I know, she smashes dirt in my face. Tipping backward in my haste to get away, I knock her into the dirty water bucket as I crash against the coffee table. The glass breaks, shattering into a million pieces, and dread pools in my stomach.

"What's going on in there?" Ms. Brown asks from her office.

As soon as the lanky caretaker enters the parlor, I rise with a concerned frown, willing my rapid heart to slow, as glass pieces fall from my worn ensemble. Thankfully, I'm not bleeding. "I just finished cleaning the floor. They tracked in mud and slipped."

It's a gamble to try to fool a human lie-detector. The thumping sound of my pulse echoes in my ears as I take slow, deliberate breaths. I'm not sure if she'll believe me; the middle-aged woman seems to know everything, but I'm desperate. A broken table could cost me a lot more than an afternoon of cleaning. I eye the basement door across the room while hiding my shaking hands in the folds of my dress.

The mousy-haired woman's steely gaze travels the length of the room. She lingers on the muddy shoe prints in the middle of the floor, tracking directly toward Abby, then at her broken coffee table.

Her nostrils flare like a dragon as the wrinkles around her eyes deepen across her olive skin. "You three, clean this up. Now!"

Abby tries to protest while scrambling to stand but slips, landing face first in the muck. It takes everything in me not to chuckle, because she kind of deserves it after smashing dirt in my face. But the owner of this place hates laughter. It's punishable by long periods in dark, confined places.

"But it's Clarissa's fault," Abby protests after spitting mud out of her mouth. She tidies her loose blond strands before tossing her long braid over her shoulders. Using the wall to brace herself, she stands. "She knocked the bucket over."

Ms. Brown glares at the handprints now marring her carefully picked floral wallpaper. "And I suppose it was Clarissa's fault the mud was tracked in here in the first place? And was it her fault you three can't read?" She points to the yellow caution signs posted at each entrance.

Abby bows her head, shrinking back from Ms. Brown's wrath. Despite her timid posture, her fists clench and her intense gaze fixes on me. Like a viper, she'll wait to strike at the right time. I just hope I'm long gone before she gets a chance.

"Clean it up, now. Since you have a newfound pleasure in creating wall art, you can clean those too. Top to bottom." Ms. Brown almost growls the last sentence. "I have clients coming soon; clean up the glass too, then bring a table in from the backhouse."

"But that's not..." Abby's friends smack her arm, stopping her protest.

"Should I make you clean the basement as well?" Carefully avoiding the mud, she towers over the girls.

Abby shakes her head. "No, My Lady."

They reluctantly take the cleaning supplies from me with a sigh. Their dirty little prank gave Abby's friends more than they bargained for. Maybe they'll learn not to follow her so loyally, but I doubt it.

"Clarissa, follow me." Ms. Brown's face is like stone.

I can't tell if this is going to be good or bad, but I instinctively clench my silver pendant hanging from my necklace. Somehow, the smooth, iridescent surface always soothes the anxiety swelling inside me.

Please don't send me to the basement, I repeat as I follow behind her, my stomach twisting as we near the unassuming door I have nightmares about.

The flowers and vines seem to almost grow on the decorative wallpaper as we approach the door. They're ready to jump out and confine me to the prison below without my caretaker's help. My breath wavers with each step as my anxiety flares, and my grasp around my necklace tightens.

When we pass the basement door, my shoulders ease, but only slightly. Just because my punishment won't send me downstairs doesn't mean it won't be any less awful. A kid in Ms. Brown's charge disappeared once. I'm sure there is a logical explanation for it, but I can't stop the wild ideas roaming around in my head, wondering if I could be next.

"Sit," she says as we enter her lavish office. She pours a cup of coffee as I sit in the plush chair next to her desk. I really shouldn't call what she makes coffee. It's more like dirt mixed with water. The dark liquid smells nothing like the drink at the local cafe.

Ms. Brown sits behind her oversized desk in a chair that makes her somehow appear taller, towering over me like a mountain. She takes a drink of the cigarette-butt-smelling liquid while I bit my lip in disgust. Both thankful and not surprised, she doesn't bother offering me anything. It's not free, anyway. Nothing in this place is. And I can't afford to spend money. I have to save every penny if I'm going to get out of here, and the Medical Apprenticeship Program is expensive.

"So," she says as she sets her cup down. She picks up her digitablet, perusing through whatever files she keeps on the device. The screen casts blue light across her face, making her pale skin appear sickly. It's probably one of the few tech items that works this far away from the capital.

"This came for you." She holds a letter in front of me. From the wax seal with the leaf symbol, I immediately know what it is—my future. I try to grab it from her, but she snatches it back. "No, no, no! All in good time. We have to settle up first."

I roll my eyes as I open my jacket, rummaging through secret pockets. Even with my recent setback, I successfully got every coin and piece of jewelry she requested, except for the one Abby stole from me.

The first bag clinks across the desk as I plop a few more coin bags behind it. Then I open another pocket, dangling a few diamond necklaces in front of her before handing them over. She steeples her fingers in complete silence with pursed lips, just waiting. I let out a huff, pulling my thin skirt up enough to get to my socks. I toss several digicards across the wood surface.

A smirk crosses her lips as she evaluates each item. Every coin is counted, every digicard balance is checked, and every necklace gemstone is closely examined with her loupe. She writes every thought and potential value in a spreadsheet, taking her time.

Of course, she doesn't trust me. I slump in the chair, waiting for her to finish as the minutes drag on. Finishing her calculations, she pauses, then silently gives me the letter.

There aren't many paths open to me that would take me away from this godforsaken place, but the Medical Apprenticeship Program is one of the few apprenticeships that would accept someone like me. I never thought Ms. Brown would approve, so I was shocked when she handed me my first anatomy book. Since that day, almost eight years ago, I've worked hard to read every book on healing available.

I don't have to rip it open because Ms. Brown has already taken the liberty of reading it. Yanking the thin paper out of the envelope, I scan the first few sentences, desperately searching for the words I've dreamed about since I was a small child, my ticket to freedom.

My breath hitches when I find them. "I've been accepted." Despite being in Ms. Brown's presence, I smile. "I got into the program."

"Of course you got in. I made sure of it," she says, glancing at me over the rim of her large mug.

The fluttering feeling in my chest disappears as my heart sinks to the bottom of my stomach. "What did you do?"

"I did what any good mother would do. I bribed them."

Heat boils under my skin. "You're not my mother."

"Oh, Clarissa, I'm hurt." Her face contorts into a pout no one would believe. "You know, I've clothed you, fed you, and lodged you all these years. Which is more than your parents did when they abandoned you in the forest. I even went out of my way to teach you how to read and write, which is not something I do with every kid that passes through these walls. I showed you how to pull your weight in this world—"

"You mean taught me how to steal?"

"Toe-may-toe, toe-mah-toe." She waves her hand around. "You have to learn how the world really works. It's the only way to survive. I'm sorry if teaching you that lesson so young hurt you. But I've done all these things for you, even paying for your extra schooling. Here you are, giving me no gratitude for everything I've done." Grabbing a tissue, she dabs at her eyes, pretending to dry nonexistent tears. "If you keep treating me so poorly, I might have to call the apprenticeship and forfeit your placement."

My fingers claw into the armrests as I try to calm my nerves. "But then you won't get whatever you want from me."

"True." She pats the side of her tawny hair, smoothing the strands back into her tight coils. "But that doesn't mean I can't get something else."

"What do I have to do this time?" My mind races through the possibilities. Whatever the headmistress wants, it can't be good.

Her lanky fingers tap the desk as she stares at me, waiting for me to crack. Finally, she leans forward with the same stony face I can't read, ready to seal my fate. "You will steal a document for me in the town selectman's office."

I blink several times as my brain tries to comprehend her words. "But the last one was just killed; security is going to be too tight."

A huge grin forms on her cheeks, making the pounding of my heart in my ears deafening. "Why don't you grab one of your fire wielding friends to help you?"

My stomach twists at her mention of my Rylari friends. Their very existence is outlawed in the country, the king going so far as calling them "Forbidden" and banning their name from being uttered. It doesn't matter their age; they are rounded up and turned into slaves of the king, destined to become his soldiers in the war.

Luna, my best friend, is one of them. But I keep it a close secret, knowing how vulnerable she'd be if anyone found out she was in town stealing food, clothes and whatever else she could carry. She only sneaks in twice a month, always on the busiest days with a few friends—timing it when the town police are distracted by the local riffraff.

That my guardian is aware of my illegal friendship sends shivers down my spine. How long has she known?

"It can't be done," I say, careful to choose my words. "Not now."

I get up to leave, tucking my acceptance letter in my coat pocket.

"That's disappointing. I'll just have to call the program and let them know you're not accepting."

At her words, I freeze. The stupid song blasts through the speakers, cutting through the silence. I bet my bottom dollar she's about to exploit me.

"In fact, now that you're seventeen, I'll have you start working at the tavern. I'm sure the boys that frequent the establishment will love you, especially with that long raven hair of yours." Despite the cold nature of her threat, her words drip with mirth.

That's the problem with her—you either have to comply with her demands or face punishment. It's an impossible situation that I've endured since someone brought me here as a baby. Even if I escape this place when I turn eighteen in a year, a part of me feels she's going to make it impossible to ever truly leave.

At my hesitation, she repeats her options. "The tavern or your dreams? You're choice, honey."

My jaw tightens. "Do you at least have blueprints of the building?"

She flips the screen toward me, then double taps the picture of the small adobe structure. Hidden within the layers of the picture are several layouts, including secret entrances I never knew existed. I flip through the images, making note of the distance between the selectman's office and the nearest exit, then examine the document she needs. It's hilarious that the man documented his bribes.

"When do I need to get this to you?" I ask as a plan forms in my mind. The only thing missing is guard rotations.

"Tomorrow."

My eyes widen. "What? I need at least a week to prepare."

"That's not possible. I need the document from the office by tomorrow." She sets her mug down. "Don't you usually see your friends today? Use them."

I cross my arms. "It's not like the Forbidden can make someone invisible."

"The White Flames can," she says, as if I could conjure one out of thin air.

From what Luna has told me, that's not a common flame intensity among the Rylari, making them extremely valuable to the king. Of the few fire wielders I've been introduced to, none of them were a White Flame.

"I don't know any."

"Pity. That would have been valuable."

Her words send a chill down my spine. Was she trying to get information about them out of me? Not that it would matter; Luna keeps our conversations to the basics, omitting anything that could be traced back to them.

I know she's about a year younger than me and lives in the Dunes with her family, but I don't know where. And I know how she, and the other Rylari, feel about King Grimrose. Their contempt isn't surprising, though, since he basically tried to massacre them nearly seventeen years ago.

"Well, I'll have to do without them." I shrug, trying and probably failing at being indifferent. "Is there anything else I need to know?"

"The king's men are in the area. They wouldn't be looking for someone like you, but that doesn't mean they wouldn't put you in prison." She turns her attention to her digitablet. "I can't bail you out of the Silver City prisons as easily as here, so don't get caught."

I nod, then head for the door.

"Oh, and make sure you grab enough digicards to pay for that table you broke. I'm not made of money."

Rolling my eyes, I push the door open to leave Ms. Brown's office, thinking about my future. The bright star of hope dims a little as the strings of the horrid woman tighten around my throat.

I can't believe she needs me to break into that office tonight. It's a sloppy move, especially for her. She wouldn't be so concerned unless the document is more incriminating for her than she admitted.

The stupid song continues to play as I pass Abby and her friends scrubbing the floor. Several younger kids are helping them, making the task faster. She glares at me with her narrow, scheming brown eyes. I don't have time for her games, but I know she won't let this go. If I want to escape this life I've been condemned to, I need to get that document for Ms. Brown.

Grabbing my cloak, I step out onto the dirt road that leads to town, closing the door and masking the horrible song that takes up too much space in my head.

Thunder booms in the distance, threatening to pour its acidic rain on me, and I pull my ragged brown cloak tighter. It will be the second storm of the day: a sign that winter is coming. We don't have protection from the poisonous skies here like they do in the cities. One good downpour could make you sick, or worse, burn your skin off.

Sighing, I hurry down the road. If I'm going to stand a chance at pulling this off, I'll need help. And I'll need to get it before the storm lets loose.

Chapter Two
Vigilance

THERE'S A BRAND-NEW SIGN that just went up outside town, a warning for the hybrid Rylari—only pureblood humans are welcome here. It wasn't there yesterday, so I assume the new town selectman put it up. A piece of wood won't stop them from entering, and no one in Paltos cares about the king's decree too much. As long as someone can pay, they will do business with anyone—including criminals.

Walking past the sign, I make my way to the adobe buildings lining either side of the single narrow road. Thick white canvas drapes across carts, protecting the owners and their animals from the elements. The street is bustling with activity, everyone rushing to get their errands done before the next wave of acid rain.

It's cumbersome at times to stop everything for the rain, but it's the best time to pocket some digicards. Maneuvering through the throng, I discreetly dip my fingers into people's bags, taking a few plastic cards and stash them in my secret pockets, only taking from those I know won't miss them: I've been hungry before.

Since that table I smashed was "gifted" by some wealthy lord, I suppose it is inevitable my caretaker will appraise it at double the cost of what it's worth. Other than the crime lords, no one in this town is that rich. If I want to pay it back as fast as possible, I may have to hitch a ride to Silver City to pick their pockets.

"Stupid Abby," I mutter under my breath.

Spotting a few town policemen, I duck behind a cart, careful to avoid splatters from the wheels. Most of them are in Ms. Brown's pockets and will probably look the other way if they notice me, but the others wouldn't hesitate to lock me up. The last thing I want is to have my caretaker bribe my way out of jail; she'd probably charge me triple what it cost, too.

Once I'm at the center of the adobe structures, I veer left into the alley between the cafe and the market. I skirt around the mud-soaked path, sticking carefully to the warm-colored adobe walls before peering around the back.

My heart stops when I see two soldiers clad in black armor, the snake pin visible on their lapels. They're carting away a young boy with red flames flickering from his skin—he's Rylari, not much older than ten.

Tucking myself in the alleyway, I press against the coarse wall. It's daytime, though, so it's not like they couldn't see me if they pass by. But they're not looking for me, anyway. I don't have the special DNA they need. If they find those stolen digicards on me, then I'm in big trouble.

I clutch my necklace as I take deep breaths. The footsteps die down, and I relax against the textured wall.

"His mom is going to be upset."

I flinch as a wild-haired girl with dark brown skin drops from the roof next to me. Her earthen tunic and pants practically camouflage her to our surroundings. Luna, while cautious, has never been subtle with her entrances—at least not around me.

I glare at her for a moment for scaring me, then ask, "Who was that?"

"My friend's younger brother. He didn't listen to me when I told him to hit the market first." She leans against the opposite wall, crossing her arms. The gesture makes her look much older than her sixteen years. "He was adamant about getting a weapon."

"He's a Red Flame then?" I ask. If that kid is a Red Flame, he can send his flames into a weapon of choice, which would be really crazy to see. Too bad he's about to become the king's property.

"Yep. He's been crying to his mother all month to come with us. She finally caved and look at what happened." Luna gestures behind her in the direction the kid was carted off. "I have to find Paytah. Maybe he can get him out of this."

She moves to leave, but I grab her wrist, stopping her. I really hate asking for help, but given the time frame, I don't have much of a choice. "I have to steal something from the town selectman's office."

Luna's gray eyes widen, her eyebrows disappearing under her curly bangs. "Ms. Brown wants you to do this?"

I nod.

"What exactly does she want you to steal?"

Struggling to find the words, I bite my lip, then release a long breath. "The old town selectman was bribed and kept a record of it to use it against others. Naturally, Ms. Brown is part of that ledger."

"And why would you help her? She's done nothing but make your life miserable." She purses her lips.

Carefully extracting the letter from my pocket, I place it in her hands. She couldn't read until I taught her several years ago. Reading and writing gives you options, and most kids in my position would never have learned. Since I basically owe Luna and her friends my life, I thought I'd pay it forward. I stole a few books so she could teach the other Rylari, too.

As she examines it, her brow furrows until she sees the wax seal. Her lips part, eyes darting back and forth between me and the letter. Then the corner of her mouth curves. "You got in. All your hard work paid off?"

"Yes. Next year I'll be living in the city, far away from all of this," I say, gesturing toward the town. When I meet her smiling eyes, a pang stabs my heart. Leaving means I might not see my closest friend anymore. She's the only one I trust in the whole world, but I really can't stay here. I don't want to have a life of crime, at the mercy of people like Ms. Brown, because I crave something more... normal.

"That's fantastic. I'll have to come visit you." She hands back the letter.

Now it's my turn to look shocked. "How would you get into the city? Don't they scan for... you know, your DNA or something?"

Luna chuckles heartily. "If those scanners were that good, the king would never complain about us, or post 'we're not welcome' signs, or throw us in that arena of his."

"Oh!" I guess I've never taken the time to think about the Rylari beyond my own interactions with them. In my mind, they are always scraping by in the desert, coming to the outlying towns for supplies. I've never imagined them traveling to the cities.

"Do you have any plans tonight?" I ask, hoping she'll agree to help.

Her brows furrow as she shakes her head. "You have to steal it tonight?"

I bite my lip. "That and make enough money to pay for the fancy glass table I broke."

"Wait up and start from the beginning. You did what now?"

I sigh, clutching my necklace. Now it's my turn to vent. I launch into a full recounting of everything Ms. Brown has done in the last few weeks, including the incident with Abby this morning.

Over the years, I've told her a few things when I had to, but I didn't want to worry her. Normally, I'd keep it to myself, but I need her to understand why I have to do this. "So, I hate to ask for help, because I know it's dangerous, especially with the king's guard here, but I'm desperate. I can't do this alone."

Her dark tresses flutter as she whistles. "I knew the old lady was corrupt, but I didn't think she was that bad."

"So, you'll help me?"

"You know you have other options, right?" she asks.

"What other options?"

She points to the tree line nearby. "Have you considered running away? You could go to Silver City and disappear. You're seventeen and could easily get away with claiming that you're eighteen."

I shake my head. "She'd just find me; she has people all over the country. Then she'll never let me go to school."

She squeezes my arms. "Clarissa, how do you know she will let you go at all? Are you sure there won't be something else? One more ask? One more blackmail?"

Luna's words are like a punch to the gut as tears well in my eyes. She's right; the manipulation will never stop, probably not even once I'm in the program. But for kids like me, there isn't much of an option. I doubt even traveling to the Southern Islands will get me away from Ms. Brown.

"I have to try," I say, my voice barely audible. There's a long silence as Luna assesses me, her steely gaze boring into me like she can see something inside me I never knew was there. I hold my breath, hoping she'll agree.

She glances at my necklace before her eyes flick back to mine. "Fine, I'll help you."

I open my mouth to thank her, but she shakes her head. "On one condition. Well, two."

Wiping the tears from my eyes, I laugh. "Now you're manipulating me?"

She shrugs. "I don't exactly have the authority to help you without talking to Paytah first. That's my first condition; he has to agree. We were supposed to leave tonight, so I don't know if I can convince him."

It seems reasonable, but I've never met her group's leader before. They call us Glyzul—snake dwellers, I believe—which suits some. Given our contentious history, a part of me wonders if he'd agree to help an ordinary human like me. "And the second condition?"

"You let me and my friends be in charge of this operation. And if things go south, you come with us."

I blink a few times, because she's never offered for me to come with her. It's not like I would survive in the hostile, sandy terrain in the east called the Dunes; it's lethal to humans like me. "But..."

She crosses her arms, looking at me like I've grown two heads. "What exactly is Ms. Brown going to do to you if you don't bring back that document?"

I gulp, thinking of the basement door. Maybe she'd leave me down there forever? Or maybe something worse than her dark dungeon. Even though I can't see it from where I'm standing, I glance toward the tavern. She threatened to send me there if I didn't succeed.

I don't enjoy working with people, let alone in a team. People have a way of disappointing you, or worse, ratting you out like Abby does all the time. But it was Luna's team that saved me, and I know I can trust her. In all the years I've known her, she's never let me down. If Luna has confidence in her crew, then I won't have to worry about incurring Ms. Brown's wrath or her condition to run away.

"Are you sure your friends can do this?" I ask.

"We can take care of ourselves. We are far more skilled than any training you received from Ms. Brown." She lifts her chin with a smile. "Don't worry about us."

When I was about eight, I was naïve enough to enter a building that was on fire, just to steal a few things the owners forgot. The second level caved in, trapping me inside. Luna appeared out of nowhere and snuffed out the flames surrounding me, then her friends carried me out before the whole place exploded. Some of the other structures in the area caught on fire, and those people weren't as lucky as I was. If there had been a healer nearby, some of them might have survived, but most succumbed to their injuries.

From that point on, I read every medical book I could find and even made some medicines for Luna and her friends. I became determined to make a difference with my life, but I won't get to do that if I don't steal that document for my guardian.

Taking a deep breath, I nod. "Okay."

"Good. I'll meet you by the town selectman's office in an hour and let you know the verdict." She turns to leave.

"How did you know I was going there now to do reconnaissance?"

She glances behind her. "It's what happens when you've been friends too long."

I smile as I watch her disappear into the crowd. The king may forbid the Rylari, but they seem decent to me.

A few minutes later, I'm hidden behind a bush, watching the guards outside the ornate two-story adobe building housing the town's records. If it were just the local police, it wouldn't be so bad, but the king's soldiers meander among them. They're more vigilant and difficult to distract. With security this tight, I may just have to forget about sneaking in tonight and go home to face the consequences. Thunder booms overhead, echoing the foreboding in my sinking heart.

I'm doomed.

"Paytah agreed to help."

I suck in a breath as I clutch my chest. "Will you stop sneaking up on me?"

Luna crouches next to me, quietly chuckling. "And miss your reactions? Never. Plus, you're not exactly well hidden."

"No one will pay attention to an orphan crouching behind a thornbush." I point at the awful thing in front of us. "And stealth isn't completely necessary for a surveillance mission."

She points at the trees behind me with a smirk. "Those work too."

"This was closer. It won't matter, anyway. There's no way we're going to get past all those guards." As if to prove my point, a hover truck pulls up with another handful of the king's soldiers. We've had them in town before, but never this many. Possibly, the murder of the last town selectman required further investigation. But bad things happen here all the time—why would they start now? Glancing at Luna, I wonder if they're desperate for more Rylari.

Luna's forehead creases as she watches them. Her jaw ticks as her eyes narrow. I turn my focus on them as well, and my gaze lingers on the taller blond with buggy brown eyes. The way he walks, barking orders at the other soldiers, reminds me of a predator stalking its prey. There's something about him that leaves me cold inside.

"We won't have to worry about them," she says. "My friend is getting your document. Our job is to create a distraction, then run."

"What?" I ask

She tugs me away from the offices, guiding me through the market without saying another word. We're nearly the same height, but I have trouble keeping pace.

When she pulls me into an alleyway, I ask, "What are you doing?"

"Waiting for the signal," she says, peering around the corner.

I open my mouth to continue my line of questions, but the acrid smell of smoke stops me. A plume of puffy white clouds rises from the other side of town.

"Perfect, let's go!" She grabs my hand, pulling me along.

I yank out of her hand. "What is going on? Tell me now, please."

"We're helping you," Luna says, waving her hands at the smoke in the distance as if that explains anything.

"You want us to sneak in right now? In the daylight?"

"We are not sneaking anywhere. I told you; we are the distraction." She tugs me behind her. "Now, come on, we've got to get going."

Luna guides me through the alley to the main road, my heart pounding in my chest. Beside me, Luna grabs a few food items and a new coat from the stalls. I shake my head and follow her lead, swiping a few digicards along the way. I'm no match for her skills as a thief. If she wanted to do this for a living, she could, but like me, she does it more for survival.

We duck into another alleyway, where a masked figure dressed in all black is etching a circle into the wall with flames sparking out of his hands, I freeze. I've only seen the Rylari use their powers a handful of times, but never like that.

"Our plan is working. The guards are noticing something is going on," Luna says beside me, but my gaze is focused on the circle being drawn. The artist sketches something inside the circle when Luna pulls me in the opposite direction.

"Luna, what is going on?" I ask, stepping out of her grasp. "And don't tell me we have to be a distraction."

"The guards are here looking for the rebels. So we're going to give them something to search for."

"You want to pretend to be a rebel?" My eyes widen as I clutch my necklace. "Are you insane? If they catch us..." I gulp, not wanting to even think about what the king would do.

She shrugs. "The plan is already in motion, and it won't work if we're late for our part. Now, let's go lead the guards on a wild chase through town."

Luna darts into the crowd. I glance over my shoulder at the person etching the wall. A fierce dragon is taking shape in the middle, ready to unleash its flame. It's just a drawing, but I can't help the twisting in my stomach.

This is what I get for asking for help.

A part of me wants to just go home empty-handed and face the consequences, but I can't abandon Luna. Against my better judgment, I push through the busy street, no one paying much attention to me as I take a few more digicards.

I spot Luna at a street cart, stuffing a few pieces of fruit in her pocket. She's not being discreet about it either, but so far, guards filtering onto the street aren't paying attention. If this was her plan to distract, it's not working.

Shaking my head, I jog to catch up. *Maybe I could convince her to stop if I promise to leave with her. At least then we can stop this stupid plan.*

She cuts past the tavern as a few drunks stumble out. The smell of cigarettes and cheap beer cause me to wrinkle my nose. I have half a mind to ask Luna to burn it to the ground, but it wouldn't help anything. Ms. Brown and the owner would probably force the workers into something much worse.

Just as I reach Luna, someone yanks me backward into an alleyway. The ground rushes up to meet me as I fall hard, sharp pain shooting through my body. I struggle to fend off my attackers, but one of them swiftly grabs my necklace and disappears into the distance. Heat immediately consumes my body. Scrambling to my feet, I go after them, Luna running with me at my side.

When I round the corner, I come to a stop then nearly run into Abby. Her wicked glare boils my blood. My silver necklace dangles between her fingers. "Looking for this?"

"Give it back," I say, even though I know it's futile. Abby isn't going to give it back. At least not without some incentive.

"No. Finders keepers and all that," she sneers.

Luna laughs. "You're the grifter."

She examines Luna like she's a bug to be dealt with. "And who are you?"

Yellow flames lick Luna's fingertip. "Your worst nightmare."

Before I can stop her, Luna unleashes her powers on Abby and her friends. Throwing fireballs at them, forcing them to dodge her lemon-colored flames. The girls screech in terror as they try to outrun the fire.

My heart hammers in my chest as my pressure builds inside like a volcano about to blow. As entertaining as it is to see her cowering in terror like this, my bully hates fire wielders with a passion. She'll likely run to the very people Luna needs to avoid. If I'm caught helping a Rylari, I can kiss my future goodbye.

"Luna, stop," I say, my voice barely above a whisper. "The guards are nearby."

"Drop the necklace. And I'll stop," she calls to them.

Abby and her friends duck behind a dumpster, throwing daggers in our direction. Despite the flames consuming my friend's body, I tackle her out of the way. We crash to the ground just as a blade whizzes over my head, clattering to the stone behind me. I flex my hands, expecting to find burn marks, but other than feeling hot, my skin is perfectly intact.

"Thanks," she says before scrambling to her feet, launching an even bigger assault on Abby.

"What are you doing?" I ask, while trying to tug her out of the way of another blade.

She just laughs at me. "What does it look like, Clarissa? I'm trying to get your necklace back."

A pang of sadness coils around my rapidly beating heart as I clutch my chest where my pendant rested. Abby has my necklace, the only thing I have from my parents, whoever they were. I can't let her have it, but I can't let Luna get into trouble either.

"Abby, stop this now," I call after her. There's only one way I could end this—give her something more tantalizing. "I was supposed to get documents for Ms. Brown. If you give me my necklace back, I'll let you give them to her."

My nemesis glares at me with a smirk from behind the dumpster, then raises her hands. "Call off your mutant friend."

"Luna, we don't want to pick a fight with her."

She lowers her flames, keeping the bright light contained within her palms. "Throw the necklace over here, and I promise not to burn you."

Abby purses her lips, slowly emerging from her hiding place with her friends right behind her. "Your kind doesn't belong in this world."

"And yet, we exist," Luna replies, completely unfazed by the slight.

My hands shake, and a tingling sensation practically consumes them as I glance between my necklace, Luna, and Abby.

My nightmarish housemate glances at me, dangling my necklace between us. I go to take it, but she pulls it back. "Where are the papers?"

I look toward the town selectman's office. "They're on their way." *I hope.*

Her brows furrow. "You let someone else do your dirty work? That's sloppy, even for you."

"They'll be here any minute," Luna reassures. "Just give back the necklace, and we can take you to the meeting spot."

She laughs. "I'm not stupid, mutant. In fact..."

Abby's friends grab Luna, and she screams, their sudden movements catching her by surprise. My nemesis raises her hand; the metal of her dagger reflects the yellow light emanating from my friend's flames.

A strange calmness washes over me as I watch the dagger, almost in slow motion, career toward my only friend.

Instead of reaching for my daggers, a molten heat surges beneath my skin, erupting from my outstretched hands in a blinding flash of light as I shoot a tremendously bright fireball at Abby. The group of friends scream as they duck, dropping Luna, and the flames smash into the wall of the tavern behind them, catching it on fire.

I'm frozen in place as I watch the tavern burn.

What did I just do?

Chapter Three
Purity Conquers Fire

THE TAVERN IS CONSUMED by bright flames so intense it's melting the metal braces. I've never seen a fire like that, and I don't know what it means. I glance at my hands, flipping them over, trying to make sense of what just happened. Other than a slight tingling sensation, they're fine, no trace of charred flesh or the flames.

"Not the distraction I was planning, but that will work," Luna says, rushing to her feet. She stares at the building. "We have to get you out of here. They're going to come looking for you."

"This can't be happening," I whisper. I'm not sure if I'm happy or sad, but I'm pretty sure from my twisting stomach I'm going to be sick. I'm transfixed by the flames consuming the building, and my body shakes.

"That fire will attract attention." She tries to pull me away, but I can't find the strength to move. "How long do you think it will be before that crazy girl runs to the authorities?"

"I can't leave. The school needs me to fill out paperwork."

She snaps her fingers in front of my eyes, pulling me out of my trance, and I finally look at her. Luna's eyes glow with a yellow tinge as flames flicker around her fingers. Her brows are drawn together as she stares at me like I'm a lost puppy.

She squeezes my shoulder. "Whatever inner turmoil you're going through right now, set it aside, because we need to run. You hear those boots? Those are soldiers coming to take us away. And whether or not you're ready to accept it, you're one of us. There will be no schooling for you."

My breath hitches at her words. "How can I suddenly be one of you? My parents..."

"Rissa, you don't know who your parents were. Maybe you're one of the lost kids. Who knows." She gently shakes me. "I'll help you figure it out, but I can only do that if we're not inside the king's dungeons."

The sound of the screams and chaos come rushing to me in that moment. Boots pound the pavement nearby, thrumming in time with my pulse and getting louder as they draw near. "The soldiers. They can't find us."

"Finally," Luna mutters.

My rapid heartbeat makes it difficult to breathe as I stand, trying to clutch a necklace that isn't there. "Where's my necklace?"

Luna grabs my arm, shoving me toward the tree line, ignoring my question.

I fight her, searching the ground for it. "I can't leave without my necklace."

"You can, and you will." She sprints, dragging me along.

"I need my necklace," I say, pulling out of her grasp.

She's quicker than me, wrapping her arms around my waist and slinging me off my feet. "We don't have time to look for it. Now let's go."

She shoves me toward the forest. I fight her the entire time, but like a shepherd, she keeps me moving forward. Tears form, blurring my vision the farther we go. It's not until I get the first glimpse of those eerie black uniforms that I finally stop fighting her, moving to sprint beside her.

I crash through the vegetation, raising my arms to protect my face. From the sound of the soldier's footsteps, they're not far behind us. I'm not sure we can outrun their massive forms; they're trained for this sort of thing.

Thunder booms above us, the clouds threatening to pour their toxic water on us. For once, I hope they do. Even the Glyzul soldiers, in their protective gear, won't last long in radioactive water.

"Come on. This way." Luna tugs at my arm, veering us toward a rock formation. Although I've lived on this mountain all my life, she knows the best hiding spots.

My legs are burning as we drop into a ravine. The giant boulders make it almost impossible to keep a quick pace, forcing us to climb over and between them. The overgrown vegetation gives us some cover, but if the soldiers follow us in, it will be easy to trap us. It's a gamble, but I don't have time to question Luna's choices.

We weave through the narrow stone walls, pushing leaves out of the way. Thumping sounds alert me to the danger behind us. Our legs propel us ahead as fast as possible. Just as I doubt my friend's plan, she pulls me between two boulders, hiding us in a shallow cavern under some foliage.

She shoves a silver bracelet over my wrist. A cold sensation rushes over me, like someone extinguishing a fire on a winter's night. Luna rummages through her pockets before taking out another one, then firmly puts it on. We wait in silence at the back of the cavern as the soldiers make their way toward our location, their boots creating a sharp crunching sound that echoes against the rocks.

My heart races as the minutes tick by. Left alone with my thoughts, I stare at my hands, wondering what this revelation means for my future. If I really am Rylari, there is no way Ms. Brown will let me stay with her. She might even revoke my application. My stomach twists at the thought. The school wouldn't even accept me if they knew about this. It's for Glyzul only.

Rubbing the ache forming in my chest, my fingers trace the empty area where my little silver necklace used to rest. I thought I closed that door to my past, killing the curiosity of knowing who my parents were. But the only clue I have about them is gone. And now, more than ever, I have a million questions racing through my head.

Are they alive? Were they both Rylari? Or did they give me up because they realized I was a hybrid?

Along with my past, my future is going up in flames too. All that work to get accepted into the Medical Apprenticeship Program was for nothing. Even if I wanted to go back and pretend none of this happened, Abby is probably there telling my guardian about the whole incident. Ms. Brown will never let me come back now.

I hold my midsection as my depressive thoughts consume me. *I'm homeless with nowhere to go.*

As the soldiers stop near our hiding place, my breath hitches. Tilting my head, I listen intently, trying to pinpoint their location.

"They disappeared around here somewhere," a masculine voice says.

"I can't pick them up on the scanners. There must be some kind of interference from the storm," a feminine voice replies.

"We get interference all the time up here," another masculine voice says. "Just look for clues for their direction."

"Maybe they're hiding," the female says.

"Check that pile of rocks out," the first male agrees.

I glance at Luna as a soldier steps dangerously close to our location. She bits her lip as she gazes behind us. There is a narrow opening that leads to freedom, but there's no way I can fit. Nodding toward the opening, I implore her with my eyes to go. Both of us shouldn't suffer the same fate when there's a chance to survive.

When she moves, my heart sinks. I'm going to be alone when they find me, with no idea what they'll do to me. It's the selfish part of me that wants her to stay, but there's no point in us both becoming the king's puppets.

"Hey. I'm over here," Luna's voice echoes through my hiding place.

I whip my head around just in time to watch her small form run away, and ominous-looking soldiers hurry after her. She's drawing them away from me, giving me time to escape. My stomach flutters as I crawl to the front entrance. Before I pull the foliage aside, I listen for any sign that one of them stayed behind. But I hear nothing.

As soon as I'm out of the crawl space, I climb the ravine, careful to check for any sign of the guards before running. It takes me a few minutes before I realize that I'm heading toward Paltos. I slow my pace and just stand in the middle of the forest with nowhere to go. There's nothing for me back there, anyway.

My hands shake as I smooth my long, disheveled hair from my face. I need a plan and a place to hide from the storm, and, ultimately, somewhere to go. The only things in my pockets are a couple of apples and some digicards. That's not going to get me far in the middle of nowhere.

Biting my lip, I search my surroundings. If I'm going to survive, I need to find Luna or the other Rylari. They could be hiding anywhere on this mountain, waiting for their enemies to leave. With a deep breath, I trudge in the opposite direction toward the place I used to meet Luna.

It's a long shot, but it's my best option. At the very least, what's left of the house will keep me out of this storm.

The wind picks up, blasting me with an icy chill that sends goosebumps across my skin. I wrap my jacket tight around me and pick up the pace. Lightning streaks across the sky, casting a reddish glow across the darkening clouds. It won't be much longer before it lets loose, but at least it will hide me from the soldiers lurking in the forest. Not wanting to be caught in the deluge, I run as fast as I can toward the abandoned cabin.

The first drops of rain sizzle across my skin just as I arrive at the dilapidated structure. I stand in the nearby clearing, watching in fascination as my burning flesh heals. A shout catches my attention, and I duck behind a bush. Several hooded figures drag a body among them. They force the man to the ground and tie him to a post, then flames erupt from their hands. When I see the man's face, my breath hitches. They've captured the new town selectman.

"Where is it?" one of the hooded figures asks, holding up a stack of papers.

"As if I'm going to tell one of you matchsticks," the selectman replies, then spits blood from his mouth. "Purity will always conquer fire."

The Rylari, with the red flames dancing in his hand, inches forward, threatening to burn the man. The selectman flinches away, but resolve quickly washes over him as his eyes narrow.

"Tell us where the schematics are now! Or your town will burn with the rest of them," another hooded figure says.

"Go ahead and try." A wide grin spreads across their captive's face.

I turn away when they smack him, his screams echoing across the clearing as they burn him. Squeezing my eyes shut, I rub my temples, trying to quell the headache forming. My pulse thrums in my ears, drowning the sound behind me. I can't believe they're torturing an old man. It doesn't matter that he's corrupt; it just doesn't seem right. There's no way I can ask these people for help.

When I open my eyes, I search my surroundings, hoping to find anything that will help me. A glistening hoverbike nearby catches my attention, and my heart flutters. I've never seen one of these things outside Silver City and have no clue how they managed to get it to work this far out.

If I can get to it, I might make it to the city, then disappear. No one would have to know about the fire, or any of this. Of course, I'll have to figure out a job, but I'll deal with that later. I have enough digicards to get me through the night.

Crouching low, I dash between the bushes, aiming for the bike. When I hop on, I search for the button that turns it on, but it's gone, replaced by a slit in the middle of a round silver disk.

"You won't get far without this."

My breath hitches as I stare at the hooded figure next to me. His glowing white eyes peek from behind the hood, his voice masked by some sort of device. A flat, toothy piece of metal dangles between his fingers.

"It's called a key," he supplies at my bewildered expression. "It comes from the time before Dragons Fall."

My mind races at his words. Technology before the world was destroyed was much more simplistic than what we have now, which means this is like a tumbler lock.

Not waiting for him to say another word, I take the key from him and shove it into the lock. He tries to stop me, but I kick him in the gut, forcing him to the ground. The engine roars under me as I take off into the forest, determined to get as far away from here as possible.

The man behind me yells something, but I don't hear what he says. Once I'm sure no one is following me, I change direction, heading south toward Silver City. It may be stupid to go to a place with technology that scans DNA, especially since I have no clue how to hide it. But since it's the closest city that will have supplies, I don't have much of an option.

My eyebrows pinch together when I realize that I've been going to Silver City for years, but not once did they flag me as Rylari. Either Luna is right, and the scanners aren't as good as the reports say, or maybe this was all an elaborate trick. Maybe I'm not really a fire wielder.

I shake off the thought, continuing my journey. I know what I saw; flames came out of my hands. Why now? Why, after all these years, did these strange powers show up now? It makes little sense. But I don't have time to figure that out; I just need a place to stay. Then I can plan my next move.

When a shrill cry echoes through the forest, I skid to a stop. "Luna," I whisper.

In all the chaos of finding those rebels, or whoever they were, I completely forgot I was searching for her. My stomach twists at my stupidity.

I turn the bike around and listen for any sound to locate her. Instead, I see smoke rising between the trees. Given her abilities, that must be where she is.

Glancing back and forth between the road ahead and my friend, I'm frozen with indecision. Those soldiers are trained fighters. If I try to help her, I could lose my life. But so could she—the only person I call a friend.

With that thought, my decision is clear. To avoid detection, I keep my distance while riding my hoverbike across the rough ground. To have any chance against the soldiers, I need to surprise them, which means staying hidden until I'm ready to strike. As I get off my stolen bike, I retrieved the key; the modified machine powers off. My feet carry me in her direction, leaping over logs and brush like a prized stallion. Luna's cries urge me faster across the forest.

When I see the yellow flames, I stop, assessing the situation. There are three soldiers brandishing weapons against one teenage girl. Sure, that girl is a hybrid with the strength of at least five normal kids her age, but even so, it seems unfair. She lashes them with intense fireballs, keeping them several feet away from her.

I lift my arms toward the closest soldier before I pivot them toward the tree. It would make more sense to hit the person, but I can't stomach the thought of killing someone. I have no clue how to do this, but I have to try. Willing the flame to burst forth, I wiggle my fingers. But nothing happens. I try again, to no avail. With my focus on my hands, I step behind a tree to figure this out when I step on a twig.

The soldier closest to me throws his head back, and we lock eyes through his dark helmet. His jaw ticks, his nostrils flaring, before he trudges toward me. Stumbling, I try to run, clasping at my necklace only to remember it's not there.

"Stop running and you won't be harmed," the soldier says in a tenor voice, still stalking toward me.

My heart pounds as I try to run while trying to activate my powers, but I trip over a log. Forgetting the stupid flames, I pull my daggers out and lob them through the air. The man dodges one and blocks the other with his vambrace. I'm about to throw another one at the only place exposed on his body when a gut-wrenching scream rushes out of Luna.

I can't help it; despite my battle, I steal a glance at her limp form. The other soldiers bind her wrists while injecting something in her neck. Heat simmers under my skin, but nothing comes out as I shake my hands.

"There's no place to run," the soldier calls out to me, snapping me out of my paralysis.

Circling around, I try to get closer to Luna, but the annoying soldier stalks toward me. There's no way I can get out of this without taking him out.

I bend over to pick up a rock, the silver cuff Luna gave me glinting as lighting crackles above. I suck in a breath and rip it off, then turn toward my stalker. Like last time, heat rises, consuming me on the inside, but the flames still won't come.

As he steps toward me, my stomach twists as my panic grows. The boiling heat roars through me in a burst of light. I don't know where the energy comes from. The wall of brilliant, blinding flame tears through the forest, burning everything in its path. My heart pounds as it passes through the soldiers. I should feel bad about hurting them, but I can't let them harm my only friend.

Remembering Luna is in the flames' path, fear clogs my throat. There's no way I can take it back now. I wouldn't know how.

Once the wave passes, I run to her side. Other than being a little groggy from whatever they gave her, she's fine. I go to pick her up when a needle plunges into my neck, and I freeze.

"Grab her," one soldier says just as the clouds release toxic water from the sky.

Whatever they gave me makes me woozy. I fall to the ground next to my friend. A shadow falls over me, my skin stinging from the rain. As I gaze into the same menacing brown eyes I saw earlier, partially hidden by the metal helmet, I face my new reality.

So much for saving my friend. We're both going to be the property of the king. My bright future is no longer possible. I guess the town selectman was right; the purity of blood really conquers fire.

Chapter Four
Cargo

THE PAIN IN MY head surges like lightning.

The substance they gave me in the forest is wreaking havoc on my body. This headache is worse than when Abby pushed me out the window. It doesn't help that I'm restrained, forced to lie on the floor of a dark cage in wet, muddy clothes.

It isn't the first time I've been locked up like this. Ms. Brown imprisoned me frequently, mostly for trivial matters, like taking too long to steal something. Whimpers and panicked breathing from other captives around me makes me think they haven't experienced something like this before.

This is not the basement I fear and fervently avoid. I blink several times, trying to clear my vision. Even when I fully focus my eyes, the bars make it difficult to see—not that there is much to see in the back of a transport. It's just more dark metal and a sliver of a window in my line of sight. The sounds of shuffling feet from time to time tell me soldiers are nearby.

"The little one is awake already," one of them says.

Little one?

I struggle to raise my head to see who is talking, but the pounding in my temples intensifies, and I reconsider. A part of me wishes I was passed out right now.

"She's awake too." The buggy brown-eyed man from earlier stares at me through the bars—his sun-kissed skin, is smudged with dirt. "We should have given them more."

"The colonel hates it when we do that to them, Major. He says..."

"I know what he says, Private." The sharpness in his voice worsens the electricity shooting through my head. "But he's not out here searching for these animals. If I say they need more, you give them more."

"Yes, Major."

The major returns his attention to me. His twitching, narrow eyes give me the feeling that he would take great pleasure in setting me free, only to chase me down for his own amusement. I've seen his type before, especially in the men who frequent the tavern. They're the men I try to avoid at all costs.

"You're old," he says while pressing his face to the bars.

I'm at a loss for words. I've never heard of a seventeen-year-old being referred to as "old" before. Considering he doesn't appear to be much older than me, I can't understand his reasoning.

"How did you escape us all these years?"

Not knowing how to answer his question, I remain silent. If I am to be this man's toy to taunt, I think I'd rather be back at that tavern. At least there I'd have the freedom to kick the boys who irritate me.

"You're a pretty little mutation, though." He reaches through the bars to touch me. Between the chains and the deep ache coursing through my body, I can barely move away from him.

"Leave her alone." Luna's voice is scratchy, but strong, even forceful.

The major huffs, recoiling his hand. "We've been tracking you for a long time, little spark. Your days of crime are over. I'm glad my team finally caught you."

"Go jump in a volcano," she spits out. Her tone makes me smile. That's the spunky little girl I met all those years ago arguing with the selectman's son.

"Insulting your superiors is a serious violation among the king's army." He clicks his stun gun against the metal bars, the piercing sound sending another wave of pain through my head. "Surely you wouldn't want to spend the night hanging from a flagpole, would you?"

Luna remains silent. If she's dealing with the same discomfort as I am, I can understand why she wouldn't try to taunt him further.

"Pity. I was hoping you'd have more stamina, little spark." He moves past my line of sight. "Maybe the boys will give me some entertainment."

"I have the extra doses ready, Major," the private says.

"I'll handle the boys. You give it to the girls."

"Yes, Major." After handing him four syringes, the private bends toward my cage so only I can hear him—his dark hair falls across his forehead. "I'm sorry. I tried to water it down some."

With my hands chained in place, it's fruitless to escape whatever poison he's giving me, but I try anyway.

"Don't worry, this will knock you out again so you don't feel as bad." He pulls on the chain, forcing my arm still. "At least the lieutenant knows how to reverse the side effects. I'll make sure he knows about your situation when we arrive."

He plunges the needle into my upper arm. The effects are immediate, causing the world to spin. My stomach turns with nausea.

His eyebrows pinch together as he watches me. "Strange… that should have knocked you out. You must be more powerful than the major thought."

I grunt in response, because his words make little sense. How could I be so powerful and not know I was a Rylari? At no point in my life did flames ever shoot out of my hands. My head is reeling just thinking about it.

He moves to the next cage. I can barely make out Luna's arm as she struggles. As soon as the medication hits her veins, she's out. Maybe he's right and it doesn't affect me as much as the others.

"It will be better if you just pretend to be knocked out. If the major sees you awake, he might give you a lethal dose," he whispers. "It's only a few more hours until we're in the city."

I clench my jaw, which is basically the only thing I can move. If he really wanted to help, he should let us go. Instead, he's making it harder for us to escape, especially with the major around. If I wasn't so groggy, I'd find the lock pick hidden in the hem of my jacket and get us all out of here. Even if the lock is a fancy electronic one, I'm certain I could crack it.

When the major comes back, I close my eyes, pretending to sleep while my nausea worsens. I would love nothing more than to be in the basement back home. Better than being trapped in a cage at his mercy.

The major stops next to my cage, and the pain in my head thumps in rhythm to the pinging sounds on the bars. I try to keep my breathing even, hoping he won't notice I'm wincing.

"Major, maybe we should go over the route we're taking into Silver City," the private says.

"What's there to go over? We show up, drop off the cargo, and wait for the others. And hope the lieutenant colonel doesn't order us to stay long. Then head back to the capital." He slams his hand on the metal, and I can't help but shudder. "Why is this one twitching?"

"They just fell asleep, sir. Even if they're sedated, they can still feel pain."

He's not entirely wrong.

"I thought they could heal themselves."

"Not all of them can, sir. Between the medication and the power dampening cuffs we use, the healing process is slower. Otherwise, they'd all be awake no matter what we did," the private supplies.

The major grunts, pausing the annoying tune he's been playing on the bars. "I think I'm going to request one of these when we get back to the capital. They're probably the best batch I've seen in a while."

"Of course, sir."

"I'll be in the front if you need me. If they wake up, give them more. I prefer them compliant until I can break them."

I hear a door slide open and shut in the distance. My body relaxes, and I exhale in relief to be away from him.

"Don't let your guard down, Clarissa. We're about to go into a den of snakes," the private says.

How does he know my name?

I don't remember telling anyone. Maybe they overheard Luna yelling my name at some point. Or maybe they have a device that can pick out thoughts, which is horrifying to think about.

To soothe my anxiety, I instinctively go for my necklace, but I'm handcuffed. The only clue to my past is gone anyway, lost on the ground somewhere near the tavern.

My gaze lingers on the sliver of light at the top of the transport, giving my only view of the outside. The dark clouds make it nearly impossible to tell the time.

I wonder what Ms. Brown is going to do when she finds out I'm gone. She's a greedy old lady, so she'll probably be upset that she couldn't cash in on turning me in. There's no way she could try to be compensated for her troubles, because if being a Rylari is forbidden, then housing one could land her in jail. It's a thought that wouldn't make me entirely unhappy, though it means I'm alone, and no one is coming to help me.

How did no one know what I was?

The psychotic major hasn't been back in a while; it's been quiet for some time. The only audible noise comes from the creaking objects as the transport moves across the uneven ground. I dare to keep my eyes open, seeking the line of light coming from the window beside my cage. It's small and barely lets me see anything, but it offers the only distraction from the nausea.

In my solitude, I almost mourn my former life. I was supposed to be preparing to go off to school. I worked for years to achieve that goal, to escape Ms. Brown, but that turned to ashes in one brief moment, and I may not survive.

Flashing lights overhead draw my attention. We're not in the wilderness anymore. Honking hovercars rushing by our transport overwhelm my senses. Silver City is the closest to Paltos and is a dirty mixture of old and new. The rich live and work in the fancy, state-of-the-art, tall metal buildings, while the poor scrape by in the adobe housing on the outskirts. It's definitely not my favorite place.

The transport turns away from the city lights, heading up a steep incline. The only places up the sides of the rocky outcrops are the homes of the elite. I doubt we're going to just anyone's home to stay the night. My bet is that we're heading for the fortress. I've never been inside; that's always been Abby's domain, the place where the elite party while the rest of the city struggles to survive.

The towering modular building overlooking the city is barely visible through the window. Lights flicker on inside the massive building, bringing the fortress to life. It's built like medieval towers from long ago, the places of refuge during a raid, but with metal and glass: the protectiveness of the past with the conveniences of today. This is the closest I've ever been to this luxury building. At one time, I would have liked to explore it, but today I'd prefer to skip the tour.

The transport stops in front of the modern fortress, leaving me with a direct view of the observation deck. The giant, enclosed 360-degree balcony, most likely used for parties, wraps around the building. Someone stands in the window, peering out at us for a moment before turning away. Maybe it's the lord of this province waiting to inspect the king's property.

"I have to give you a stimulant," the private whispers, making me flitch from his sudden reappearance. "The major doesn't want to carry you into the holding cells."

Alarms go off in my head, warning me of the consequences of mixing medication. "But that will—"

He tugs the chains, pulling my arm straight, then plunges the needle into my arm without letting me finish. At the same time, the doors to the back of the transport bang open.

"Wakey, wakey, little beasts. It's time to get inside," the major says while opening the cages. "This lot is a handful; have your guns ready to fire."

"Maybe one of them will run," someone chortles.

"We can only hope," a man replies.

The private moves on to the next cage, and my slowed heartbeat already starts to increase. This is going to be bad. I'm not even a medical student yet, but I know you don't combine those medications. If I weren't one of his victims, I'd hit him over the head for being so stupid.

Major Psycho presses a button on the wall beside me. The chains connecting to the power dampening cuffs around my wrists drop with a sudden clatter. My door swings open before he pulls me out. After spending hours stuck in one position, I can barely stand.

"Move," he says.

"I'm trying," I snap while using the cages to brace my shaky legs.

Instead of helping me, he shoves me forward. "Go faster."

Barely catching myself on the next cage, I take a deep breath, trying to muster some strength to comply with his words before he hurts me. When we get to the edge, I stop, searching for a way to step out safely in my current state. Instead, I'm shoved off the transport. Before I face-plant into the cement, powerful arms wrap around me, holding me in place.

"Are you okay?" the owner of the arms asks.

Pressed against his hard chest, I glance up into piercing green eyes. My heart skips a beat. "I think so."

"Can you stand on your own?" he asks.

A part of me wants to say no, but I nod, it's the only thing I can muster in my current drug-induced state. The world around me seems to warp and twist peculiarly. My savior releases me from his hold but doesn't take his arm away from my waist. From the pips on his collar, he appears to be a lieutenant colonel, but he looks a little young to hold that rank.

"Don't damage the cargo, Major Prescott," he barks at the menacing-looking psycho who threw me off the transport. If I was in a better state of mind, I'd be offended at being called "cargo," but I'm in no shape to argue.

"What am I supposed to do? She was going too slow. It's not like we have all day to wait for them," Major Psycho replies.

"If you don't want them to move so slow, don't drug them." Colonel Green Eyes glances over his shoulder. "Get them to their accommodations."

"Colonel, can I have a word with you?" the private asks, his focus shifting between me and his superior officer, who's keeping me steady.

"Going to tattle on me, Private?" the major asks.

He hesitates, twisting his hands.

The colonel's eyes narrow as his forehead creases. "Major, clean off the transport. I don't want any of the desert radiation leaching in my driveway."

"If we were back at court, you wouldn't be able to tell me what to do, Gabriel."

"But we're not, Ty." He points behind me. "Go, now."

Major Psycho grumbles while closing the doors to the back of the transport.

As soon as he's out of range, Green-Eyes—or I guess his name is Gabriel—stares at me for a moment. "How much did you give them?"

"Three times what I should. I tried to water it down," the private says.

He takes me by the shoulders. "You shouldn't be awake right now, let alone standing."

"I guess I'm more resilient than I look." My voice sounds strange again; it's moving too slow.

"She's... powerful, sir," the private says, shifting his weight. I don't know why he feels uncomfortable; I'm the one being taken to a prison.

"Get Luna upstairs too. Make sure Major Prescott isn't allowed on that floor," he says, before turning his attention to me. "I'll take this one myself."

How does he know my friend's name?

"Is that an order, sir?" the private asks.

"Yes," he replies with a smirk.

The private dashes off somewhere, but I don't pay attention because the world is spinning again and stars are forming in my eyes.

"Come on, let's get you upstairs." The colonel guides me forward, letting me lean on him to stay upright.

I shake my head, which is a bad idea because the world wobbles more. My pulse is throbbing in my ears as the nausea worsens, and I'm almost certain I'm going to throw up. "I can't take stairs."

"There's an elevator."

"Oh! That's nice," I reply. "I've only taken an elevator once. It's a fantastic place to steal stuff."

He laughs at my admission.

"Ms. Brown would not like a military person knowing that," I admit, much to my horror.

"Is Ms. Brown your guardian?" he asks.

"No. Yes. Sort of. She's my employer." My heart is racing way too fast while my breathing becomes shallow. *Why am I talking so much?*

"Did she know about your fire abilities?"

"I doubt it. I only found out about them this morning because someone took my necklace." If only I could tape my mouth shut.

"Do you still have your necklace?" he asks. The steel-enforced glass doors open automatically. I've never seen a door revolve like that before.

"No. It's probably still by the tavern. Do you think we could go look for it?"

He guides me into the lobby. A few steps inside and I'm hit with an intense stabbing pain in my stomach. It intensifies as it radiates across my back. My knees buckle, but Gabriel catches me before I tumble over.

"Get the medic," he yells. My warden is quick on his feet, picking me up off the floor, then ushering me into an empty room. He lays me down on something soft, but the pain doesn't subside. I squeeze my eyes shut because I can't take this agony anymore.

The throbbing ache increases with each breath. This is it, I'm sure of it. I'm about to die. Maybe it's for the best. There's no way I'd survive in this world, anyway.

He unlocks my power dampening cuffs, tossing them to the side. Heat surges through my body. The pain subsides, a little better than before.

"This may hurt," Gabriel says before lifting my shirt.

Something warm lands on my chest, causing my entire body to tremble, as if I'm on the verge of bursting. My cries fill the room, growing louder and more desperate until my voice is completely lost. Maybe I won't become the king's precious cargo after all.

Chapter Five
Shades of Gray

I FEEL LIKE I'VE been run over by a transport.

I don't know what day it is when I wake up, but I'm in a gray room with a wall of windows overlooking the city. The only color comes from the potted plants strategically placed around the room. I start to move to get a better look, but pain pulses through my head. I squeeze my eyes shut and cradle my head, trying to ward off the impending throbbing.

"Moving is probably not a good idea right now."

Slowly, I peel open my eyes. A handsome young man towers over me. Even though a stabbing pain rips through my head, I study him, Ms. Brown taught us how to read people, though I was never as good as Abby. From the creases marring his perfectly chiseled olive-toned face, I think he's concerned. But I don't know him, so I could be wrong.

"Where am I?" My voice doesn't sound like mine. It's scratchy and deeper than normal.

Without a word, Green-Eyes helps me sit up, tucking the pillow be-hind my head. He pulls up a chair beside my bed, then grabs a glass of water and brings it to my lips for me to sip.

I try to take the cup from him, but he shakes his head. "Let me help."

Instead, I glare at him, but he shrugs and lets me take the full weight of the cup. My hands shake, and I spill the water all over me. Before I dump the whole thing on myself, he grasps my hands. I glare at him again.

"If you really want to take a bath, it's right in there." Mr. Green-Eyes points to the door on the opposite side.

Frustrated, I sigh, allowing him to assist me with the water. The cool liquid soothes my aching throat, and all I want to do is consume the entire thing in one gulp.

"Slowly," he says as I take my fill.

Once I rest my head against the upright pillow, he sets the cup down on the table beside my bed. He watches me with an inquisitive gaze, studying me like I'm a puzzle with a missing piece. From his black uniform, I assume the mystery man is my warden. I suppose he's better than the other guy who captured me.

"My name is Gabriel."

Why does that name sound familiar? It's all a blur. The one thing that's crystal clear is the pain. Knife-like agony that surged through my body until I blacked out.

"Clarissa." My voice sounds almost normal. "So, are you going to answer my question?"

He glances out the window. "You're in Silver City. This is the bed-room you're staying in for now."

"Really?" I roll my eyes. "I thought I was at a carnival or something."

"For all I know, you grew up in the Dunes without ever knowing the comforts of a bedroom. There wasn't much time to get that kind of information from you before you passed out last night."

Massaging my temples, I will my mind to stop lagging like a digitablet with a bad connection. The memory of running through a forest and being caged in the back of the transport forms in my mind. Heat creeps up my cheeks when I remember falling into the mystery man's arms.

A slight twitch at the side of his lips is the only sign that he might have noticed my flushing face. "Until you're fully recovered, you'll stay in this room. It's in my father's home, but most people call it the fortress. Do you remember anything?"

Bruises on my wrists capture my attention, my body growing cold. "I was captured, and I am now the king's property."

He winces at my words. "You started a fire in Paltos. My squadron chased you, eventually captured you, and confirmed that you are a Rylari."

It's strange hearing a person of his station use the term Rylari. I thought it was forbidden to even mention what the fire wielders call themselves. But the colonel doesn't seem to have a problem using the proper name.

I rest my arm across my eyes, wanting to block out the daylight. "Why is this happening? I was supposed to be at the apprenticeship program."

"You discovered your powers at the wrong time."

"Way to state the obvious." If the memory of burning the tavern down wasn't seared into my mind, I would think Gabriel was crazy. The fact that I'm in this place is unbelievable. Peeking at him, I ask, "What happens now?"

"Once you're feeling better, we'll start your training here. Eventually, we'll take you to the training center in the capital. That's where the other Forbidden trainees stay."

"Trainee?"

He sits back in his chair with an arched eyebrow. "You may have just found out you're a Rylari, but you can't be this ignorant of the world."

I purse my lips, knowing he's right. Didn't I just make the argument that I wasn't ignorant? It disturbs me he can read me so well, while I can't read him at all. Even though I might not understand fire wielder culture, I am well aware of the training center in the capital. More importantly, I know about what happens on graduation day.

"How long do I have before I die?"

He stands, then moves toward the window. "My job is to make sure you survive graduation day."

I met a soldier like Gabriel once. He was kind, but he just used me to get information about my Rylari friends. It took me a while to figure out he was manipulating me, but once I did, I misled him. After that, I never saw him again. It's a reminder that I have to be careful around Gabriel, too.

"So, are you going to be my handler?" I don't know if I want him to be my handler, but he seems a better option than Ty.

"Those assignments haven't been handed out yet." He crosses his arms as he stares off into the distance. "Complete basic training first. Depending on the trainers' ranks during training and your abilities, a handler would pick you as their lesser after graduation."

My face scrunches at his derogatory word. To call someone "less" is a harsh term that we don't use in my village. To hear it used now is like a shock to the system. I'm not sure if I should get used to it, but given where I'm going and what I'm about to face, that word is going to be used a lot. I set my feelings aside for now. "When is it?"

"When is what?" he asks.

"Graduation day."

"Because of your age, spring."

My stomach suddenly feels queasy. Graduation day typically happens around Dragons Fall, the festival that commemorates the destruction and rebirth of our planet. They rarely graduate new recruits so quickly. "They're only letting me train for seven months?"

"You're not the only one," he grumbles. "The king needs more soldiers in the West. So every Forbidden over fifteen is going into the arena in spring."

"No," I say, throwing off the covers. "I have to find Luna."

As soon as I try to stand, I fall to the floor. My headache comes roaring back to life, leaving me stuck on the ground. Gabriel lifts me off the floor like I weigh nothing, then he sets me back in bed.

"I suggest you avoid walking or any physical exertion until that stuff clears your system." He takes something from the drawer next to my bed. When I see the cylinder, I flinch.

"It's alright," he tries to reassure me. "This will help with the headache."

When I frown, he rolls his eyes. "If I wanted to hurt you, I could have done it already. You're not exactly combat-ready at the moment."

"The last Glyzul soldier I encountered was a little too trigger-happy with your poisons. I want to see the bottle it came from." I extend my hand, waiting for him to comply.

He just stares at me. "Will you be able to understand the words?"

"For the past several years, I've studied medicines and herbs. There are substances that will help and plenty that will make headaches worse. I want to read the ingredients for myself. Is that too much to ask?"

"Interesting." He chuckles as he sets the needle down.

"What's interesting?"

He rummages through the drawer. "Luna didn't mention you studied medicine."

"Luna. You've seen her?"

He takes a small brown glass bottle out, then hands it to me. "I'm overseeing her recovery from this stuff. She's a more compliant patient."

I take the bottle from him, ignoring his dig at my attitude. If the roles were reversed, I'm sure he'd be equally upset being in this position. "Is she okay?"

"Her headache will subside in a day or two. She'll be weak for a while, but she'll be fine."

I read through the label. Everything appears remedial, but then I have to trust this label is accurate. Though Gabriel seems like he wouldn't harm me, I have to remember he's the enemy. "This is just acetaminophen."

"A highly concentrated dose only allowed for extreme cases. Which seems fitting for your condition."

"I am not an extreme case." Pinning him with a glare, I take the needle and inject the pain reliever into my arm.

"Whatever you say, Rissa."

It's a nickname my only friend gave me. I only thought it was a shortened form of my full name, but Luna told me it's because I always rise to help others. It's unsettling hearing it from a stranger.

Setting the tube down, I repeat, "Rissa?"

A knock comes at the door, ending our conversation.

I really don't know what to make of this man. On one hand, he's a soldier in the king's army, my warden. But he's kinder than Ms. Brown ever was. She never tried to make sure I was okay and, half the time, gave us expired medicine that rarely helped.

"Enter." Gabriel rises, pressing his broad, muscular shoulders back like a highly trained guard.

A solider comes in, wearing the full black uniform with a snake symbol on the arm, then salutes. "Colonel. The general is requesting an update on the new recruits, sir."

"Of course he is." Gabriel shakes his head. "Let him know I'll be there in ten minutes."

"Yes, sir." He exits without even casting a glance at me.

"Can you handle your own medicine?" Gabriel asks, pointing to the drawer.

"I'll figure it out."

"Good. Maybe when your headache subsides, I can have you help with the others," he says.

"The others?"

"You weren't the only one Ty overdosed, but you're the first one to recover. Which makes sense if your flame is as intense as the reports indicate." He shakes his head as he heads for the door. "I'll have food sent to your room."

"Thanks," I say.

Before he leaves, he says, "Just know that you're not permitted to move beyond your room without an escort. So don't do something stupid, Rissa."

He doesn't even give me time to respond before exiting the room, leaving me weak and alone in a prison of gray. It could be worse; Abby could be here with me. That's at least some improvement in my new situation. As for the broody Glyzul soldier keeping me prisoner, the jury is still out. He may seem nice, but he's still my warden.

If I try to escape, he'll come for me, maybe even kill me. That's what he's trained to do, right? My body won't let me flee this fortress, anyway. I need to build my strength as quickly as possible; that's my only way to survive. For now, I'll bide my time and wait for the right moment.

Since I activated my flames, my body heals so much faster than it ever did. Even the arm I injured after falling out of the window is better, giving me full range of motion. My childhood makes a little more sense now. Ms. Brown always told me I was a lucky kid for healing so quickly, which, when translated from her warped mind, only meant that the evidence of her abuse disappeared quicker.

It's been two days, trapped in a room in the fortress with nothing to do but exercise. I've made the most of it, coming up with a strength training routine I remember reading in one of my medical books. There is more than enough space for me to jog back and forth, too. This is the only way I'm going to escape—by being at my physical peak.

I pause by the giant window when I spot a vehicle coming up the long drive from the valley below. From the camouflage coloring and snake symbol, I assume it's another military vehicle dropping off more Rylari kids. This is the fifth one I've seen in the past two days.

While I can't make out faces from this high in the tower, I can count bodies. The only soldier I can distinguish is Gabriel. With his messy light brown hair and scruffy face, he looks unlike the other guards. He holds himself differently when he's outside around the king's minions somehow, barking out orders so effortlessly, you'd think he was the king.

As if he can feel me watching him, he glances in my direction, giving me a subtle salute that I'm certain no one else notices. He's spotted me watching every time.

Two kids are shoved out this time, bringing the total to fifteen—that I know of. It's not like I've been out of this room to verify. I've tried multiple times, but Gabriel has guards posted every few feet on this level. He sure is paranoid about us escaping, I'll give him that much. Since I'm actively trying to escape, I can't call him stupid.

With a sigh, I continue back to my training. It's time for push-ups. Sinking down to my knees, I brace my arms while pushing into a plank, then begin. Yesterday, I made it to twenty without getting fatigued. I'm hoping to beat that record today, but I know my body is still recovering from my cardiac arrest. I'd be more worried about having it at seventeen, but if I don't get out of here, my life span might be too short to deal with any consequences later on in life.

After a few minutes of exercises, sweat drips from my forehead, pooling onto the concrete floor.

"You're doing them wrong."

I'm about half ready to throttle the intruder, but I'm not strong enough yet. Instead, I pause and glare at him. I don't know when my warden came into my room. Usually priding myself on being aware of my surroundings, it unnerves me I was so distracted I didn't hear him enter. "No one asked for your opinion."

Gabriel's lips twitch. "It's not really my opinion; it's fact. You can't do push-ups well with your rear-end in the air."

Heat rises to my cheeks as I sit, embarrassed for being called out and self-conscious of his attention on my backside. "What are you doing here?"

He pushes off the wall and settles in front of me, his presence commanding my attention. The sight of his tousled hair falling across his forehead makes me want to tuck it back. "If you're strong enough to do this, you're strong enough to train properly."

"That's it? You, the person I assume is the leader of this operation, came here just to tell me to train?"

"Those are my orders." He shrugs and then stands. "Since you're the only one strong enough, I'll take you to the training facility we have here. It's crude compared to the capital, but it's a start for you."

The Colonel extends his hand to me, but I ignore it, pushing to my feet myself. "I'm perfectly fine training here."

He raises his eyebrows. "You can't train properly in this room, and it won't let you."

"What do you mean 'won't let' me?"

He points to tiny nozzles recessed in the ceiling, which I assume is a sprinkler system. I didn't notice them before, which is unusual for me. In my defense, they are practically camouflaged against the smooth surface.

"Basic physical training isn't enough. If you want to survive the arena, you need to learn how to control your flames," he says.

"You, a Glyzul, are going to teach me how to control my fire ability?" I ask, not understanding how that is even possible.

"There's a reason the general put me in charge of the training facility. I've trained several Rylari kids over the years and helped some of the toughest cases survive. I may have chosen not to take a lesser, but I can help you."

Almost laughing, I say, "That's the funniest thing I've heard all month."

He steps closer to me, invading my space, forcing me to look up at his towering form. My heart thumps in my chest. If he's trying to make me feel uncomfortable, it won't work because I won't let it.

"You're seventeen and have no experience with your fire. Out of all the Rylari we've rounded up, you're going to struggle the most. Even though your flame is powerful, Luna could run circles around you. If you want to die on graduation day, fine, be my guest."

"I'm not..." My voice trails off when Gabriel grabs my wrist, forcing red flames out of my hand. They dance between us, heating the space.

"Red, from a person as powerful as you, is the sign of a beginner." His fingers remain firmly around my wrist.

I stare at the flames, captivated by their presence. There was a time I dreamed of having this power, but now that it's a reality, I wish it never happened. "Maybe this all I'm capable of."

He squeezes my wrist harder, causing the flames to strengthen. I wince, and when I do, the fire in my palm glows brighter. Then it grows hotter, changing to a bright yellow color.

"You're more powerful than you think, Rissa. Use it to your advantage, survive this path." He drops my wrist and my flames disappear, leaving a chill in its wake.

I stare my hand, wondering how to unleash the fire. It's been days since I last used the ability. I started to question whether the whole thing was real or just a product of my imagination. Setting the tavern on fire with this ability was not planned, but it was a bright yellow color, maybe even white, not the hue of a normal flame from nature. Then I used my abilities again in the forest. Everything happened so fast, I struggle to remember the details. Now that I see the power in the daylight, the cynical part of me fades away because the evidence lives inside me.

"How do you know I'm a powerful Rylari?"

"The Rylari may be resilient and heal faster than a full-blooded human, but only a White Flame can heal themselves the way you do. Your body fights against damping cuffs. If you were a Yellow, or even a Red Flame, you wouldn't have been conscious at all during your journey here." He heads toward the door. "Enough questions for now. Let's train so you can stand a chance against the other kids."

Gabriel waits for me in the hallway, standing at ease with his hands behind his back. I flex my fingers, trying to make my palm burn again, but nothing happens, not even a spark.

Given the circumstances, learning how to control these flames wouldn't be such a bad idea. I'd choose a Rylari to train me rather than an over-confident Glyzul military puppet, but I can't change my situation, at least not yet. If I really want to get out of here, I need to gain knowledge, and he's offering me the opportunity. Despite my hesitation, I follow him.

The corridors are not as sterile as I expected. Plants and artwork adorn the walls on one side, while the other side is a row of windows overlooking the rocky desert terrain. It's the nicest prison I've ever seen—at least, nicer than the basement. Each door we pass is guarded by a soldier who salutes Gabriel. I can't imagine it's fun to stand like that all day, but maybe they only do it when their colonel is around.

With each step, I count doors, paces, and turns, making a note of which direction we go. For once, I'm glad to have grown up with Ms. Brown as a guardian. If it wasn't for her, I'd be confused right now. This place is a puzzle and anyone could get lost, but unsurprisingly, the tousled-haired soldier walks with confidence in his childhood home.

Two soldiers stand on either side of the elevator. A small digipad sits on the wall next to the shiny doors. Gabriel places his palm on the device before typing in a code he won't let me see.

Gabriel gestures for me to get onto the elevator first, then enters behind me. He presses the bottom button, indicating the basement. As soon as the doors close and the elevator moves, he leans against the railing and his shoulders relax.

"It's exhausting being a soldier, isn't it?" I ask.

"Only when I am here. It's easier in the capital."

Before I can question him further, the doors open to reveal a vast gym filled with strength training equipment, cardio machines, and fire pits. In the center is a small platform, ringed by flames. The heat of the room envelops me as we move farther in. I've never seen something like this before, but then I've been surrounded by Glyzul up until now, who'd have no need for something like this. A military commander who trains Rylari for a living certainly would need a war room to train his soldiers. And now I'm his next project.

Chapter Six
Into the Flames

I FIND MYSELF IN a strange new reality.

Rows of weights, their metallic surfaces gleaming faintly, line the walls of the basement, interspersed with curious-looking contraptions designed to aid in calisthenics. The assortment creates a cluttered but functional space. Enormous glass walls in the corners of the rectangular room separate the firepits.

"We'll start in a fireroom." Gabriel heads toward the flickering red light in the corner, casting dancing reflections on the surrounding surfaces. The flames sit on a slick-looking square pad. There isn't a visible heat source; I'm not sure how it works.

"What do I do?" The heat radiating from the contraption envelopes me the minute we pass the pivoting glass door.

He stops in front of the smaller flame sitting on a square pad. "To start, walk through it."

I shake my head. "I can't walk through fire."

"All Rylari can pass through a low-level flame like this without it affecting them, even the toddlers."

"It will burn my clothes. And I'm not about to do something stupid just because you tell me to."

He rolls his eyes, then shoves me in.

A scream rips from my throat as I stumble into the blaze, the flames licking at my clothes. I'm surrounded by dancing red flames, a fiery inferno that spikes my core temperature; I can feel the heat intensifying with every breath. My heart hammers against my ribs, a frantic drumbeat accompanying the tendrils of panic that claw their way through me. I hurl myself from the platform, colliding painfully with an unseen wall. My impact sends a wave of shimmering distortion through the force field; the light fractures for a second before disappearing.

I bang on it, desperately trying to escape the certain death that's coming for me. "Let me out!"

Gabriel stands in front of me with that calm, unfazed demeanor that irritates me. "I think you're fine where you are."

"You're killing me," I scream, practically crawling up the wall as I continue my desperate search for an away out.

"Clarissa, you're standing in the flames."

"Because you pushed me into them."

"But you're not burning."

I glance at my feet. The blaze reaches halfway up my body. The standard issue uniform they gave me remains untouched. My mind races to reconcile my knowledge of flames with what I'm witnessing.

Tentatively, I touch the fire with my exposed hands. Instead of burning me, the red light dances across my fingers. When I pull my hand away, the crackling light sticks to me like they've been longing for me. I stare at my burning appendages. Instead of inflicting pain, the flames covered me with a pleasant light tingling.

"Do you understand now?" Gabriel asks.

"I think so."

"There are four classes of flames."

"Luna said there were five." I close my palm, extinguishing the fire. It's strange not having the flame with me anymore, almost feeling like I lost a friend.

"Officially, the Artijan government only recognizes four flame classes."

I focus my full attention on Gabriel. Whenever someone uses the word "official," there's always a secret to learn. "And unofficially, what's the truth?"

"There have been no records of a Blue Flame in at least a century. It's a genetic anomaly the current and former government haven't been able to figure out." With a sigh, he crosses his arms, the fabric of his black uniform stretching across his chest. "But the Rylari hope for one to rise."

"Why? What would it do for them?"

"Hope is a powerful force, capable of motivating people even in the direst circumstances."

There've been very few times in my life when I've truly felt hopeful. It was an incredible experience that made me believe I was invincible, like anything was possible. Then the bubble would burst, and I'd fall from the lofty heights hope had carried me to.

For years, I hoped I'd get into that healers program, studying every free minute I had, because I was sure it would get me out of that town. I didn't want to be a part of the corruption; I just wanted to help people. It was within my grasp until I discovered this stupid power. The fall has been a harsh, sickening drop into a cold, unforgiving reality. Now, I find myself a prisoner in a hopeless situation where instead of helping, I'll be hurting.

We're teenagers—we shouldn't be in the military, let alone forced into servitude. But until I can master this power, I will be useless, like I was in the forest. Still, every cage has an exit. Maybe there is a way to get out of this nightmare, but until I can form a plan, I have to do everything I can to survive long enough to get me and Luna out of this.

"You were saying there are four flames classes?"

He presses a button on his wrist, and the force field drops. "Yes. When the flame gets too intense, step off."

"You're going to make the flames hotter?"

"It's the only way to know how far to go. I don't want to push you past your tolerance."

I fold my arms. "And yet you push poor, innocent young girls into a giant firepit."

"It was for your own good." He presses another button, and the surrounding flames slowly change from red to orange. "Anything?"

"They feel fine to me," I say, not acknowledging the jitteriness that's making me flinch. My mind is still not convinced.

"Good." With the press of another button, the flames intensify to yellow.

Beads of sweat form on my skin. This flame doesn't feel as friendly as the red and orange. They're a little more aloof, like they want me to come to them. Still, it's not too hot.

Gabriel intensifies it more, the flames losing their color. The heat is so strong I feel like I'm in a furnace. I shift a little, willing myself to not run away.

He pushes another button, and I half expect them to change to pure white, but the flames turn off instead. "That's enough for today."

"So what's the verdict? Am I as powerful as they think I am?"

He helps me off the platform. "It's still too early to tell."

"The flames were yellow. Does that mean I'm a Yellow Flame?" Knowing my flame class feels important, like a rite of passage or something.

"It's too early to tell."

I roll my eyes. "But you said earlier that I'm probably a White Flame. Why were the flames yellow?"

He chuckles. "The fire world isn't as black and white as you think. Even within a flame class, there are a variety of intensities. Since you haven't trained in the flames and have had them suppressed your entire life, I don't want to push you beyond your capabilities."

"What happens if you do?"

His lips thin. "You explode."

My enthusiasm disappears. No one told me about the consequences of pushing your flame too far. "Explode?"

"Yes, explode, which is why I want you to take this part slow." He guides me to another rectangular firepit. "Let's do something that's easy for most Rylari."

"Have you seen someone... um, explode?" It's a horrible question and I don't know why I'm even asking.

His features darken. "A few. It's not something I ever wish to see again."

This world is getting stranger and darker the longer I'm in it. Luna told me bits and pieces over the years, even talking about her struggles for food and clothing. Since I was in a similar situation, we bonded and became friends. But she never really talked in too much detail about her abilities or the dangers of being powerful. Maybe it's because she thought I was a Glyzul.

He points at the line of fire on the floor. "Extinguish it."

"I don't know how." It's strange how my powers come and go—inconvenient, too.

"Then it's a good thing I'm about to teach you." He steps closer to me, reaching toward the flames as if he has the power to control them. "Imagine the flames as an extension of you, a part of your body. They're there for you to command. "

I laugh because he looks like he's in one of the superhero comics from before Dragons Fall. The world seems different from the time before those metal beasts fell. "You look ridiculous."

He completely ignores my comment, grabbing my arm and extending it toward the flame. "Your goal is to learn this to survive. Fewer comments and more action, please."

I let out a breath as I focus on the flames, imagining they're just another part of me, but nothing happens. Concentrating harder, I stare into them until my eyes glaze over, but still, I feel nothing. Gabriel's presence looms over me as he inches closer, close enough for his breath to tickle my neck, causing goosebumps to rise all over my body.

"What makes you angry, Rissa?" his voice is soft, almost soothing. "Don't say it, just think about it."

Picturing Ms. Brown, I think of all the times she exploited me and the other kids. The time spent in the basement, the torture, and all the contracts form in my mind until all I want to do is burn the place down. Heat rises in my body as my pulse pounds harder, and I clench my fists.

"Good job." Gabriel steps away from me, leaving me cold.

The floor is bare. The dancing orange flame vanished, replaced by a faint haze of smoke that rises silently, carrying the faint smell of embers. I don't know how it happened, but a goofy, uncontrollable smile spreads across my face at the victory.

"Do that again, but improve the speed." He pushes a button on the wall, igniting the flames again.

I nod, extending my hand, picturing every time I've been wronged in life. The fire goes out again.

"Good, but faster."

"How fast do I have to be?" I ask.

"A two-year-old is faster than that," a tenor voice says from somewhere behind me. "Why is she getting special treatment?"

The major stands in front of Gabriel with his chest puffed out, like he wants a reason to shove him into the fire. His intense, narrow eyes make him more menacing than when he captured me and Luna.

Gabriel either doesn't notice or doesn't care. He's at ease, as if the major is just a speck of dust on his uniform. "She's the first one to recover from the drug overdose."

"Then maybe I should escort her to the capital myself while you heal the others," he says, yanking my arm and causing me to stumble. Yellow flames erupt across my skin, forcing him to let me go. "You little..." He raises his hand to slap me, but Gabriel steps between us, stopping him.

"You should know better than to touch a Rylari while they're training, major. That's a rookie mistake," Gabriel says, shoving him away from me.

His eyes dart between us. "I'm going to report her to my father."

"Go ahead," Gabriel says. "I've already talked to him about her case at length. He would be thrilled to know she can call upon her flames when she feels threatened."

With a twitching eye, the major just stares at him. I slowly inch away from the two, because usually, when young men act like this, it leads to a confrontation. Living in the orphanage, I've seen my fair share of brawls.

These are two highly trained soldiers. If they fight, I can only imagine the damage they'd do to me if I'm caught in the middle.

"Just wait until we get back to the capital," the major replies.

"We won't be at court, Ty. You can't use your title at the Forbidden Training Center just to get your way."

The major gets in Gabriel's face. "But we will be after the arena."

"I can't wait," Gabriel says. "Go back to your post."

Saying nothing, the major walks out of the training room. I don't know why that man has a problem with me, but I plan to stay as far away from him as possible.

"Why does he hate you so much?" I ask once the major leaves.

Gabriel brushes his hair back. "Ty wanted my job, but his father picked me instead."

"Who is his father?"

"General Richard Prescott."

"Who's that?"

His eyebrows shoot up so high, I think they might jump off. "Seriously, you don't know General Prescott, the leader of the Artijan army?"

I shake my head. "Our country's politics isn't something that I had time to study."

"Right. I should get you a book." Shoving his hand through his hair, he blows out a breath. "He's the head of the Artijan army and the king's right-hand man. Nothing in the army or the country happens without going through him first."

"Is he the one with the enormous mole near his ear?" I ask, remembering the way Luna describes people she's seen during her travels.

"That's the one," Gabriel says while staring into the flames. "Ty can't stand that I was promoted over him."

"General mole-a-lot." I smirk to myself, imagining the description Luna has given me.

"Huh?"

"It's what Luna called him." I shrug, wishing I could talk to her right now.

Gabriel laughs, pinching his nose. "Of course Luna would call him that."

"By the way you talk about my friend, it sounds like you know her."

He shakes his head. "I haven't met her before, but she has a reputation for getting into trouble. The Forbidden Task Force has been tracking her for some time. I'm just glad she was caught here and not somewhere else. They probably would have killed her in another province."

"Little Luna?"

Smiling, he says, "Little Luna is a Yellow Flame Rylari who, just by crossing the border from the Dunes, commits a crime."

"And that's dumb."

"I don't disagree with you, but it is the law," he replies.

I think about the things the major said on the transport, about how he'd been after Luna for a while. It makes me wonder how much I don't know about her. Can you ever truly know someone? But one thing is certain: the major doesn't like her or Gabriel. "Why is Ty so worried about getting back to court?"

He frowns as the temperature rises from the firepits. "At court, he outranks me."

Shaking my head, I admit, "I don't understand. How does he outrank you?"

"The king doesn't have an heir. It seems unlikely he's going to have one." His face contorts as if speaking the words is painful. "He appointed Ty as the presumptive ruler, should something happen to him."

"The major is the crown prince?" My jaw drops to the floor.

"Steward. He's the crown steward," he corrects me.

A shiver runs down my spine as I think about him being in charge. "Whatever. It's basically the same thing."

Gabriel just grunts in response. I can understand why he wouldn't want that guy in charge. He's ticking off all my red flags, and I've only been in his presence for a few hours. Things are already bad with the current king. With people going hungry, a war in the west, and the oppression against the Rylari, I can't imagine what Artijan would look like with Ty in charge of our country. And I don't want to.

"Come on, let's get back to training," Gabriel says, pulling me out of my musings.

The future just keeps on looking worse and worse.

Training is more exhausting than I imagined.

All I want to do is sit in the shower for a few hours to appease my aching muscles. Or, if I knew how to swim, a pool might be nice. Using my powers is a lot more complicated than I thought. I don't know what I was expecting, but this wasn't it. It's frustrating training with them; I'm not picking anything up.

Whatever Gabriel's instructions were, I did the opposite. Instead of snuffing out the fire, I intensified it. Then I struggled to snuff it out when he asked. He said I've improved, but I don't feel like that's true. I had it at the beginning, following his instructions exactly, then nothing. It might be Major Psycho's visit that bothered me, like the colonel thinks. Or maybe it was just beginner's luck or some silly thing like that.

Stepping onto the elevator, I can't wait to get to my room. I never knew using fire like this would cause a physical reaction. Overuse can drain you and make you sore like regular physical exercise. I wanted to be a healer all my life, but not once did I read about this Rylari peculiarity in any of my medical journals. If I had, it would have stuck in my brain. I always thought the fire wielders were invincible, but I guess I was wrong.

My prison feels more like I'm a guest in a swanky hotel. It seems nothing about this experience is what I expected.

"You won't see Ty on your floor, so you don't have to worry about him," Gabriel says. Though he's relaxed, his stance is still rigid, like he's on guard for an attack. I wonder whether he ever feels at ease.

"Doesn't that put the guards on the floor at risk of disobeying a superior officer?" I ask, studying the subtle twitches in his jawline.

"The guards on your floor are loyal to my father and, by extension, me," he replies. "They're not on the king's payroll."

I take a minute to process his words, because I've never heard of anyone having their own private military personnel.

He must see the surprise on my face because he answers my internal question. "My father is the lord of this province. Since our territory sits on the eastern border, King Grimrose allows us to patrol with our own private force. He's been sending us a few Forbidden to help find border crossers."

"Wait. You're Lord Caldera's son?"

"That's what he tells me."

The doors open, preventing me from asking any further questions. The guards may be on his payroll, but I doubt they would approve of our conversation. Even though he's my warden, I don't want him to get in trouble, son of the lord or not. I'd rather have him in charge than Major Psycho. We head down the hallway, but instead of continuing straight to my room, Gabriel guides me into another corridor. There are no guards here, which is strange. Most of them seem to be gathered around the elevator and in front of my room.

He opens a door and invites me through. The room is like mine, but with fewer windows. What captures my attention is a familiar person lying in the bed.

"Luna," I say, forgetting my sore muscles, and I run to her side.

She sits up, smiling, before embracing me. We stay like that for a while before we pull apart. Her face is more sunken than the last time I saw her, but other than the ashen skin, she looks fine.

"So, how was the training?" she asks. "Did my girl pass?"

I glance between Gabriel and Luna, not understanding what they're talking about.

"She exceeded expectations." My warden comes closer, taking a seat on the other side of the bed. "Luna is still healing from the effects of the sedative and stimulant combination. She had a similar cardiac event like you, but doesn't have the internal healing capabilities. I've had some Rylari healers up here, but it hasn't been as effective as I hoped."

"What medicines have you given her?" I ask, my mind searching through the millions of texts I read recently. I know there is a medicine that can help, but if it hasn't worked, it won't work now.

Gabriel points to the drawer next to me. "The bottles are in there."

I sift through them, careful to read each label. "No oxymorphone?"

"Oxy what?"

"You never brought in real healers?" I ask.

He bows his head. "Most Glyzul healers refuse to work on the Forbidden."

I purse my lips as I think about his choice of words. The more I'm around this strange soldier, the more complex he grows. "Why do you switch your terms?"

"What switch?"

"Sometimes you call fire wielders 'Rylari' and other times you call them 'Forbidden.' Why do you do that?"

He laughs while rubbing the back of his neck. "It's probably just a habit. I don't have a problem with calling you Rylari, but the king does. All military personnel are required to say Forbidden, but we're a little more relaxed here."

"I see." It's another thing to look forward to when we reach the capital. "As for Luna, if you haven't given oxymorphone, it's probably a matter for IV fluids at this point."

"Is that what's needed for cases like this?" Gabriel asks.

"Generally, yes, but I'm not a doctor." The painful thought stabs me in my already delicate heart. I'd be going to the capital for a different reason right now, ready to become the healer I always wanted.

"You're the best one we've got," Luna says, clasping my hand. "Do you know how to make that stuff?"

"It's a delicate process, but I'd need poppy seeds and a bunch of other stuff."

Gabriel grabs a pen and paper from the desk, then hands them to me. "Write down what you need, and I'll see if I can get it."

"You actually want me to make the medicine?" I ask.

"Clarissa, there are other Rylari here who are worse than me," Luna says, squeezing my hand tighter. "They need something to help."

"She's not wrong. Besides you, we only have one White Flame and two Yellow Flames in this entire province helping," Gabriel adds. "One of those Yellow Flames is currently sick in bed."

"You want me to heal Luna so she can help the others?" I ask.

"It's that or I unleash your untrained flames on them."

Luna perks up, her eyes widening. "So she's a White Flame?"

"We didn't get that far in training yet, but I'm pretty sure," Gabriel confirms.

"Why is that so amazing?" I ask. White Flames are rare, but I can't imagine that it's so rare to warrant this much excitement.

Luna laughs, but then is thrown into a fit of coughing. "I forget how much you don't know. There is talk among the Rylari that we're due for a Blue Flame, but none have been found yet."

"What does that have to do with me?" I ask.

"You're the first unknown White Flame we've found since..." Luna stops herself then glances at the colonel. "Let's just say it's been a while."

"Remember how I said you could explode if you push yourself too hard too fast?" Gabriel asks.

I nod, recalling his advice from earlier.

"Blue Flames can only be cultivated from a White Flame."

"What do you mean 'cultivated'?" Sitting back against the headrest, I stare at him.

"Just like learning a musical instrument, you start with basics like we did today. Most beginners are on a level playing field at that point. But those with natural basic abilities and those who practice become stars of their craft." He leans forward, resting his arms on his knees, looking almost lost in thought. "It's the same with your fire abilities. You may have higher heat potential than most, but without practice, you'll never find out your true flame."

"It would be amazing if you were," Luna says.

"And also life threatening," Gabriel adds. He studies me for a moment. "There are many people in this world who would love to exploit a powerful Rylari like you. Don't let anyone know how powerful you are, Rissa. If you do, you may live to regret it."

His ominous words send shivers down my spine. I hope I'm not a Blue Flame because I don't want to be anyone's savior. I need to be patient and wait until Luna's stronger. If I can just survive this training and get past the arena, maybe I could find a way for Luna and me to escape the king's grasp. The war front is in the wilderness, and there are a lot of places to hide there. I just hope I don't have to wait long.

Chapter Seven
Uncertain

Gabriel provides me with a shadow.

The honorable lord of the tower is too smart for his own good. I didn't expect him to trust me with my medical duties completely, but neither did I expect to have a babysitter. Now, everywhere I go, my shadow, Zane, follows me.

It could be worse, he could have assigned Major Psycho to watch me, but I doubt he'd do that. The fact that those two don't get along is fine by me. And at least when I need to go to another floor, I have protection from the major, but it's sad it even has to be that way.

My world isn't so bad, being locked in the fortress tower. It's far better here than the basement back home. I shudder every time I think about the beatings I endured from Ms. Brown. They were always for stupid things, like complaining that I didn't want to steal from a family that had barely enough to eat.

"Do you need anything, Clarissa?" my shadow asks. The lieutenant is so silent, I forget he's there sometimes. His stealth skills are beyond anything I've ever seen. Maybe he'll teach me his secret.

"No, Zane. It's nothing you can help me with." I let out a breath before continuing through the corridors. The sleek gray has grown on me these past few weeks, especially the areas filled with sunlight: my only connection to the outside world.

As far as I can tell, we're in the highest section of the fortress on the eastern side, overlooking the city. I enjoy the view and getting to know some of the other Rylari, like Bobby. He's only seven, but his imagination is wild. The older captives are less talkative, staring at me like they're awestruck or something.

In some ways, it's the life I was hoping for, healing the sick. It just has a few more guards and a lot less freedom than I imagined. And the training Gabriel has me go through is rigorous.

At least three times a day, I train physically: sit-ups, push-ups, and squats, more if I'm not working on my flames or healing one of the other Forbidden. The line between freedom and captivity is blurred, especially since the guards fetch me whatever I want. If my shadow wasn't always a few steps behind me, you'd think I was just a part of the staff.

"I bet you I could help you with your problems," he replies.

Pausing in front of a giant fern far away from the other guards, I cross my arms, ready to face the lieutenant. "Will you let me and the others escape? Because being a prisoner here is my problem."

"I think you already know the answer." He smirks, sharp eyes studying me, his uniform nearly vanishing against his dark brown skin. "Trust me, you don't want to go downstairs without an escort. Specifically, you'll want to go with Gabriel lower than the top four floors."

"Why?"

He shifts uncomfortably, then glances out the window. Following his gaze, I see Ty and some others shooting objects with their guns, but they're not the electrical kind I'm used to seeing. They have live ammunition. I thought those types of guns were banned within city limits, saved for areas with extreme radiation.

"While you're here, Lord Caldera and, by extension, his son, have jurisdiction over you."

"What about Lady Calera? Does she have jurisdiction over me too?" As soon as I say it, I realize I've never heard anyone talking about our provincial leader's wife.

Zane ignores my question. "Just know that the minute you walk out the door, you enter the king's jurisdiction. The highest-ranking officer in this area willing to represent his majesty in this manner is your 'Major Psycho.'"

"I thought the colonel outranks him?"

"He does, but they are at odds over transporting everyone to the capital. After appealing to the king, the compromise is, if one of you escapes, you're well enough to be transported to Segura."

Rolling my eyes, I reply, "A prison is a prison, no matter what it looks like."

"I don't disagree with you, Rissa."

"Great! Now you're calling me by that name?"

He shrugs. "It's what Luna calls you, and so does the colonel."

"That doesn't mean I give you permission."

"So Gabriel has permission?"

Groaning, I head to the supply room to drop off my medical bag, then Zane and I head toward the only door to freedom: the elevator. He presses the lowest number on the keypad. The basement is the only other floor I'm allowed to go—with an escort, of course.

At least I won't be alone during training today. Some of the Yellow Flames have healed, including Luna, which means I get to see them use their fire. The anticipation of seeing the others use their abilities makes my hands tremble: a nervous excitement tempered only by the unfortunate situation.

When the doors open, the heat that rolls out feels more welcoming than the first time. I've embraced the heat and even welcomed it. I honestly don't know how I functioned before under the cold guise of a regular human.

My fellow Rylari stop what they're doing when I enter, staring again as if I'm important. Clenching my fists, I enter the dark room, searching for Luna.

"Why can't they see that I'm a nobody? I'm no savior, just an orphan, nothing more. I'm not a fable."

Zane smiles at me, shadowing my footsteps. "Blue Flames aren't a fable: they actually exist, Clarissa. Any time the Forbidden find a White Flame, they get hopeful."

I get why the Rylari are excited about someone with Blue Flames, but I don't understand their obsession. One person can't take on an entire country, no matter how skilled they are, especially if the people in charge are trained warriors.

Searching the closest firepits, I say, "Putting hope in me will just leave them disappointed. I can barely snuff out a fire."

He shrugs. "Sometimes people need hope, and that's more powerful than having the real thing. Besides, how do you know you're not a Blue Flame?"

"I can barely reach the White Flame, let alone strive for something unobtainable." I shake my head, then check the next walled off room.

"You're only seventeen and have just started practicing with your abilities. Most of the kids here have been practicing with their flames their whole lives." A yellow fireball zooms to the other side of the wall, incinerating its target. It came from a little kid about half my age, almost like he timed it to prove Zane's point. "None of you reach your full potential until you're fully grown and have had years of practice."

Crossing my arms, I watch the little kid command his flames a few more times. I feel so inadequate watching him. "They shouldn't put faith in me. I can't even control my fire yet. They'd do better to unite behind someone stronger if they want out of this situation."

"The arena is going to push you to your maximum flame, whether or not you're ready. If you don't have faith in yourself, who will?"

I study my shadow. "For a guard who's supposed to hate me, you sure speak like you care for the Rylari."

He squares his broad shoulders. "There was a time when my people were enslaved. I think I can empathize a little."

"Then why do you work for the oppressors?"

"Because changing people's minds takes time." He nods toward the fire room on the opposite side. "Now are you going to visit Luna today or not?"

He's got a point; it's normally a slow process. From the few cons I've run for Ms. Brown, I've learned it always depends on the change. It's easy to convince someone who's ready to listen, but the stubborn ones hold on to their values like their lives depend on it. Each side has a different trigger point to push them the way you need them to go. It's the people in the middle my former caretaker told me to avoid: too unpredictable to bother with.

"Whatever you say, Shadow."

"Shadow?" he asks.

"I thought we were exchanging nicknames? Don't you like it?"

"I'd prefer not to be associated with the creatures in the desert," he replies, keeping step behind me.

"Stalker?"

He shakes his head.

"Lurker?"

"No."

"Ghost. Because you seriously don't make a noise."

"No."

I weave around the line of treadmills no one uses because they don't go fast enough for us human hybrids.

"Got it. Wolf."

His lips twitch. "If you really must give me a nickname, you can call me Z."

"How original!"

I pause outside Luna's training room. I consider her my friend, but watching her skip her flames around the room reminds me that there's a lot I don't know about her. "How does the arena push Rylari beyond their flame intensity limit?"

Zane bites his lips.

"I'm a big girl, I can take it."

"You'll have to face your worst nightmares. Many don't make it out."

My body shivers with the thought. I've lived through a lot of nightmares for most people; what more could I possibly face? "Why does the king want this?"

He shrugs. "King Grimrose has his reasons. I don't pretend to understand them."

Can anyone really understand a lunatic? I open the revolving glass door to join Luna.

She allows her yellow flames to cascade across her fingers so effortlessly, I'm almost jealous. It's bizarre seeing her like this. I've known she was a Rylari from the first time we met, but I've never seen her use her flames so openly.

"That was amazing," I say, hesitating to come closer.

She extinguishes the flame with a smile. "I think it's funny you're still afraid of my flame, especially since you could extinguish it without a problem."

My body tenses. "Sorry, I'm still not used to all of this."

"I'd imagine this is a lot to take in. You just find out you're Rylari before you were carted away." She shakes her head, allowing her coiled curls to bounce around. "It's my fault you ended up in this mess. I lingered too long after you started that fire when I should have dragged you away to find Paytah. He would have protected you."

"I got myself in this mess. If I hadn't gotten Abby into trouble that morning, she might not have come after me in the first place. Then neither of us would be here." It's only been a few weeks, but the whole incident feels like ages ago. Of course, Abby never needed a reason to pick a fight with me. Tormenting me was one of her prime hobbies. It's entirely possible she could have put me in this position even if I hadn't taunted her.

"The soldiers have been gunning for me for a few years now. I grew careless and entered the town when I knew I shouldn't." Luna joins me on the side of the longer firepits. "And you know Abby would have caused trouble no matter what happened that morning."

"So, what are we going to do now?"

Luna knows more fire wielders outside this prison. If we could get a message to them, then maybe we can figure out a way to escape.

"Nothing," Luna replies.

"What?"

"We do nothing."

"I don't understand. Won't your Rylari friends come for us?"

She takes my hands, squeezing them as if to emphasize her next point. "If I know our leader well, they aren't going to risk exposure by storming a heavily guarded fortress. If they didn't come for us while being transported here, they won't come at all. There aren't enough resources."

"Maybe they'll rescue us on the way to the capital?"

She shakes her head. "Clarissa, there will be no rescue mission. There are thousands of Rylari in servitude to the king. Even if they decided to come after someone like you, I doubt it will be soon. Our only option is to prepare and train for the arena. Maybe after we receive our assignments, we might escape. Or, at the very least, fight some of the discrimination against us."

"But..."

"You haven't been in the Rylari world long enough to understand. Just trust me when I say staying put is the best possible option for everyone here. If others come for us, then we'll figure something out." She hugs me, then points to the flames, making them hotter. "Now let's practice."

Luna isn't the best teacher. She can tell me what it feels like to have the heat boiling through your blood, but she can't articulate the exact action I need to take to copy her. It's strange that a regular Glyzul soldier is better at teaching someone to use their fire than an actual fire wielder. Instead of making progress, I feel like I'm reverting to that first day Gabriel threw me into the firepit.

It doesn't help to have the other kids watch me. When I fail, it feels like I'm letting them down, and I watch hope drain from their faces. This is why I can't be their savior. I'm a nobody who can't even master my ability, let alone lead a people.

"Come on, Rissa, just let it out," Luna says.

Tired and hungry, I lift my arms, willing the heat to form an orb above my hand. But all I get is a tiny spark. "I can't do this."

Sinking into a chair, I rest my head in my hands. It's all just too much.

Luna squeezes my shoulder. "It's just going to take time, Clarissa. Be patient with yourself."

That's what everyone keeps saying, but it won't be long before graduation day. If I'm not capable by then, I'll probably be the first to die.

I stare at the fire pits, my mind wandering back to Luna's friends and the incidents that happened in Paltos. The Rylari were going to get my document in broad daylight. Then I found them by that cabin harming the town selectman. Between the guards, the rebels, and the tavern, I never had time to process everything. Further thought only generates more questions.

"Why were your friends pretending to be rebels?"

Luna laughs. "Every single Rylari out there is a rebel; at least, that's the way the king sees it. To us, though, we're just doing what needs to be done to survive."

"So you're not part of the rebels?"

She spreads her hands wide. "It's all a matter of perspective. Why are you so worried about rebels, anyway?"

"It's time to go," someone announces before I can answer.

We stand and head out into the gym. It's empty; my escort is nowhere to be found.

"Did they forget about us?" Luna asks.

"Zane would never leave me unless the colonel was here." Since neither seems to be around, I wonder how true that is as we move further through the massive room.

Voices carry down the next hallway. We move closer, the masculine voices becoming crisper, and I instantly know it's Gabriel and Zane. I bite my lip, trying to figure out what to do. Having information is always a good thing, but the consequences of eavesdropping in a place like this could be much worse than back home.

Luna doesn't hesitate and bounds forward like they're expecting her. I take off after her, pulling her back just in time. They're talking about me.

From my limited view, I see Gabriel sitting at a desk using a digitablet to communicate with someone while Zane sits across from him in a smaller chair.

"Yes, general," Gabriel says. "The cargo should be ready soon. The girl has been helpful in getting them ready for combat training. She was studying to become a healer, so she could prove useful in that area."

Luna moves closer to the door and I try to stop her, but she's too fast. She pauses right outside, silently listening. I join her, even though it goes against my training. Eavesdropping in such close proximity without an exit strategy is grounds for punishment in Ms. Brown's home. But this isn't her home; it's Gabriel's. His punishments could be worse.

"No, I don't think so, sir," Gabriel says in reply to something I don't hear. "As far as she knows, her parents are dead. Our database isn't conclusive; I can't confirm anything."

I'm not sure why knowing my lineage would be important to them. *Do they do this for every Rylari?*

"There are a few that still need recovery time, sir," he continues. "Of course. Tomorrow. We'll have them ready for transport."

There's a click, followed by a loud sigh. "We've run out of time. The general wants the Rylari in the capital the day after tomorrow."

"But there's a storm coming," Zane says.

"The general doesn't care. He wants Clarissa to train in the capital."

"Why? What does he want with her?" Zane asks.

"She's likely a White Flame. He wants to see how she measures up with the other two. Maybe run their tests, who knows? And, apparently, her story has reached the king's ears."

Tests? I hate medical tests; the irony of my choice of profession isn't lost on me. Ms. Brown signs up the disobedient kids as test subjects for money. It's been a while since I've been in the basement undergoing those trials, but the prick of the needle is still fresh in my mind.

"Gee, I wonder who told the king?" The sarcasm in Zane's voice is thick.

"There's nothing we can do about it now. We just need to keep the major from meddling further," Gabriel says. There's a long pause, and I can't help but hold my breath. "Clarissa and Luna will ride with me. Distribute the rest of our forces between the other transports. Put at least two of our men with Ty. I don't trust him."

"I thought you were going to stay behind to meet up with that girl you've been seeing," Zane says.

"The plans have changed. I'll see her another time. If the general wants Clarissa, I'll hand her over myself."

My heart thumps loudly in my ears. There's no way I can let them run experiments on me. I'd rather die. I back away from the door with trembling hands, flames flickering at my fingertips.

"Clarissa, what are you doing?" Luna asks, her tone hushed.

I shake my head. "I don't want to go there. They can't run experiments on me."

She reaches out for me, squeezing my hands. "It will be alright. I'll be there with you, and I won't let them run tests on you."

"You have no power here. How would you stop them?"

"Are you telling me all those years living under Ms. Brown didn't train you for oppressive situations like this? How did you survive?"

Taking a deep breath, I squeeze my eyes shut, then clutch for the necklace that's not there anymore. It was the one thing that would calm me, even on my worst days. I'd do almost anything to get it back.

When I open my eyes, Luna smiles at me. "There will always be someone watching out for you. I promise."

The chairs scrape across the floor in the office, grabbing my attention.

"Come on. We don't want to be caught eavesdropping."

I grab her hand and hurry back into the gym, but I slam into a solid form, sending us crashing to the ground. When I look up, I tense at the sight of piercing brown eyes—the last things I want to see right now. My stomach sinks.

"You wouldn't be attempting to escape, would you?" There's a sinister edge to Ty's too-friendly voice.

I shake my head. Technically, I was eavesdropping, not running away, but I don't think Major Psycho will see a see a difference.

"Really? Then why are you running through the hallway without an escort? Hmm?"

Nothing comes out of my mouth. I don't have an excuse. It's the first time I can't just lie and make up some kind of explanation, which is baffling.

"That's what I thought." He reaches for me, but I roll out of his grasp as Luna screams for help.

Scurrying to my feet, I try to run, but the major is faster, circling his arms around me before lifting me off the floor. I scream, hoping Gabriel and Zane hear one of us, while Luna takes off, leaving me in the major's grip.

"Stop squirming," he says, tightening his grasp.

"Fat chance," I say before biting his arm.

He roars with pain but doesn't drop me. Instead, he slams me on the ground, then pulls my arms around my back and pins me to the floor.

"You listen to me, you filthy little mongrel..."

"Get off her, Major."

His grip loosens, but only slightly. It's not enough to wiggle out of his hold. "She was trying to escape. That means she belongs to me, Colonel."

"Is that true, Lieutenant?" Gabriel asks.

"No, sir. Clarissa is authorized and scheduled to be here in the gym. Since our meeting took longer than usual, I told her she could have more practice time with Luna," Zane answers.

Ty grumbles. "You let her roam without shackles?"

"They're in the training room, Major. The goal here is for them to use their fire," Gabriel says. "If you're worried about something getting burned, I would worry that she'll burn you. Especially since she doesn't have full control of her flames yet."

The mix of gym socks and alcohol emanating from him makes me gag. I try to shove him off me, but he doesn't budge.

"As I said before, Major, get off her. That's an order."

With a huff, Ty roughly releases me, jabbing me in the side. "Just wait until we're out of here. My father—"

"We're leaving tomorrow, Major. Ready your men," Gabriel cuts him off.

I crawl to the wall, using it for support as I stand.

"Why are we leaving so suddenly, sir?" Ty asks.

"Because I said so. Now get out of here, or I'll reassign you to the Dunes," Gabriel says.

Grumbling, Ty leaves.

As soon as he's out of sight, Gabriel stands in front of me. I've never seen his eyes so tense before. "What did you hear?"

"All we heard was the end of your conversation with the general," Luna supplies. "That they want Clarissa and we're leaving tomorrow."

He runs his hands through his hair. "The capital is going to be a lot stricter, and I won't be able to get you out of things like this as easily. If you step out of line there, even if it's perceived, I won't be able to protect you from the consequences. You understand?"

I nod, completely grasping his meaning. It won't matter if I actually break the rules or not; they will punish me regardless, and he might be powerless to stop it. "Why does he want me?"

"I told you, White Flames are rare. With your origin story, you're even more curious." He squeezes my shoulders. "Do you understand?"

His tense energy unnerves me, and all I can do is nod.

"Don't mess this up." He stalks off, leaving me alone with my shadow and Luna.

"Come on, let's get you back to your room," Zane says, letting me lean on him for support.

My ribs are sore from the jab, and it's radiating across my chest. Major Psycho might have cracked something, which is going to take time to heal. If we're traveling to the capital tomorrow, I'll have plenty of time to mend them.

"You want me to heal them?" Luna asks with a glance at where I clutch my ribs.

"Maybe when we get upstairs." Between Ty hitting me and the medical test conversation, I have a sudden need for a window. Despite the wide-open space, I feel stifled by the prospect of living in a much worse version of the orphanage.

Chapter Eight
The Journey

IT SHOULD BE ILLEGAL to be awake this early.

We're forced out of our rooms before the sun is up. Zane cuffs my hands as I stand outside my door. There's no sign of Gabriel anywhere, but then I don't have a view of every hallway. He was mad after the incident with Ty, that much I could tell. It doesn't really matter where he is. To be honest, I'm upset the general ordered him to bring me to the capital.

"This way," Zane says after chaining my leash to his belt. "Sorry about this. It's protocol for cargo transport."

"We're not cargo," I say through gritted teeth.

He stops in his tracks, causing me to bump into him.

"Listen, Clarissa, let's get one thing straight. I know that you're a human being, just with a little more flair. The thing is, if we transport you to the capital in front of the top brass, we have to follow their rules. If we don't, all of us will be six-feet under. I get it, and I don't like this anymore than you do." He gestures to the soldiers, leashing the other kids down the hall. "No one here likes this. In Segura, they're happy to do much worse to you."

"I bet Gabriel enjoys locking us up," I mutter.

"He has his part to play, too." Zane continues down the hallway, dragging me with him.

"What is that supposed to mean?" I ask, trying to keep up with his long stride.

"You're smart. You'll figure it out, eventually." He stops in front of Luna, binding her with another pair of power dampening cuffs attached to a leash. "Sorry, kid."

She shrugs. "It's nothing I can't handle."

Zane stares at me. "See, now that's the type of attitude you should have."

I glance the other way. Sure, I've been in tougher spots than this and got away, but this is different. No one, not even the elite or Ms. Brown, has treated me like cattle. I may have been a commodity to her, but at least she gave us a little more dignity.

The elevator ride to the bottom is quiet. Luna glances at me a few times but says nothing. It's almost like she's mad at me, too. But that could be the paranoia I'm feeling right now. As we exit into the lobby, I sigh at the sight of hundreds of waiting guards. At the head of them is Major Psycho himself.

"I can take it from here, Lieutenant," Ty says.

"Sorry, Major. I'm under orders to deliver these two directly into the colonel's vehicle." Zane doesn't flinch when Ty steps into his space.

"I'm in charge of this transport, Lieutenant. Are you going to disobey an order from your superior, officer?"

"No, sir."

"That's what I thought." Ty moves to grab our leashes, but Zane grasps his hand.

"Lieutenant Colonel Caldera has ordered me to take them directly to his transport, Major Prescott." He emphasizes his lower rank. If Major Psycho wasn't here, I'd laugh. I'm not into fights or anything, but if Zane punches Ty, I wouldn't hate it.

The look on the major's face, with his twitching brown-eyes, tells me there's a high probability of that happening. I step back as far as my chain will let me. We might get hurt if those two start a brawl. Luna takes my hand, giving me the silent support we both need right now.

"Is there a problem here?" Gabriel strides through the lobby doors.

Ty brushes imaginary dust-off Zane's uniform before backing away. "No problem at all, Colonel."

"Good," Gabriel says. "Get the rest of the cargo in the transports quickly, I want to leave by the top of the hour."

Ty stares at him for a moment before saluting. "Yes, sir."

If I didn't know any better, I'd say Gabriel's eyes were glowing like a fire wielder using their powers. His strong dislike of the major is puzzling. Other than being overzealous about protocol and punishments, he'd be more irritating than anything. Ty seems to just be doing his job, so there must be something more going on between them.

"This way, Lieutenant." Gabriel leads the way outside, completely ignoring me. It doesn't bother me; I plan to do the same. He holds the door open as we pass. "Don't try anything stupid, Rissa."

I don't care what he says; this is my life on the line. And I'll do whatever it takes to survive this, with or without his support.

There's no way to escape this transport.

Unlike the rest of the Rylari, we are transported in a fancy hovercar, where we get to sit in plush seats. The only reminders of our situation are the cuffs chaining us to our captors. They have us boxed in the small space, keeping us at the other end away from the doors. I guess it could be worse, because at least I don't have to sit between two bulky guys.

Once the car heads down the driveway, it dawns on me that this will be the first time I'll have traveled beyond Silver City. On top of that, this will be the first time in my life that I'll be out of Ms. Brown's reach. It should be a joyous occasion, and it would be if it weren't for our wardens.

How are we going to get out of this?

"Don't even think about it," Gabriel says.

Squinting my eyes, I give him my most withering stare—at least that's what I hope I'm doing. "I said nothing."

"It's the look on your face that told me exactly what you were thinking," he replies, completely unfazed by my glare.

"Shows you how little you know about women," I mutter.

He tips his head back and laughs. "I'm not dealing with a woman right now. No, I am dealing with an angsty little girl who thinks she knows the world better than me, but really has no clue."

"Little girl?" If it wasn't for the cuffs, the inferno I never knew existed would have this hovercar burned to a crisp. "You're what, at a maximum two years older than me, little boy?"

"She's got you there, Gabe," Zane interjects.

"Whose side are you on?" Gabriel asks.

"The side of reason. You are only nineteen," he replies. "I don't exactly want to listen to this stubborn back-and-forth argument between you all the way to the capital. You guys are like two sides of the same coin, so I won't hold my breath."

I roll my eyes, turning my attention to the world outside my window. Unlike my entrance into Silver City, I can fully see everyone going about their errands without a care in the world. If I hadn't landed in this mess, I'd be picking their pockets or convincing them to buy me something. Those days are over now, and it won't matter if I get out of this or not. My life will never really be the same again.

A few hours into our journey, my arm is numb. Luna fell asleep an hour ago, choosing to use me as her pillow. I don't mind, but I wish I could adjust so it wasn't so painful. The only things keeping me awake are my curiosity and Ms. Brown's training. If I don't stay alert, I won't be able to track the landmarks as we pass by them. It's one of the first rules she taught us. But so far, there isn't much to see that could help me navigate.

"Here, let me," Gabriel says, crawling toward me. He presses the button on my cuffs, and when they come off, my flames surge under my skin, bringing much needed warmth back to my body.

Pins and needles prickle my arm, making me wince. "I thought you weren't allowed to take off our cuffs."

"We can't bring you into Segura without them, but if you haven't noticed, we're not in the capital yet."

"Aren't you afraid of fire?" I ask.

He looks up at me with intense eyes, holding my gaze. "I'm not afraid to get burned."

I don't know if it's from my powers or his words, but heat runs through my cheeks. Thankfully, Gabriel crawls back to his seat next to his sleeping friend. Zane fell asleep a half-hour after we entered the desert. It makes me laugh because Luna held out longer than him.

"What's so amusing?" Gabriel asks.

"Your friend." I nod toward Zane, who's drooling all over his uniform.

Gabriel laughs. "He hates trips through the desert. He falls asleep every time."

"I can understand. It's a little boring out here," I say while staring at the reddish hued sand dotted with tumbleweeds and cacti.

"Be glad for the boring view. The alternative is much worse."

"Worse how?" There's nothing wrong with getting a little information about the desert, especially if I ever plan to escape.

"For one, the storms are horrible out here." He points to billowing dark clouds sweeping through the dunes in the distance. "If you're caught in one, powers or not, you may not survive."

"How does a Rylari survive out there?" I ask.

"Luna would be a better person to ask than me; I've never been beyond the chasms."

"Right, Glyzul can't even step foot in the Dunes."

"It's not the Dunes so much as the wastelands on the other side. Our sensors tell us the wreckage is still leaking Star Poison, which makes the storms worse for the surrounding areas. If the king wants to visit Gadrar on the other coast, he has to go through Vathosen to the north to avoid the radiation."

"But Rylari can walk right through it?" I ask.

"More or less, depending on their flame class. I doubt a Red would be capable of making it to the center on their own."

"Right." If no Glyzul could survive, it would be the best place to escape to if we get a chance.

"Then there are the Shadows, too. It's said they live in the wreckage, or even came from it, but we have no way to confirm that."

Everyone has heard of the Shadows. It's a story used to frighten kids into obedience. "Those aren't real."

"You don't have to believe me, but you can ask Luna about it when she wakes up. Everyone knows not to wander in the desert at night and to avoid the wreckage at all costs," he says.

"You're just saying that to scare me into staying here. Ms. Brown used to tell us the stories all the time."

"And where do you think those stories came from, Rissa?" he asks. "Trust me when I say they came from some shred of truth."

Despite the heat running through me, I shiver, never wanting to run into a Shadow if they're real. I would love nothing more than to prove him wrong, but how do you prove a mythological creature doesn't exist?

"You talked about Ms. Brown before. She was your boss, right? Was she kind?"

I'm pretty sure my eyebrows are merging with my hairline right now. "No one likes Ms. Brown, not even her patrons. She makes herself a necessity that you have to deal with."

"Then why work for her?" he asks.

"She doesn't give you an option." Talking about Ms. Brown reminds me of my contract with her. She'd still get what she wanted, even if I am in custody. I'm curious about what kind of punishment she'll give me for failing my mission. She'll show up somewhere; I'm sure of it.

"How did you meet her?"

"What is this, interrogation hour?" I ask.

He puts his hands up. "I'm just curious. Out of all the captured kids, you're the most mysterious. I thought it would be good to get to know your past better."

I laugh. "So that you can use it against me? No thanks."

His eyebrows pinch together. "I didn't mean to make you feel uncomfortable. Sorry. If it makes you feel better, you can ask me questions."

Staring at him for a moment, I contemplate my options. Knowledge is power, and the closer I get to the capital, the less information I possess. It couldn't hurt to know what I'm about to walk in to before I get there. "What's it like? The arena, I mean?"

"And here I thought you were going to ask me a tough question." He leans forward on his knees. "Only those who've been through it know for sure. You fight against your own fears, both known and unknown. Everyone whose survived has a different story and slightly unique experiences."

"How is that even possible?"

"I don't know, just that it has something to do with the floating crystal above the field." He sits back, brushing his hand across his face.

His guess is better than mine. I've only ever caught glimpses of the arena on the stray digitablet or digiscreen. If it's just going to show me my fears, I shouldn't have too much to worry about. Ms. Brown forced me to confront most of them.

Staring at him a moment, I think of my conversation with Zane. It's odd that he ignored my question about Gabriel's mom. I don't know why I'm curious. It's not something that would directly help me in the future—but you never know.

"How come no one speaks of Lady Caldera?" I ask.

"You mean my mother?"

I nod.

He glances out the window. "My mother died during the Purge."

My breath catches in my throat. The Purge was nearly seventeen years ago. Most of the adult Rylari that didn't get out of the country were killed during the massacre. After that, speaking the name "Rylari" was punishable by death, and they became known as the Forbidden. Now that I know I'm one of them, I understand why I was left at an orphanage so long ago. But it doesn't make sense why Gabriel's mother was killed. "Why? I mean, how?"

"She was a Rylari sympathizer and helped some of them escape. My father paid a heavy price to get back in the king's good graces."

I want to ask what the price was, but from the hardened look on Gabriel's face, I stop myself. Some things are better left unknown. It's not something Ms. Brown ever taught me; it's just something I feel in my gut. To let people deal with their emotional trauma as they wish. Turning back to my view, I continue searching through the desert, committing our route to memory.

A few hours later, the flat desert plain transforms into rocky hills and steep ravines. I've seen lakes and streams before, but nothing like this. Evergreen trees fill in the barren landscape, and before I know it, they surround us on all sides. Above our heads, gigantic, snow-peaked mountains tower above us. It's been a long time since I've seen snow, as I most only deal with the radioactive rain. It's like this part of the world remained untouched by the accident of the past.

The road becomes narrower as we climb higher, and the elevation change makes my ears pop. I rub them, but it doesn't help much. Even though the hovercar is heated, I can feel the chill creeping in through the windows. I didn't know winter comes so early here.

Luna wakes up, stretching her arms like she isn't a prisoner about to die. She glances out the window, taking in the sights. She's never been here either, but she's mentioned she always wanted to visit.

Zane sneezes himself awake. He blinks several times before he glances out the window. "Good, we're almost there."

"Here." Gabriel hands him a pill that the sleepy soldier pops in his mouth. Noticing my gaze, he adds, "He's allergic."

"To what?"

"Everything," Gabriel answers.

"It's not everything," Zane retorts. "There are a few plants that grow here that I can't stand."

"A few dozen." Gabriel chuckles under his breath before picking the cuffs off the floor. He kneels before me. "I'm sorry, but this is required."

Instead of shoving them on my wrists, he extends them toward me, patiently waiting for me to put these on willingly. I don't know what's worse: being forced into them or choosing to give up my freedom. If I had a real choice, I'd prefer to jump out of this window, but with twenty transports behind us, I doubt I'd make it far. With a deep breath, I extend my arms, placing them in open cuffs. When Gabriel clicks them closed, the icy temperature from the window worsens.

"Here." Gabriel wraps a blanket over me and Luna as if he knew we'd be freezing.

"Thanks," Luna says, scooting closer to me for warmth.

"Yeah, thanks," I reply.

A half-hour later, we come to a stop in front of a smooth, towering wall. Guards stand on either side, with guns and staves charged and ready to fire. They're bedecked in a black uniform similar to what Gabriel is wearing, but they don a patch on their arms of a crown surrounded by a snake.

Gabriel opens his window. "Lieutenant Colonel Caldera, heading for the Forbidden barracks with twenty transports."

"Yes, Colonel. General Prescott is expecting you," the guard says. A few guards take a long, glowing, cylindrical contraption and pass it over the hover car before heading toward the transports behind us. "You're good to proceed. Welcome to Segura! It's good to have you back."

"Thank you, Sergeant." Gabriel closes the window as the giant gates open.

The city is filled with tall black buildings towering over the smaller city buildings. People on the street are bundled up in brightly colored jackets as they go about their errands. It hasn't snowed here yet, but from their foggy breath, I can tell it's icy cold.

We head up a bridge that takes us to an elevated roadway. The hovercars whiz by us as we join the fast-paced vehicles.

"It's called a freeway," Gabriel says. "It allows us to move faster than streets with the lights."

I roll my eyes. "I know what a freeway is."

"But we've never seen one," Luna adds.

If Segura were next to Silver City, the capital would dwarf it, making it look like a tiny village. There are so many buildings of all sizes crisscrossing the flat valley and heading up the surrounding mountains, I can't even count them. The closer we get to the capital city's center, the more skyscrapers dot the landscape. I don't even want to know how they build those things; the thought of standing on an unfinished building creeps me out.

"This is the palace." Zane points out the building in the distance. Twin towers connected by some type of bridge arch into the sky, surrounded by a thick brick wall. It reflects the setting sun like it's on fire from all the glass. In the heart of the palace grounds, a lake is encircled by a meticulously landscaped garden and buildings. Trees flank the grounds on one side while the other is filled with tall buildings, though much shorter than the palace, making the towers more foreboding.

"You'll have time to visit after the arena," Gabriel adds. "They usually have a celebration ceremony there."

"I'm not sure if I'll feel like celebrating," I say.

Gabriel shrugs. "The king makes it mandatory."

Of course he does. It's probably never occurred to him we might need time to recover from seeing people die.

"Is that the arena?" Luna asks.

I glance out the window. An enormous black oval building is nestled between the skyscrapers. Long ramps curve up each side, making the arena look like a giant spider ready to eat you. Above it floats a glowing stone. The king supposedly has one just like it; at least, that's what Luna told me. Even though it's far away, I can't stand to look at it. I turn away, focusing on my hands instead.

Gabriel reaches across and grasps my hands. "You're going to survive it."

I meet his gaze. "How do you know?"

"Because I'm going to teach you how."

My new lodgings lack the luster of Gabriel's home. Other than the trees lining the hillside and the grass coating the grounds, the barracks of the Forbidden look just like a gray prison of concrete—probably because it is a prison. They may call it a training center, but I'm not so naïve as to think it's more than a place to keep us out of the way until we can prove useful to the king.

Our hovercar stops in front of a short, round building with concrete walls that look like they could withstand several missile blasts. An older man stands outside, dressed in a black uniform with a fur-trimmed cloak wrapped around his shoulders. His dark eyes, and angular jaw resemble an older version of Major Psycho, with a little more discipline and patience. Flanking him are a few dozen guards and what I can only assume are medical staff by their white robes.

"I hate it when he greets us," Zane grumbles. "Doesn't he have better things to do?"

"You know why he's here," Gabriel replies while glancing at me.

"Why am I so special?" I ask.

He glances out the window as the hovercar continues around the circular driveway with a statue of a soldier in the center. "Do we really have to spell it out again?"

My heart is pounding in my ears as I stare at the healers.

"It's not as bad as it sounds," Zane says, but Gabriel cuts him off.

"Let her be fearful of him." He places his hand on the door handle. "He's not a man to let your guard down around under any circumstances."

Gabriel exits the car, saluting his boss. His body is more rigid than I've seen since meeting him. I guess I'd be the same if Ms. Brown suddenly showed up.

"He's not wrong about the general," Zane says while unlatching our chains from the console.

"What does he have planned?" I ask.

He shrugs. "I don't know. The king is searching for something, or I guess someone. Anyone presenting as a White Flame is to be brought in for inspection. Combine that with your unique circumstances—well, you can imagine how interested they are to see you."

"Great," I say as I follow Zane out of the car. Despite my desire to defy both Gabriel and Zane, I follow their orders. The last thing I want is more attention. If we have any chance of escaping, I need to blend in with everyone and become an afterthought.

"Let's see her then," General Prescott says.

Zane pulls me forward by the leash. I keep my head down, not daring to look him in the eyes. The menacing man, in his swirling fur coat, circles and studies me.

"And this is the one she was found with?" he asks while sweeping around Luna.

"Yes, sir," Gabriel replies.

"Interesting," he says. "And she doesn't want to tell you how she evaded detection for so long?"

"It appears she doesn't know and was unaware of her own origins," Gabriel says.

General Prescott returns to his position with his guards. "There are a few others with similar stories. We'll keep them together in Bunker A for now."

"Yes, General," Gabriel says.

"Take them to the medical ward for evaluation," he says to the fair skinned woman next to him.

She writes something down on her digitablet before glancing at us. "Follow me, gentlemen," the doctor says, she avoid eye contact with us. "It's just a few tests."

Her words send shivers down my spine while my mind conjures thoughts of terrible machines and needles. With all the guards surrounding us, I have no choice but to endure whatever torture this woman has in store.

Chapter Nine
New Recruits

WE'RE HERDED ALONG BEHIND the healer by Zane and Gabriel.

She leads us toward the nearest round building, the woman's long white lab coat billowing behind her. Beneath her coat, she's wearing a military uniform, so she's not just a regular doctor. Her red hair is coiled so tightly, I'm surprised her eyes don't bulge from their sockets. Not a thing is out of place, but given the pips on her collar, I gather she's a colonel. I suppose you don't become one if you're undisciplined.

The computer pad scans her hand, then her retinas. I've never seen a retina scanner in person. Silver City is about the closest place with technology like this, and it's nowhere near as advanced. The colonel opens the door for us to enter.

A few desks with busy secretaries are the only things that interrupt the gray. The circular, domed building is even more boring on the inside. Aside from our entry point, three other doors mar the smooth walls.

Two of them appear to lead outside, but one looks like it leads to another building, and that's the door we're going through.

She places her palm on the scanner, letting us through. "I'm sorry, gentlemen, this is as far as you go. Medical personnel and patients only from this point forward. Though for you, Colonel, you can use the officers' entrance if you like."

I haven't known Gabriel long, but from his shifting gaze, I think this woman makes him uncomfortable.

"We'll wait out here, Colonel." Gabriel nods and takes a position like a sentinel beside the door. Zane hands her our chains, then stands on the opposite side with twitching lips.

The strange lady guides us into a sterile room that looks more like a laboratory than a medical facility with beakers and foul smelling liquids brewing.

"This is where we're inventing new medicines, with the help of your kind, of course," the colonel says. "This way, ladies."

I take a deep breath, squeezing my hands as tightly as possible. Inventing medications at a military compound filled with people they consider "other" feels wrong. And the way she says "with the help of your kind" makes my stomach roll. A few weeks ago, I might have been fascinated by this, but not anymore.

She takes us into another room that looks like a hospital, with beds lining the walls on either side. A girl about my age with red hair lies on one of them, a nurse wrapping her arms.

"Burn victim," the colonel points out, as if catching my gaze. "It happens all the time during training. Right here, you two." She pats two beds side by side, then hands us funny looking blue robes with little diamond patterns on them. I'm pretty sure my behind will stick out if I put this on.

"Disrobe please. Do you have any known allergies?" She closes the curtains, then picks up a digitablet and starts typing.

I don't move, completely frozen in place.

She glances at me over the top of the device. "Don't worry, this is just a basic physical before we send you to training. It's standard protocol."

I still don't move.

The colonel sets her notes aside, then places her hands on my shoulders. "Did something happen to you before coming here? You can tell me. I'm under doctor-patient confidentiality."

I want to laugh in her face. She's a member of the military, and the general wants me here. If he wants to know something, I'm sure she's going to tell him.

She separates our beds with a privacy screen made of thick mesh, though it's essentially just a piece of cloth. Anything she says will be heard by at least Luna, who was already changed and sitting on the gurney.

"The general filled me in on your situation. You were in an orphanage, right?"

I nod.

"Did I hear correctly that you'd like to be a healer?"

I nod again.

"That's a great goal. Though, if you have a fear of basic medical exams, it might be difficult for you to do this for other patients."

Sitting on the bed, I sigh. "It's not like that's going to happen, anyway. Just by the definition of what I am, I have no rights in this world."

"Honey, stranger, things have happened." She grasps my wrist, giving it a little squeeze. "And from the report I read from the Colonel, you may just be the thing your fellow Rylari need."

I glance up at her. "I thought that word was banned?"

"It's just a word, Clarissa: a label. Only those who are afraid of what's different need to fear it."

"Then why does the king fear it?" I ask.

She studies me for a moment. "That's a good question. In a place like this, we should probably keep that one to ourselves."

I catch her warning and bow my head.

"Now, are you going to tell me why you have a fear of medical exams? It might help me make this experience a little easier for you."

The image of the basement wells up in my mind, making my eyes water. I was maybe twelve the last time I ended up down there. "I was caught stealing. My caretaker hated it when we were caught and would punish us. So she forced me—really everyone who falls short of her standards—to be part of what she called 'medical trials.' They drew blood until I passed out..." My voice wavers, and I rest my head in my hands.

"Thank you for sharing that with me, and I'm so sorry you had to endure that. I can understand why you may have an issue with me." She loops her arm around my shoulders. "By the way, my name is Doctor Lacy McMasters. I'm the resident doctor and healer of the Rylari. Or officially, healer to the Forbidden. Actually, I'm probably the only doctor in Artijan that will help heal the Rylari, but that's a different problem."

She picks up her tablet. "I have to give you this exam, but why don't I let you help me?"

"How can I help you?"

She smiles at me, then hands me her digitablet. "I find if someone has been through a traumatic experience, it helps to give them some control over the situation. Eventually, it may desensitize you enough to trust me with your medical care. But if you can perform some of the exam yourself, I can still get the data we need, then I'll assist you where you need help."

I glance through the medical chart she started for me.

Name: Clarissa

Last name: Unknown

Town: Paltos

Province: Silver

Age: Seventeen

Flame Class: White?

"Why is there a question mark by my flame class?" I ask.

"We classify the Forbidden by classic colors of their flames. But medically we usually place a maximum temperature with it. If the patient is reaching beyond that maximum temperature, we can take steps to stop it. Since we haven't measured yours, we can't place the mark yet."

"I see," I say as I read through the rest of the report. "It's just a standard physical."

"Yep, with a few extras that are special for Rylari physiology. Then you get to go to your room and rest before tomorrow."

"What's tomorrow?"

"You'll be woken up early and taken to the training center. The general and facility director will assess the abilities of the Rylari who will graduate this year. You'll unfortunately be part of that group. And I can say you're behind. Most of the other trainees have been here for months, and some kids have been here for years."

"And how will they assess us?" My mind is filled with countless ways they could terrorize us.

"It will just start with basic weapons and fire usage training. Eventually, it will lead to battle simulations. Those are the ones I hate, because that usual means my beds are filled. But nothing is ever life threatening."

I let out a breath, then grab the robe. It's not like I have a choice to be here or a part of this. "Okay, let's get this over with."

I have to wake before the sun again, and I'm more exhausted than yesterday. The stress from the medical exam probably doesn't help either. It wasn't as bad as I thought: just a few questions, routine physical checks, and a blood draw. After I read through the ingredients, the colonel even let me perform my own vaccinations. Lacy certainly doesn't act the way I expected, but she seems nice. The entire ordeal has shaken my confidence, making me wonder if I was ever cut out to be a healer.

To make matters worse, Luna and I had to share a bunk in the communal sleeping quarters for the night. We'll be sharing it until they assign us to a temporary trainer. It was cramped with all the other teens, but with my friend next to me, it wasn't as cold. The heating in this part of the compound isn't great, which wouldn't be a problem with our higher internal temperatures. Luna thinks they have power dampening devices in the walls, robbing us of our natural heat. I can deal with it, but the worst is definitely sharing a tight bathroom with too few showers and a single toilet alongside a crowd of kids and teenagers.

"Can you cover me?" Luna asks.

I use our blanket to shield her from view as she changes clothes. Everyone fifteen years or older was given matching black pants, shirts, and jackets trimmed with red and emblazoned with the Artijan crest—a crown with a snake coiled around it, ready to attack. The younger kids are in a dark gray version with white trim. Regardless of the color, none of us looks like we belong in a military training center.

"How do I look?" Luna twirls for me, then ties back her wild black curls.

"Like you belong to the king."

She swats me then shrugs on her jacket. "Everyone belongs to someone or something."

"How do you figure that?" I ask, tucking the sheet onto our bed.

"It's what my momma always told me. Then she'd add that people complained about the previous rulers, too. But they didn't know how good they had it until they were gone."

I suck in a breath. Talking about the previous king and queen is treasonous. I've only heard a handful of people ever mention them, so I know next to nothing about them. Those who dared to mention them either kept it simple or criticized them harshly. To hear Luna mention them so casually is unusual.

She shoves my jacket in my arms. "Lighten up, Clarissa. You're with your people now, and no one here is going to turn you in for talking about the former Rylari king and queen. Or for talking about the current king."

"No one here was alive during that time. How can you even talk about them?"

"Our parents told us the stories. Some of them even worked in the palace, and others used to be commanders of this facility." She leans in so only I can hear her. "Like my mom."

My eyes go wide. "Your mom was a commander?"

"Yep. And my dad was a junior senator—barely made it out during the Purge."

"Why didn't I know this about you?"

"Don't take this the wrong way, Rissa. You're like the sister I never had. Seriously, my brothers annoy me to no end. I'd have loved at least one of them being a girl. But as much as I appreciate you as a friend, I couldn't trust you when I thought you were a Glyzul. Not with this kind of information, because it was too dangerous if it fell into the wrong hands. And it would have put you in danger, and, despite what the media says, we don't enjoy getting innocents in trouble."

Her words are sobering. It makes sense that she'd have to keep things from me to protect her family, but it still hurts not being included.

She loops her arm through mine. "You'll learn a lot more about our world in the coming months; we just need to get past this training bit."

"Why would that matter?"

"Once we graduate, we'll have a little more freedom to talk." She gestures to the walls. "For now, we need to be careful."

We meet in the hallway where Gabriel and Zane are waiting. Several armed guards stand quietly behind them. The colonel counts us, making sure we're all here.

He nods, and the soldiers force us into two straight lines, then slap cuffs around our wrists. My body instantly chills, cutting me off from my flame.

"Today, you'll be together with your fellow graduate trainees in the training center. Be on your best behavior, because it won't just be me and your other trainers. The general and his staff will evaluate you. Failure is not advised." He stares at me, like those words are intended solely for my ears. "Follow me."

Gabriel and Zane lead us through several wide hallways to the lower levels. There are at least fifteen of us walking behind them in two haphazard rows. I recognize most in our group from Silver City. I have no idea where the younger kids disappeared to, and I hope they're alright, given the circumstances.

Where the upper floors were practically empty, the lower floors are lined with guards. Two large metal doors come into view. As we approach, my hands twitch, and I can feel the heat before I see the flames inside.

Fire lanterns burn along every inch of every wall of the training chamber. Exercise equipment stretches across the room, enough for at least a few hundred people to train simultaneously. Despite the early hour, people are already here warming up. Some are stretching on mats while others are using weights. If it wasn't for the flame symbol on their uniforms, I would assume they were Glyzul soldiers.

Gabriel leads us farther inside to a raised square platform with fire burning in each corner. At least three dozen teens sit in the middle, while black uniformed Glyzul guards mingle around them like this whole situation is normal.

I follow behind Luna as we step into the open area. The other kids sit, but Gabriel and Zane guide me and Luna to the back. They do it so smoothly it looks like they're just directing us to sit, but it feels like they're placing us here on purpose.

Once we sit, the boys leave us to take their place among the guards. I forget sometimes that they're different from us. Zane and Gabriel talk to us almost like equals, and it isn't until moments like this that I remember they are our wardens. Their job is to keep us here by any means necessary. I wonder how he'd react if I successfully made it out of here? Would he shoot me?

"I don't know what the fuss is all about." The girl in front of me with long, dark hair twists around, assessing me with narrowed eyes.

"Excuse me?"

"You heard her." The girl to the right of the first girl looks at me. She looks so much like her friend, I thought they were twins at first. A slight smirk plays on her lips. "Word around the compound is that you're a White Flame, and you brought General Prescott here. And didn't Colonel Caldera train you personally?"

Despite their curious demeanor, the tone in their voices is one that I would recognize from miles away. They already know who I am, so their words are nothing more than a disguise to get more information about me. And information in the wrong hands is always dangerous. Abby taught me that lesson early in my life when she convinced me to divulge my plans to get a nice couple to adopt me—I ended up in the basement for a month.

I shrug. "I don't know what you're talking about."

The first one sneers at me. "You won't get Caldera as a trainer. I can tell you that much."

"Wait. You're mad at me because a certain soldier took time to train me?" I knew people could be insane, but this is the next level weird. As if any of us could choose our captors, let alone be here.

"Colonel Caldera is the best trainer here. Everyone wants to be paired with him," the second one replies.

I glance at Luna, and she nods. "Serene is telling you the truth. Caldera is well known among the Rylari. If we end up here, he's usually the one everyone goes to for help."

My gaze drifts to the man in question. Unlike the other guards, neither Zane nor Gabriel are relaxed. They stand stoically in the far corner by a fire pit, watching over everyone as if they're ready to strike.

"Wouldn't you rather get out of here than fight over who's going to be your trainer?" I ask.

The first one huffs. "There is no getting out of the training facility. Trust me, I would know. My brother tried to sneak his girlfriend out once, and it didn't end well. With the king searching for someone special, our only way out is through the arena."

"Someone special?" Luna asks. "Victoria, what are you talking about?"

"Out of all the people here, *the* Luna doesn't know?" She shakes her head.

"The rumor going around is the king is searching for a Blue Flame," Serene answers. "He needs one to help the queen or something."

"There hasn't been one for at least a century." Luna glances at me with worried lines marring her forehead.

"Well, he's focusing on White Flames for now, so we need Gabriel and his team to train us," Victoria adds.

General Prescott sweeps into the room, ending our bizarre conversation. His boots pound the stone floor, echoing in the silent room, as his long coat swishes behind him. Everyone snaps to attention, saluting as he passes them.

"Up," Gabriel says.

We scramble to our feet. The other soldiers push us into neat, staggered lines. I'm shoved between the look-alike girls as my cuffs are yanked off. Heat surges through me, enveloping my vision in a shimmering light before settling. The general reaches the platform just as Gabriel and his guards salute. My group tries to do the same, but it lacks precision with some bumping elbows.

"The next time I see this group, I want the salute precise," he says.

"Yes, sir," Gabriel says.

"Major Prescott and Colonel Caldera will be team captains. You'll each pick your Forbidden and begin training immediately. We need these new recruits ready for graduation quickly, and I expect to see results."

The general paces around us like a hunter searching for his prey. He stops near me, staring at me for a chilling minute, then scrutinizes the two girls next to me. "In the coming months, we'll let the war games begin. My team will evaluate you throughout this learning phase, then pick your trainers. Based on your progress and how well you do in the arena, they could become your permanent handlers—providing you survive graduation day."

He smiles like the thought of us dying in the arena brings him joy. A small breath escapes my mouth when he moves away.

"Major Prescott, please make your first selection," the general says.

"With pleasure, sir," Ty says.

My shoulders tense. I thought working with Gabriel was a given. The possibility of being trained by Major Psycho is less than appealing. I think I'd rather take my chances trying to escape right now in front of everyone than be on his team. And now I realize why these girls want to train with Gabriel: the alternative is much worse.

Ty circles the group, occasionally glancing at faces. It appears he's looking for someone specific, and I hope it's not me. My hands tingle the closer he gets to me. The girls on either side of me have long raven hair like mine. Even though our complexions and body shapes are a little different, I hope he won't notice me.

Am I horrible for hoping he'll pick them over me?

He's standing right behind me, and I hold my breath. He lingers there, a tormenting silence hanging heavy in the air, and all I want is to scream at him to choose. My heart pounds in my chest as spots cross my eyes.

The world around me almost has a white fog to it. If he doesn't decide, I just might pass out.

"This one," he says, tapping Victoria's shoulder. The girl falls in line behind him with a disgruntled face. I feel bad for her because I wouldn't wish Ty even on Abby.

Gabriel steps forward, heading directly toward the back with purposeful steps. I eagerly wait for him to tap my shoulders, but he passes me, grabbing Luna instead. Her gaze lingers on me for a moment, then she follows him to his side of the platform. While I'm grateful for Luna being kept away from the blond-haired soldier, I can't stop the sting in my chest. His rejection gives Ty another opportunity to choose me.

"Isn't she a Yellow Flame?" Ty asks, scoffing at Gabriel's selection.

"I have my reasons," Gabriel replies, completely neutral in tone and facial expressions. If I wasn't trying to stay under the radar, I would say something that would wipe that neutral expression off his face.

The major walks into the center of the group, appearing to be coming straight for me. I bow my head, trying to stay out of sight, wishing I had left my hair down so I could conceal my face better. He's picked on me so much over the last week, I know he'd relish being my trainer. Luckily, a tall boy in the middle distracts him, and he chooses the kid that looks like a giant boulder.

I don't get to relax, though, because Gabriel picks another kid, again skipping me. Every time it's Ty's turn, a palpable tension hangs in the air, tightening with each passing moment. The flames, like restless serpents around my fingers, pulse with a dangerous energy that I have to contain. I tune everything out, squeezing my eyes shut, because I just want to forget this anxiety-inducing ritual.

By the time I feel the tap on my back, the teams are almost full. And I realize I have no clue who's picked me. With a gulp, I whirl around.

For once, I'm grateful to see those green eyes, but I'm equally perturbed. There are only ten people left; he didn't have to wait so long.

I give him what I hope is a stink eye. He either doesn't notice or doesn't care, because he turns, expecting me to follow him. I'll confront him later when we're alone. Once I'm standing next to Luna, I sigh, letting some of the tension ease from my shoulders, until I see Ty glaring at me. It wouldn't surprise me if tries to steal me away from Gabriel's team.

The last ten are chosen. The two raven-haired girls are on Ty's team. As I assess the rest of his team, I see how formidable they look together. From the tall, muscular boys to the hardened-looking girls, I can see why he selected them. Gabriel's team just looks like a series of misfits, tiny kids and scrawny teens like me. If we have to battle each other at some point, I'm not sure we're going to win.

"Battle simulators will begin three months from today. Have your teams ready, team leaders. And handlers, please be at the top of your game in the meantime. We will watch your performances to make our decision on which Forbidden you can choose," the general says as he heads down the platform for his entourage. They distribute around the room, like little birds ready to spy from their perches.

"Follow me," Gabriel says before heading toward a door on the far wall. We follow him in two lines.

As I walk past Ty, I can't ignore his intense stare. I'm thankful he missed me, though I can't explain how it happened.

Chapter Ten
Combating Fear

I'M EAGER TO LEAVE Ty behind.

I hurry to stand right behind Gabriel as he leads us through the gym. The facility is even bigger than I thought. The interconnected domed buildings appear small from the outside, but the insides are surprisingly large. Upon seeing several wide glass doors leading to different spaces, I wonder if we're underground.

Guards open the doors for Gabriel as he leads us into a wide, almost-empty warehouse. The only thing inside is a large table filled with weapons and several alcoves with targets.

Ms. Brown trained us with daggers, but that wasn't for combat-style training like this, it was purely for survival. Even then, we didn't practice with them all the time, so I'm an amateur at best. I've never killed anyone, and I don't want to start.

"For those of you who don't know me, I'm Lieutenant Colonel Gabriel Caldera. I'm here to help you prepare for your assessments.

Please ask me or any of the other handlers if you have questions. Because we're rushing everyone's arena preparation, you'll all need to master both armed and unarmed combat." He gestures toward the handlers at the armament table. "Each of the handlers is adept at different weapons. I want you to work with each weapon for at least ten minutes before you choose which one you want to become proficient with."

"You're giving us a choice?" someone asks.

"Over the last few years, I've trained hundreds of Forbidden. I've found allowing people to choose their own fighting style and tools leads to confidence and better results, and most survive the arena." He rubs his hands together like an eager kid. From the way the other Rylari are practically bouncing on their toes, Gabriel doesn't appear to be alone. "Everyone head over to the table and choose your first weapon."

While others rush to the tables, including Luna, I'm frozen in place. Something is holding me back, but I don't know what. The possibility that we'll one day use these weapons against each other might be the reason. Maybe I'm undecided because I never thought about weapons or fighting before. Sure, I may have gotten into fights with Abby, but it never led to serious harm or death. I will be ordered to inflict deadly harm for no reason, and that just makes me sick to my stomach.

"Why don't you try the crossbow?" Gabriel stands beside me, staring at the fray of teens testing out their weapons.

"I think you've forfeited your right to counsel me, don't you think?"

He assesses me with his piercing gaze. It bothers me how easily he can see through me. "What did I do to upset you now?"

"You left me standing there until the end. What if Ty picked me? You know he has it out for me."

"Oh, that." He grins. "You were kind of hard to find. For someone who struggles to control her powers, you sure know how to use them when you need them."

"Huh?"

"White Flames can bend light around them. It's a unique trait that you apparently have mastered."

"I used my powers to become invisible?" Flipping my hands over, I make sure everything is still intact.

"You weren't exactly invisible, just hard to see, like looking in a mirror that's reflecting another mirror. Having the other White Flames around you probably helped. I think that's why Ty chose Victoria first."

Thinking back to that moment, my eyes narrow. "But you knew exactly where I was. You placed me right next to them."

He rubs the back of his neck. "That may have been a strategic choice on my part. I knew Ty barely spent time with you and the other girls. And he always goes for perceived strength rather than strategically picking a team. Given his unnatural obsession with you, I hoped by placing the three of you together, he'd get it wrong."

"You based my future on hope and a chance he wouldn't find me?"

"That's life. You make a plan and hope it works out the way you want. And in this case, it did. Besides, being chosen first wouldn't have spared you from Ty and the general's attention. If anything, it would have drawn more attention to you. With three White Flames to fawn over, this kind of makes you less of a target."

"I thought they already put a target on my back."

"Yes, so why make it bigger?" he asks. "And for the record, I didn't pick you last. I picked her last." He points to the redhead I saw in the infirmary yesterday. She wields a sword as if it's an extension of her hands until she trips on the mat and nicks herself. A guard picks her up and guides her out of the room.

"Is that why you picked her last?" I ask, wondering how often she ends up visiting the colonel.

"No. She's part of my plan."

"What's your plan?"

"To make sure you survive graduation day." He points to a group of Rylari training with a crossbow. "It's not as inanimate as a sword. I figured with your desire to be a healer, close combat might not be your thing."

He guides me toward the table, ending our previous conversation. I glance up at him, still stewing from my earlier anxiety. The hard lines that mar his face whenever Ty is around are gone, replaced by the friendly, soft eyes that make him approachable. He's wise, with a strong sense of duty to protect those under his care. But it's still perplexing that he supports a system purposely trying to eliminate us.

A single crossbow is left. The surface is smooth, and I'm surprised how lightweight it is despite its bulk.

"Here, let me show you," Gabriel says, taking it from me, then he holds it to his shoulder. "You want to anchor it like this to keep it stable before you shoot."

"I don't want to shoot at all." Watching the kids excitedly learning their weapons makes me sick.

Gabriel sets the bow down. "You probably won't need these weapons in the arena."

"Then why are we training with them?"

"For what comes after surviving the arena—the war."

I've been so focused on the present problems, I completely forgot about the consequences of survival. Luna and I would become soldiers for the king's war with Thevania, the nation with water wielders. Just thinking about fighting a person who could drown me sends shivers down my spine.

"So, this training is for surviving the war?" I ask.

"More or less. Most of the time, you'll fight with your flames. If something should happen where you lose that ability, you should know how to protect yourself and your unit."

"Defense," I say, trying to convince myself that this is strictly for protection and not for hurting others.

"Exactly." He grabs the crossbow and guides me to the training station. "Since you have medical knowledge, they may not assign you to the front lines. They may keep you at a base camp or something."

"Base camp," I repeat, thinking of the possibility of using my healing skills again. After my freak out with Colonel McMasters, I'm not sure I can handle using those skills anymore. It leaves me conflicted and lost, the fact that I have no choice in my future. But a small part of me hopes I could use my knowledge and skills, even if I don't enjoy being the patient. Despite the odds, it gives me hope. That emotion is risky here because there are no guarantees. The arena could kill everyone here before the war ever affects them, for all I know.

I join some others with crossbows while Gabriel observes from a distance. The trainer teaches the fundamentals of holding and dry firing the thing. The instructor then helps me find a comfortable stance before he lets me shoot.

He loads the crossbow for me then hands it back. I get into position, holding the crossbow steady against my arm with my elbow at the correct height. Getting ready to aim, I peer through the scope. I breathe in, relax, exhale, and then shoot. The arrow sails through the air, hitting the very top of the target.

"Good job," Gabriel says. "Everyone switch."

"I didn't exactly hit the middle," I say, placing the weapon on the table.

"With an energy discharge, that won't be necessary."

"That thing shoots energy discharges?" I ask.

"Not that model, but the one they'd issue to you after graduation would. Training with them from the beginning isn't effective, though, because it's harder to improve your aim."

"Which one should I choose next?"

"If you want to stick with low mortality, try the staff." He points down the line. "The real ones are electrified, but it's better to train without that feature when you're learning."

"Thanks." I turn to head toward that station but stop. "Gabriel, can I ask you a question?"

"Of course."

"Why do you care about the... Forbidden so much, when the government you work for is so intent on destroying us?"

"Do you remember when I told you my father paid a heavy price for my mother's mistake?"

I nod.

"I'm that price he had to pay."

My breath hitches. "The king took you away from your father as punishment?"

"Military servitude, living with Ty, and rarely seeing my father: that's basically my origin story. Now get back to training before you lose more time."

As he ushers me toward the next training station, his gaze hardens ever so slightly. I wonder if it's because he mentioned Ty or if it's the entire problem surrounding his family. Maybe it's a little of both. But it certainly sheds some light on his situation, making me wonder what he'd be like if his mom never got caught helping during the Purge. Would he be here now? Or would he have chosen a different path?

After an hour of trying every weapon here, I'm ready for a break. My skills are limited to the crossbow, staff, and daggers; I'm awful with most of the others. Luna seems to master all of them.

"I don't know which one to choose." She takes a big gulp of water. "I'm used to daggers because those were easy to come by in the Dunes. But the long ax was fun, and so were the swords. I don't know if I liked the long-range weapons much."

"Have you trained with those things before?" I ask. *Am I a little off-put that a fifteen-year-old showed me up? Yes.*

She sets her drink down. "Not all of them, but my family trained me young. Between the occasional raid and the Shadow Monsters, it's kind of necessary to learn how to defend yourself out there."

"I see." I grab an apple and take a bite. Its juices explode in my mouth. Food in this place is one thing I can't complain about; it's far better than anything I had at the orphanage.

"What's wrong?"

"I just feel like I'm behind in everything." I sit at a table, setting down my plate. "In my old life, everything came easily to me. All I had to do was read a book on a subject or watch someone else do a task a few times and I picked it up. But after a few hours of training here, I'm just all over the place."

Luna places a hand over mine, giving it a gentle squeeze. "Sorry. I guess I didn't think about how much this would affect you."

"It's not your fault." I take another bite of apple.

"Still, I should look out for you instead of droning on about weapons." She digs into her food. "You know, maybe we can ask Gabriel if you can have extra training after hours. Maybe he can give me a pass, too."

"Is that even possible?"

She shrugs. "Asking can't hurt."

After lunch, Gabriel guides us to another training room. He's standing among the other handlers, though his expression is light, he doesn't laugh and joke like the other officers. I fall in line with the others, staying against the walls.

"It's time to test your flames," Gabriel says as the floor reconfigures. A gigantic fiery platform rises from the ground, its immense size dominating the room and with larger fire pits in each corner. "Let's start with something simple, like hitting a moving target. Please don't try anything fancy that could hurt you or the others in this room. Just stick to a fireball or throw your flame, whichever you like."

With sparks illuminating their fingertips, everyone gathers around the platform. An invisible shimmering wall forms a barrier humming with an electrical current—a force field. With holographic targets encircling him, Gabriel explains the rules.

A slender young man steps into the middle with him, wearing a black uniform with a flame pin on his jacket. He's followed by a broad-shouldered man, but from the stripes near the collar, he's a corporal and a Glyzul. The larger man rolls his sleeve up, revealing a cuff resembling a watch that shimmers when he touches it. The young man abruptly assumes a combat posture as fire erupts from his hand.

"I can't stand the idea of being cuffed like that," Luna whispers.

"What?"

She points to the corporal. "He's controlling the movements of the Rylari, his 'lesser,' like he's a pet robot or something."

The thought of someone doing that to me suddenly makes my stomach squeeze. I sort of knew about handlers and lessers, but I didn't understand how the whole thing worked.

Gabriel steps away from the ring, joining us on the side. "Ready, go."

The holographic targets swirl around the fire-wielder, but he's fast, taking out several targets with a single burst of flames. After a few minutes, the targets move faster.

When the Rylari takes out a larger target, it bursts into multiple objects, flinging around him like tiny little daggers. His flames gradually shift from red to a brighter orange. The young man's flames intensify to a deeper yellow, the simulator pushing him to the limits of his ability. Beads of sweat form as he leaps out of the way. His handler grunts a little, then taps something on his wrist. A bright flash blinds me, dotting my vision in its wake. Gasping for air, the young man collapses to the ground.

"Match. Thank you for the demonstration," Gabriel says, stepping back in the ring. "Each of you will come in here one by one. The simulator will automatically match your skill level until you can't continue."

He says something else, but I can't take my eyes off the young man lying on the floor. Slowly, he rises on unstable feet as his handler observes him from afar. I knew the Rylari were mistreated, but I never knew how bad it was until now.

I need to escape this deadly Glyzul-inflicted situation as soon as possible, before I have to face the inevitable drowning from the water wielders on the front lines. There's no way I can handle being a prisoner like that.

Being forced to do someone else's bidding makes me want to reach my maximum flames just to destroy everything.

"Clarissa," Zane says next to me. "You're up."

The entire room is staring at me. In my trance, I lost track of time. Half of them have already faced the hologram, their clothes smoldering slightly, hair tousled, and faces etched with exhaustion. This is going to hurt; I know it.

Luna whispers, "You've got this White Flame."

With sweaty palms, I nervously step onto the platform next to Gabriel. I haven't really grasped control over my powers yet, barely able to spark a fire on command. They only appear to function right when I'm under pressure.

Gabriel assesses me for a moment, his face softening. "Just like we practiced last week, but keep the flame intensity at a minimum."

"You want me to fail?"

"You can't best a simulator, no matter how good you are. Don't let your flame go past what you're ready for, so keep it to a yellow intensity at maximum."

The image of me exploding into a million pieces forms in my mind, and that twisting feeling in my stomach returns.

He points to two black devices in the corner. "That's the simulators. They can only project an object in the light's beam. If you treat this like a heist, I know you'll succeed." He pats me on the shoulder before stepping off the platform.

"Easy for you to say," I mutter.

I take a deep breath as the force field closes me inside the simulator. The first object flies at me, and I barely have time to duck out of the way. More objects hurtle toward me, the rush of air preceding a painful impact on my arm as I scramble out of the way. Thirty seconds into the game and I've not hit a single object, but the stinging impacts of the holographic drones are numerous. I duck past more ghostly targets, their edges blurring in the heat haze near the fires, like a glitch. A smile forms on my lips as an idea forms in my mind.

Diving across the platform, I roll into the flames. A vortex of objects spins and twirls, a silent, colorful storm, but none approach my spot. Using the flames from the pits, I pluck them like flowers before hurling them at the flying tokens. One by one, they go down. As the simulation speeds up, a dizzying rush of holographic targets streams past, but I take them all down.

"That's enough," Gabriel says after several minutes. The simulator stops and the force field opens, allowing him to take his place in the center. "What did Clarissa do right?"

"She conserved her energy by using the flames already available to her," Luna shouts.

"Exactly. Sometimes using your own fire is necessary, but when you can use the surrounding resources, use them. What else?"

"She found a strategic location, standing in the flames," the red-head I saw in the infirmary says. Her arm is bandaged, but she seems fine.

"Location is key in any battle." He glances at me, his eyes beaming with pride. I don't know why, but my heart flutters. "Seems we have a natural leader in our midst."

His words sober me, and my smile drops. I have no desire to be a leader. Considering what's happening, or rather, what is going to happen, I shouldn't be happy about this. War isn't something I look forward to, and I don't want to lead anyone into battle, even if it's self-defense.

Gabriel dismisses me, calling up the next trainee while I sit against the wall. The rest of the kids take their turn, copying my stratagem. They come out looking a little less disheveled than the others.

The Rylari from earlier stands next to me, clapping his hands, encouraging the teen fighting in the cage. The young man looks about my age and adds a little flair to my strategy by skipping the flame around, taking out more targets faster than me.

"It's not as bad as it looks," he says. "Well, provided you get a handler that's kind, one that will give you some respect."

I hug my knees to my chest as I glance at his handler joking with the other Glyzul. "Yours didn't exactly help you off the ground."

He shrugs. "If certain people weren't watching..." He points up to a blackened window near the ceiling. "Charles would have helped me, but he has to appease them. I learned quickly not to take offense at him becoming indifferent like that. This world is what it is."

It's sad he's had to learn that, but I guess I'm not any different. How long have I lived with Abby tormenting me? At some point in the past, I just became used to it. Unless she directly attacked me, I just chalked her mean girl tendencies up to her being who she was. I didn't stand up for the other kids in the house either, making me, in a way, complicit in her crimes.

He claps again. "Go Gregory."

"You know him?"

"Greg's my little brother."

My eyebrows lift. "Really? Both of you were taken?"

He shakes his head. "I volunteered. Greg... let's just say, he made a few poor decisions."

I nod, remembering some experiences Luna told me about the Dunes. It makes me consider what will happen next. It seems everyone is fraught with serious problems. If I escaped, where would I go?

"And if you get a bad one? A bad handler, that is?" I ask.

"Then death will be a mercy for you."

His statement isn't unexpected. Once I met Major Psycho, I had a feeling that was how it would be all along. I either have to escape this place before graduation or do everything in my power to stop Ty from becoming my handler. I sigh. Without knowing much about this world, figuring out the selection process is going to be difficult, and escaping is going to be even harder.

Zane steps onto the platform with Gabriel, drawing my gaze. *Unless I get a certain shadow to talk.*

Chapter Eleven
Insomnia

I think I'm becoming an insomniac.

It's been over a week since I stopped sleeping. I stare at the top bunk with Luna curled at my side snoring. My mind is racing, and every day is a step closer to graduation. Instead of holographic targets, we fought actual drones recently. They knocked me off the platform more than once, breaking a couple of my ribs, but the operator of the machine might have had something to do with that part.

If I was just a regular human, it probably would have been worse. Until they heal, Colonel McMasters has me on light duty exercises. If I could rest without the power dampening devices and focus my energy on repairing my ribs with my abilities, I probably would be fine right now. But with the devices plaguing me everywhere I go, my healing powers are diminished. At least it should be better in a few more days instead of months. Either way, it's a setback I can't afford.

I got to see a glimpse of Victoria and Serene the other day. Their flame abilities are wild. Apparently, White Flames can create fire tornadoes. They couldn't quite get the ability under control; for a brief second, the wind nearly tore the warehouse apart. I can only imagine what they could do if there was a wind wielder here.

Letting out a deep breath, I run my hands over my face. I'm never going to be as good as them, not at this rate. Luna's right—I need practice beyond the designated hours, away from prying eyes. But we're not allowed to leave the sleeping quarters without power dampening cuffs and an escort. Other than in one tiny corner near the showers, I can't even create a spark in this place.

Luna keeps telling me to talk to Gabriel or Zane, but with the general and his entourage lurking around, watching us with beady eyes, I can't seem to get a moment with either of them.

I glance at the clock. It's only midnight. They won't wake us up for five more hours, and I can't lie here anymore.

As quietly as I can, I crawl out of the covers, my bed squeaking when I sit up. Other than a few moans from some kids as they turn over in their bunks, everyone stays asleep. Grabbing my uniform, I tiptoe into the bathroom, careful to close the door before turning on the shower.

Once I'm done, I put on the uniform and look at myself in the mirror. My face is fuller than it was a few months ago, probably from the food, but my bloodshot blue eyes lack their normal luster. It's likely from insomnia and anxiety. I need to do something about my situation, but until I can, I'm going to go insane.

"This has to work," I whisper to myself before heading through the dark room toward the exit.

Taking a deep breath, I turn the knob and walk out the door. The guards surround me with their electrified guns drawn.

"Get back inside," the private barks at me.

I put my hands up. "I just need to speak with Lieutenant Colonel Caldera, please."

"He's not on duty. Go back to sleep," the private says.

I don't want to press my luck, but I have to try, even if it means lying. "The colonel told me to call him if I was having problems with my flames." For dramatic effect, I make a few sparks fly from my fingertips.

"I'll ask." He steps away, then speaks into his digipad. "Lieutenant Colonel Caldera, come in, please. We have a problem."

"What is it, Private?" Gabriel asks. His voice is scratchy.

"Sorry to wake you, but we have a certain Forbidden asking to speak with you. She said you told her to call you if she was having problems with her flames?"

My heart is practically pounding out of my chest waiting for his reply. He could call my bluff, turn me in, and punish me. But I'm hoping the compassion he has shown occasionally will extend to me now, despite the late hour.

"Take her to the gym. I'll be there in twenty," he replies.

"The gym, sir? Shouldn't we take her to the infirmary?"

"Yes, the gym, Private."

Ten minutes later, I'm in the gym practicing with daggers. The private stands back, not offering critique, just watching me with a frown. His hand rests on the hilt of his gun, ready in case I bolt.

This is much better than staring at the ceiling and doing nothing. The movement for throwing the blades doesn't bother my ribs as much as the other weapons. Which is why I've been practicing with them all week instead of the crossbow.

I pick up another blade, trying to line my body up with the target. The dagger leaves my hand with a satisfying snap, arcing through the air before it hits the target with a loud thwack. It's still nowhere near the center, but at least it hit the board.

Practicing with objects is easy, but I can't escape the goal of cultivating this skill. I still don't like the thought of hurting someone, but Gabriel's words from the other day play on repeat.

"What if it's a sneak attack and the enemy is already at close range?"

He's not wrong, and in a den of vipers, I need to protect myself.

I throw another dagger. It hits the inside of the outer circle. The sound is satisfying, much better than lying on my bed listening to Luna sleep. The only other thing that could be greater than this would be to explore this place without an escort. Maybe then I could find a way out of here. With every corridor lined with soldiers, this place is locked down, basically a prison.

What frustrates me more is that Major Psycho is back in my life, and it's his fault I got injured. His team trains alongside us a couple of days a week. His Rylari trainees are fine. I even talked to a few of them. But they attack a little harder than us, which leads to injuries to both teams. It's not their fault; their leader punishes them if they don't obey his commands. When one of them failed to win their match, the major used the drones to attack us, which was how I injured my ribs. Gabriel had words with him about that incident, but I don't think it made a difference because Thomas, one of Ty's trainees, ended up in the infirmary yesterday.

I throw another dagger. It lands in the middle ring, and I jump up, dancing around until my ribs remind me they're still sore. Doubling over, I let out a breath, clutching my side. With the power dampening cuffs on, I can't even ease the pain.

"It's okay, Private, I got this. You can go back to your post," Gabriel says, his boots pounding on the surface as he comes to my side.

"I'm fine," I hiss.

"Clearly." He ignores me, taking my wrists and pulling off the cuffs. Heat roars through me, and I sigh in relief as the pain subsides. "Better?"

"Much." I lie back on the ground, just taking deep breaths as the flames heal my side.

"You're healing faster, which is good." He kneels next to me, discarding the cuffs. "It's probably from the training."

"Good, but not good enough."

Gabriel studies me for a moment. "Perfection is unrealistic and will only lead to disappointment."

A chuckle escapes my lips, but the sharp stab of pain in my ribs forces me to stop. "Victoria and Serene would probably be healed by now. I can barely create a flame from nothing, and they're creating fire whips. How am I going to survive an arena like this?"

"Comparing yourself to others isn't going to help your situation, either. It just saps you of joy and places unnecessary self-imposed burdens on your shoulders."

I roll my eyes. "Ty's team moves like they're battle-hardened robots. We appear like clueless kids who don't know what they're doing."

"That's because you are kids that don't know what you're doing."

"They beat us every time we spar. Doesn't that worry you at all?"

"No."

This is so frustrating, I want to scream at him, but my ribs won't let me. "Why?"

"Because they're not your enemy."

I brush a hand across my face, then sit up. "Then who is?"

"Right now, you're your own enemy. And until you stop comparing yourself and instead focus on how far you've come, you'll never reach the level of success you crave." He extends his hand, helping me to my feet. "How long has it been since you slept?"

"I sleep."

"How long has it been since you slept a full eight hours?" He looks at me pointedly, and I know I can't avoid his question.

"Almost two weeks."

"Then you don't need to train right now. You need rest." He tries to guide me to the door, but I shake my head.

"I'm behind, Gabriel. If I don't practice, I'm never going to survive graduation day."

He runs a hand through his hair. "You know training more doesn't make you better."

"Then what does?"

"Balance, starting with a regular sleep pattern, for starters. Lots of people view the Rylari as these unstoppable forces, but you have the same weaknesses as a Glyzul. It's two in the morning, and you're still healing from an injury. You could get away with it a little longer than a full-blooded human, but you still need rest."

"Major Psycho's team operates without sleep all the time, and look at them. We're going to lose."

Gabriel moves closer, towering over me as his sandalwood scent envelops me. He studies me, and my heart races. I'm normally upset when someone invades my personal space like this. But it doesn't bother me. "Why are you so worried about losing this battle?"

"Because then he'll... I don't want to be his lesser." I scrunch my nose, having used that word.

"Who do you hope to be your handler?" he asks, completely unfazed by my blunder.

I bite my lip, trying not to blurt out the one name I don't want to pass from my lips. For lack of remembering anyone else, I say, "Zane."

"Zane?"

"That's right, Zane."

"That's a good choice, but I don't think he'll choose you. And even if he picked you, I doubt the general would approve for a long-term pairing."

"What?" I ask. "How do you know? We haven't even competed in the battle."

Gabriel chuckles as he shakes his head. "General Prescott didn't say the battle would determine your handler. He said it would determine your trainer until after graduation."

"Oh!"

Pointing to the dark observation room above, he says, "They've been evaluating your progress, watching how each of you works with your instructors. They ask for our opinions before determining the pairs. The battle is just for training exercises to increase your skills for later. It also ends the day early. Which is why they announce the pairs after. Besides, that's weeks away; you still have time to improve."

"Can you honestly say I'm going to improve enough without extra practice?"

He lets out a breath. "You're right. You could use a little more training. And if you promise to go to sleep right now, I'll give you some extra training."

"You'll give me training?" I ask, practically bouncing on the balls of my toes.

"Either me or Zane, but only a couple of extra hours a day. But you have to promise me you'll get sleep."

"I don't know if I can."

"Why not?"

I bite my lip. "Besides the anxiety and the pain, Luna sleeps loudly. And she gets right into my ear."

"Well, that I can fix." He takes my hand, his touch sending goosebumps along my arm.

"How?"

"Come on." He guides me out the side door, past several guards. They acknowledge Gabriel as we pass by before returning to their stiff postured stance.

"Where are we going?" I ask, trying to keep up with his long stride.

"You'll see." He smiles, and for once it reaches his eyes. It makes me want to bring it back. He's handsome even when he's brooding, but the mischievous glint makes him more charming.

He's not my friend. I remind myself as I follow him. *He's the enemy.*

Sometime during my stay here, the seasons changed. Crossing several enclosed bridges, I catch sight of the snow-covered courtyard. It must be freezing outside; I've never seen snow this thick before. The mountains where I grew up were dusted with the white powder a few times a year, but it never stuck around for long.

"Segura's elevation is higher than Silver province," Gabriel says. "The winters are harsher here, and even a Rylari could die of hypothermia."

"Are you warning me not to escape?"

He shrugs. "Always, because it will be a suicide mission no matter when you try."

"How can you be so sure that I'd try?" I ask.

"Let's just call it a hunch based on previous experience." He guides me away from the window, and I'm hyper aware of his hand on my back. Despite the layers of clothing, a comforting warmth, a feeling like a feather-light touch, radiates through our connection, making my skin tingle pleasantly.

We arrive at a door with Gabriel's name and rank etched across the plaque. When he presses his hand against a keypad, it hisses before sliding to the side. As he pulls me inside, a deep, guttural bark from the inside makes me jump. A giant fluffy creature jumps on me, slamming me into the wall. The dog barks at me, its paws pinning me in place.

"Hi," I say, hoping the dog doesn't take it as an insult and eat me. I've seen wild dogs before; they were friendly enough in that "don't bother me and I won't bother you" kind of way. Never have I interacted with someone's pet.

It tilts its large, honey-colored face before it licks me. I clamp my mouth shut, but I'm covered in drool.

"She likes you," Gabriel says. "That's good, because she rarely likes anyone. Come on, Fireball, fetch."

The dog jumps off me, running after a toy, while I use my sleeve to wipe off the slobber. "And you were planning to let her eat me if she didn't like me?"

"Fireball usually obeys when I tell her 'off.'" He hands me a wet cloth, then presses the buttons on his replicator.

"Fireball?" I ask while washing my face off.

"She likes to chase fireballs." He hands me a cup, taking the drool covered cloth. "I replicated a warm tea that helps me sleep."

"What's in it?" I sniff the cup. It has a sweet floral smell.

"A blend my father used to make me when I had nightmares. It's a little mixture of chamomile, lavender, and valerian."

"I thought you didn't see him much?"

"I didn't start my servitude until I was about six. There were a few years between the Purge and when the king found out about my mom's involvement. So, I had some time with him. We still see each other when I'm working in his province or when he visits the capital. And he still makes this for me every night." He holds up his cup.

I take a sip of the warm liquid. It soothes me, giving me enough of a mind to notice that I'm in a small apartment. The black and tan dog sits on the couch chewing its toy while Gabriel stands in the kitchen observing me. There are two hallways on either side of the space that I assume lead to bedrooms.

"What is this place?"

"It's where I live most of the time," he says. "Other times, I might stay in my dad's city home."

It figures he has multiple places to live in, while I have to share a bunk in a cold, damp room. I can't imagine living in luxury like this, dashing off to random homes whenever I feel like. I, for one, would hate to pay for the upkeep.

"So, Zane lives with you?" I ask, pointing toward the bedroom doors.

"He lives across the hall."

"Then is the extra bedroom for your dog?" I ask. Fireball looks at me, tilting her head like the answer is yes.

"No, that is for a lesser when I have one, or a guest," he says, then takes a drink.

Gabriel told me his recruits usually survive the arena, but he doesn't have a lesser. Because of his position as a teacher to the Forbidden, he rarely goes to the war front. And I doubt they'd send him into actual combat. Which makes me wonder, "What happened to your last lesser?"

"I've only had one, and she died." He sets his cup down in the replicator, a technology I wish we had in the orphanage. "I promised myself I wouldn't take another."

"How did she…?" I can't quite let the "d" word slip through my lips.

"She joined a resistance cell. The rebels were more about gaining power through force. She made a few mistakes, and it led her down a path to her death."

My attention is fixed on the cup of tea, the somber subject weighing down on me, causing a sinking feeling in my stomach. A mixture of disbelief, anger, and a touch of something akin to hope swirls within me as I process his confession.

The very fact there is someone resisting this oppression excites me, but that the girl died in the process makes me sick. I saw the rebels back home the day I ended up in this situation. The one I kicked seemed nice enough, but what they did to the town selectman was gruesome. But on graduation day, I might have to face worse.

Then there's the fact Gabriel just admitted he wouldn't take another Rylari to train. It's both infuriating and endearing. The whole master-slave thing is horrible, but if I have to endure it for a while, I want to at least have a good trainer for now and eventually a good handler. If I want to avoid Ty becoming my handler, I'm going to have to get to know the others, especially if Zane is already assigned to someone.

"You should sit. You look like you're going to pass out," Gabriel says.

"Your dog isn't going to bite me?" I ask.

She tilts her head at me like I've offended her or something.

He takes me by the shoulders, guiding me to sit down. Fireball shakes with excitement as Gabriel sits on the other side of her, then she practically slams into his lap and lounges across him. There is definitely something strange about that dog. I'm pretty sure she thinks she's human.

My hand moves across the soft fabric. We weren't allowed to sit on Ms. Brown's couches; they were for guests only. The unknown Rylari girl could have sat here before. Did Fireball like her? Given the age of the furry creature, it's possible Gabriel replaced his lesser with the dog.

"So tell me, has anyone picked me as their trainee?" I ask, slightly afraid of the answer.

"The general hasn't decided yet. He plans to take his time with the White Flames, especially you, because of your unique situation. But there are several trainers interested in you."

I stare at the plant on the coffee table, its waxy green leaves almost inviting me to touch it. "Is Ty one of them?"

"I don't think I have to answer that one. You already know."

"Ugh." I rest my head in my hands.

He pats my back. "Let Victoria and Serene look stronger than you. Ty always goes for those who appear the strongest."

I glare at him. "Is this another one of your hope plans?"

"Maybe."

"You know that if I were to step into the arena tomorrow, I would die. I need to figure out how to survive this."

"Let me worry about that. Just focus on getting stronger and learning how to control your abilities."

I stare at the plant again, my eyes growing heavy. "Why are you helping me? I'm a nobody orphan."

He drapes a warm, fuzzy blanket over me. "Because you're not a nobody."

He mutters more, his quiet, soothing voice fading as I drift off to sleep.

Chapter Twelve
Paradigm Shift

THE SUNLIGHT FILTERS THROUGH the curtains against my wishes.

The weightless, silky soft blankets envelope me, caressing my skin. I rub my eyes, not knowing how I ended up in a bed. From the gray walls and plants, I assume I'm still in Gabriel's apartment. A heavy, furry creature lays across me. I try to shift in the bed, but the dog growls, keeping me pinned in place.

"Fireball?" I ask. She licks my face, forcing me to turn away.

Fireball jumps off me, then barks. When I don't move, she twirls in a circle, then barks again.

"You want me out of bed?" I ask as I slowly push the covers off, swinging my legs over the side. She wags her tale excitedly as I stand.

Marching toward the door near the bed, she glances between me and the handle.

"I got it." I move slowly, careful not to startle her. When I peek in, she jumps on me, shoving me into the bathroom, then barks, nodding at the shower. "What are you implying?"

The little German Shepherd just sits there, waiting for me to comply. I mutter as I go to pull my jacket off, then stop when I realize the throbbing pain is gone. Pressing on the broken ribs, I find them completely intact. It's strange I healed after only a few hours; I've never healed that fast before.

With a glance at the dog, who looks at me like I'm the weird one, I turn on the shower. *I can't believe I'm being ordered around by a dog.*

Unlike the water in the common room, the water here only takes a few seconds to heat. My body practically begs to jump under the steamy liquid. When I come out, my clothes are gone, and so is the dog. A fresh practice uniform is waiting for me on the door.

After drying off, I shrug it on, then head into the bedroom, where the bed is already made. There's no way a dog can do that, right?

When I come out of the room, Gabriel is setting plates on the table, filled with delicious smelling bacon and scrambled eggs. We never get food like this in the cafeteria. It's usually some type of milky porridge or a protein bar for breakfast.

"Good morning," he says, as if it is normal to have me here.

"I don't remember falling asleep," I reply. "Isn't it some kind of rule violation that I slept here? Aren't I going to get in trouble for missing training?"

"I talked to the general about your insomnia already. You have a medical pass for today, so he's ordered that you be placed in my care for the time being."

"I'm too far behind; I should be training with the others."

"You needed sleep, and I wasn't about to carry you all the way back to your dorm. The others needed their sleep too." He points to the plate. "Eat. As soon as you're ready, we'll start."

"Start what?"

"You wanted specialized training to fast track you? Well, the general agrees, and it starts today." He points to the chair. "You're going to need your strength, so sit and eat, please."

I take my seat, picking up the fork. Gabriel sits across from my place, his napkin in his lap. He takes a small bite, not looking up from his plate before he takes another one.

"So, does this mean you'll be my handler?"

He finishes chewing. "Officially, no. This is just a temporary arrangement, just until the battle or until the general says otherwise."

I nod, taking a bite of the scrambled eggs. Salty, buttery flavor cascades across my mouth, and I close my eyes to savor the moment. Two pairs of eyes meet mine when I open them. Gabriel is frozen mid-bite, staring at me, while Fireball sits beside me, her head on the armrest.

"What?"

"Have you ever had a decent meal?" he asks.

"I've had enough food, if that's what you mean."

"Being full and having a decent meal are two different things." He sets his fork down. "You'll stay here with me, so I can make sure you're eating properly. The food in the cafeteria is terrible, anyway. I'll ensure you get enough rest for early individual training without disturbing others."

"What about Luna?"

He smiles. "I'll make sure Zane looks after her for you. Though I doubt she'll mind having the bed to herself."

I pick up a piece of bacon. "You would if you knew how cold it is in there."

His eyebrows pinch together. "What do you mean, it's cold?"

"Luna assumes there's dampening devices in the room, preventing us from regulating our temperatures. It's always freezing in there; well, at least to Rylari, it's freezing in there. I'm not sure how a Glyzul would feel." I almost laugh at myself for differentiating myself from a human, because I think it's the first time in my life I've done that. My whole life, I considered myself a Glyzul, thinking I was just a regular human. Turns out, I'm not human; I'm a hybrid, some altered form of human. My fire obliterated my self-perception, creating a void I'm not sure I can fix.

Gabriel stands abruptly. "Keep eating; I'll be right back."

Fireball moves toward his full plate.

"Stay, Fireball," he says without looking back.

With his departure, I suspect I just unknowingly tattled on someone. Which I shouldn't really care about in this place, especially if it makes our stay just a little better. He's supposedly the director of this facility, and it's curious that someone might have done something to our room without him knowing about it. What would be the goal?

Fireball barks at me, drawing my attention. She nods toward the food in my hand.

"So demanding." I roll my eyes and eat the bacon. "Wow. No wonder they serve this stuff at the fancy parties I crashed."

I really shouldn't get used to this luxury, because I know it won't last forever. At some point, the bubble will burst and everything will come crashing down around me. But I'll leave that thought for another day, because right now, I'm going to enjoy the food while I can.

Every day I eat, sleep, and train, then I repeat the next day. I'm always the first to roll call and the last to leave, but that's because Gabriel has me up early to work on my flame abilities. And in just a few weeks, I'm already hitting the targets with more precision. I still can't do all the fancy stuff Victoria and Serene can do, but at least I can throw my flame now.

After everyone is gone for the day, I use the extra time to work on my fighting or weapons skills before dinner. Occasionally, Zane brings Luna over, and after we eat, the boys disappear into Gabriel's study. Which is what I'm looking forward to after dagger practice.

I throw another blade; this time it clangs against the board before clattering to the floor.

"You really should relax. You'll get better results," Gabriel says.

Taking the cloth on the table, I wipe the sweat from my face. It's been an hour, and I feel like I'm getting worse. I pick up another knife. "I have daggers, you know."

Gabriel shows off four blades in his hand. "So do I. But I've had longer than a month to train with them." To prove his point, he doesn't even look at the target as he throws the blades across the room. Of course, they land near the center. "Try again."

"Unbelievable." I roll my eyes, then take a drink of water, the cool liquid soothing my throat.

"You'll get there, eventually." He exchanges my empty water bottle for two throwing knives.

With shoulders back, I stand ready at the line. "Will 'eventually' be before or after we lose to Ty?"

We're less than a week away before our first battle simulation and they announce the handlers. At close range, though, I might be deadlier with these blades than the other teens in our group. Unlike them, I've read every anatomy book Ms. Brown gave me. I know exactly where to strike to either kill instantly, kill slowly, or keep alive. That's knowledge I'd rather not have to use; it was meant for healing, not for hurting. Every time I see Major Psycho's group training, I'm reminded that I might not be given a choice.

"He doesn't matter. And it's just one practice battle. What's more important is improving your skills before entering the arena."

Letting out a breath, I follow his instruction and throw the first dagger. It hits the target landing on the upper rings.

"Your powers can make your aim truer." Gabriel stands next to me. "That's what makes Red Flames so deadly when they're given a weapon."

"But I can't make my flames wrap around the weapon like they can."

"True, that's their specialty. But as a White Flame, you can use a similar technique with the abilities in your body to increase functionality. You did that the other day when you sparred with Freddy. But one thing you haven't naturally done is let your flames consume your eyes: it would enhance your eyesight."

I've seen other Rylari's eyes glowing when they use their powers and just assumed I did the same thing. "Okay, how do I do that?"

"Remember how Luna said your powers are tied to your emotions?"

I nod.

"Start with that. What makes you sad? Fearful? Angry?"

"You realize those are all negative emotions?"

"There is no such thing as a negative emotion." He glances at me. "Just negative responses to the emotion. And if you want control over your powers, gain control over your emotions."

I take a deep breath and adjust my stance while finding the pinch point. *What is my greatest fear right now? What would make me angry?*

When the person's face appears in my mind, I release the blade. It lands with a satisfying thwack in the dead center of the target. I scream, jumping up and down at my success, then somehow end up hugging Gabriel. But I don't care; I hit the center.

"Preferential treatment, I see."

I jump back at the intruder's voice, freezing at the terrifying voice. Ty stands next to the table of daggers and picks up one to inspect. Either he'd been standing there for a while or picturing him in my mind before throwing the blade conjured him.

"What do you need, Major?" Gabriel's entire demeanor changes, his hard muscles flexing.

"You know you're going to have to burn that uniform, Gabe. With that thing all over you, I don't understand how can you stand the smell."

I scrunch my nose while clenching my fists. It's strange he always has snide remarks about fire wielders, but then practically obsesses over us. Maybe he's jealous or something.

"I doubt you came here to worry about my laundry. What do you want?" Gabriel doesn't move from his place beside me, which is a slight comfort because I feel anything but confident with Major Psycho around.

Ty twirls the blades around his fingers. "My father said something that caught my attention, and I had to confirm it myself. I mean, the moral colonel who always prattles on about being fair is giving extra lessons, and not just to anyone, but to a White Flame. Even with little knowledge, she'd have a clear advantage over the others just on raw talent alone."

He shakes his head then comes around the table, his gaze locked on me. "Here she is, being given special treatment above the others in your group—or my group, for that matter. And she's not being trained by just any handler, but the director of the facility himself. I mean, how fair is that?"

I want to hide behind Gabriel, but he grasps my shoulders, keeping me in place.

"Are you done whining, Ty?"

"I told my father how unfair it is for you to train with her, the one that concealed herself during selection. And how you seem to be so captivated by her. I mean, it's one thing to give an extra hour to practice here and there, but she's living in your apartment with you?" He inspects his fingers. "It's like you already claimed her as your lesser when she hasn't been assigned to anyone yet. That's really not fair at all, is it?"

"And what did you do about it?" Gabriel's jaw ticks, his features growing harder by the minute.

"Oh, nothing much, just leveled the playing field a little." He walks toward us, flipping a dagger in his hand. With each step, my heart rate increases until he's in Gabriel's space. "Whoever's team wins gets first pick."

Gabriel doesn't react, keeping that calm exterior that infuriates me. "And how is that fair, exactly?"

"Since you rigged the selection in the beginning." Ty throws the dagger over my head, causing me to flinch. It hits right next to mine in the center. "I'm rigging this one. Good luck with that misfit crew of yours."

He turns to leave, then pauses for a moment. "Clarissa, don't get too comfortable in that apartment. You'll be moving soon. Into mine."

My heart sinks because he's right about our team. We're not nearly ready enough for this battle, so there's a real possibility I could become Ty's lesser.

Chapter Thirteen
Battle Simulation

I really wish we had another month of training.

Ty's little rant snapped Gabriel into action, and he finally listened to me, increasing not only my training but his entire team's. We're more efficient and can hit our targets, but we lack the talent and discipline of the other team. This worries me, because I'm certain Major Psycho will do everything possible to win.

Despite the reassurance from Gabriel, my stomach twists as I follow our team captain through the hallways toward the simulator. I'm not ready for this battle, and neither are my teammates.

The battle simulator is on the opposite side of the compound. It's basically a warehouse twice the size of the one we practice in. The room is colorless, mirroring the snow-covered peaks outside. There are no windows except for the observation box where the general and his entourage sit, waiting to make their judgment.

The major stands on the other side, surrounded by his team, who chants some mantra I can't quite make out. They're ready for this, probably because he's threatened them if they lose.

Gabriel takes his place in front of our group, talking to a few of the other handlers while I find Luna. She's chatting away with the red-haired girl from the infirmary, who always seems to get injured. I'm slightly worried about her.

"You weren't at the warm-ups this morning. Where were you?" Luna asks.

"I couldn't sleep. Gabriel made me sleep in." I don't really want to tell her about my nightmare of being forced to marry Ty. That is definitely the worst thing I could think of on the eve before this battle, but there's not much I can do about it.

"You didn't sleep again?"

"Sorry," I say. "I was worrying about today."

It's not a lie because this battle was occupying my mind before Ty's declaration last week.

"You're not in this alone, you know. We are more capable than we look." Luna shakes her head. "This is Ginger, by the way."

The red-haired girl with freckles scattered across her fair skin smiles. The bandages from her last accident are gone. "Hi," she says.

"I'm Clarissa." I put my hand out.

She shakes it enthusiastically. "Oh, I know. Everyone knows who you are."

"Of course." White Flames are famous and all that nonsense keeps following me around.

Gabriel calls us to gather around, drawing the crowd of twenty teens forward to hear his words. He's not projecting like he normally does. I glance at Ty's team; they're doing push-ups in sync with a drumbeat.

When a boy in the back doesn't quite follow the beat, one of the other guards kicks him. If anyone needed a resistance cell, it was one of those Rylari.

"Just remember your training. Be patient with yourself and your team. Think through every situation, and remember, it's a lot harder to take you out as a unit than as an individual. Helping each other is better than saving yourself." Gabriel points to little projectors in the ceiling and walls. "The emitters are off, but in a few minutes, they'll conjure up a battlefield. This is a Capture the Flag style game. We steal theirs and we win. They steal ours and we lose. Remember, this is only a game. Don't do something that will get you hurt just to save the flag."

Ginger groans beside us. "He's talking about me," she whispers. "I'm the only one who gets hurt around here."

"That's not true; the major's team gets hurt all the time," Luna replies. "And I'm pretty sure their team captain is the one who causes it."

"Okay, then I'm the only one on this team that gets injured," Ginger says, then follows the group toward a yellow flag.

I trudge after them. Zane hands out the gear while Gabriel designates assignments. I'm only half-listening because I feel eyes on the back of my neck. Searching for the source, my gaze is drawn high to the window above. The general sits in the loft high above us, feasting on an assortment of food. Our eyes lock, and I feel an awful chill running down my spine. He has the same angular features as his son, but with his darker coloring, he looks like a cobra ready to devour his prey.

As the emitters activate, my environment transforms into a forest, obscuring my sight of the observation room. It takes me a minute to regain my senses, the world slowly coming into focus as the image settles into place. The nearby tree is so realistic I can almost smell the pungent aroma of pine needles and the earthy scent of the forest floor. I'm left wondering if I could climb it. My breath hitches when my fingers brush the rough, textured tree bark.

"Yes, you can climb them." Gabriel stands beside me. "But they will disappear when the simulation is over."

"Be out of them when we win, got it," Ginger says.

"I want you three with me and Zane at base camp," Gabriel says.

"What are the others going to do?" I ask.

"They're going to clear a path toward the other camp, hopefully bringing back the flag."

"You want us to sit around doing nothing?" I ask.

"It's called guarding home base." He nods toward the flag a few paces away. "And I have my reasons. Now go lay the trip wire."

Grabbing the wire from the pile of supplies, I pick my way through the foliage until I find a suitable spot. If it wasn't for the warehouse ceiling, I would think I was in an actual forest. I blow out a breath as I string the wire across, connecting it to a small disk that will simulate an explosion if someone walks through here. At least I hope it's just a simulation. My gaze drifts to the general. Would his game place us in danger?

Once I'm finished, I move on to the next trap until the entire area is covered. I go back to find out my next orders, where Zane hands me a few electrical daggers and a small crossbow.

"None of the weapons are lethal, but they will hurt if you get hit by one," he explains.

"Yeah, provided the major doesn't change his," Luna mutters, then swirls her crackling short sword.

Ginger frowns while taking the staff from Zane. "He would do something like that, wouldn't he? You know, to get an advantage?"

"Let's not worry about what he did or didn't do." Gabriel comes into the clearing with dirt covering his face. "Focus on protecting the flag at all costs."

"And if he modified his weapons?" Luna asks. "What do we do then?"

"We adjust accordingly." He pauses for a moment, staring directly at me. "And get evidence of it if we can." He picks up a long sword along with a few light grenades, then distributes four small disks that look like flat batteries. "Everyone has their communication devices?"

I place mine behind my ear and nod.

"Let's roll out."

Zane stays behind, while Luna and Ginger travel further into the forest to hide. I follow Gabriel, carefully picking our way through all the booby traps we set.

When we reach a clearing, Gabriel points to a branch above me. "Anchor yourself up there. You should get a good view to shoot anyone who comes out of that line of trees over there."

The last time I crawled up a tree was to sneak inside a manor house. And because of Abby, I fell. This time, I hope I can get out of the tree before the simulation is over. "Where will you be?"

"Not far." Gabriel sinks into a bush. If I didn't know he was there, I would never see him, especially with the dirt on his face.

I copy him, picking up a handful of dirt and smearing it on my face. Then I strap the crossbow to my back and start climbing. With the added weight at my back, I take my time placing each foot and hand across the rough bark. Once I make it to the mid-level, I straddle a branch, bracing myself between two branches. Then set up my crossbow, waiting for the first sign of movement.

This is taking ages. Forests are normally very loud. Other than an occasional whistle in the distance, which could be from either team, it's too quiet. I glance at the window above, where the general is speaking to another officer, pointing to something along the tree line to my left.

With my heart pounding in my chest, I adjust my weapon, using the scope to check the area out. The opposing team, identifiable by their red scarves, is approaching. My jaw clenches when I see the two dark-haired White Flame girls who can unleash flames that could hurt everyone but me. My stomach drops when I realize they're heading toward Luna and Ginger. I signal Gabriel using my mirror, flashing the light toward him.

"Where?" he whispers over the comms.

"Ten o'clock." I point in their direction.

He nods. "Hold for now. G and L, you see them?"

"Not yet. Do we know who it is?" Ginger asks.

"White Flames," I reply.

"Then they could be concealing themselves," Luna says.

I peek through the scope. "I can see them clearly. Only about a hundred paces to your right."

"Yeah, but you're a White Flame, Rissa." Luna says. "You can see past their disguise."

"Clarissa, be their eyes for them, on my mark," Gabriel orders.

Beads of sweat form on my forehead as I get into position. They're far enough away that my discharges might not hit their targets. But when I see the glimmer of one of our devices nearby, I smile.

"Girls get back," I say. Then I unleash my discharge.

A bright flash fills the area, and the next thing I know, ten other people run from behind the trees. Cries come from all directions—it's an ambush. At least half of Ty's team charges toward us. I rely on my training and fire my weapon. The electrical charge from my gun is so powerful that it incapacitates two people at once. I fire another round, and another two go down. Using electrical discharges is far simpler than arrows, enabling me to neutralize more incoming forces.

With my confidence bolstered, I continue my tirade, shooting in all directions. Some get past my attacks, but Gabriel finishes them with his electrical sword. The open field is covered with kids trapped by electrical netting, keeping them stuck to the ground until the battle is over.

I'm so focused on the battle ahead of me, I don't see the blast heading in my direction until the last second. Confined by the limited space, I risk a daring leap to the next branch, just managing to grab it. Dangling painfully by my arms, I squeeze the tree trunk, the rough wood digging into my skin, while I struggle to hook my legs onto the log.

"Watch out!" someone yells.

When another energy discharge hurtles toward me, I do the only thing I can—I let go.

My breath escapes me as I crash and roll to the ground. Shaking off my pain, I heal myself, then scramble to my feet, only to find several red arm banded enemy combatants running for me.

The crossbow lies in a jumbled heap on the ground. My chest pounds as I reach for my daggers. Feeling the heat, I realize the daggers aren't needed.

Focusing on my abilities, I unleash my flames, forming a ball in each hand. The group hesitates, then runs in the other direction when I throw them. A few go down while the others dive out of the way.

For the next wave of combatants, I skip my flames like a stone across the water. Gabriel takes out the people I miss, locking them to the ground. With each second, my flames grow in intensity, and I relish in the power as it consumes me.

The air crackles with energy as I dodge the weapons' fire. Red flames shoot toward me, but I reflect them back as if they had come from me.

I've never used my abilities like that, and I pause, staring at my hands as if they were a foreign creature, the residual energy humming faintly beneath my skin. A yellow fireball grazes my arm, pulling me out of my stupor. It stings, but doesn't burn me.

When I see the kid it came from, we lock eyes, then he halts with wide eyes before running in the other direction. I don't know why he's scared; it's not like I would hurt him on purpose. That's when I glance at my arms. They're not just the normal light yellow color—they're pure white, and my breath leaves me. From the color alone, they're burning brighter than anything I've seen out of Victoria or Serene. I could do a lot of damage with these flames, even hurt my friends.

Someone screams, and I look up just in time to watch Ginger go down by Ty's hand. And he's not exactly gentle about it either. Luna runs to her side, trying to heal her despite the electrical webbing pinning the girl to the ground. Ty rounds on her with his sword held high above his head.

I don't think, I just run as I launch a wave of light across the clearing, blinding everyone. Gabriel's voice calls out to me through the comms, but I don't listen because I have to help Luna.

I push myself as fast as I can, crashing through the foliage just in time to take the blow from the sword. It slices through me, causing me to cry out. Pain explodes in my side as I feel a warm liquid gush out of me. Ty yanks the sword back as the electrical netting forms over me, pinning me in place.

Major Psycho takes a blade from his side and throws it at Luna as she tries to escape. "I knew you wouldn't resist saving your friend."

He steps over me with a gleeful smile while I clutch my side. I struggle against the restraints, but it doesn't help, they just get tighter.

The forest disappears suddenly, along with the netting. I scramble to my feet, my mind completely disoriented as I take in the gray warehouse.

"Congratulations, Major Prescott! You captured the flag," General Prescott says from the glass box above. "Line up the Forbidden, Captains."

The world spins when I try to move. Luna and Ginger come to my aid, helping me to my feet. My uniform is wet from my blood, and it appears I'm losing a lot.

"Quickly now," the general urges.

My breath comes in short bursts as I clutch my side, pushing myself to move into our formation. Luna tries to heal me, but a guard shoves her away.

Ty stands at attention with a smirk on his face as he waves our yellow flag in his hands. Gabriel, meanwhile, looks like he's going to explode. There's nothing we can do about it now.

"Major Prescott, as the winning captain, choose whichever Forbidden you'd like to train for the arena."

My heart pounds in my chest, begging for him not to choose me. We lost, and now my fate is sealed.

"Thank you, General." He turns around, walking through the rows of Rylari like a lion stalking his prey. His menacing gaze assesses each one. He even grabs them by the chin, a gruff hand cupping their faces, inspecting them, before passing them by. My body grows tense the closer he gets to me. I almost feel like my stomach is shoved into my chest.

When he stops in front of me, he smiles, his fingers graze my cheek. "Such a pretty little mutant. You'll be my new favorite pet."

Chapter Fourteen
Chained

I TREMBLE AS Ty places a gold cuff on my wrist.

I shiver from the loss of my powers, and it doesn't help the pain either. My side feels like it's going to burst. How did I survive all those years living like this?

Oh, that's right, I didn't have lunatics trying to stab me all the time because I'm different.

Sure, Abby and I had our fights, and Ms. Brown forced me to commit crimes for her. It wasn't the best, but at least there wasn't a constant fear of dying looming over me. It was torture living in the orphanage, but nothing compared to this.

"Follow," Ty commands

My body moves against my wishes, staying only a few steps behind him despite the searing pain from my wound. With the bracelet on, I can't even heal it. I think I'm going to be sick.

By the time I make it to the front, I nearly fall over. Gabriel catches me, and when he realizes I'm bleeding, I swear his eyes are like fire.

"General Prescott, I invoke my right as facility director for an examination of cheating," Gabriel says, holding up his hand coated in my blood.

"You can't do that." Ty whips around. "Father, he can't do that."

I'm frozen, not really understanding what is happening right now. I clench my fist as I watch the general appraise the two young men. He clenches his jaw, clearly unhappy with the situation. His dark gaze travels to me, sending shivers down my spine.

"Do you wish to take her as your trainee, Colonel?" he asks.

"Yes, General. I've already been working with her." He's infuriatingly confident, almost like he already anticipates the outcome.

"Are you sure you're ready for one? Especially now." He arches his eyebrow.

"Father, he's making it up," Ty says. "If you grant this review based on an injury, then I won't get to pick the person I want."

The general purses his lips then glances at the man next to him who holds up a digitablet for him to view. "Unfortunately for you, Major, the cameras caught it when you struck the girl with the sword. Given that she's bleeding, your weapons have clearly been modified. If you wish to forfeit having second choice, you can appeal."

Ty moves away, his lips curling

"Granted, Colonel. The White Flame known as Clarissa will officially be your trainee until after the arena," General Prescott says. "But unless I see an improvement in her rebellious behavior, it will not be guaranteed you keep her should she survive the arena."

"I'll keep her on her leash," Gabriel says, taking my wrist and placing his thumbprint on the cuff. It makes a beeping sound, then heat floods my body, soothing the pain.

"Heal yourself as much as you can," Gabriel whispers. I'm now his new pet, forced to follow his every order, but thankfully, I'm not Ty's. There's something seriously wrong with this world.

Despite having an injury, I'm required to stand next to Gabriel as the others choose their trainees. My powers are trying to stitch the wound, but I lost a lot of blood, making the process excruciating. Gabriel stands close to me, keeping a steady hand on my back to help me stay upright.

Guilt pools in my stomach when Ty chooses Victoria in my place. I wouldn't wish him on anyone, including Abby. No one deserves that. When Zane's name is called, my shoulders relax. He beelines straight for Luna, settling the bracelet on her wrist before walking her back toward me.

He whispers something to her, then she clamps my arms, sending soothing flames through our connection. I take a deep breath and close my eyes, finally relaxing. I shouldn't because this place is full of surprises, but for now I'm fine with just easing my pain.

"Congratulations to everyone. If you acquired the Forbidden that you wanted, make full use of your time with them. If you didn't, do better next year," General Prescott says. "I expect these Forbiddens to be ready for the arena by April. If you do well enough, you may even get to keep them permanently."

The word "permanently" sours my stomach. We're not property, but his little speech reminds me that this is a completely different world from the one I'm used to.

"Dismissed," he says. "Gabriel, come see me, please."

"Yes, sir," Gabriel answers.

Ty glares at us. "My father is going to skewer you. He doesn't like his plans disrupted." He leaves with Victoria following behind him, not giving Gabriel a chance to reply.

Gabriel shakes his head, then glances at me. "You okay to walk, or should I send you to the colonel?"

"I'm fine now. Just a little tired.

He nods, then says, "I'm sorry about this next part."

Pressing a button on his watch, he says, "Follow. Say nothing."

It's like I'm in someone else's body because it's moving against my will as I follow Gabriel through the corridors. We take several turns before ascending a staircase up to the next floor. Once we reach the top, he turns to me, and that fire I saw in his eyes has returned.

"You will say nothing while we're in there with the general. Do you understand me?"

I blink at him for a minute, waiting for the command to settle over me, but it never comes.

"It only works if I command you to do something." He lifts his arm, showing off his watch with a command switch. Next to it is a silver band I never noticed before.

"Then why don't you command it?" I ask while inspecting the bracelet.

He leans in so only I can hear. "Because I'm not a heartless monster."

Instead of waiting for my reply, Gabriel turns down the hallway. This time, I decide to run after him. We arrive in front of a door guarded by two menacing-looking guards. They knock on the door before announcing us.

The general is lounging in the chair I saw him in during the battle, but it's turned inward. A woman pours more red liquid from a crystal jug, and from the acidic, sweet smell, I assume it's wine of some kind.

The other men and women lounge around the observation area, scarfing down a banquet of food.

"Why did you accuse my son of cheating?" the general asks while swirling his glass.

"Because he did." Gabriel points to my bloody side, which still needs at least a day to heal.

He examines the wound with his icy stare. "So he did. But you didn't have to make a spectacle, did you?"

Gabriel bows his head, making him look like a little boy disappointing his father.

"That's what I thought. Now, convince me why I shouldn't take away your new pet."

My eyes widen with horror as my stomach jumps up in my throat. I shake my head as my lips part. Gabriel's grip on my wrist is like a vise, silencing the words struggling to escape my lips.

"Major Prescott would not be a good fit for her continued development. I've been working with her and have seen significant improvement these past few weeks," Gabriel says, not skipping a beat.

"You said, and I quote, 'I'll never take another lesser again.' Yet, today, you took one." His hooded gaze travels to me, assessing me in his half drunken state of mind that makes me want to recoil. Normally, I'd say something snarky, but I don't think Gabriel will let me. "You choose not just anyone; you chose her, of all people. I want to know the real reason, not the answer to put on a report, Colonel. Is she special to you?"

The way he says special makes me want to throw a drink in his face. If Gabriel wasn't digging his fingers into my wrists, I would.

Unlike me, he doesn't flinch. "She is special. There is a lot we don't know about her past. I feel it is prudent to learn about her origin story.

Given the major's behavior lately, particularly with her, I think it's important—my duty actually—to take up this mission."

I'm just a White Flame who doesn't know who her parents are. That doesn't make me special. Sure, my flames became hotter than ever before, but I can't understand why that is anything to get this upset over. Victoria and Serene have similar intensities as me.

"To what end?"

"We need to find out how she evaded us for so long. The orphanage caretaker had no clue, either. If she could evade us, then there could be others like her."

My gaze snaps to Gabriel. I had no clue he's talked to Ms. Brown, but I guess it makes sense. If he wanted to learn my origin story, I'd talk to her too. There isn't much of a story to tell, considering I was left under a tree as a baby and someone took me to her.

The general takes a sip of his wine. "Alright. Find out as much as possible. You only have a few more months with her. I expect to know everything. And consider us even; no more favors." He waves his hand toward the door. "Dismissed. Oh, and you know how Ty can be when he doesn't get his way. Be on guard. I don't want to report a dead White Flame or colonel to the king."

Gabriel salutes before leaving, dragging me behind him. I follow Gabriel out of the room, grateful to leave. If I can avoid the general in the future, I'll go out of my way to do it.

We walk through the corridors without a word. The only sound is our boots pounding on the smooth cement surface. Instead of heading for the dormitories, Gabriel strides toward his apartment.

He shuts the door behind us, then points to the room I've been sleeping in. "There's your room." He files past me before shrugging off his jacket.

I have no clue why he's so angry with me. "I-I thought..."

He rounds on me. "That's the problem: 'you thought'. Because you didn't listen and stay at your post, I had to give up a lot today. You have no idea what you just did."

"Luna was—"

"You really think I wouldn't be watching or commanding?" he asks.

"Yes, but Ty—"

"Would have been taken out by Zane. He was going to shoot them when you stepped in his line of sight."

"Oh!"

"And because of that, they won. Then I had to give up..."

"Give up what?"

He slams his fist on the kitchen counter. "Never mind. There are fresh clothes in the closet. Take a shower, finish healing yourself, and get some rest before dinner."

My body mechanically moves toward the room.

"Sorry." Gabriel pinches the bridge of his nose. "I didn't mean that as a command."

The bracelet relinquishes control as Fireball trots out of Gabriel's bedroom, stretching before greeting us.

"I'm going to wash this stuff off." He takes a drink of water, then heads for his room. "Fireball, watch her."

She sits on my feet, her amber eyes locked on me. I try to move, and she growls.

"I'm just going to the shower."

She wags her tail.

"You are a strange dog," I say. "Can't we just come to a compromise? You let me get away with things and I'll give you a treat."

Her triangle ears perk up at the word "treat," and I smile. Just give me a few days, and I'll be running this place instead of the dog. I search through the kitchen but don't find any dog treats.

"Do you know where your treats are?" I ask, as if she'll answer.

She glances at me, then dips her head toward Gabriel's door. "Figures."

I fill a cup with water and take a drink. I try submerging the bracelet under the facet, but it doesn't come off.

Rummaging in the kitchen, I search for tools to crack it open. Every device has a battery source. The only thing I find that might be useful is a butter knife, but the surface of the cuff is completely smooth, with no opening of any kind for me to slide the knife into.

"That won't work."

I jump, the knife tumbling from my hands and clattering on the marble countertop. Gabriel's hair, still damp from his shower, sticks to his forehead, adding to his already striking appearance. My cheeks heat at the thought, and I rub them to make them stop.

"Why won't it work?" I ask.

"You can't take this kind of device off with a butter knife."

"Then how do you get it off?"

A smirk tugs at his lips. "I'm not that dumb. But there is nothing in this apartment that can take it off besides me."

"You expect me to take a shower with it on? It's going to get gross underneath."

"If you earn my trust, I'll take it off when we're inside this apartment." He points toward the front door. "When you're out there, you wear it, no matter what. I can't change that law."

I sigh. "How do I earn your trust?"

"You listen to me without me having to command you." His gaze is intense, emphasizing the command part. "I don't enjoy commanding people any more than you like being forced. It's why I vowed to never take a trainee or lesser on again."

I swallow. "And if they found me without the bracelet, what would they do?"

"Best case, they'd kill you. Worst case, they'd force you to kill your friend."

Despite my need to escape this thing, I nod. "Can I at least take this thing off to shower? You can send your dog in to watch me."

"Fine." He presses his fingers on the side of the cuff. A light glows around the side, followed by a click, and the device falls off in his hand.

"Thanks." I rub my wrist to get the ache out.

"You're welcome."

I head toward my room to take a shower.

"Fireball, watch her."

The dog nudges me into my room, and I shake my head. Between a man and an overbearing furball, I'll take the dog any day.

Chapter Fifteen
Transcending Boundaries

Every day, Gabriel wakes me up to train before the sun comes up. Or should I say, Fireball wakes me up, then almost drags me out to the living room while I'm half asleep, where Gabriel is waiting for me. There's always a protein shake and a thick jacket to go over my uniform.

Once I'm ready, we head outside in the blistery winter weather. My powers give me an extra layer of warmth, but even a Rylari can't keep it up forever. While I am adjusting to the routine, I continue to resist it, choosing to stay up late at night and remain in the cozy walls of my prison. It doesn't help that my bed is the most comfortable ever. But Gabriel likes the solitude outside, away from the prying eyes of the others, and if I'm honest with myself, so do I.

I hate it when he's right.

"Ready?" Gabriel asks at the start of the snow-covered trail near the edge of the compound. Everything is coated in white, including the city, but the snow isn't as deep as it was a week ago. With spring coming, the temperatures are rising, encouraging the trees to sprout. In a few short weeks, the ice will be gone and it'll be graduation day—a moment I'm not looking forward to.

"Let's go," I say before taking off at an even jog. My breath is visible as I run through the forest, but I'm warm inside. Unlike some of the other Rylari, my handler doesn't cut me off from my fire; it's always at my fingertips. He limits my powers in training to push me to use other fighting styles, constantly emphasizing preparedness if my powers fail. I suppose he's right. Having fighting skills could have helped me avoid capture in the first place.

Although he trains everyone, he always finds extra time for my improvement. My fire sparring was weak, but now, thanks to Gabriel, I'm just as skilled as the others.

The Rylari are watching me like hawks—they notice every little improvement or slip-up. I see hope forming in their heads, especially because of my white flames, and I don't need that kind of pressure. The only mildly amusing part is the Glyzul soldiers that shift their weight nervously every time I practice. I may have occasionally sent a stray fire blast in their direction to watch them run.

At least out here in the mountains, no one has to be afraid of me or enamored by me. I can just be me, free to train, to triumph or fail, however my roommate dictates.

Despite growing up in a mountain town, the altitude in the capital makes it a little harder for me to exercise. When we first started working out in the freezing cold, I could barely run. It took my body a month before I could keep up with Gabriel's pace without wheezing or doubling over. He could easily outrun me, but he chooses not to, likely out of consideration for me.

After the first mile, I head up a steep trail with my trainer right behind me. With each step I take sprinting up the incline, my heart hammers in my chest. Unlike a few months ago, I make it to the top of the plateau without stopping.

Targets dot the clearing, with weapons sitting in a neat row on a cloth in the center. This is where I love to train and spar. My flames surge under my skin in anticipation of the next task. I don't know when Gabriel has time to reset fresh targets every day, but the round discs are always here when we arrive.

I take my place several paces away from the first target, ready to unleash my flames, but Gabriel stops me. He pulls back my sleeve, his fingers grazing my skin and sending goosebumps up my arm. Then he does something I've only dreamed about for the past few months: he takes off my golden cuff.

Gabriel doesn't back away, instead focusing his gaze on me. "I want to see exactly how powerful you are. And you won't get there with this on."

This is the first time he's ever taken this thing off outside our room. We're not even near the barracks, far enough away that if I wanted to, I could try to escape and possibly get a good head start. He really shouldn't trust me because every dream I have is running away from this place.

"And how do I do that?" I ask, still in shock.

After spending every day training with him for the past few months, Gabriel is still a conundrum to me. In one instance, we laugh and joke around while he's showing me exactly how to improve. And the next minute he's distant, like a brooding storm about to heap a pile of snow on your head.

I can't help but imagine a scenario where we could be friends in some remote location rather than whatever we are now. The king, the capital, whoever makes these decisions on morality, would never allow us to be anything more than a handler and his lesser. And from what I can tell, Gabriel likes to follow the rules. Mostly. There are times like this when he bends a few, but those are always those gray rules everyone argues about. I doubt he'd ever really go against the king.

He holds up the cuff. "This has a suppression system built into it. Even if I commanded you to reach your hottest flame level, it would automatically prevent you from reaching what it thinks are explosion levels. It's why you don't wear them in the arena."

Panic sets in as I comprehend what he's about to do. "No. You can't push my flame any hotter."

He chuckles. "As long as you don't go too fast, you'll be fine. You've reached pure white flames on your own, but let's see if you can exceed that limit now that you're unrestrained."

"I can't."

He grabs my wrists, preventing me from backing away. "The flames are part of who you are. There's nothing to be afraid of."

"Except exploding."

"Do you really think I'm going to let that happen?"

I pause in my protests. He's right. I don't believe he'd let me go beyond what I'm capable of. He's shown that on multiple occasions. With me wearing the heavy metal bracelet every day, my handler could make me obey his every command, but he doesn't—not even in the simulations where the general watches, allowing me to choose to obey him. The only time he used it was when I almost stepped on a trip wire, and that was the singular moment I was grateful for the confounded thing.

"What's your plan to stop me from going too far?"

He holds up the golden bracelet. "Automatic fire suppression."

I let out a breath. "Fine. How do I do this?"

"You reached pure white flames during the first battle without building up to it like most young Rylari do. What were you thinking about then?"

"Survival mostly. And then Luna being attacked."

"Luna was a distraction," he says.

I roll my eyes. "You don't have to rub it in. It was a mistake, and I'll own up to it."

"I'm not rubbing it in. Your flames dimmed when you stopped thinking about surviving and focused on Luna. And it has happened in every battle simulation we've entered."

My instinct is to snap back at him, to remind him we won those battles, but it won't help me improve. I constantly have to remind myself that Gabriel is not Abby. Then I have to remind myself he isn't my friend either. "What am I supposed to do with that? Shouldn't I be helping people in battle?"

"Yes, but you have to keep yourself in survival mode while helping people. Otherwise, you leave yourself vulnerable for others to attack."

He makes it sound easy; battles are filled with distractions. Somehow, he remains focused, but how long did it take to make him that way? "Well... teach me how to do this, oh wise one who's only two years older than me."

He shrugs. "I've been in the service officially since I was twelve, but growing up in the Prescott household, I started my training the minute I arrived."

"And working with flame throwers?"

"I've been working with the Rylari longer. It's probably why they assigned me here rather than some remote outpost."

"How long were you working with the Rylari?"

He shrugs. "All my life. My dad trained them before me. And I already told you, my mother helped them during the Purge."

It makes sense now why he has such an affinity for helping people who are so different from him. If his dad trained them and his mother was sympathetic toward them, then Gabriel is following in their footsteps. The Rylari were free and in charge around that time, which would make a big difference in their attitude.

King Grimrose took the throne around the time I was born, killing off most of the adult fire wielders in the Great Purge. From the talk I've heard over the years, he changed the history books, but that doesn't surprise me. History is always written by the victors, and everyone else becomes a footnote. Officially, the record says the Rylari begged him to take charge because they realized the Glyzul were the superior species and bowed down to him. If that were true, there wouldn't be any rebels running around.

"Now focus on the primal emotions of survival," he says.

"And what are those?" I ask.

"For being a medical student, I'm surprised you can't name at least one of those emotions."

Of course he won't let me off easy and just tell me. "I suppose if someone were to attack me, I'd be afraid."

"Yes. What else would you feel?" he asks as he circles behind me like a predator.

It makes me feel uncomfortable, but maybe that's the point. "Angry."

"Exactly. What else?" He's so close, I can feel the heat of his breath on my neck.

"I guess I'd be a little anxious."

"Maybe not a little." He points to the target in front of me. "Close your eyes. Imagine the person who makes you angry."

"Ms. Brown, for all the times she locked me in the basement." The older brunette woman with her perfectly coiled hair fills my mind.

"Now imagine the person who makes you the most anxious."

I don't have to think for long. My blond nemesis appears alongside Ms. Brown. And another face appears beside them. Ty's menacing brown eyes bore into me, and I almost shutter. "Abby, because I never knew what she was going to do to me. And Ty, because he's a lunatic."

He lifts my arms, straightening them out in front of me. "Now, what do you fear the most?"

"Losing Luna." My voice almost breaks as I say it out loud. He's forcing my emotions to the surface, and with it, my flames surge under my skin.

"And what does losing her really mean for you?" he asks, his voice barely above a whisper.

A tear falls down my cheek. "That I am alone."

"Then stop that from happening."

Without opening my eyes, the flames rip from my hand, hotter than ever before.

"Imagine being locked in that basement," he says before encouraging me to lob another fireball. I open my eyes to see the flames are even brighter than I'm used to, incinerating the fire-resistant target and leaving nothing but ash behind.

"Imagine Abby and Ms. Brown hurting Luna," he says.

The flames grow brighter, almost blinding me, as they flow from my hand. The target bursts into a million little pieces.

Gabriel doesn't stop, pointing toward the next target. "Now imagine your parents abandoning you."

My hands shake as flames erupt from my fingers, filtering the world around me in a blue light. With a primal cry, I hurl the flame across the snowy patch, melting it before it hits the target, the combustion in a gigantic explosion almost reminiscent of the bombs described in my history books. My chest heaves as I focus on the destruction. The fire, though dying down, still casts a mesmerizing blue flicker across my fingers, its heat a lingering ghost.

"That's what I thought," Gabriel says, his gaze resting on my hands. "You're a Blue Flame."

A shiver runs down my spine despite the heat coursing through me. Even though the evidence of his words is right in front of me, I can't believe him. It's not real. Blue Flames are just a fable the Rylari tell their kids to give them hope. As I stare at my hands, I realize it's not as much of a myth as I thought it was. My future just became so much more uncertain than before.

"What does that even mean?" I ask.

"It means you don't tell anyone, not even Luna."

I don't know what I expected him to say, but that wasn't it. He brought me out here to see if his suspicions about my flame were right, and I just proved them. "I don't understand."

"This power is dangerous. If certain people find out, the war in the west won't be the only thing you'll have to worry about. The king will try to exploit it."

"But you're the king's soldier. Why wouldn't you tell him about this?"

His broody, sour face returns. "Because this power that you have will make you a target. And it won't just be from the king."

"You mean the rebellion?"

"They're a bunch of renegades who've lost their power; the king made sure of that. But that doesn't mean those outside forces wouldn't use you."

"What outside forces?"

"Hey, Gabriel," someone yells from behind us.

Zane is running toward us, with Luna right behind him. "What was that explosion?"

Gabriel pulls me behind him before snapping the bracelet on my wrist. My blue flames disappear on contact.

"It was a little trick we concocted, combining flames and a substance," Gabriel lies so smoothly, I almost believe him.

I'm not sure if I should obey Gabriel or not, but I know having more focus on me would be a curse. But Luna is my best friend. I held her secret for years, and I know I can trust her with this. If someone overheard us, this could leak to the wrong people. Escaping the king would be impossible for me if I was under his control. A thief needs invisibility and stealth, and being the focus of the king's attention won't give me that.

My trainer reminds me all the time, the arena pushes the Rylari to their hottest flame. Since no one here is a Blue Flame besides me, I think I'm going to stand out. Yet another thing to worry about, and I only have a few weeks left.

How am I going to keep this a secret in the arena?

Chapter Sixteen
The Last Chance

I push the food around my plate.

The dining room is filled with noise, with people chatting away about receiving their assignments. No one wants to talk about the elephant in the room—the arena. And I have the added problem of my new flame intensity. My mind can't even comprehend what I saw earlier today. Gabriel told me not to say anything, but how can I keep this a secret? I have a million questions, but my handler is nowhere to be found.

After our training session, he deposited me in Zane's care, then disappeared. He said everyone would be after me if they found out I was a Blue Flame. I can't help wondering what he plans to do with that information. Will he turn me in? Maybe not. He could have done it already, but his abrupt absence worries me. I sigh. The longer I'm here, the worse it will be for me.

I glance at Luna. She's happily eating her roast beef, chatting away with the red-head girl named Ginger. They're only a year a part—fifteen and sixteen. Luna told me she came from a neighboring village in the Dunes, but the accident-prone girl was picked up two weeks before us crossing the border. Since I've been practically glued to Gabriel's side, I haven't had the chance to get to know anyone, but Luna knows everyone.

"What's wrong?" Luna asks, pulling me out of my thoughts.

"Nothing," I reply. It's an automatic response, and I can tell by the way she scrutinizes me she doesn't believe me. "Nothing important. Just thinking about the arena." *It's not a complete lie. If Gabriel wants me to keep this a secret, I have no idea how he's going to pull it off inside the arena.*

"I try not to think about it," Ginger says. "I've gotten injured for silly things, like being overzealous when swinging my sword. If the arena really taps into our worst fears, I don't know what will happen in there."

"It's best not to think about it," says the skinny boy in the next seat—Eric, if I remember right. He takes a sip of water. "The more we dwell on it, the more likely the crystal will find our true fears and use them against us."

"It's an advanced alien technology. How does not thinking about it keep it from probing our minds?" Gregory asks. The light-brown-haired boy carries himself like a leader, and the way others listen when he talks, I figure they follow him.

"He's right," a dark-haired girl—Becky, I think—replies. "The thing will figure it out regardless of what we do right now. I think if we talk about it, maybe we can overcome the fear before we get there."

"Or at least how to cope with it," a ivory skinned girl—Olivia, I believe—adds.

Like a wildfire, the entire room erupts, discussing strategies for overcoming their fears. I don't know if it's better than avoiding talking about it, because the minute someone mentions spiders, I shiver at the thought.

"Not a spider fan?" Luna asks.

"Who is?" I ask.

"Me," the bulky guy—Freddy—says. "The key to spiders is remembering they serve a purpose. Sure, it's annoying walking through their webs, but they keep the bug population under control."

I shake my head. "That doesn't stop them from being creepy with their spindly little legs. If this crystal is going to create our worst nightmares, then what if the spider is a giant and traps us as its prey?"

The boy blanches. "I don't know."

"You overcome it the same way you do with everything in the arena." Luna pats him on the shoulder. "Use your imagination. Think about it. If the crystal is just an advanced computer creating our worst fears, then we have the power to imagine ourselves overcoming them. How do we take out giant human eating spiders?"

"With our flames," Ginger replies.

"With our weapons," Freddy adds.

I open my mouth to reply, but Luna shakes her head. "Don't you dare, Clarissa, not unless you have a way to overcome that negative thought you were just about to spit out."

Biting my lip, I think about the fear. There are several techniques I read in my psychology books about overcoming fear. But somehow, I don't think those studies took into consideration being thrown into an area where facing those fears might literally kill us.

"Fear is a chemical response with the release of adrenaline and cortisol. It can cause rapid heart rates, breathing, and tense muscles." With the perplexed looks on everyone's faces, I realize repeating medical jargon will not help in the arena. "What I'm trying to say is it's a fight-or-flight response. If you know the symptoms, you can use that to calm yourself so that you don't become paralyzed by fear."

"And how do we overcome the symptoms?" Eric asks.

"I'm not sure which one will work, but sometimes tensing and releasing the muscles will work. Keeping yourself rooted in the moment can help. Exposing yourself to your fear can help too. You can also reward yourself when facing your fear."

"You mean like a dog?" Becky asks.

I can't help but think of Fireball chasing my flames the other day. Gabriel gave her so many treats for obeying him, I didn't understand how she wasn't getting fat. "Basically. We have similar reward centers in the brain."

"So, if we have to face a giant spider, then we can find spiders around the barracks and reward ourselves with chocolate for facing it?" Olivia asks.

"That could work," I admit. "But we don't have access to chocolate."

"How about an extra helping of that purple juice drink they serve?" Eric adds. "It's the closest thing to a dessert we'll ever get."

I glance at the buffet, wrinkling my nose at the monotone sustenance they call food. It makes me feel guilty that I have access to the replicators in Gabriel's apartment. I could get chocolate for me and Luna, but it might look suspicious if suddenly everyone had some. When my eyes land on the pile of bread, an idea forms.

"How about the reward can be cinnamon toast?"

"I like your method, Blue." Becky nudges my shoulder. "But how would we get cinnamon?"

My body tenses at being called "Blue." Did someone find out already?

"She shouldn't be called 'Blue,'" someone says behind me. I don't have to turn around to know who it is. Victoria circles our tables, viciousness in her eyes. "She can barely control her flames, let alone become a legend like a Blue Flame."

"Seriously, Victoria, you were just going on about how she looks stronger than she appears," Becky says.

"I'm a hybrid; I can be wrong," Victoria replies. Unlike me, her dark hair is perfectly braided, not a strand out of place. She's lined her eyes, making the dark blue stand out. With the subtle glow surrounding her iris, it's clear she is using her flames to intensify their color.

She holds everyone's gaze as if she ruled this place. "If anyone is a Blue Flame, it's me. All of you saw the tinge of blue in my flame this morning. So why don't you stop making this imposter your queen and focus on more important matters?"

"And what are the important matters?" Luna asks.

"We need to be focused on how to make ourselves strong enough to impress the king. This is our last week of training, little spark."

I flinch at the derogatory term. It's strange hearing it come from her lips. Victoria might be picking up Ty's speech patterns because he's her trainer. But my gut tells me something else is going on.

"You know not to call me that, Vic," Luna says in a sickeningly sweet voice. From the way Victoria winces, I assume she doesn't like being called by that nickname.

"I would call you by your real name, but it's so contradictory to your skin color," she says.

I freeze and hold my breath. There are no words to fully classify the feelings flowing through me.

Luna stands slowly. Victoria towers over her, but the rage running through my friend's body is evident by the flames flickering across her skin.

Victoria's eyes twitch. "Go ahead and hit me, little spark."

The paralysis leaves me because none of this is adding up. Sure, Victoria is intimidating, but she doesn't pick fights like this. She's not like

Abby; she usually is just trying to survive. And that's the second time I swear she's mimicking Ty's words.

I stand, searching the room; it doesn't take me long to find Major Psycho. He's lurking in the corner, pressing buttons on his bracelet that connects to his trainee. His wild gaze meets mine as he smirks. When the general arrives in the room, I know exactly what he's planning.

"Luna, no." I practically dive over the table, but it's too late. Luna's fist clashes with Victoria's jaw, sending her backward onto the table behind her. The kids at that table smash into others, which cascades through the crowd. Then chaos breaks out.

It's not long before flames fly across the room. The sounds of splintering wood and scraping metal fill the air as tables and chairs are overturned, hastily repurposed into both barricades and weapons.

I grab Luna's hand and pull her away as soldiers break up fights. A wall of white fire engulfs the room, and I fight the urge to scream as I dive under a table. I don't wait to see what happens.

Luna crawls with me, keeping low to the ground as we head for the door. The mixing of flame intensity makes the consequences the other kids will suffer unpredictable, let alone the measures the soldiers will take to intervene. My instincts tell me to get out of here as soon as possible.

I don't know what Ty was thinking, manipulating Victoria like that, but I'm sure he has a plan beyond sending everything into pure chaos.

When the white flames dissipate, we crouch, making our way toward the door. Something smacks me across the face, cutting my cheek and sending me flailing to the floor. Warm liquid spills from the wound as I clutch my jaw.

I freeze when I see an unconscious guard next to me. The device that masks our golden cuffs from the building's electronic sensors sits in its holster at his side. As Luna helps me up, I take it—my chance at freedom.

Victoria launches more white flames at everyone, and a short guy—Thomas, I think—gets hurt as he tries to run away.

Although I've used white flames for months, seeing others use them still frightens me. I don't know if I'll ever get past this handicap, but that's a problem for another day.

Just as I reach the door, a sudden gust of wind slams us against the wall. I didn't think it was possible, but a giant flame tornado is circling in the middle of the dining room. How stupid could Ty be? From Victoria's wide eyes, I can tell she's afraid.

Luna and I peel away from the wall and slowly reach for the door. It takes both of us to yank it open, but when it does, we bolt for the corridor on the other side.

I head to the left, pulling Luna along with me as the mental map I've been creating these past few months fills my mind. The hallways are practically empty, probably because the guards are all heading toward the cafeteria to resolve the situation. Sticking to the shadows and avoiding the windows as much as possible, we make it to the back door of the barracks.

"What are you doing?" Luna asks, halting me in my flight.

"Getting us out of here," I whisper while checking the hallways on either side of the door.

"We can't leave, Clarissa." She pulls me back before I can cross the open space.

"The guards are distracted. I know how to get us to the training plateau. It won't be hard to get out of there."

"Um, yes it will." She holds up her wrist with the shining gold bracelet that matches mine. "Did you forget these link us to our trainers?"

I hold up the device I stole and smile.

She laughs at me, which sours my mood. "That's not the device that lets us pass through the front doors with an escort."

"What?" I examine the device and realize I've broken one of the first rules of stealing: know what you're going for. If this were happening on Ms. Brown's watch, she'd lock me in the basement.

"It looks just like it, though. This one just has a wider base." She takes it from me, inspecting it. "I think they use this for the force fields in solitary confinement."

My fists clench in frustration. "I can't believe I stole the wrong thing."

"It doesn't matter. Trying to escape from this place is probably not a good idea." She pulls me with her back the way we came, handing me the useless device. "We can at least head for your apartment and get cleaned up."

"Fireball doesn't like it when you come over without Gabriel around."

Sometimes I think the dog is more human than animal. She gets a lot more rambunctious if Luna comes too close to me, even snipping at her. It's like she wants to keep me to herself.

"She just takes her job of guarding you seriously. As long as I don't approach you, I'll be fine."

Before we can make it to the elevators, we run into a group of soldiers, and at the head is the Major Psycho himself. Of all the guards we could have run into, he is the last one I want to see right now.

"Well, funny that we find the girl who started the fight and her friend in the hallway, unescorted, near the exit," Ty says matter-of-factly. He takes the device from me. "And stolen equipment from an officer?"

I keep my flame under control, though it bubbles just under the surface. Gabriel advised me to keep it hidden while I'm in the barracks, pretending that he's locked my flame down, and now facing this situation with Ty, I see why. Not only does it give me an advantage to defend myself, but it also leaves me at full strength. But if we can't get these bracelets off, fighting the guards would be futile because we would have nowhere to run.

"We didn't start the fight in the cafeteria," I reply. It's not the whole truth, but it's clear Victoria instigated it. After seeing the smirk on Ty's face and seeing him here now, I am more confident he used his influence over her to start it. What I don't know is why.

"So Luna didn't punch my trainee?" Ty asks.

My heart sinks to my stomach because he has a one up on us. There's no way I can prove he was controlling Victoria to instigate the fight. And it doesn't help that I stole that useless device from a guard.

"That's what I thought," he says. "And now here you are, escaping. This will give me what I need to take you out of Gabriel's control."

My lips part as my body tenses. Was this his plan? To get me to escape, to take me away from Gabriel?

He steps closer so only I can hear him. "Why do you think there were no guards at the door? I knew exactly where to find you. Since Victoria's flame appears about the same as yours, I can easily doctor the video."

I glare at him as my stomach twists.

"We were not escaping," Luna says. "Yes, we ran out of the cafeteria after everyone started fighting, but we got lost on our way back to our rooms to get a first aid kit."

"I don't believe you, little spark." Ty's eyes twitch as he looks me over. "Arrest them."

I have no idea how long we're in the prison, but the way my stomach growls, I'm pretty sure it's at least a day. Several more Rylari prisoners have come down here over the past few hours. All of them look worse than me, but their eyes are haunted, like they don't remember what happened. Given what I saw and what Ty said, I'm going to bet he did something to them. But if it's my word against his; no one is going to believe me.

The jail cells are enclosed by three cement walls, with a seemingly unobstructed space to the oval corridor where a fourth wall should be. I think it's made of some type of electrified glass force field. It kind of reminds me of the giant dome that covers the cities around the country, except this one you can't pass through. It makes me wonder what would happen if the electricity went out. Would the wall just disappear?

I sit on the tiny bench in the back of the cell alone. Luna is across from me on the other side. Despite our efforts to communicate, we can't hear each other. If only I knew sign language.

Being in this place doesn't worry me as much as Major Psycho's words. That he's actively planning to take me away from Gabriel sends shivers down my spine. I have no idea what his intentions are toward me, but I don't think they're good.

The day Gabriel called out Ty's cheating in front of everyone and used his favor to take me from Ty's grasp, I knew he was upset. I just didn't think he was crazy enough to orchestrate a fake fight in the middle of the dining hall. That is the problem with psychotic people; you just never know what they're going to do. With Gabriel and Ty in a virtual war with me caught in the middle, I don't know what will happen to me.

Clutching my middle, I lean my head against the icy wall and close my eyes. The freezing temperature of the stone makes me believe it's an exterior wall. Freedom lies on the other side. Without tools or flames, I can't blow the wall open and escape. They took that away with the power dampening devices in the wall. All I can do is rest and hope I don't freeze to death in here before they decide my fate.

"I can't leave you alone for one second, can I?"

My eyes snap open at the familiar voice, and I stand. Gabriel smirks at me on the other side of the barrier next to the intercom. I run to the wall, never in my life so glad to see those green eyes again, shaking my head. "I didn't do it."

"What didn't you do?" he asks.

"I didn't start that fight. Victoria, she provoked Luna, and then everyone went crazy. All I wanted to do was get out of there," I say. I've never talked this fast before, nor have I ever felt this desperate for someone to believe my words. Then I add all the other crazy things that I saw, including my suspicions about Ty. Of course, I leave out the part about escaping, because he doesn't need to know about that. I'm not sure if Gabriel's belief in me matters or if he even has the influence to help me. For some reason, I need him to believe me, just this once.

His face remains unreadable as he stares at me. I really hate that about him. He's not like this all the time, but when he is, it's always at the worst times when I need to read his emotions. I think he does it to annoy me.

After what feels like forever, he says, "I saw the video."

"Then you should know I didn't start the fight—"

He puts up his hand. "I believe what you just told me. The real video of the fight convinced the general to release you."

"He's releasing me?"

"Into my custody, yes. But he's worried you're going to 'lose control,' so I had to make some unpleasant promises."

"But I didn'—"

"I told you, I believe you." Gabriel presses a button, and the invisible wall crackles before it disappears. He removes my restraints, unleashing the glorious warmth of my fiery power. I never thought I would love my fire as much as I do right now. "The target on your back is getting bigger, Rissa. So please don't do anything to get into any more trouble."

When I open my mouth to protest, he shakes his head. "Save it for later."

I file past Luna's cell. "What about Luna?"

"Since she hit Victoria, she's going to have to stay there for now," Gabriel says. He nods to the prison guards, and they open the doors for us to exit.

"But she's—"

He glares at me. "Not. Another. Word."

As I peek around him, I find Major Psycho sneering at us, his father next to him. I immediately clam up and follow Gabriel without a word.

"Good to see you finally have her under control, Colonel," the general says. "See that you keep her that way."

I clench my fists, keeping my flames under control. The absolute last thing I want is to start a conflict with a group of highly trained military veterans. Plus, I don't want to place Gabriel in that spot again.

"Yes, sir," Gabriel says as he walks with more confidence than I would in his shoes. I follow behind him, almost holding my breath as I pass by the crazy family that raised him. My shoulders don't relax until we reach the elevators leading to our apartment.

Once we're inside, Gabriel grabs a sandwich from the fridge and hands it to me with a glass of juice. "I assume you're hungry. They don't feed prisoners much."

"You mean at all," I reply, then take a bite of the turkey sandwich. Just chewing the food makes the knots in my stomach feel better. Once

I swallow, I head to the dining table and finish the rest. When I'm done, I sigh with contentment.

"Why did you try to escape?" Gabriel asks. He hasn't moved from the kitchen, and I'm pretty sure he watched me eat.

"I thought you said you believed me."

"I do."

"Then what's up with the interrogation?"

He comes around the kitchen island and leans against it as he hovers over me. His muscular, towering figure used to intimidate me, but after living in close quarters, it doesn't have the same effect. "I believe what you said downstairs. But I'm not stupid; I know you don't get lost. You're very meticulous about mapping everything in your mind."

I hang my head in defeat, then hold up my wrist where the golden bracelet sits. "I thought about it, but I didn't steal the right device."

"Thank you for your honesty. And I'm glad you didn't walk through those doors, even if you stole the right device."

"What would have happened?" I ask.

"The devices are coded to the guard's DNA. The building scans the devices together. When your trainer, or in the future, your handler, isn't with you, the building would electrocute you. That's not including the other security measures surrounding this place. That's why I don't worry about you going to the gym in the middle of the night. You won't get far without me."

I blow out a breath, trying to wrap my head around what might have happened if Luna didn't stop me.

"Go take a shower." He nods toward my door. "As soon as you're ready, we'll go up to the plateau and train."

"You trust me out there?"

"You're impulsive about things sometimes, but you're not stupid, Rissa." He runs his hands through his unruly hair. "We have a week before you're thrown into the arena. Despite your power, you're still behind on some of your abilities and control. Do you want to waste your energy trying to escape? Or do you want to use the time to learn how to survive?"

After seeing the immense power used by the other Rylari in the dining hall, I have to admit he's right—I am behind. Not as much as before, but I could still use more training. If getting through the arena is the only thing that will get me and Luna out of here, then I'll do what it takes to get better, faster, stronger.

"Survive," I say.

Chapter Seventeen
Humanity's Enemy

T HERE'S NO WAY I can sleep tonight.

Despite drinking Gabriel's herbal tea earlier, I still can't stop the racing thoughts that are keeping me awake. Unable to bear my constant movement any longer, the dog moves to a cushion on the floor. I laugh at myself, because I feel bad for disturbing Fireball.

Blue flames dance across my fingers in the darkness. As soon as I see them, I immediately lower the intensity to a bright white color. After an intense training session with Gabriel, adjusting the temperature is becoming easier. But it doesn't alter the simmering fear that might trigger a flare-up.

I check the time on the digital clock by my bed. A glowing "two in the morning" glares at me, confirming that there will be no sleeping before the arena.

I throw off my covers and begin pacing, stretching, and jogging in place. Then I drill the fighting techniques Gabriel has taught me. He refined my stances this week, showing me how to use them against larger and smaller opponents. During practice, I may have partially dislocated Zane's arm, which led Gabriel to use it as a lesson in healing others. Among the skills I've gained recently, I appreciate this one the most. But I still don't feel ready.

Blowing out a breath, I move to planks, using my flames to increase my stamina. And after testing my endurance against Luna yesterday, I'm certain my abilities are much higher than the rest of the Rylari.

Really, I'm just happy they released her. Despite having a week of very little food, water, and training, she still beat me more than I'd like to admit. She gloats after each loss, though Gabriel suspects I throw the game. Maybe he's right. Let's just hope the crystal doesn't pair us up in a fight. If we are, I don't know what I'm going to do.

Not knowing what happens in the arena isn't helpful, either. The Rylari with that experience are useless. Though they entered the arena together, each person's story differs. I disagree with Gabriel's assessment that trauma and differing viewpoints are the sole causes, because the dark crystal that hovers over the games controls them. From my limited knowledge, I know it's advanced alien tech left over from Dragons Fall. What's that thing really capable of?

"You're doing that wrong."

I jump, not expecting to find Gabriel in my room. Fireball moans her exasperation, annoyed with the disturbance of her beauty sleep.

"Sorry, I didn't mean to scare you. I just heard some noise in here, and thought I'd come check it out," he says. He's wearing sweats and a sleeveless black undershirt that set off his muscular arms. And I can't help but blush.

"I can't sleep." I stand, then point to my head. "It won't shut off."

"Come on." He waves me to follow him to the living room.

He grabs a remote and sits on the couch. A thin digiscreen appears out of nowhere. Gabriel pats the couch next to him. "Sit."

"I'm not a dog," I reply as I sit.

"Could have fooled me." A smirk touches his lips. He presses another button, and the screen turns on.

A series of colored drawings move across the display, and I swear my jaw is on the floor. I've never seen anything like it. I stand and walk to the digiscreen, trying to figure out how they made the drawings move.

"It's called a cartoon. Apparently, our ancestors loved them," Gabriel explains. "Most of the ones I've seen are funny. I like to watch them when I feel anxious about something."

"Cartoon," I repeat, then take my seat on the couch again, not taking my eyes off the strange rabbit with a carrot in his hand. "How do they do that? I mean, how do they make the drawings move and talk?"

"A lot of still frames and voice actors."

I sit back down, in total amazement, watching the loony little characters play pranks on each other.

I don't know when I fell asleep, but when I wake up, I'm leaning against something warm. At first, I think it's Fireball, but it's not fluffy. I'm so comfortable I don't want to move, but my curiosity gets the better of me, so I slowly peel my eyes open.

"Good morning," Gabriel says.

When I discover that not only did I fall asleep on Gabriel, but I also drooled on him, I practically jump to the other end of the couch.

"Sorry, I wanted to make sure you got some sleep, so I decided not to wake or move you." He tosses the blanket off, showcasing a silver bracelet. I saw it once before, but I hadn't noticed how intricate it was. "Go get ready. I'll make us some food."

"What's that?" I point to the band.

He clutches it like it's a lifeline for him. "It's the last thing I have of my mother."

"Oh," I say like an idiot. Then, I hastily add, "I'm sorry."

"Me too." He drops his arm. "It's graduation day, Rissa. After today…"

"I know." Neither of us are much for words right now, because both of us are worried about what happens next. "I'll get ready; we don't want to be late."

He just nods and moves to the kitchen. I make my way into my room, where Fireball stretches across my comforter like it's her bed. Maybe after today, she'll get it back to herself. I don't know if it will better to survive the arena or not, because sometimes death is a mercy for the living. But for Luna's sake, I need to keep us both alive.

I'm riding to my doom.

I read somewhere that graduations are supposed to be joyous occasions. Families come together offering gifts and congratulations with a wish for a bright future for the graduate. But as we near the arena, I can't help but think it's going to be the opposite for me.

Even from this distance, I can see the sinister, dark gemstone that somehow hovers above the oval building out the transport window. It glows with flames like a dragon about to unleash its deadly breath. My heart thumps loudly in my ears. If I wasn't chained to the wall, with my neck locked into place in this transport, I'd look away from it. But

I suppose that's the point of chaining us at the window. They need our fear at its peak before we fight to the death.

Luna is the closest thing to family that I've ever had in this life. I wish we didn't have to arrive in different transports. My only hope is to catch a glimpse of her before we're shoved into that chamber buried beneath the field. This might just be the last time we see each other, but the alternative of meeting her on the field is worse.

The transport rattles as we turn into the driveway. A sea of people cheer as we glide to a stop near the entrance. They have banners with our names written across as if we're their heroes. A few have digiscreens with numbers scrolling next to everyone's picture. I am pretty sure they're betting on which of us will live or die. Humans are always like that, quick to make a buck off an event that has nothing to do with them. I hope they lose that buck and it goes up in flames.

The archway in front of the stadium is emblazoned with the words *Moriuntor Hostis Humanitatis.* It means something like the dying enemy of humanity. Another warning for half-breeds like me: I'm not really human and not welcome here. The thought is still so foreign to me, because my whole life I thought I was just like them, and now suddenly, I'm an animal in their eyes. But really, besides our flames, what makes the difference between a Glyzul and Rylari? What really makes someone a human?

The transport comes to a stop as soldiers swarm around us, pushing the crowd behind the barrier. Their electrified guns are drawn, already charged and ready to fire. Although the weapons aren't aimed at our transports, I suspect their purpose isn't to protect us. Since death is imminent for most of us, those guns are a means of control, ensuring our entry into the arena.

My transport door swings open, drawing my attention. I'm greeted by the piercing green eyes I've known so well these past few months. He's quiet as he unlocks my power dampening chains, leaving only the hand-cuffs in place, completely focused on his task. In his dress uniform with the coiled snake pin signifying him as a Glyzul, he's scarier than normal. Somehow it makes that rough stubble he calls a beard look like the hood of a cobra. When he trained me, he didn't look this intimidating. Just this morning he made me breakfast, all of my favorites. He didn't seem so callous then, when we were just two teenagers trying to figure things out.

Perhaps the crystal's effects are amplifying my fear. Or could it simply be the enormous group of people surrounded by more soldiers than I've ever witnessed?

Wrapping his arm around my waist, Gabriel effortlessly picks me up from my kneeling position. He sets me gently on the ground, steadying me and waiting for me to regain the feeling in my legs.

Across from us, a Rylari is thrown out of the transport van. I can't remember his name right now, my mind is so jumbled.

"Get up," his trainer screams at him while he cowers on the floor.

He tries to stand but, like me, his legs are too weak to support him, and he wobbles. Being crouched in the same position for over an hour left my legs numb, and the kid is probably no different. The Glyzul soldier takes a whip out, slashing it across the boy's arm. Cheers increase around us, drowning out his cries.

My hands clench together. I'd love nothing more than to face that soldier in the arena, but the stadium isn't for our Glyzul masters; it's for us Rylari slaves. Its purpose is to separate the strong from the weak. Only the fearless will survive to witness the water war on Artijan's western border. But, for the weak kids, today will be their last.

"You can't help him," Gabriel whispers as he tries to guide me away. My resistance only causes him to pull me closer until his face is the only thing I see. "We can't linger here."

His words pull me back to reality. If there ever was a time for sparking a rebellion, attempting something while standing alone in the middle of a hostile crowd probably isn't the smartest idea. Even though I'm walking away, I send up a silent prayer, hoping that the kid is strong enough to face his Glyzul handler when this is all done.

Entering the confines of the glistening, dark gray walls leaves a chill in my bones I can't shake. It's so cold in here, I think the building might actually freeze into a solid ice castle.

"It's protecting us from the crystal." Gabriel places his jacket over my shoulders. "There are a bunch of power dampening devices installed in the outer rim of the arena. It prevents Rylari from escaping, and it stops the crystal from exploring your mind until you're inside."

"How comforting." My gaze travels toward the tall windows, exposing the glowing obelisk hovering above a platform. Much like the infamous Crystal of Death that king wields to keep us in line, the stone making up the sinister structure casts an eerie reddish glow across the field. They say the giant crystal's minerals match those found in caves north of here. All I can think is that it somehow looks hungry.

An electrified force field crackles around it, protecting the spectators. The power funnels to the platform beneath. And under the field, my destiny awaits.

Gabriel guides me through the three-story glass entryway, toward a hallway on our left. Instinctively, I search for Luna. She should be here, but with so many people around, I can't find her. I just hope she's alright. Of course, I shouldn't worry. Having grown up using her flames, she's more skilled with her powers than I am. She proved that to me just yesterday.

As if reading my mind, Gabriel says, "She'll be fine. Zane is looking out for her."

"Maybe so, but you can't stop that thing from incinerating her."

His jaw clenches, probably because I've irritated him again, but he says nothing. It's typical of him to just keep to his brooding silence. If I'm about to die, at least he could have the decency to keep my mind off it.

I glance out the windows, showcasing the crystal I'm about to face. Banners hang around the arena to prepare the crowds for our battle. But really, they're just the decorations for the Dragons Fall festival. If I survive, I might just see how the people of Segura celebrate it.

As we turn a corner, Gabriel pulls me to a stop before we crash into a towering figure. Ty's eyes twitch as he assesses us, lingering on the jacket draped across my shoulders.

"Make sure you wash that before you wear it again. I don't know how you can stand their smell." He wrinkles his nose, his gaze not leaving me.

Gabriel steps in front of me, blocking me from Ty's line of sight. "You're really obsessed with my laundry. And I'll handle my trainee the way I like."

"You treat them like they're human."

"If you stopped treating yours like animals, you might end up with a lesser that actually survives."

Ty gets in Gabriel's face. "I'm the king's heir. I'm the better trainer."

Gabriel's shoulders tense. "Maybe. But the king appointed me as the head of their training for a reason."

Ty just growls as he passes us by. I don't know where Victoria is, but I feel terrible for her. He's yelled at the poor girl so many times, I've lost count. I wouldn't doubt if he hurts her; he seems like that kind of guy.

A strange low rumble pulses through the speakers. Gabriel meets my gaze. It's almost time. The slight crinkling of his forehead is the only thing telling me what he's thinking. He's afraid for me. If I'm honest with myself, I am too.

In silence, we walk to his viewing room. My name is emblazoned on the digiscreen next to his more permanently etched sign. If I die in there, or if he doesn't become my permanent handler, the next time he comes here, my name would be replaced with someone else's. It's like they can just erase us with a push of a button. As I glance down the corridor at the looming crystal, I suppose they can.

After Gabriel uses the palm scanner, the door swings open, revealing a plush, finely decorated sitting area. Even though the furniture looks expensive, the gray walls make the space appear smaller, almost oppressive. But the green throw pillows stand in opposition to the utilitarian decor.

As I swirl around to glance at him, he smiles. "There are a few benefits to being the son of a provincial lord."

"Green pillows? That's all you do in this place?"

He shrugs before he unlocks my chains. "I said 'son of a provincial lord,' not a prince. But I do have a minibar."

Shaking my head, I step inside.

"I'm only seventeen, remember? I can't drink."

"You know, minibars aren't just for alcohol." He hands me a soda and my favorite lollipop to prove his point.

Staring at the food and drink in my hands, I can't help but laugh. This might be my last meal. Despite the strange thought, I drink the cool liquid. I might as well enjoy myself while I can.

Plopping down on the couch, I peel back the lollipop wrapper. The raspberry flavor dances on my tongue. I let out a sigh as I take in the room. This is where my trainer will watch helplessly as I face my worst fears. I've been training for this for months, with extra thanks to Gabriel. He somehow taught me all sorts of skills that would hopefully help me survive this death trap.

I can't help but think about the last girl that was here. She probably sat on this couch and ate these foods before she plunged into the arena. "Did your last lesser survive?"

"I told you she did," he says. "And so will you."

"How do you know?"

"You have the training for it," he says.

He's right. With all the extra private lessons, my flame is hotter than ever before. I turn to thank him, but I'm distracted by the silver locket dangling between his fingers. It's my necklace, the only clue I have of my past. After I was captured, I thought I'd lost it forever.

"How did you get that?"

His lips twitch. "When a powerful Rylari living like a Glyzul for seventeen years with no one noticing comes through the processing center, everyone asks questions."

"How did you even know what to look for?" I ask, pulling my braid aside for him to drape the necklace over my collarbone. His fingers graze my neck, sending goosebumps across my skin. My breath hitches as he adjusts the necklace, straightening it across the fire-resistant uniform.

His cheeks subtly curve into a small smile. "Luna may have helped me with my investigation."

"Why are you giving it back to me?" I'm about to go into the arena to fight against a powerful, advanced alien crystal. Silver dampens Rylari powers. It seems absurd that he'd give this necklace to me now.

"I assume this necklace hid your powers your entire life. I had it altered." He sits next to me, finding the spot concealed under my sleeve where the Rylari brand is. Tracing it through the cloth, he says, "You can't hide your Rylari heritage anymore, but you can conceal your flame intensity."

My lips part. "They're not going to know I'm…"

"You'll at max appear as a White Flame. Powerful enough to make sense of what everyone has seen, but not so powerful as to draw too much attention to yourself."

"Why are you doing this? Why are you helping me?"

He's silent for a moment, but I can see a war brewing behind his eyes. "Besides the king… let's just say, there are people searching for a Blue Flame like you. I think the longer you keep quiet, the better."

I shake my head as I stand, suddenly too jittery to sit still. "What would they want with me? Sure, I'm a Blue Flame, but what could I actually accomplish? I've just learned how to control it. I'm just a nobody trying to figure this out."

"With your powers, you can be used as an object of hope or an object of fear. And people just 'trying to figure it out' are easier to exploit." He comes to my side and points to the floating obelisk. "That thing is going to test everything you've got. It's going to push you to your maximum flame."

"Is that what it's really for?" I wrap my arms around my stomach.

"Honestly, I have no clue what the king really needs it for."

I snap my gaze toward him. "Really?"

"I didn't need to use a dark Sky Crystal to push you to unlock your blue flames, did I?"

Smoothing my hair, I let out a breath. "I suppose you're right."

The low hum of the bell rings again, reverberating in the room. With him so close, it suddenly feels a lot smaller than it did before.

"Don't take this necklace off." He squeezes my shoulder. "The crystal is going to test your fear response. The first test will be the easiest, but the longer you're in there with that thing, the worse it gets."

"I'll remember."

"It's all an illusion, but it will feel real. Hold on to that truth. It will help you get to the next stage faster."

"But not all of it will be simulated. What if I have to face Luna?" It's been the worry that's dominated my mind for weeks. I can't kill her.

"You won't."

A doorway appears next to us, illuminated by glowing red light. It swivels open, waiting for me to step to my doom. It's time for the games to start.

"How do you know I won't face her?" I ask, my focus not leaving the tunnel leading toward the field under the crystal.

"Because facing Luna isn't your worst nightmare," he says, guiding me inside.

"What's my worst nightmare?"

The pivot door slams shut before I can find out his answer, blocking out anything he might say. I touch the door where he was, somehow thinking it will give me strength. It's silly, but I'll take any help I can take at this point.

Facing my imminent future, I head down the long tunnel. Out of habit, I clutch the necklace, kissing it before tucking it inside my uniform. Now that I'm outside the protective confines of the enclosed stadium, I can hear something whispering in the wind. It presses on my mind, probing my every thought, trying to find a weakness. I don't know what that crystal is, but it's certainly something otherworldly.

As soon as I reach the end of the tunnel, cheers from the crowd fill the air. It's graduation day, and it seems the entire city is here to help me celebrate.

Moriuntor Hostis Humanitatis is scrawled across the digiscreens around the stadium. With the jubilant crowd screaming in favor of the coming bloodbath, I wonder who humanity's enemy really is. Is it these kids whose DNA is mutated from a past we didn't ask for? Or is it the people desiring the depraved entertainment?

I guess those are questions for another day, because today is graduation day. Since I have to face my greatest fears, it could be my last.

Chapter Eighteen
Crawling with Fear

THE STADIUM IS BIGGER in person.

There are forty or more of us around the giant crystal, ranging from fifteen to eighteen years old. The crowd's deafening cheers and the pounding music reverberate in my ears, each pulse of sound a sharp stab of agony that makes me want to scream.

With every step nearer the immense structure, the mental pressure builds, along with a rising dread and chilling whispers from unseen sources. Searing pain like lightning bolts rips through my head as the alien structure probes my mind, each jolt making it nearly impossible to move. If it doesn't stop soon, none of us are going to make it into the chamber.

My picture and flame status appear on the massive screen above me, catching my eye. Gabriel did a good job concealing my secret, because it still says White Flame, along with my weapons proficiency: crossbow and daggers.

It's no surprise to me it's silent about my healing abilities. Why would they even be interested in that when we're marching toward our potential deaths? No one here cares about our welfare; they just want entertainment at our expense and to fight their wars for them. It makes me wonder what they'd do to the water wielders in Thevania if we are successful in taking over their country. They'd probably do the same to the water wielders: torment them, then turn them over to the obelisk that rules this place.

Gabriel showed me the true apathetic nature of the people of Artijan. When no healer would come to help the fire wielders here, they were left with my limited medical knowledge to save them. As I stand in the middle of the arena overflowing with a cheering crowd, I wonder if saving those kids was a blessing or a curse.

Luna is a few walkways over from me; she glances at me, then nods. She's a lot gaunter than she was a week ago, but being imprisoned didn't help her strength at all. I hope her abilities will see her through this, but I have my doubts. We're going to help each other if we can, but there are no guarantees.

The shadow of the massive crystal engulfs me as I approach the circular platform near the base. It hums with an otherworldly energy, and I take my place on a glowing circle next to the lower step. A bright blue light spills from the crystal, washing over the smooth surface of the cement platform.

Seeing it in person, standing under it like this, differs vastly from sneaking a peek on someone's digiscreen. The circular disks beneath the crystal seem to float on an invisible track, their smooth surfaces reflecting light as they slowly rotate. I've never seen technology like this before, which makes me wonder how it was built.

There are so many questions popping in my mind, it's difficult to concentrate. Combine that with the pressure, and I feel like I might just collapse right here before we even start the ceremony. Gabriel told me multiple times this week to stay in survival mode, and that's what I plan to do.

A woman appears on the screens above the stadium. Her dark hair is piled on her head with a string of sparkling lights strategically pinned into her weave, making it look like the night sky. Her lips and eyes are painted metallic blue, matching the glittering, high-slit dress molded to her body. She's one of a handful of celebrities that rotates through hosting duties, depending on who is available, but I don't remember her name.

"We welcome everyone to the graduation day of our newest recruits."

The crowd cheers even louder this time, but the crystal's hum makes their chant impossible to understand. With all the smiles and waving flags, it's clear the person speaking, whomever she may be, is adored.

She lifts her hands, showcasing her absurdly long acrylic nails, as she calms the crowd. I don't know how anyone can function with nails like that, but I suppose if this is all she does for a living, her nail length is more about style than practicality.

"The Handlers of the Forbidden Foundation would kindly ask that you support the war effort. To effectively combat the attackers of our royal family, our troops need more financial support. You can transfer credits through the digiscreens to place your bets on your favorite graduates. Every credit counts to support our troops."

Numbers appear on the screen next to our faces, with mine near the top, along with Victoria. I glance at her across the platform. Since the incident last week, I haven't had the time to talk to her. She smiles as if she's pleased by the cheering crowd, which seems strange.

"And now the moment you've all been waiting for: a message from His Majesty, King Grimrose."

The view changes to a large platform at the top of the stadium, its metallic gleam catching the artificial light as it detaches from its place among the spectators. It slowly circles the stadium, the king's regal figure waving to the cheering throngs below. As he floats by, everyone bows or curtsies to him. When he reaches us, I panic slightly because I've never done it before. Awkwardly, I bend my legs while bowing my head, only coming up when he passes us by.

"Thank you everyone. Graduation day is such a special time of year for us all. This year is exciting because we have forty-two graduates here with us today." The crowd roars. "This is also a time for mourning and remembrance, honoring the lives of so many of our children who were taken from us, murdered by our neighboring kingdom."

The crowd turns solemn as the screen displays the bombing of the capital so many years ago. Images of children crying, their faces streaked with tears and grime, flash across the screen alongside scenes of people running frantically through smoke-filled streets. It all happened before my time, at least before I can remember. After this event, anyone who could wield elemental power became Forbidden. They fled to the Dunes, the only place they could be free from persecution.

"As you know, this has been a tough year for the Queen and me. We've lost another child, but we will prevail." He takes a tissue to dab his eyes that don't appear wet. The crowd chants again, drawing a smile from the king. "These graduates we have today are ready to test their abilities. Only the strongest will survive, and the weak will serve a higher purpose to make the will of the shadow crystals stronger."

The crowd holds up dark crystals, the air buzzing with anticipation. From this distance, I can't tell if the crystals are real or novelty items, but the people's sick fascination with this alien crystal is apparent from their wide eyes and smiling faces. They practically jump with excitement, as if they were touching the infamous dark crystal that hangs from the king's neck.

"And we have a special treat for you. Unlike other seasons, we have White Flames among our graduates. We haven't had a White Flame in the arena for a very long time, but when we do, it's always very entertaining."

"I'll say," the fancy blue-dressed woman agrees.

"But it's not just one White Flame. My men found three White Flames hiding from us in the wilderness. I'm so sorry that my soldiers have been so careless. Can you imagine the chaos these mutants must have caused for our friends in the outer provinces?" He shakes his head. "I blame myself and the grief I've been going through for this mishap. And that is why my advisers and I are going to double our efforts, finding every Forbidden hiding in our country."

The crowd cheers in approval as our faces grace the digiscreen. This time I know exactly what they're saying: "Eradicate!"

"Maybe if one of them turns out to be a fabled Blue Flame, we'll have an explosive good time." He laughs along with the crowd, but his mention of my flames makes me flinch. "Either way, today should be entertaining. And with their help, we will destroy our enemies in the west. I hereby open the seventeenth graduation day. Let the celebrations begin."

The crowd roars before the woman comes on the screen again.

"Each graduate will step into the middle of platform one by one before being transported to the underground arena. Betting for your favorite Forbidden will last until they step into the rings. Good luck, everyone."

A white light appears from somewhere above, focusing on Ginger. She adjusts her long braid with a gulp, then slowly climbs the stairs to the middle of the platform. Video of her appears on the screen above as credit amounts I never knew were possible increase as people bet on her ability to survive. Her triumphs and failures in the battle simulator and practice sessions are shown to the world.

She winces, then stands directly under the glowing black crystal, her arms glued to her side. The rings, suspended in the air, plummet down, enveloping her before a dazzling blue light erupts. When they ascend again, Ginger is gone. I know it just transports people below, but it doesn't stop the shiver running down my spine.

Several more kids disappear through the rings before it's my turn. I clench my fists as I make my way to the platform. With each step closer to the crystal, I feel its energy pulsating through my skull, attempting to pierce the veil of my thoughts. I reach the center and turn toward Luna, my heart pounding as I grip my necklace. She nods at me before the disks swoosh around me, lifting my braids with the wind.

Despite myself, I glance toward Gabriel's viewing suite. I don't know why I do it, because I can't see him and he's technically my enemy, a member of our suppressors. He's done everything he can to prepare me for this moment. A part of me wants to think of him more like my friend, and that thought gives me strength.

The bright blue light fills my vision, blurring out the arena and the remaining graduates around me. There's no turning back now, because the only way to escape is through the tournament. What fears await us inside is anyone's guess.

My stomach drops as the blue light fades, then all I see is darkness. The chill of fear creeps into my bones. It's time to face my worst nightmares. Maybe I should have reaffirmed my belief in a higher power before graduation day. Hopefully, he hears my prayers now.

It's so dark I can't even see my hands. I can't hear anything but the powerful drumbeat of my heart. A faint musty smell envelops my senses as I take a few deep breaths to calm the tension in my muscles, trying to think through my options.

Gabriel explained that the crystal would use its understanding of my fears to challenge my limits. It makes me hesitate to use my powers. If I push them to their limit too soon, the stone might attempt to force my flames beyond white and maybe cause me to explode. Despite my necklace's power-dampening effect, I'm hesitant to overexert it, but I can't stay in the dark.

As my trainer taught me, I raise my hand; heat surges through my veins, leaving a tingling sensation in its wake. Flames emerge from my palm and cast a delicate red glow on my surroundings. The cement walls are narrow, only allowing a foot of room to move on either side. The darkness snuffs out my light a short distance ahead, but it's better than not seeing anything at all.

I move forward a bit and then hit my head. Rubbing the sore spot, I glare at the offending low beam in the tunnel. I'm not tall, so I can't understand why they'd build something like this so low.

My breath catches in my throat when I notice thick, milky webs clinging to the wood. Aiming my fire at every nook in the space, my body shivers. This small alcove is filled with a network of spiderwebs that drapes over the support beams, concealing the spiders waiting in the corners with their watchful, beady eyes.

Easing myself under the beam to escape, I inadvertently walk into an even bigger spiderweb. I fling my hand, trying to remove the sticky substance clinging to my arm, but freeze when I feel something moving on my neck.

Adrenaline surges through as I set my whole body on fire while brushing the creatures off. They fall off like crispy pieces of bacon. *Ugh, I don't think I'll ever be able to eat that stuff again.*

I take a deep breath to calm my nerves. "Keep your head on straight, Clarissa. They're just spiders. Creepy crawly creatures that haunted your nightmares as a kid, but they're just spiders. They can't really hurt you."

Taking a few more steps away from the alcove, I extinguish the fire, only keeping the flame in my palms glowing. "Unless they're poisonous. Or bigger than you."

The tunnel seems to go on forever into an unknown darkness that could lead anywhere. I'm desperate to escape this spider-filled hallway, so I hurry as fast as I can, ducking under rotting beams and pushing past sticky webs. Even though I know spiders likely still surround me, I try to ignore it.

There's no point focusing on something I can't control, a lesson Ms. Brown taught me often. I followed that advice for most of my life, getting out of several situations where I was almost caught. It's always better to focus on what you can do to get out of a predicament. That served me well until I ended up in here.

Just when I lose hope of finding an exit, I come across an opening on my left. The walls widen on either side of me, becoming indistinguishable from the darkness. The air is thick with a sickly, musty smell, a blend of rotting wood and decay. My only comfort in this vast, cold room is the warmth from my red flames, barely illuminating the surrounding space in a small circle of light.

Cautiously, I extend the flames, holding my arm up like a torch, slowly intensifying them. My heart drops when I see dozens of dog-sized spiders, their hairy legs twitching, spanning the full length of the ground in front of me. As soon as the light hits them, their large, beady eyes turn toward me. Their oversized pincers click together in an eerie sound that echoes through the hallway, then they lunge at me.

I cast aside my dignity and scream, sprinting into the cramped corridor in the opposite direction. My heart slams in my chest, the rhythm echoing with the frantic flickering of the flames in my palm.

The fuzzy spiders, with their thick, hairy legs, chase after me, scrambling over each other in their haste to reach me. Panic surges through me as my mind races to find a way out, but every path leads to a dead end, and the feeling of being trapped with the spiders is driving me to the edge.

Just as I lose hope, the tunnel abruptly turns. It takes all my effort not to crash into the wall. I scrape past webs, brushing smaller spiders off me, as I bolt as fast as my legs can carry me.

As my anxiety escalates, I struggle to contain my flames. The red hues are quickly becoming hotter, and if I don't get them under control, they're going to turn completely orange. With the hotter flame dancing in my hands as my boots pound on the floor, I can see farther ahead. It's a curse in disguise, though, because the corridor ends, leaving me in a giant cavern covered from floor to ceiling in spiderwebs.

I skid to a halt inches from an enormous web, then spin around. The dog-spiders aren't behind me anymore, staying farther back in the corridor. I can't say for sure if they're keeping me here or if they're waiting for something. My arms shake as I examine the sticky spiderwebs surrounding me. I think I know why they're staying behind. If the webs are large enough to entrap a human, the spider in this cavern has to be huge.

This whole situation feels strangely familiar somehow. It's almost the exact nightmare everyone talked about in the cafeteria last week. We didn't just talk about our fear; we created a plan to conquer it. Spiders don't like fire, and I'm a human torch.

Careful not to go beyond the orange stage, I set the webs next to me on fire. They ignite within seconds, spreading quickly, until I'm surrounded by the friendly flames. The inferno spreads into the corridor, engulfing the entire place. A few gigantic tarantulas wither on the ground as they burn, and the rest of the creatures scurry away in fear.

My shoulders relax, happy to get away from them. I sigh in relief. But before I've had a chance to revel in my victory, a low clicking sound echoes in the burning cave, and my body tenses. I'm almost frozen in place, too scared to turn around, but I force myself to look. A colossal, bulbous spider descends gracefully on its silk webbing toward me.

The eight-legged creature tries to poke at me with its needle-like pincers, but I duck into the flames just like Gabriel taught me. Apparently, not all spiders are afraid of fire, because this one still tries to come after me.

As I roll around in the flames, careful to avoid the rocks, I think of something else that my trainer encouraged me to learn—weapons. I grab a jagged stone, heat it intensely, and hurl it at the spider. It screeches in pain as the rock scorches its back side. The creature slows down its pursuit, but it's not giving up.

It ascends a nearby rock and leaps ahead, redirecting my escape. In my haste to get away, I trip over the uneven ground. The spider takes advantage of my stumble, pulling me toward it with its spindly legs.

I clutch a boulder, determined to avoid becoming its next snack. Kicking and twisting, I free one of my legs long enough to move closer to a stone that's just out of my reach. I stretch my arm to its extent and manage to pick up the rock, then I lob it at my captor, hitting one of its eyes. It releases my legs and I scramble to my feet, carefully running over the terrain.

I have no idea where I'm going, but with the flames moving their way through the cave, they reveal a rectangular, glowing rock in the distance that looks like a door of some sort. My heart flutters at the prospect of leaving this place behind. But when I see that vast empty space between me and freedom, the sheer impossibility of it crushes my spirit. Peering over the edge, I realize the gap is too deep and too wide to jump.

The spider screeches behind me, drawing my attention. Running alongside the gaping chasm, my muscles strain as I desperately search for a way to cross. A sticky web brushes my arm, then attaches itself to the far wall. My stomach drops as I quickly realize what I have to do.

I scramble to the top of a massive overhanging rock above the canyon. The spider follows me, shooting long webs that I have to swerve around as I step farther back to get a running start.

"Please let this work," I say before letting out a deep breath.

Taking off at a sprint, I propel myself along the ground before pushing off the boulder, launching myself across the void. For a few minutes, I'm weightless, soaring through the air like a comet. Then gravity takes over, and I plummet in my arc. I'm close to the edge, but I know I won't make it.

Just when I think my plan has all gone wrong, something hits me in the back, propelling me to land on the ground on the far side. The webbing wraps around me as I roll to a stop. Despite my near-death experience, I laugh as I gaze up at the ceiling, probably looking like a mummy in a long-forgotten cave. I ignite my flames to melt the silk strings binding my body while the spider searches for a way over.

Once I'm free, I jump to my feet, then head for the doorway. Without hesitation, I jump through, glad to have survived the spider.

I freeze when I walk through at the same time as another fire wielder. The boy shakes when he sees me, knowing that my flame burns much hotter than his red ones.

"Congratulations. You've reached the next stage. Battle simulation activated. The loser will not advance," the computerized voice says.

Suddenly, I want to go back to the room with the spiders.

Chapter Nineteen
Red Drone

THERE'S NO WAY I can do this.

The boy clenches his fists, hesitating to move. A few months ago, he was almost a stick, but after training on Major Psycho's team, he's broad like a tree trunk. He's didn't arrive at the training center with me, so I can't remember his name, but I think it starts with an E.

Ethan? No. Everett? No. Elli? No.

I'm terrible with names. I wish I had taken more time to get to know everyone more. Maybe that was a mistake, but I was so behind everyone else and prioritized needed additional training.

Eric! That's right, that's his name.

From what I can remember of the last battle simulation, he took out several of our operatives. So I know he could kill me if given the chance.

"Ready yourselves, graduates," the mechanical voice warns.

My opponent shifts, his palm igniting with flickering red fire. The space separating us isn't extensive, and with his longer legs, he could probably reach me in a few strides. If I'm forced to use the maximum temperature of my flame, the kid is toast. It will take a lot more flame from him to take me down. From this distance, he won't even leave a mark on me. My advantage lies in speed and keeping the distance between us. I need a place to take cover, but other than a few columns, there's not much to hide behind.

I try to match Eric's intensity, but the pounding in my chest makes control nearly impossible. Before entering this world, I didn't know the distinctions between Rylari flame classes. To me, it didn't matter if one person's fire was more intense than the other because it was still fire—something to avoid. But my flame can melt metal. It would be easy to inflict actual damage to the feebly fleshed humans, even to the Rylari who are a lower flame class than me, which is literally everyone here. I have to remain in control.

Maybe that's the point of this challenge. If the crystal is trying to push us to panic, pitting us against each other is likely to force us to the next flame intensity. Since I outmatch him in flame and he out matches me in strength, it is only a matter of time before one of us makes a fatal mistake.

On each side of the oval room, alcoves open to reveal weaponry: daggers in one and a sword in the other. Anticipation makes my hands tremble as I prepare to grasp the short, snake-hilted blades.

Adding the weapons to this fight gives me a new sense of fear. I've never killed someone before, and I really don't want to start now. But this is a survival situation. I might be left with no other option than to take drastic measures.

"Chose your weapon," the voice says.

Without hesitation, I lunge to my right, running at top speeds before Eric has time to attack. I barely have my fingers wrapped around the hilt of a dagger when a blast of sweet-smelling gas fills the air, flowing from a vent above me. I scramble away, but it's too late. My surroundings start to tilt. Glancing at the kid behind me, I watch him stumble backward, coughing, before grabbing onto a nearby column, the same noxious gas from his alcove choking him.

I pin myself against the smooth cement, using my dagger to cut a piece of cloth from my sleeve and covering my mouth.

"Cover your mouth and nose," I say between coughs. If the room keeps filling with gas, we'll end up unconscious on the floor, or worse, dead.

I only have one dagger. Regardless of what the computer allows, knives could be helpful for future challenges. Having them around during my spider battle wouldn't have been a bad thing. With the world spinning, I launch myself at the alcove, bracing myself against the wall as I attempt to grab the rest. My hand fumbles through the air, desperate to find the handle, before finally closing around one of them. It takes a few more minutes to grab them all, and I nick my hands more than once on the blades.

With the toxic gas filling the air, I don't have time to secure the daggers in holsters. I cough as I stumble away from the vent, holding the daggers in one hand and the holsters in the other. The floor is completely covered in gas by the time I crash into the column. Somehow, I keep a hold of the daggers but lose the holsters. Letting out a breath, I tilt my head back against the cold stone, trying to get my bearings.

"How are we supposed to fight each other if we're drugged?" Eric asks, clearly not able to move much. He's maybe only two years younger than me, and he's strong enough to wield the heavy sword. He grips it like it's the key to surviving this place.

"Maybe the challenge isn't what we think," I say through laborious breaths. The effects of the poisonous cloud strain my already hammering heart, making it difficult to remain vertical.

"I don't want to kill you."

"I don't want to kill you, either." To prevent myself from falling, I press tightly against the stone surface. Breathing more gas won't help the spinning world that's beginning to make me feel nauseous.

"Truce," he says.

A chuckle escapes my lips, growing louder with each passing moment. The last time I really laughed like this, I was locked in a dark basement. Maybe it's because I've suppressed it for so long that I apparently laugh at inappropriate times now. This situation is so stupid, I can't help myself. "It's not like we have any other choice right now."

"You're right." He laughs too, making me wonder if this stuff is laughing gas. "Did you face spiders?"

"Oh yeah, the mother of all spiders," I say, trying to regain my composure.

"I wonder if the others faced the same thing."

The reminder makes me think of Luna for the first time since being here. I really hope she survived the spiders, or whatever challenge she faced. She's lived on the run for so long, she's probably fine. She might have even passed the challenge faster than me. "Since it was an awful lot like the scenario we talked about in the cafeteria, I'm going to guess they did."

"Do you know what's strange?" he asks.

"What?"

"We only thought of that a week ago. How did they find a giant spider that quickly?"

Eric's words almost sober me because there are no spiders that large in the world, unless they had help. But changing something like that takes a long time. No way they got this done in a week unless they already had a plan.

"I don't know. Maybe they planted the story." Thinking about what Ty did to Victoria to start a fight in the cafeteria, it makes me wonder if he was the instigator.

"Maybe you're right, but I don't know what good it would do for anyone," he replies.

"It keeps us alive longer because we've already figured out how to defeat the spiders. They don't want us dead yet."

He grunts something when a loud beeping noise comes through the speakers, blocking out his response. I freeze, glancing at my surroundings, waiting for something to attack me. The toxic fog stops coming through the vents, then another alcove opens, revealing about a dozen oval-shaped drones.

"Defend yourselves," the computer says.

As soon as the computer stops speaking, the tiny machines come at us. I use my flames first, thinking it will be much easier than trying to throw the daggers, but I'm very wrong. The flames spread around a force field, rendering my powers useless against the drones. It's possible that they are just resistant to lower-level heat, but I don't want to push myself to a higher flame yet.

"We need to work together," I say while ducking out of the way of the flying contraptions. I throw a dagger. It grazes one of the slender wings, sending a drone careening into another one. They explode into several pieces before falling to the ground.

"We're supposed to be enemies," he replies while swinging his sword wildly. He hits one, sending it flying into a wall, but misses the rest. When one charges him, he's forced to jump out of the way and crashes to the floor. He screams, and I run over to him, dodging the annoying metallic beasties. When I touch his shoulder, he screams again.

"Get off the floor," I say as I cover his mouth.

He tries to sit up, but his arm gives way. It hangs limply at his side, apparently dislocated from the fall.

"Come on, we're getting out of this gas." I help him sit up, then lean him against the wall.

Two drones come flying at us. I grab his sword, then crouch in anticipation. The metal blade is heavier than I like, but I'm sure I could swing it enough for this attack.

When the first drone comes, I swing, clipping the tip of the wing and sending it in the opposite direction. The second one prepares to fire its laser beams on us, but before it can shoot, smoke blocks my view. I turn to find Eric using his low-level flames to create a smoke screen, making it difficult for the contraptions to aim at us. Combined with the gas surrounding us, we could become invisible to their sensors.

"Good thinking," I say, following his lead. By the time the smoke fills the area, I can barely make out the nearby column. The blinking lights from the drones are the only things I can see in the dark fog. The more smoke that fills the room from his flames, the slower the drones travel, making them much easier to hit.

"Let's move," I whisper before helping him a few feet from our previous location.

He continues to create smoke while I form a fireball and throw it around a column. It distracts the drones and illuminates them long enough for me to lob a dagger at them. The closest one to us crashes to the ground, lost in the gas. Growing more confident in my plan by the minute, I lob a few more daggers at the attackers. With my flames inching dangerously close to reaching the yellow level, I send more fireballs through the chamber, increasing my chances of hitting the drones with my blades.

"Careful, you don't want to push yourself too hard. We don't know what's coming next," he says while keeping the smoke rising in the room.

I clench my fist, extinguishing my flames to reset them. He's right. My default flame intensity is bubbling to the surface. I need to calm down to maintain control. Before I have time to reset, the remaining drones come at us. I grab Eric and yank him out of the way. One of them crashes into the wall where he sat, but the other four swerve just in time.

"They must have triangulated our position," he whispers. With his good arm, he leans into the wall to help him stand. "We have to move."

Following him around the perimeter of the oval room, I keep my gaze toward the middle, catching a few glimpses of the drones through the smoke. They continue to attack our previous location, confirming his assumption. We take refuge behind a wall in the alcove I arrived through. It's not as concealed as I'd like, but it's better than nothing. This part of the chamber has less gas in it, which will make it easier for the drones to find us.

"I don't suppose you know how to fix my arm?" he asks.

From my studies, I've read about fixing dislocated limbs. But there's a difference between reading about something and actually performing it. Sure, I've seen Ms. Brown do it loads of times at the orphanage. There was always one kid or another that would make a rash decision and end up injured. Ms. Brown even set my arm back into place after Abby pushed me out the window.

"Sort of," I whisper back. "I've never done it myself, but I've read about it and seen it performed several times."

"On a scale of one to ten, how confident in your knowledge are you?"

I bite my lip. Knowledge wise, I know exactly how the muscles connect, but my fear is doing it wrong and making the injury worse. "Six, maybe seven."

He lets out a breath. "Good enough for me."

He maneuvers himself down to the floor. I tentatively place my hand on his shoulders, knowing full well this is going to hurt. If I use my white flames on him, I could lessen that pain, but I don't know if it's a good idea.

As if reading my thoughts, he shakes his head. "Just do it with the pain. I can take it."

"I'm Clarissa," I say while I gently take his arm.

He winces. "Everyone knows who you are. You, Victoria, and Serene are famous."

My eyes widen.

"Don't look so shocked. We keep track of our elite fire wielders like they're rock stars. It's been that way since before the royal family was assassinated and might be more so since they're gone."

I blow out a breath, then move his arm behind his head. "I'm sorry that I didn't take the time to talk to you more than that one time in the cafeteria."

"Don't be. I'm just another red drone. My name's Eric." He takes a deep breath as I push his arm farther back.

"You ready?"

He nods. I shove his arm, and he gasps as the shoulder pops.

"Thanks. Best doctor I've ever been to." His shoulder relaxes as he closes his eyes, relief washing over his dark features. "Now let's take these little pests out."

Together, we emerge from our hiding place. The smoke is almost clear from our previous hiding place, and the flying contraptions stop attacking it, instead scanning for us. I stay low, keeping just above the gas to conceal us from their sensors.

"Do you have a dagger?" Eric asks. "I lost my sword."

I nod, handing him two of mine, leaving me with the final three. We emerge from our hiding place, each of us unleashing our fire. The drones come at us in attack formation, passing through our flames effortlessly. I throw the remaining three daggers at them. Two of them land, but the other just misses its target. Eric lands one of his shots, leaving us with only two drones left.

"We need weapons," I say while searching the ground.

"Not necessarily." He ignites his palm. "We can always force them to become their own worst enemy."

I smile, latching onto his plan. "I'll go right."

He nods, then disappears. Before I go to my side, I send an arching red flame ball down the middle of the chamber. It distracts the flying contraptions long enough for Eric to throw another flame ball between the two drones, causing them to spin around.

I run for the right, sending another fireball between them to disorient them further. Together, we keep up the pace, going one at a time before they finally decide to split up, each of them taking on one of us.

Ducking out of the way of one of them, I fall to the ground, landing on something soft. My eyes widen as I grab the holster I dropped earlier. When the drone comes for me in a nosedive, I swing the holster around, smacking the drone across the room. It swirls like a baseball as it crashes to the ground.

"Winner. Congratulations, you can proceed to the next stage." A door opens in another hidden alcove. It's difficult to make out what's on the other side. I'm not sure I want to know what we have to face next, but at least I won't be facing it alone this time.

The gas is vented from the room, revealing my daggers and the remains of the drones. Picking my way around the room, I strap the daggers into the holsters as I tie them around my waist and legs. Eric grabs his sword, though his grip isn't as good as it was before he injured his arm.

"Ready," he asks.

"Probably not," I reply.

He chuckles. "A pessimist. I like it."

"I'm not pessimistic…" I pause, thinking about his words in relation to our surroundings as we walk to the next challenge. "Okay, maybe in here, I am a pessimist."

"The hardest step is admitting your problem. Good job." He extends his free arm toward the open door. "Ladies first."

"So chivalrous."

"Artijan may think we live like renegade filthy animals in the Dunes, but we have manners."

I eye him. "Either that or you want the spider to eat me first?"

He shrugs with a smirk. "It was always the women sacrificed to the beast in those old movies from before Dragons Fall."

"You have movies in the Dunes?"

"Yeah. Digiscreens are easy to steal."

"But I thought…"

"That we were renegade filthy animals with no class, hellbent on killing everyone in Artijan?"

Heat rises in my cheeks. "Well, not that exactly."

"Don't be embarrassed, Clarissa." He pats me on the back. "We Rylari are well aware of our reputation among the Glyzul population. But I guess it's time to learn that you're a part of us now. Despite the propaganda, all of us are human… we just sparkle a little more than the Glyzul."

"If we survive—"

He shakes his head, silencing me. "When we survive."

"When we survive this, you're going to have to teach me to unlearn all my prejudiced notions."

"Of course." He smiles again, showing off his dimples. "Now, are we just going to stand here talking, or are we going to survive the next challenge?"

I squeeze his arm, then step through the doorway to the other side. The world surrounding me blurs before I'm in a very familiar room. From the fancy floral wall paper to the decorative molding and overly frilly curtains, I've known this place since birth—the orphanage.

Turning around toward the door I stepped through, I see Eric on the other side. He's banging on an invisible surface as if it's solid. I tentatively try to reach through the doorway, but I'm met with resistance; a force field of some kind is blocking my path. Eric's face twists in fear as tears flow from his eyes. It takes me a moment to see why he's panicking. The gas is back on, but this time, it's completely flooding the room.

I pound on the force field, even attempting to use a dagger to penetrate the invisible wall. As soon as the gas surrounds him, his body ignites in flames, slowly pushing him further.

"No," I say, paralyzed by fear.

His body convulses as his fire reaches for the yellow stage.

"We both took those drones down," I scream, pounding on the electrical field. "Let him go."

I ignite my hand, forcing it through the field. It glitches and weakens.

"Error. Contestant breach," the computer says.

An electrical pulse shimmers through the field, forcing me backward to crash into a table. Once I untangle myself, I glance at the doorway, but it's gone. A shiver runs through my spine when I remember what the computer told me at the beginning of the challenge. "The loser will not advance." I should have known it meant death.

I rub my face as tears flow down my cheeks, trying to figure out how it determines winners and losers. The only thing I can think of is that I took down more drones than Eric, but I could be wrong. After letting out a deep breath, I pull in another one, slowly trying to calm my racing heart.

"Now, Clarissa, you know what breaking a table means in this house."

Her words send a shiver down my spine. I haven't seen her in months, and I relished not being around her. But now, she looms over me with a menacing arched eyebrow and stern, thin lips. Ms. Brown.

"How is this possible that you're here?"

"This is my home," she says before dragging me up from the broken tables. "You, however, will be punished a week for your insufferable behavior."

She flings me forward, pulling me to the door I've grown to fear my whole life—the basement. The vines and flowers seem to grow the closer I get to the door. It's silly because it's just a room under a house. But with Ms. Brown, it was never just a room. She turned it into a torture chamber. After opening the door, she practically shoves me down the narrow wooden stairs, trapping me in the damp, musty darkness.

Chapter Twenty
Controlled Burn

I can't tell what's real anymore.

Lying on the cool, damp ground, lost in the darkness, my head spins. The space is familiar because I've been here before. This is where Ms. Brown would keep us when we disappointed her, while the good kids stayed upstairs working away to steal a fortune for her.

Were the last few months all a dream? A concoction of my imagination, because I've been down here too long?

I don't know how long I've been stuck in this basement, but my rumbling stomach is convinced it's been a month, which can't be right. People can't go that long without food or water, right?

Wincing at the pain in my bruised ribs, I clutch my stomach and roll to my side. The chains that bind me to the wall clink as I move. Ms. Brown clarified that breaking a table is cause for the most severe punishment. My side has taken the brunt of it when she practically shoved me down the stairs.

But she didn't punish me for breaking the table. She sent me on an errand to steal those papers. Right?

Ms. Brown would certainly lock me in the basement for a day for breaking something of hers, but she would never shove me down the stairs. Any physical punishment was always minimal because it would eat into her profits if we couldn't do our job.

Using the wall for support, I stand, then let out a breath. It's dark down here, and I can't see much past my hands. When I extend them to stretch, flames spark out of them, illuminating the area.

That's new. Or is it?

As the heat courses through my body, my memories return. Everything comes into sharper focus as I take steadying breaths, the flames stitching my ribs back together.

"Not a dream," I whisper. Since I have fire coursing in the very fiber of my being, this basement can't be real. And it also means Eric really died.

Squeezing my eyes shut, I hold back the tears. This is the arena, and its graduation day. But how did they orchestrate such an elaborate replica of my childhood home?

Before I can fully realize the thought, squeaking hinges alert me to the intruder, then the light flickers on, practically blinding me. After extinguishing my flames, I rub my eyes. With a deep breath, I turn, waiting for whatever torture she has planned for me today.

"My, my, you continue to destroy my house, Clarissa. You're very disappointing. Maybe that's my fault because I had such high expectations for you." Just like in my memories, her hair is perfectly coiled, not a strand out of place. She stops in front of me with a stern, thin-lipped frown that I've seen on more than one occasion. "If you do not learn your lesson, I will just have to continue with more punishments."

I roll my eyes because if this is just an actor playing a part, she clearly didn't do her homework.

The Ms. Brown lookalike scrutinizes me, her expression unreadable, as if trying to understand my every thought. "Being beaten doesn't scare you, does it?"

"You already know what scares me."

She steps closer to me. "I want to hear it pass from your lips."

"You with your face smashed in the mud." I brace myself for a slap, but it doesn't come.

"Always the little jokester," she replies.

It's another lie. I was the quiet, obedient one. Well, mostly obedient. Abby made it difficult to keep my head down. But I never said anything like that to Ms. Brown because I wasn't stupid. If she punished me for laughing, I can only imagine what she would do if I talked back to her. This just confirms my theory that she is not my real caretaker. My former guardian is a master at figuring me out, like an evil mother you never wanted.

If she is an impostor, who is she? Or what is she?

"Since you're in such a snarky mood, I guess you can come out of the basement." She unchains me, which would normally shock me. "You can clean the floors. We have a special guest coming soon."

Rubbing my wrist, I ask, "Who?"

"You'll see."

When I reach the top, I find the bucket and sponge waiting for me. The table is different, likely changed when I was locked up. The doorway where I witnessed Eric's death is gone. It's like it never happened, but every time I close my eyes, he's there with his terrified eyes and screams burned into my mind. Even though it wasn't by my hand, I can't help but feel guilty.

Maybe I should have let him go first?

"I want it spotless," Ms. Brown says. Her heels click on the floor as she leaves for her office.

I sigh before dropping to my knees. At least this is a simple task that doesn't require facing instant death. After dunking the sponge into the soapy water, I scrub the wood floors, grateful for the reprieve. Then it happens: the stupid orphan song blares over the speakers.

"Of course," I mutter, almost wishing the spiders had eaten me. It's just a tune, nothing to be afraid of, except I have listened to it nearly every day since I can remember. To drown it out, I hum, changing the lyrics to suit my mood.

There'll be no light, tomorrow
Promise shadows will bring so much sorrow
There'll be death.

I quietly chuckle while continuing my work. This should have been my go-to method all along; it makes the chore a breeze and even more comical.

It's not until a shadow looms over me I remember where I am. Ms. Brown watches me with her hands on her hips.

"You missed a spot." She points to the floor in front of her with her perfectly polished nails.

I blink a few times when I see the mud tracked in. This is too much like before, except the last time Abby was in front of me, not Ms. Brown.

How could they know my memories like this, however twisted they might be?

"Hurry up and clean, Clarissa. We don't have all day." She taps her foot on the ground, waiting for me to comply.

I let out a breath, picking up the bucket of water as I stand.

This isn't Ms. Brown. I repeat the words over in my head because what I'm about to do goes against everything I've ever been taught.

"And you messed it up," I say, pointing to the signs at all the entrances. "You tracked in the mud, not me."

"That was the wrong move, young lady," she sneers.

"Was it?"

Just as she tries to grab me, I swing the bucket of water. The pail smacks her in the face as the water sloshes onto the floor. She screams, but I ignore her, taking off in the opposite direction toward the kitchen.

When I push open the door, I pause. The place is loaded with food from fresh bread to roasted meats to vegetables. It's a full banquet that I've never seen in this house before. I slow my pace, my stomach grumbling, pleading with me to take a bite.

With the footsteps behind me, I shake out of my hunger delirium. It's probably poisonous or something, anyway. Then head out the back door onto the perfectly landscaped backyard. I run at the fence at full speed, then climb over, but I'm not prepared for what I find on the other side.

Instead of the half dead forest I expected, I find myself in front of a burning house. It's the same one Luna and her friends rescued me from, a place that doesn't exist anymore.

"Save me. Rissa help, please."

I stare at Luna standing inside the fire. She's somewhere in the arena with me, that much I know, but is this really her? From this distance, I can't tell.

Reaching out my hand, I connect with the flames. They feel unruly and violent, very different from the fire I'm used to. With a deep breath, I close my hand, and the flames slowly snuff out, leaving smoke in its place, but the energy from them isn't gone.

"Watch out," Luna says.

I turn just in time for the Ms. Brown lookalike to tackle me to the ground. Without thinking, I unleash the unruly malevolent fire that was burning the house. She screams as it burns her, turning her to dust.

Sucking in a breath, I settle my rapid heartbeat. Watching her disintegrate because of what I did is unnerving. Despite the torture I endured over the years, I've never wanted to harm her. I would have loved to see her in jail, but that's not the same. Despite the trepidation twisting my stomach, a part of me feels liberated by the prospect of purging her from my life, to let go of all that pain. Still, did it have to be like this?

When her ashes float away, an iridescent door appears in the fence, waiting for me to step through. I glance back at Luna. She's gone too, along with the house.

Shaking off the unsettling experience, I head for the door. Once I'm on the other side, I look back just as the doorway shuts, leaving me locked in a rectangular room eerily similar to the one Eric died in.

"Congratulations. You've reached the next stage. Battle simulation activated. Losers will not advance," the computerized voice says.

My hands shake as I glance at the boy and girl in alcoves on either side of me. Their eyes are wild, reflecting my fear like a mirror. This time the computer says "losers," meaning only one of us will advance. I close my eyes, remembering what happened to Eric and wishing for this moment to be over.

"Injections."

My eyes snap open just as a needle pricks my skin of my arm, depositing a translucent green liquid. My head starts spinning, and my vision goes blurry—I'm definitely feeling the effects of whatever they gave me. The symptoms are similar to the gas from earlier, but it's a lot more potent in this form. I have no idea how we're going to battle like this, but we're going to have to figure it out. And if I can help it, we're going to figure out how to stop the computer's twisted kill switch.

For now, I focus on the poison. The only way to get rid of it is to burn it out of my blood. As I increase my internal temperature, sweat beads form on my skin. To produce a fever, I need a hotter flame, which plays right into the computer's demands. At this point, I don't care. I can't function in this drug-induced state, and neither can the others.

The young boy on my right is maybe fifteen. His short golden locks are in chaos, making him look like he just got out of bed. Like Eric, he was on Ty's team during our training exercises. I think his name is Freddy. I could be wrong, but I remember his flame class: Yellow. Yellow Flames can't heal themselves, but healing others is his specialty, just like Luna.

I really hope Luna's okay.

On my left is the girl is about my age. She has her chestnut hair pulled into a ponytail that's a little out of sorts. Her name is Becky. She's a Red Flame on Gabriel's team with me. She can't heal herself or others, but she can ignite objects and use them with deadly accuracy.

"Good luck, graduates."

Three alcoves open on the opposite side of the room, revealing three glowing crystals. I'm not sure how the stones will help, but last time there was an unexpected twist, so I bet there will be one here too.

The world gradually stops spinning. Releasing a breath, I lower my internal temperature. If my fellow graduates will let me, I can burn the poison out of them too. Judging by their fiery eyes and skin, I doubt they'll allow it, but I'll give it a shot. We need to work together against the computer, not fight with each other.

"Reach the crystal, win the challenge," the computer says.

"That's it," I say out loud.

As if the computer is listening to me, the room morphs. The crystal alcoves slide backward as the ground drops, revealing a deep cavern of molten hot liquid. Rock pillars rise from the ground spaced several feet apart, close enough to jump across if I judge the distance right. The way they taper in the center makes me question their ability to support my weight.

"You had to say something, didn't you?" Freddy asks, then shakes his head.

"It probably has nothing to do with what she said," Becky defends me while bracing herself against the wall of her alcove. "This challenge was probably already preset."

"Touch the lava, and you lose. You have twenty minutes to reach your crystals, graduates. Begin."

My heart accelerates in my chest as my mind races to calculate the distance between me and the first pillar. Before I can think, Freddy leaps across, landing hard on his shoulder, then he nearly falls off the other side. He groans while trying to hang on the ledge.

"I'm coming to help you, Freddy," I say, trying to back up to get a running start.

Freddy glares at me while he tries to pull himself up. "You've got to be kidding me. We're enemies."

"Do we have to be?" I ask.

"Freddy's right. Only the winner will get out of here alive. We can't trust each other; we're on our own now," Becky replies. Before I can stop her, she leaps over the space between the alcove and the closest pillar. In her drugged state, she misjudges the distance and falls off the side. Her arms flail as she tries to grab onto something, finding purchase on a ledge just below the flat part of the pillar.

Clutching my chest, I let out a long, deep breath. Their harrowing near-death experiences are doing nothing for my control over my flames. I press myself against the back of the alcove as I prepare myself for the jump. Victoria can use her heat in combination with cooler air to create a tornado. I thought Gabriel was lying when he told me it was possible until I saw her attempt it twice. Never had time to try it myself. I'm still a novice, but I wonder if I can use my flames to give me enough boost to reach my target.

Keeping my flames in the red, I run toward the end of the alcove, leaping into the air with all my strength. I move my hands behind me, intensifying the fire like an old combustion engine I read about in my history books. It gives me the extra boost I need, allowing me to roll onto the smooth platform at the top of the pillar.

I redirect the flames to counter the force pushing me toward the lava below, skidding to the opposite side just before the ledge. I shake off my anxiety, slowing pulling my flames under control again, having almost reached the white flame level.

Scrambling to my feet, I assess my companions. Freddy is almost back on top of his pillar, but Becky is too short to reach the ledge above her. There's only a tiny gap between our pillars, and I barely register the jump as I race to help her up.

"Give me your hand," I say, reaching for her.

"No, you'll just drop me," she replies.

"If I wanted to do that, I could have just left you here and gotten my crystal already." I extend my reach, clinging to the rough stone to prevent myself from tumbling. "It's this or death; your choice."

She purses her lips, then jumps to clasp my hand. The weight nearly pulls me over, but Freddy grabs my feet.

"Don't look so shocked," he says as he pulls me back.

My muscles feel like they're going to rip apart by the time we get Becky on top of the pillar. We topple over, none of us getting up for a few minutes.

"You have fifteen minutes left to complete your task," the computer reminds us.

The computer's words revitalize our energy, and we jump to our feet to assess the path toward the other side. From this vantage point, I can tell there are pillars with narrow middle sections that will probably crumble if we jump on them. If we can, we'll need to avoid them.

Freddy sways a little as he nears the edge, and I pull him back.

"Let me heal you," I say, hoping they'll both agree. "It will make it easier for you to jump across."

He shakes his head, then sits down. "This is too dangerous."

"I don't feel so good," Becky says as she sits down next to him, clutching her stomach.

"If we don't unite against the computer, it's going to pick us off one by one. We need to work together."

"We'll never make it across; there's no point in trying." Becky slumps to the ground.

"What is wrong with you guys?" I ask.

They stare at me like I'm crazy. I let the yellow flames dance over my hands, deciding to use a different approach to reach them. "I've already burned the poison out of me. It's probably making you sick. Let me get rid of it for you so we can win this challenge together."

"But you'd have to use your white flame, wouldn't you?" Freddy asks.

"A low level one for you guys, that's it." I've only recently used my healing abilities on others, so it might be a lie.

Becky is the first one to cave, stretching her arm toward me. I grasp her hand and let my bright yellow flames flood across her body. After a few minutes, she sighs, and her agitated glare is gone.

"Thank you," she says as she pulls her hand back. "That stuff is toxic."

"You're welcome."

Freddy studies the flames in his hand but doesn't reach for me. I bite my lip, trying to figure out how to encourage him to let me heal him.

"Let go of your pride and let her heal you. You know she's a White Flame. The tests are going to favor her over us anyway," Becky says.

"What?" I ask.

"As if you didn't know," Freddy says, rolling his eyes. "This game the king makes us play never kills the strongest flame in the room. Well, not unless they do something really stupid like one kid a few years back, but that's beside the point. White Flames will never die in these things, but loads of Red and Yellow Flames will."

Becky clears her throat. "More Red Flames than Yellow."

"Sorry," Freddy says. "But you get my point."

"Why?" I ask.

He shrugs. "I guess the king only wants the higher flame levels to win. Usually the hotter the flame, the more likely they'll live. Every once in a while, the system will favor a lower level flame, but it's rare."

I glance at Becky.

"Yeah, that means I'm for sure going to die in this. That's why I figured taking your help couldn't hurt," Becky says.

"If I take your help, it will put Becky at a disadvantage," Freddy says so softly I can barely hear him.

From his twitching limbs, I'm sure he won't make it across this labyrinth at all. He needs to burn off the poison to stand a chance.

"Has anyone tried to win these challenges together?" I ask.

"Not that I know of," Becky says.

"Me either," Freddy adds. "I don't think the computer would allow it. Not after what I..." He closes his eyes, a single tear falling down his cheek.

I reach for him, knowing it's futile unless he accepts my help. "Then let's see if we can do this together. We won't know unless we try."

He wipes his face on his sleeve, then grasps my hand. I send the smallest flickers of Yellow Flame toward him.

"At least I won't be sick to my stomach when I die." He lets out a breath, then releases my hand.

I roll my eyes, gaining control over my fire before extinguishing it. "Have a little more positivity, will you?"

"Honestly, I don't know how you're staying so positive after the last challenge." He stretches his arms, swinging them around to get limber. "Some guys murdered my sister. I was about ready to lose control."

"Same here, but it was my mom," Becky adds. "What was your challenge, Clarissa?"

"Um..." I bite my lip because I'm not sure I should tell them. If the last challenge had something to do with family or losing family, then it must have failed with me. I've already lost my family, so there's nothing for me to fear. "It was... I'd rather not talk about it."

"Totally agree," Becky says. "It's probably better to forget all of this when we're done."

Freddy points to the next platform. "I think I see a pattern. The columns that look like this one, with the perfectly smooth square platform at the top, are sturdy. We can probably land on those and not worry. The ones that are uneven on top will probably break if we touch them." He focuses our attention on the middle of the room. "But we need to use them when the gap between them is too big."

I nod. "So rest on the solid ones before we jump on those. Got it."

Together, we follow Freddy's pattern toward the center of the room. When the gaps are larger, Freddy and Becky use their fire to give them an extra boost, just like I had earlier. It makes getting to the center platforms easier.

With a running leap, I ride the unstable column toward a solid one, jumping just in time to roll onto the platform in the center of the room. Wiping the sweat from my forehead, I study the columns on this side of the room while tracing my necklace through my shirt.

"We made it this far," Becky says. "But I'm not sure how we're going to make it through this side together."

She's right. Most of the columns are the kind that will fall if we jump on them. It wouldn't be too much of a problem if there were more of them, but with the pattern I'm seeing, we're going to be playing dominoes as we run. If our paths cross at any point, one of us is going for a swim.

"If me and Becky stick to the sides, you can run down the middle." Freddy points to an almost perfect path to the other side.

"One of you should take that path," I say.

He shakes his head. "You're shorter than us, the gaps are too large, and you've already started tapping into your hottest flames."

I glance at the platform with the crystals, then at the three paths. It's like the distance between the pillars was determined by our height. There's no way I can make it safely on the side paths without using my powers.

"Fine, but you two go first," I reply.

"Are you sure?" Becky asks.

"If these games are rigged toward my flame class, then it's going to be easy for me to get across. If either of you get into a trouble, having the extra columns will help you."

"But then you wouldn't..." Freddy trails off when he sees my glare.

"I'll figure something out. When you get to the other side, don't pick up the crystal until we are all together. We will grab them simultaneously to ensure all of us are winners."

"Sounds good," Becky says. "Good luck, guys. We've got this."

"You too." I give her a small smile, my mind already trying to focus on the task in front of us.

"Hey, don't die. I mean it. We need more people like you," Freddy says, then hurries toward his path.

"Ten minute warning," the computer says.

I roll my eyes while prepping to jump. Giving them a head start is a gamble, but I'm not about to let anyone else die. Not if I can help it.

"Begin liquefaction," the computer adds.

I don't have to ask what that means because the columns in front of us are sinking into the lava.

"So much for your plan," Freddy says. "Jump."

Chapter Twenty-One
Illusions of Truth

I DON'T THINK ABOUT it. I just jump.

As soon as my feet touch the surface, the column lurches, my momentum sending it sideways into the next pillar. Bracing myself, I run up the slope just in time to leap to the next one. The domino effect has started, and I don't have the luxury of thinking through any problem solving right now. It's just running, leaping, and breathing repeatedly as I pick my way through the sinking columns. While the pillars in front of me are sinking slowly, those behind me are already submerged.

I pick up my pace, misjudging the next leap enough that I nearly fall off. I grasp the edge of the rocky surface as it leans forward. With the adrenaline coursing through my veins, I get my feet up to brace myself, just in time for it to hit the next pillar.

My heart pounds in my chest. I've lost my momentum, and I'm not sure how to get it back. Climbing to the side, I get back to my feet, running across the surface that's dangerously close to the boiling lava below. The next pillar is already falling to the side, thankfully in the direction I need it to go. But if I don't get to the next one in time, it might not fall forward like I need.

Using my flames, I try to propel myself faster as I leap toward it. When I land, I'm more than halfway down the side of the giant pillar. I race to the top as my column lists to the right. It's falling in the wrong direction, just enough to push the next one toward Freddy's side. I have no choice but to follow the falling columns, even if they take me to the wrong side.

Leaping onto the next one, I see Freddy slightly ahead of me, riding a column toward a stationary one. I decide to push the next pillar in that direction, hoping it will give me just enough reprieve to regain my momentum.

The giant rock smacks into the column, nearly knocking me off. I leap at the last second, grabbing onto the edge of the platform before the other pillar lists sideways, then melts into the lava.

I let out a breath, then climb to the top. As soon as I roll onto the platform, Freddy's angular face greets me.

"You were supposed to stay on your side," he says.

"I tried." With effort, I pull myself to my feet, the remnants of the pillars looming around me. Only six more on my lane of columns and seven for Freddy's.

"Your plan won't work."

"How do you even know my plan?" I ask.

"Logic." He points to each one, showing me how it would play out if I took one of his columns. "You want to get back to your lane, but you can't, not without taking out too many of mine."

Rubbing my forehead, I let out a breath, because he's right. My only option is to watch as the molten lava consumes the pillars, and with them, my only chance of escape.

"I might regret this, but come with me," Freddy says.

My eyebrows rise in disbelief, wondering if he's actually serious.

"What can I say, your little speech inspired me to be chivalrous." Before I can protest, he guides me to the edge.

"Five minute warning," the computer says just as the ground rumbles beneath our feet. Fountains of lava erupt from the ceiling, making it even more impossible for me to go back to my lane.

"Keep up." He forces me to jump with him. I brace myself for impact as we free fly toward the next pillar.

Freddy lands ahead of me, looking like an elegant cat and making me wonder if he played sports back home. I land just behind him, nearly falling over, but I remain on my feet. As the pillar tilts forward, we run up the side, his long legs giving him a greater advantage to reach the next platform.

He leaps just in time, pushing the next column enough to avoid a lava fall. I leap after him, following his lead, and we jump to the next column and the next until there is only one left. The only problem is it's too short to reach the top. We're going to have to make a leap no human is capable of, but a fire wielder may have a chance.

Pushing myself harder, I practically fly across the stone column just behind Freddy. We land on the last pillar concurrently. It leans just in time to avoid a new lava flow. I race up the incline as fast as I can. The pillar crashes into the side of the platform where the crystals sit. To my surprise, this pillar isn't sinking yet.

When I reach the top, Freddy is already scrambling to the platform, then he disappears. My stomach lurches when the column falls a few feet, making my jump impossible without help. I call to Freddy, but I don't see him. My heart thumps loudly in my ears as I try to find another way up.

Hopefully, he hasn't betrayed me.

Moving backward, I take a deep breath. There are jagged little rocks that I could climb if I can reach them, but my muscles are already burning from my flight through this deadly puzzle. I get a running head start and push my legs as fast as I can. The pillar tilts further, dropping a few feet more. I make my last leap toward the platform. My fingers dig into the rocks as the column completely gives way to the lava below.

My feet scramble for purchase as I dangle above the liquid hot rock. Sweat pours down my neck, and my hands aren't faring any better. With a grunt, I haul myself up, fingers scraping against the rough rock as I reach the next handhold. My fingers, slick with sweat, lose their grip as I reach for the next handhold, leaving me dangling precariously by a single arm. Against the rock, my other hand slides, and tears well in my eyes.

Just when I think I'm doomed, someone grabs my wrist and starts pulling me up. I find Freddy and Becky working together to help me. Using the last bits of strength I have, I leverage myself to make it easier for them. Once I'm safely on the platform next to the crystals, I laugh again. This whole arena is ridiculous.

"One minute warning," the computer says.

Together, we leap up and take our positions in front of the crystals.

"Together," I say.

"Together," Freddy and Becky echo.

I count off, "One. Two. Three."

We grab our crystals at the same time. A force field erects across the lava filled room as the remaining pillars, including the stationary ones, are swallowed by the molten rock.

"Congratulations, graduates. You will proceed to the next stage."

I smile at Becky and Freddy.

"I've never been so happy to be wrong," Becky says.

"Yeah, me too," Freddy agrees.

Looking around the platform, I can't find the familiar shimmering door that leads to the next challenge. It's strange because they always appeared when I completed them.

I open my mouth to ask the others when the ground disappears beneath my feet, and I'm falling into a tunnel. The only source of light is above me, but it's getting farther away by the second. I clutch my necklace like it's going to save me, and it pulses against my skin, like a familiar friend waiting to help me.

The tunnel twists and turns for what feels like forever as I slide toward the bottom. My stomach churns with a sickening anxiety, picturing the ghastly creatures and treacherous pitfalls that could lurk in the darkness. I don't know what the computer thinks is a fun slide for humans, but this isn't it.

Just when I think this falling sensation will last the rest of my life, I tumble across the bumpy floor. The world turns, but there's no light. No way to see what monsters live in this place. I come to a stop, smashing against a jagged rock. I reach for my head, feeling the warm liquid spilling from my skull. The world spins more before I give into the need to sleep.

My eyes flutter open. Everything hurts, from my head to my toes. Instead of seeing a rocky cave, I'm staring at an overly flowered canopy that hangs above a very cushy bed. From the large, bright gold flowers all the way to the tiny white flowers, the bizarre pattern reminds me of Ms. Brown's wallpaper, but in cloth form.

I search my memories for the last thing I can remember, and I'm pretty sure I didn't land here. In fact, I'm almost confident I should be inside a cave, probably with some creature about to eat me. Clutching the cloth on the back of my head confirms my suspicions: I hit my head pretty hard.

It takes my vision a moment to adjust to my new surroundings. The fancy golden wainscoting lining the room makes the gaudy floral decoration worse.

I've seen rooms like this in Silver City when I traipsed through fancy homes, but I never slept in one before. The soft mattress makes me wish I had at least stopped to test them out. I shift in my bed to sit up when someone pushes me back.

"You're safe, I promise."

I blink a few times in disbelief. "Gabriel? What are you doing in the arena?"

He gives me a half smile. "You're not in the arena anymore. You survived, mostly intact."

"I did?"

"What's the last thing you remember?" he asks.

I think back to the lava room and Freddy and Becky. My heart hammers in my chest because I don't know what happened to them after I fell into that tunnel. "I landed in a cave and hit my head. Are Becky and Freddy okay?"

He glances away from me. "In a manner of speaking."

I sit up more and instantly regret it as the dull pain in my head makes the room spin a bit. Clutching my head, I brace myself against the bed rest. "What do you mean?"

Gabriel lets out a breath, seeming a lot more aloof than normal. "They survived the arena. But the king handed out the assignments a week after the event was over."

"And?"

Gabriel runs his hands down his face. "As with most Rylari, they were assigned to the front lines. Becky was drowned by a water wielder. Freddy was killed by an electrical discharge when he tried to heal someone in the middle of the same battle."

My breath hitches as tears fall. They were such great people; I was hoping to get to know them better. Now, I won't get a chance.

"Wait. How long have I been out?" I ask.

"About a month," he replies.

"A month? You mean it's May already?"

"Yes, almost June actually." He smiles. "I should say congratulations for surviving, but it seems silly."

"What about Luna? Where is she?"

He opens his mouth to reply when the door swings open. The last person in the world I ever thought I'd see again comes bounding into the room. Her blond locks are coiled on her head, adorned with a small glittering tiara. The pink satin dress swishes as she bounds over to Gabriel and hugs him.

"You wouldn't guess what I found in the shop today, sweetheart," Abby says, then kisses him passionately in a fierce embrace. My heart sinks into my stomach. I'm not sure whether it's the sight of Abby kissing my trainer that unsettles me or if I simply find public displays of affection disgusting. Either way, I just want it to stop, so I throw a pillow at them.

Abby gasps, then her face scrunches with shock.

"Um, honey." Gabriel pushes her back, then points toward me.

"Oh, Clarissa. I didn't know you were awake," she says in that sickening sweet voice of hers. It's a facade I know all too well, and it means she's about to torture me with something. "I supposed you don't know, because of the injury and all. Gabriel and I are getting married next week. Isn't that so wonderful?"

I clutch my stomach, trying desperately to keep the bile down. The last thing I ever suspected was Abby being attached to Gabriel. But the more I think of it, the more it makes sense. She was grifting a provincial lord's son. Gabriel is a provincial lord's son, and his home is the closest to the orphanage.

All I want to do is sink under the covers and never come out. I thought I had gotten away from Abby. Instead, she's going to marry my trainer. And if he's been appointed as my handler, I'm going to have to see her every single day for the rest of my life. It almost makes me want to go to the front lines. At least there I could have some peace.

"Aren't you going to make her answer, sweetheart?" she asks.

He bites his lip, and from the way he looks at me, I almost think he's going to force me to do something. "I can't anymore. I'm not her handler."

"What?" I ask at the same time as Abby.

"She didn't finish at the top because of the head injury. I could have pressed to get her again, but I decided with the wedding and a new wife, being in charge of a lesser would be too much." He shrugs. "So I gave up the burden so I could focus on you, beautiful."

Abby's face contorts with anger, but she smooths it out before Gabriel notices. "That's so sweet of you."

Swallowing the bile rising in my throat, I ask, "We were being graded? If you're not my handler, then who is?"

He glances nervously away. "There was a petition filed with the king for you. There were several, actually. But one petitioner held more sway than the others."

"Who is it, Gabriel?"

"Ty Prescott."

"What?" I practically leap off the bed with a surge of adrenaline, throwing the covers into a big heap on the floor. "How could you let Ty be my handler?"

"I can't go against the king's wishes," he answers. "He is giving the crown prince whatever he wants. And he wanted you."

"I thought he was an unofficial heir, not a crown prince."

"The queen died during her pregnancy while you were unconscious, ending any hope for a prince. Which means Ty was officially adopted as the crown prince of Artijan."

"No. No. No. No." I pace the room, ignoring the throbbing pain in my head. "This can't be happening."

"I'm sorry, Clarissa," Gabriel says.

I stop to look at him. "Where's Luna?"

"She's with Zane here in the palace." He stands, removing Abby's arms that entangle him. He reaches for me, but I back away. "I promise she won't be going to the front lines."

"How can I trust that promise?" I ask.

He inches closer, and I can feel the heat of his body envelop me. "Because Zane is one of mine. I get to say where he is deployed. I will make sure Luna never sees the war."

"And if the king sends your unit to the front lines? What then?" I ask.

His fingers graze the skin of my neck, sending goosebumps down my neck. "I can still keep them safe at base camp." Biting his lip, he adds, "If only you weren't an abomination, we could be together."

My eyes narrow at him. He's never used those words with me before. This behavior is so unlike him, it makes me wonder if Abby bewitched him.

This is too overwhelming for me to handle, so I pull out of his touch, nodding toward Abby. "I think you should just focus on your grifter fiancée."

He nods, stepping away. "Since Ty is your handler, I look forward to having you at our pre-wedding celebration ball tonight."

Clenching my fists, I watch him walk out hand-in-hand with Abby. She gives me a smirk and a wink, then closes the door. As soon as I know they're gone, I belt out a guttural scream. Flames ignite across my arms as I continue to unleash my voice, growing from yellow to white. It makes me feel powerful and yet weak, because I can't do anything about my situation. I'm trapped.

Too tired and dizzy to stand, I crumple to the floor.

I don't know how long I remain on the floor, but I'm pretty sure there is a permanent burn mark on the rug. Even after I dozed off for a while, my flames continued to burn. Which is strange because they've never done that before, always going dormant when I slept. Nothing makes sense anymore, and I can't handle this drastic change in my world.

Clutching onto that last thought, I sit up. *Nothing seems right.*

There's a knock on my door, but I ignore it. If Gabriel's come back to talk to me, I don't want to hear anything he has to say, especially if he's not real. I wipe the tears from my cheeks, hating myself for being like this. The door creaks open, and I steel myself for anything he has to say to me.

"Hmm, I thought you'd be dressed by now."

My body shivers when I hear that tenor voice. It sounds just like my worst nightmare. My fists clench when his menacing gaze fills my vision.

"Maybe you are broken like everyone says you are," Ty says, clamping the golden bracelet on my wrist.

I glare at him, waiting for my powers to go cold, but they don't. "What happened to your precious Victoria?"

"Oh, well, she fell into the lava." He shook his head. "Clearly not up to the task. But you made it across, and you're a White Flame. Having you as my lesser just makes sense, and you were a bargain compared to Serene."

"I'm glad I could be so accommodating."

"Me too." He rubs his hands together. "Now, get dressed."

My body moves without my permission, and despite trying to resist the command, I march into the bathroom to get ready.

"I hope this is fake," I mutter I as I close the door. Ty takes a seat on the bed with a smirk on his face. Never in my life did I imagine hoping to be in the arena, but that's how I feel right now.

A half hour later, I'm dressed for a ball. The dress Ty makes me wear is practically a nightgown, barely covering the important parts. I constantly have to tug the thin layers of fabric across my chest just to make sure they stay in place. The long slits up both thighs leave me feeling exposed, but I'm not the only one wearing these barely-there dresses.

Ty guides me around the perimeter of the ballroom, greeting people as we pass them. It's a circular room with vaulted ceilings, with a few embellishments near the top, and painted motifs I can barely make out in the dim lighting. I've never been to a ballroom before. Sure, I've been in many homes that have a designated party room, but I was always upstairs during the events. Seeing all the glittering jewels, delicious food, and ornate attire, I can understand why the elite like these parties so much. It's a way for them to show off their wealth.

My new handler stops in front of the dais. The king nods to Ty, then lifts his hands. The music stops, and the dancers face the dais.

"Where is the happy couple?" the king asks.

Gabriel, in his black military dress coat adorned with all sorts of medals, steps forward with a gushing Abby at his side. Unlike me, she's swathed in a light purple dress that clings to her upper body before flowing outward into a billowing skirt. Silver beads embellish the cloth, forming the snake motif of the capital and the motif of Silver City. The thought that she's going to have some authority over others makes me almost want to vomit, but I hold it together. I can't make a scene before I find Luna.

"Congratulations to the future province leader and his soon-to-be wife," the king says before lifting his golden goblet.

The crowd follows his lead, except for me and Ty. We don't have drinks in our hands.

"I have another wonderful announcement." The king extends his hand toward us, and Ty guides me up the stairs toward the dais. "My adoptive son, Tyler Prescott, as you know, was announced last month to become my heir apparent."

The crowd claps enthusiastically, except for Abby. She's glancing at me and Major Psycho.

"But what you don't know is that Ty has decided to follow in my footsteps." The king prattles on about the importance of tradition and unity. "As many of you know, my late wife was from the Forbidden. It was a sacrifice I made for the good of Artijan."

With everyone staring at me, I fight the urge to roll my eyes. I'm in a room filled with people who would love nothing more than to find an excuse to kill me.

"You'll obey me, or I will command you," Ty whispers in my ear.

"And he has chosen Clarissa, a White Flame victor as his wife," the king announces.

Ty squeezes my hand as my eyes widen with shock. This is the last thing I wanted or ever expected to happen. I can't let it happen, but right now, I have no clue how to stop it. My head is swimming with confusion as Ty kisses my cheek, then shows me off like I'm his property. I guess as my handler, I technically am his property, but that doesn't give him the right to treat me like this, like his dress-up doll to show off to the world.

Heat rushes through my body, but it doesn't bubble forth. It can't anyhow; the cuff will prevent any flame from escaping. The crowd is clapping and cheering and chanting Ty's name.

I don't know how long I stand by him before he lets me go, but it feels like forever. The crowd parts for me, already treating me like I'm something more than I am. It's all fake and, frankly, stupid. What difference does it make for the Rylari if I'm married to the future king? Absolutely nothing. The last queen did nothing, and my role will be the same because we are slaves to the fake picture they're painting.

Once I'm at the buffet table, I take a cup and dip it into the liquid, then down the pink drink in one gulp. It's disgusting because it tastes pink; there are no other words to describe it. But I do it again at least three more times before someone grabs my arm.

"I'm sorry," she says.

Sighing, I drink the last bit of liquid in my cup. "What does it matter, Luna? We all knew we were going to become slaves at one point or another."

"Yes, but you have to do it on Ty's arm in front of the cameras. I know you hate being the center of attention."

Setting my cup down, I embrace her. "I'm glad you're okay, my friend."

"Me too. About both of us."

Rubbing my temples, I say, "We have to find a way out of this."

"Why? The Glyzul are excellent masters," she replies. "This is way better than living in the Dunes, barely scraping by."

That's not the Luna I know. She'd never say living as a slave is better than being free, even if she has to sacrifice a little comfort. This is the third person not acting like themselves. Which either means everyone has been body snatched or I'm still in the arena, in some kind of illusion.

As soon as the thought forms, an iridescent door appears on the other side of the room.

I try to run for it, but Luna grabs me and pulls me back. "Where are you going?"

I clasp her hand. "I have something I need to do."

"No, you don't."

Reminding myself that this isn't real, I shove Luna off me, then run toward the door. I'm almost there when I trip and tumble head over heels across the smooth floor.

An annoying laugh reaches my ears.

"She's wearing granny underwear," Abby says.

"I knew she was a lost cause before this. I don't know why Ty thinks she could be a queen," Gabriel replies. "But I'm glad he didn't find you." Then he passionately kisses her.

I shake off my embarrassment and run for the door, shoving anyone out of my way. Crashing through, I let out a sigh of relief when I'm on the other side, until I see four other Rylari kids with me.

"Congratulations. You've reached the next stage. Battle simulation activated. Losers will not advance," the computerized voice says.

I groan in response. Not only am I going to have survive whatever trap they have in store for us this time, I'm going to have to do it in a dress.

Chapter Twenty-Two
Rejection

I NEED TO FOCUS on the next challenge.

The room has a strange octagonal shape to it, but that could change once the computer starts its twisted games. I wrap the long material of my dress between my legs and tie it off, then I kick off my heels, leaving them in the alcove's corner. My companions look as bewildered as I feel, and their clothing looks just as out of place as mine. The boys are wearing top hats and tails while the girls are in gowns. It makes me wonder if they experienced the same strange ball I did.

"The only way we're going to survive this is if we work together," I say.

There's no point arguing this time. I've had enough of these games; the emotional toll they're taking out of me is unreal. If I have to, I'll blow through the walls of these illusions with my flames to show them the truth.

Between experiencing that strange world I just left and the weird constructs of Ms. Brown, I'm sure we're in a simulator of some kind. I could be wrong, but Gabriel said that everything would be fake. I just didn't know how real it would all feel, or the disorientation of each challenge. The only thing I know for sure is that not everyone will make it out alive.

"Clarissa's right." The boy next to me rips off his hat, revealing his curly black hair, then removes all the fancy bits of his outfit that impede his movement. "I wouldn't be here if we hadn't worked together in the lava room," he says. "I'm Edgar, by the way."

Edgar was on Ty's team in the barracks. Even before this training, he had an athletic build, but now he's like a pile of muscles.

"I'm Beatrice," the girl on Edgar's other side says. "Clarissa, how did you tie your dress?"

I bite my lip as I look at her billowy ball gown. Where mine fits my curves and already has slits, her legs are swallowed by layers of tulle. If she has to leap or run, the thing will probably imprison her.

"Rip the tulle off, then tie the skirt together," I decide.

"What about mine?" the girl on the other side of me says.

For the first time, I take her in with a smile. "Glad to see you, Ginger."

Gabriel and I were both worried about her in the weeks leading up to this. She visited the infirmary more than anyone else. To see her come this far brings me some hope that we'll get out of this alive.

I assess her dress; it's almost a mermaid silhouette, way too tight to run or do much of anything. "Rip slits on both sides until you have a full range of motion for your legs."

"Right. And how do I do that?"

"Here." The sandy-haired boy tosses her a knife.

"Thanks, Mark," she answers, then gets to work cutting up her dress.

The groaning sounds of stone reverberate through the room as it morphs into a swimming pool. This time, there are no pillars rising to provide a path to the other side, where five buttons wait for us on stone pedestals.

"Great, swimming. Every Rylari's dream vacation," Edgar says.

My breath catches in my throat because I don't know how to swim. The lake near the orphanage was practically dead, no one would dare go in it or drink from the water, let alone swim in it.

"It's not like it would be difficult," Beatrice says, then points to a set of stairs on the other side.

"The water isn't the scary part; it's what they put in the water that I'm afraid of," Edgar replies.

I ball my hands into fists, the tightness in my chest mirroring the pressure in my grip, knowing he's right. Every experience we have is like a building block, molding our fears into reality.

"Don't add to our problems," I chide. They look at me like I'm crazy. "We are in some type of simulation. Whatever we fear is coming true."

"That makes so much sense," Mark says. "I mean, why would my mother be here?"

"So, don't think about our fears?" Ginger asks.

"The more we feed into it, the more likely we're going to experience it," I reply.

"Why?" Beatrice asks.

"Because fear gets us to use our maximum powers," Mark answers.

Every simulation, my flames have intensified. If the next stage pushes me, I'll struggle to bring a stop to it. My only hope lies in my necklace, which Gabriel altered for me. Despite my costume change, it's the one thing that made it through to this challenge.

"Make it to the other side and push the button. All paths are open for a limited time," the computer announces.

The ceiling transforms into a dizzying array of pulleys, rings, and intricately shaped hand grips, while narrow beams and platforms extend from the surface, creating a precarious obstacle course over the water. It gives me a glimmer of hope that I can make it to the other side without taking a swim. I just have to time everything perfectly.

"Good luck, graduates. You have ten minutes to cross on my mark," the computer says as stone objects start swinging across the platforms.

"Creatures in the water." Edgar points to a triangle swimming nearby.

"Great, an obstacle course," Ginger says. "I might just need to take my chances with the creatures."

"Use your flames to give you strength or propel you across," Mark says.

"At least get as far as you can before you chance it with the beast," I say. "If we help each other, we can all reach the other side on time."

"On your marks."

Glowing lines on the ground appear in front of me, marking where I should place my feet. I follow the instruction, igniting my flames for the first jump, which is thankfully not as far away as the lava room pillars. The memory makes my skin crawl, and I desperately hope Becky and Freddy are alright, no matter where they are.

"Get set."

I take a deep breath, already crouching to leap across and preparing for whatever unseen surprise is in store for us. Scanning the area, I try to find a path forward that will play to my strengths. One thing I am good at is climbing things: trees, buildings, mountains, doesn't matter what it is. Unless there's a surprise, I should make it to the other side quickly.

"Go."

I jump, flying almost in sync with the others. We land on our platforms at nearly the same time. The surface tilts, threatening to throw me in the water.

"Run," Mark yells, clamoring toward the other side of his platform.

I follow the idea, running as fast as I can to the other side. The platform moves with me, dipping dangerously low, making it impossible to jump to the next platform.

"Stop," Beatrice yells. "We won't make it unless we tilt this thing right."

I come to a sudden halt, then back up to the center, and the platform levels off. My companions do the same, searching for a way to get to the next platform without falling.

"I can reach it now," Mark says.

"But if you move, we won't make it," Edgar replies.

"There," Ginger says. "There's a slide under the platform. If we time our jumps right, we can reach that even if the platform crumbles."

"But I can't see where it leads," Beatrice says. "What if it leads into the water?"

"Nine minutes, graduates."

"We'll have to take our chances," I say, preparing myself for the leap.

I push my legs into a sprint. With the platform hurtling toward the water, I time my jump perfectly, landing on the metal slide beneath the next platform. After sitting, I search for the end, preparing myself for the next obstacle. Gravity will carry me to the bottom before throwing me into the air to catch tiny little loops several feet above the water.

With a deep breath, I push myself down the slide, with my bare legs hovering slightly over the metal so it doesn't burn me. The drop makes my stomach twist as I hurtle faster and faster toward the water. If there wasn't the threat of death, I can see how someone would think this is fun. Just as I'm about to reach the bottom, a huge pendulum swings across the slide. I plaster myself against the slide as I narrowly pass under it, making me lose some momentum.

Instead of gracefully flying toward the rings as I planned, I'm flailing through the air, desperately trying to reach them. I reach out at the last second, barely catching one as I dangle over the water by one arm. Just to add to my anxiety, a toothy fish swims under me.

With a deep breath, I swing myself over to grasp the next ring. It doesn't take me long to get into a rhythm, and I'm suddenly thankful for Gabriel pushing me to strengthen my upper body.

I reach the next platform, happy to find it stable. The metal surface connects to several others with climbing walls that reach all the way to the ceiling. My arms are too sore from the rings to attempt an upper body obstacle course now. I consider my next options.

Edgar leaps across to a platform near to me, then heads up to the next level. The others are picking their way through the course, and I'm grateful we all made it. Deciding to go up, I jump to the next level until I find a narrow beam. Three pendulums swing across it, and I decide to take it.

Closing my eyes, I visualize running across to the other side. When I open them, I time the swings, then take my place. Once the first rock passes, I step onto the beam, quickly making it past it before it whooshes behind me. The second one swings in the opposite direction, but at a faster pace. Once it passes me, I scurry past it. The wind it creates as it travels across the beam nearly makes me lose my balance, but I tighten my stomach as I reach my arms out to stabilize myself.

I square my shoulders, watching the next one. It's much faster than the others, so I inch closer to it until I can almost touch it. I let it pass by me several times before I make my move. Scurrying across the beam,

I almost leap for the platform as the pendulum nearly hits me. Once I'm safely on the other side, I bend over, trying to calm my racing heart.

"Seven minutes left, graduates."

"As if I need the reminder," I mutter before continuing on my journey. From what I can see, Edgar is slightly ahead of everyone, and Ginger is slightly behind. I watch her jump to the next platform, being more cautious than normal. I can't blame her; if I was as accident prone as her, I'd be extra cautious too.

The next several obstacles are a blur as I pick my way across. My muscles scream at me to stop, but I have a few more apparatuses to go before crossing the finish line. Edgar is already safe on the other side, coaching everyone.

"Two minute warning," the computer announces.

A part of me wishes we can turn it off, but we need to know how much time we have to complete this. I shake my head as I hop down to the next platform.

Taking a deep breath, I jump to grab the handlebars above me. Once I make sure I'm stable, I swing back and forth, rocking the circle bar out of its locking mechanism and onto the next, continuing through the obstacle until I'm nearly to the other side, with sweat pouring from my forehead.

Mark joins Edgar safely on the other side. It's just girls left with a little over a minute to go. Only one more obstacle stands in our way.

I take a deep breath. It's a hanging wall with bars protruding out of it. It's another crazy upper body challenge, and I can only hope my muscles are going to hold up. The tricky part is going to be swinging onto the surface on the other side.

I grab the beam and jump, dangling high above the water. If I fall from this height, I'm sure it's going to hurt. I inch my way across the beam to the end. The next beam is higher, which means I have to jump with my arms. I've done it once before when Abby threw me out of the window; this should be easier.

I build momentum by swinging, then I jump. Gripping the bar with whatever strength I have left, I stabilize myself before I scoot across to the next smaller beam.

"This one's tricky," Edgar yells. "Make sure you go for the upper one. The lower one is angled wrong."

I nod, unable to use words.

"One minute warning," the computer says.

I make the leap, and while midair, the apparatus descends toward the water, messing up my calculation. Barely catching the bottom bar with one hand, I try to regain my footing, but there's nothing for me to gain purchase. My muscles are burning, but I use my fire to give me strength as I reach with my free arm.

Something splashes in the water behind me, and I make the mistake of looking. My awkward position makes me lose my grip, and I slip off the bar. I plummet to the water and brace for impact.

The frigid water is numbing, but it brings a welcome relief to my aching muscles. It absorbs all sound, leaving me alone with the drumming of my heartbeat in the unsettling silence. I thrash and struggle, my limbs flailing in a desperate attempt to reach the surface, but I'm utterly helpless. My lungs burn, an agonizing reminder I need air. If I don't get there soon, I won't make it. Just as I'm about to burst, something grabs my waist, hauling me up.

I gulp several greedy breaths, my chest heaving, barely taking in Ginger smiling at me.

"Come on, we don't have time to float here. We probably only have forty seconds to race up those stairs and push that button," she says. "And there's a creature heading our way."

"What?" I glance behind me, watching that gray triangle swimming in our direction. "I don't know how to swim."

"I gathered that. Just don't fight me." Ginger grabs my waist again and swims us both toward the stairs.

I try to kick to make it faster, but the enormous toothy fish gains on us. Just when I think I'm about to be eaten, Ginger reaches the stairs.

"Thirty seconds," the computer says.

The toothy fish snaps at us as Ginger and I race up the stone stairs, trying not to slip. Edgar and Mark stand around their buttons, urging us to hurry.

"Fifteen seconds," the computer says as we reach the top.

I take a minute to realize we're missing someone. "Where's Beatrice?"

Mark points to a red spot in the water, and I nearly fall to my knees.

"No time for that now," Ginger says, holding me up. "We'll mourn her later."

Tears are pouring down my face as I stand by my button.

"Ready?" Edgar asks. "One. Two. Three. Go."

We push our buttons simultaneously, ending the obstacle course of death.

"Congratulations, graduates. You will proceed to the next stage."

I sink to my knees as I hold my head in my hand. We've lost another one. How many more were killed that I don't know about? I'm not sure I can take much more of this.

An invisible force drags me back through a newly formed doorway, and the surrounding air rushes by as it pulls me through. Landing hard on the cold floor, I find myself in a room of countless mirrors, each one showing a different perspective of my fall.

I look like a rat drowning in a body-size diaper made of sequins.

I pull my damp hair away from my forehead, the chilling memory of the pool's murky depths still fresh in my mind. Being the novice of the Rylari in my class, I should not be here. Another person is dead, and I, somehow, am still alive. If it wasn't for Ginger and Freddy, I probably would be gone.

Smoothing my hair out, I pick myself off the floor and assess my new challenge. The illusions I've encountered so far are incredibly realistic, making me question whether I'm actually trapped in a simulation, watched by millions across the country.

As I examine each mirror, I wonder how this plays on my fears. While I'm not always fond of my appearance, I've never been afraid of it, not even when Abby gave me two black eyes. How a person looks is what it is and makes no difference to the person within. At least, that's how I've always felt, so this challenge makes no sense to me.

Freddy told me he'd seen his parents in one of his simulations, where I was stuck with Ms. Brown. Both Freddy and Becky were shaken by the experience where I felt irritated more than anything. The injections and the gasses also don't have the same effect on me, making me wonder if I'm supposed to experience more fear than I have in this part of the testing.

The only one that really affected me was the one with Gabriel, Abby, and Ty. But I hit my head, which reset my perception of being in a simulation, and maybe that's the key. As long as I'm fully aware and in control of this nightmare, I won't have to be filled with fear. *Maybe that's why White Flames always have an advantage?*

Letting out a deep breath, I walk toward the mirrors, trying not to think about what would scare me. Of course, as soon as I tell myself not to, the thoughts just flow. From seeing myself deformed to dying, the mirrors morph to show me my worst fears.

"Come on, Clarissa." I run a hand down my face as I try to shake off the thoughts.

When I face myself in the mirror, the reflection's face contorts as its eyes examine me. "You should be dead."

I blink a few times, trying to process that my reflection just talked to me.

"And you're apparently dense." She puts her hands on her hips, reminding me of Abby. "Look at you. Even with all that food and training, you still look like a scrawny weakling."

Glancing at the other mirrors, I watch my reflection morph, their faces contorting into various facets of emotions.

The one next to me looks doe-eyed and sighs. "Isn't he dreamy?"

"Oh, don't get her started," the one in front of me grumbles.

"Who cares if she's in love with him? It makes no difference," the one on the other side says. "She'll move on to another crush, eventually."

I point to each one. "Lovesick, critical, and indifferent."

"Oh, finally, a stray neuron kicked in," the reflection in front of me says.

With my curiosity increasing, I leave the three mirrors behind, choosing to explore the myriads of other mirrors, each one embodying aspects of my personality in their unfiltered forms. Each one speaks to me as I pass, then completely ignores me, going back to reflecting on the emotions it represents. I don't know how many mirrors there are in this labyrinth, but it feels like they multiply as I weave through them.

When I come to a dead end, I pause, finding two mirrors there. Instead of reflecting me, there is a man standing in one and a woman in the other.

I don't recognize either of them, but they feel familiar, as if we've met before.

As I inch closer, I see the woman has my blue eyes and long black hair. But where mine is in braided, hers coils into a neat bun. When I examine the man, I instinctively touch my nose, because I can see my nose on him. Mine's more feminine, but I can see the similarity. It makes me wonder if the simulation can pluck a memory I don't remember out of my head. Are these my actual parents? Then again, it could just conjure a potential match based on my DNA. I move closer, gently touching the mirrors.

When the man grasps my arm, I scream, then try to tug myself free. The woman clamps onto my other arm, making me feel like my arms are about to pop out of socket.

"You are an abomination," the man says. "No daughter of mine."

"Even as a Forbidden, she's still a disappointment," the woman says. "She couldn't save that Eric kid."

"Finally, something we can agree on," the man replies. "We should just kill her."

To my horror, they step out of the mirror. With a sharp kick, I break free from the woman's desperate grasp, but the man's grip remains firm, his fingers digging into my skin. Twisting around, I throw all my weight against the man, pushing him into the mirror, sending thousands of shards of glass scattering everywhere. The body is gone, maybe shoved back inside the mirror world he came from.

The woman wraps around me, but I shove my elbow into her gut, then take off at a full-blown sprint. Somehow, she keeps up with me in her heels and pencil skirt.

It's not until I turn several corners, with my reflections yelling at me, that I remember I'm in a simulation. Running isn't necessary; I just have to search for the exit. I take another turn, ducking between the mirrors, and conceal myself in darkness as the woman passes by me.

"Where is she?" the woman asks my reflections.

"We didn't see her," they say simultaneously.

It's really creepy hearing my voice like that, but I shake it off. I continue in the narrow space between mirrors, careful not to nudge anything. When I find an area with fewer mirrors, I push out the one I'm behind, keeping myself out of the reflection. The last thing I need is one of them alerting that woman to my whereabouts.

Once I arrange a few more mirrors to block my path, hopefully redirecting her steps, I take off in another direction, trying to stick to the spaces between the mirrors when I can. Searching through the dark warehouse, I look for the exit, that elusive shimmering door that appears when I need it.

"You won't find it like that," my reflection whispers to me.

"What do you mean?" I ask.

"Think about It. The doorways don't appear until you complete the challenge. You won't find it until you complete this one."

I study my reflection for a moment. "Logic."

She shrugs. "The one and only."

"Then, logic, how do I get out of here?"

"Clarissa, I can't do everything for you. This is a computer construct."

My teeth nervously graze against my lip. "I have to feed you with knowledge."

"Exactly."

"Alright." I take a deep breath, then spin around, taking in the mirrors surrounding me. "I am in a room with mirrors reflecting my personality. There are a man and woman who look similar to me trying to kill me." Pausing for a moment, I think about the purpose of the arena. It was designed to push us to our maximum abilities through fear, feeding off painful memories. "I have to face a truth."

"Yes. But which one?" she asks. When I hesitate, she asks, "Why do the man and woman look similar to you?"

"They are not my parents."

"Maybe, maybe not. But what do they represent for you?"

"A possibility of having someone who loves me in my life."

"And if they don't love you?"

I suck in a breath as tears stream down my face. "Fear of rejection."

"Bingo!" She snaps her fingers at me. "Now, face your fear."

Someone slams into me from behind, knocking me against the mirror. It topples over, shattering into hundreds of pieces, as I desperately try to roll away from the woman. From this close, she really looks like an older version of me. But I have to remember that this isn't my mother, just a figment of my imagination.

She snarls at me as I kick her off me. Tiny slivers of glass dig into my skin as I scramble to my feet, a sharp pain shooting through my body. Matching move for move, I fight against the woman, even picking up shards and throwing them at her, but nothing seems to work. Then I think of how I got rid of the man, and a burst of hope flutters into my chest.

Slowly, I circle until I'm in front of a mirror. When the woman lunges at me, I step aside, allowing her to collide with the reflective surface before shoving her inside. My flames roar to life, consuming the glass in a fiery explosion, leaving behind a pile of tiny broken pieces. There's no way that thing will get out of there now.

Just as I suspected, a shimmering doorway opens next to me.

"Thank you, logic."

Discarding the glass, I step through, ready to be done with this.

Chapter Twenty-Three
Facing Fears

THIS IS NOT WHAT I was expecting.

I'm in the middle of a mountainous desert, surrounded by water. The sun is setting over the horizon, reflecting a warm glow on the placid surface. There are ten of us this time, each standing on a platform on the narrow beach. It feels so real; the breeze causes goosebumps to form on my skin. Unless teleportation devices were invented recently, we're still underground. This scenery proves my theory that this is just a simulation.

Beatrice's body floating in the water floods my mind, forcing me to confront that I might be next. It almost reminds me of those nature documentaries our town selectman always watches where a predator stalks a herd, picking off the weaker members one by one. They're killing us because we're different. Maybe this is all for the king's sick entertainment, but it could be something more, like being afraid of something.

"Congratulations. You've reached the next stage. Battle simulation activated," the computerized voice says.

My mind goes into overdrive. If this is all in our minds, we can wake ourselves up, ending this insane competition. I could be wrong, though. And if this is just a holographic projection, and I do something stupid to wake myself up, I could be the next one to die. I'm totally in the dark about what awaits me, and with my inability to swim, my survivability seems grim.

We're on a beach in the middle of nowhere. This was created to exploit our fear and force us to use our powers. What are fire wielders afraid of the most?

Besides water, the only thing I can think of is the war front. The lake likely holds a deadly secret, I'm sure of it, a surprise the simulation has waiting for us. If we don't comply, it will come for us.

"Good luck, graduates. All paths are open. See you on the flip side," the computer says.

I blink a few times, trying to understand what it means. Then I glance at the group of fire wielders with me. Some of them I've met at least once or twice during training, but the others I've only seen around.

"Are we supposed to swim?" Gregory, a tall, lanky boy, edges closer to the water, peering under the surface. I remember talking to Gregory in the cafeteria about the spiders with Eric.

"I wouldn't get so close," a girl in a giant torn ball gown says. "You never know if there's a mermaid in the water."

The guy next to me laughs, his eyes bloodshot like he's medicated or something. If he's a Red Flame, he wouldn't have been able to burn off the poison we've been given as easily as the others. "There is no such thing as mermaids, Olivia." To prove his point, he wades into the water.

"See." He jumps all around, splashing like he's not in the middle of a battle simulation hellbent on killing us all.

"But there are such things as water wielders, which are basically like a mermaid," I yell at him.

"And we are in a simulation that preys on our fear, Thomas," a smaller girl in a glittering black dress adds.

Thomas's face blanches, and he trudges back to the shore. "Okay, maybe I should be a little more cautious."

With a startled cry, Thomas slips and tumbles into the cold, dark water, then he skims across the water at an incredible speed. My jaw drops because I've never seen anything move that fast. Gabriel showed me footage of the water wielders once; they're fast, but their powerful strokes and the spray of water still couldn't match this impossible speed.

"Should we go after him?" Gregory asks as Thomas sinks under the surface.

"I don't know," I answer. This is a simulation preying on our fears, possibly making our fears worse than reality. "Water wielders are strongest in the water. We would have to get them on land to stand a chance."

"She's right," Ginger's friend Olivia agrees.

"But how do we do that?" a girl in a shimmering gown asks.

Searching the dry land, I see nothing that can help us until I turn to look at the tree behind us. It's huge, probably tall enough to cross the entire surface of the water to the other side. And in this barren landscape, it doesn't belong.

"We build a bridge," I say, while encouraging everyone to follow me. I explain my plan, and because it's the only one we have at the moment, they go along with it.

"Someone else will have to go in after him," a girl in a blue gown points out. "That's the only way we're going to get Thomas back."

I glimpse him screaming as he thrashes in the water; it makes my stomach sink. Whatever the computer conjured, it's probably using him as bait, waiting for us to get there before they attack us. Closing my eyes a moment and envisioning Beatrice, I take a deep breath. Whoever is going into the lake will probably end up like her if we aren't careful.

"I'll go into the water," another tall boy says. Everyone stares at him like he's insane, then argues that it's too dangerous. Maybe he is crazy for volunteering, but arguing won't help anyone, let alone Thomas.

"If there is an opportunity, I'll get him out," he repeats more animatedly this time. "We just need to find that shimmery door, and we will be out of here."

"Are you sure, Robert?" Gregory asks.

"No one else is going to help us except each other." He points to Thomas, still struggling in the water. "We have to try."

"Then we'll all help," Gregory says. He launches into a quick plan to spread our flames around the water to prevent the water wielders from surfacing. "Try not to get knocked in."

"I can't swim," I announce.

"Then definitely don't fall into the water," he says, then points to the girl in the glittering black dress. "Stephanie, go with our White Flame to the other side. Make sure she doesn't fall in, but give her the clearance to use her powers. We need a flash flame."

I just nod, hoping I can create a flash flame. Gabriel pushed me during training to make one in a controlled environment, but it only worked once. Either I create an uncontrolled one when I'm stressed, or I just can't seem to make the power work at all. If I don't keep it under control, I could endanger everyone on the log.

"Let's do this," Gregory says, getting to work on the tree.

Five of us work together to burn the bottom of the tree while the Red Flames pick up rocks to infuse with their heat. Apparently, we can outmaneuver a water wielder by burning off the water, turning it into steam. Of course, that's only going to work if the thing holding Thomas is a water wielder and not some other computer construct.

The tree lists forward, creaking and snapping, before falling over. Just as I suspect, it reaches the beach on the other side with a bang, giving Robert direct access to Thomas.

"Clarissa and Stephenie first; the rest of us will follow." Gregory waves us up. "Keep Yellow Flames dispersed evenly between the Red Flames. That should give everyone enough cover while we try to heat this water up."

I give him a questioning glance.

"The water is likely shallower near the beach; if you fall in, you can walk out. Stephanie will help if something happens before you reach the other side. Use your blinding flash toward the opposite side of Thomas. We don't need him blinded for hours."

"Right." I nod before jumping on top of our tree bridge. *This should be interesting, since I have no idea what I'm doing.*

I walk across the log carefully, with Stephanie right behind me. It's a struggle to navigate around the thicker branches, but we avoid falling into the water. As we reach the middle of the fallen tree trunk, I glance at Thomas splashing frantically in the water but going nowhere. He's right there, with wide, fearful eyes, making me feel nauseous. Even though he's a short distance away, he can't reach the larger branch dipping into the water. Just the thought of drowning sends shivers up my spine.

"Come on," Stephanie says, urging me forward. "The sooner we get to the other side, the quicker we can get this over with."

Knowing she's right, I move forward, my fear for Thomas propelling me across the log. The sooner I take my spot, the faster Robert can help him.

Once we're near the other side, with only a sliver of water between us and the land, we prepare to launch our flames as the others take their positions. It wouldn't take much to knock someone off, and it makes me wonder if we just fell into a trap.

"Do you think..." I start to ask, but a person jets out of the water and fires his laser weapons across at us, then practically flies to the other side, knocking one of my companions into the water. She goes under, but unlike Thomas, she doesn't come back up.

"Flames across the water now," Gregory yells.

Fire erupts along the surface as my companions aim their flames around Thomas. A few more water wielders fly from the water, knocking more of us off the log. Stephanie and I try to take them out, but we're too far away to do enough damage.

"Do your fire wall, Clarissa!" Stephanie inches toward the middle but doesn't stray too far from me as she knocks one wielder out of the sky by throwing her fire like a skipping stone.

Taking a deep breath, I let the heat inside bubble under my skin. I need to keep this under control or I could knock everyone into the water, or worse, burn them. Sparks crackle out of my fingers as I let the pressure build like a volcano. I'm not sure if I would describe the feeling that way, but it's the term Gabriel used to teach me to do this.

I open my arms wide, letting the white flames dance across my arms until they reach my fingertips. My chest heaves as I prepare to bring my arms together. Just when I push the blinding fire forward, several water wielders jump out of the water, knocking more of my companions off the log. Panic seizes me as my hands come together, releasing the flames across the surface, but they don't go in the direction I was aiming. Instead, it engulfs the entire lake, setting the log ablaze.

"No!" I cry out as my friends scream.

With the momentary distraction, my flames falter, and it's too late that I notice the water wielder knocking me into the burning water. I thought I was close to the shallows, but I've fallen into a deep part that seems to go on forever. It's quiet, just like last time I was drowning, and the light is fading from view. If I knew how to swim or to dive, this might almost be a peaceful hideaway from the chaos of the real world. I remember this is just an illusion to spike my fear, but I can't use my flames under water, which seems the opposite of what the computer has wanted this whole time.

I try to swim toward the surface, clawing at the cold liquid like Ginger did, but something is dragging me down toward the dark depths of the bottom of the lake. Whatever current is pulling me, I can't fight it, not without swimming lessons. The only thing I learned the last time I was drowning was how to float.

Instead of focusing up, I look down at what will become my watery grave. Something rectangular shimmers, and I realize it's the door that leads to the next challenge. "All paths are open. See you on the flip side," the computer had said.

My strength returns, but I'm running out of oxygen as I try to fight the current toward the door. I struggle against it, just burning up more precious fuel for my lungs. Instead, I relax, allowing my body to flow with the water. To my surprise, the current releases, but it's too late. Spots form in front of my eyes. My mouth opens, and I suck in a breath of water. Just as I'm about to pass out, the doorway pulls me inside.

I reach the other side and collapse, my lungs burning as I cough up water. When I open my eyes there is nothing. No light. No smell.

Nothing. It is so dark I can't see my body or the surface I'm lying on. I only know that it's rough and feels like cement. Assuming you can't feel anything when you're dead, I must be alive. I might have gone blind while letting myself drown, but deep down, I feel like this is just another test.

This is all about facing fears, right? So what is this fear?

Moving my hand in a circle, I test my surroundings. Everything feels solid, but that doesn't mean it's like that everywhere. Instead of standing upright, I opt to crawl to further feel my way through the darkness. I have no idea where I'm going or what direction I should take, so I count each crawl so I can get back to where I started if I need to.

My knees ache as I move across the rugged surface. If I don't find my way out of this soon, my skin is going to break open. Just as I'm about to stand up, something crinkles under my hand.

I pat the ground, picking up what I think is a small strip of paper. Sitting on my knees, I hold it up. The writing glows in the dark, shimmering like the moonlight.

Embrace who you are -Gabriel.

"What does that mean?" I ask, my voice echoing back to me.

I take a deep breath, then slowly let it out while I think about the message.

"Who am I?"

When I was little, I labeled myself as an orphan with bad luck. But as time went on, I changed to view myself as a kid who was going to make a difference. With everything I've had to endure these past several months, I don't know who I am or where I fit into this world. My flames have been more of a nuisance than something that saves me. Releasing my frustration, I let out a breath, knowing exactly what Gabriel is encouraging me to do.

"When surrounded by darkness, I can become the light," I say, then I ignite my free hand with my flames, illuminating the area.

I'm deep inside a cave. The ceiling is adorned with stalactites, their smooth, white surfaces reflecting the dim light. Turning in a circle, I search for a way out and find one behind me.

Like this cave, the next one has no source of light, but the ceiling is much lower, forcing me to duck. Since there's only one way in and out of each opening, I continue through the maze, looking for a way to the surface, or at least another shimmering door.

Even though I'm certain I'm alone, I can't help the feeling of being watched. Considering I'm in a simulation of some kind, I wouldn't be surprised if there were hidden cameras.

The feeling something is watching me increases with each cave I enter. I bite my lip as I think through the possible fears I might have, careful not to give them too much detail to prevent them from manifesting.

There is, of course, the possibility that a creature of some kind could be following me, but I think I would hear it moving. In terms of my flames, most creatures would perish, even with a low-level heat. It could be some robot, but even that doesn't frighten me because they are easily disabled.

When I reach the next cave, I freeze, staring at what appears to be a night sky dancing across the ceiling. I hold my hand higher, illuminating it further. Millions of tiny crystals cover the gray surface, but they aren't the beautiful gemstones I was expecting. Instead, they're black, with a swirling light inside that reminds me of dragon's breath. These stones are just like the one the king wears and the one that hovers over this arena.

I pull my flame back, instinctively trying to conceal myself from them as I try to look for an exit. A shiver runs down my spine because I realize where that eerie feeling came from—the black gems. It's some kind of cavern where they form freely, and my gut is telling me to run.

The cave is enormous, and I circle the walls, searching for the exit. No matter what I do, I can't find one. If there is no exit, then I haven't faced my fear yet. I glance at the ceiling, taking my place in the very center of the room.

"This is just a simulation," I whisper to myself.

With a deep breath, I let my flames explode out of my hand, filling the cave with a blinding light and the crackle of fire. The heat envelops the dark crystals, causing them to emit a soft hissing sound, like whispers of ancient power. They appear to almost melt from my power before long, shadowy figures emerge, leaking out of the crystals like tears.

"Shadow creatures," I say, remembering all the childhood stories that gave me nightmares. My hands tremble because I don't know what to do until I remember Gabriel's words: "Embrace who you are."

I'm a fire wielder, and we were practically built to take these creatures on. At least, that's what Luna told me.

Stretching my arms wide, I unleash my white flames. They roll over my body, illuminating the cave. I launch an attack on the Shadow Creatures flying toward me. My blinding light keeps them from slamming into me. As they weave around me, I realize they are just as afraid of me as I am of them. The sudden revelation steadies my resolve to keep melting the crystals while intensifying my defense against them.

A Shadow lands, then morphs into a woman who looks like me. It's like the creature from the mirror room, making me wonder if we've been chasing Shadows all along.

"You're a true disappointment to us, Clarissa," it says.

I know it's not my actual mother, but it's certainly the one I always imagined as a kid. "My lack of family, that's what you are."

The woman smiles before morphing into General Prescott. "Doesn't mean you don't have fears, darling."

"Fears can be conquered," I say, surprising myself that I can talk so calmly.

"You're right." The creature morphs into Gabriel as another Shadow lands, transforming into Abby.

"But there are some fears that will always just be too much," the one that looks like Abby says before kissing Gabriel.

My heart hammers as I repeat over and over that this is just a simulation. Still, it hurts to see her doing this. If I have to be in his life, I really don't want her around. Shaking off my momentary distraction, I send a fireball in their direction, forcing them to morph back into their shadow form.

Fed up with this simulation, I send blast after blast toward the sinister creatures. I hit some of them, making them go up in smoke, but not enough to stop them from attacking me.

Another Shadow lands, morphing into Luna. "I thought you were my friend, but you just want to get me killed."

"That's not true," I say, chiding myself at engaging with it.

"Really? Then prove it. Stop hurting us." Her voice transforms into a sinister, deep voice that echoes through the cave. Several Shadows dive at me as the Luna lookalike runs at me.

I duck out of the way, but not before one of them hits my arm with some black substance. It burns my flesh, causing me to cry out. The cavern falls to darkness without my fire. I clutch my arm, trying to heal it, when something slams me to the ground. Without thinking, my entire body ignites. The creature screeches in pain.

When I look back, Luna withers, partially melting as a shimmering door appears on the other side. I passed the test, but at what cost to my sanity?

Scrambling to my feet, I step over what looks like Luna's body. She grabs my leg, burning my skin where it touches. I send a flare of fire toward the creature while yanking my leg free. It just laughs as it melts further.

"You can't save her," it says before completely dissolving, the ominous words sending shivers down my spine.

I don't know if Luna is alive or dead, but I can only hope I'll find her on the other side.

Racing for the doorway, I use my flames to mend my scorched flesh, desperately wishing for an outfit change. After my experience fighting for my life in a barely-there dress, I may never wear one again.

Passing through the doorway, I expect to feel the same strange electrical current, but this time, it feels like a thousand needles press into me at the same time. I cry out as I tumble to the ground on the other side. Gas pours out of the vents from the ceiling, quickly filling the entire space, giving me no choice but to breathe it in. It leaves a metallic taste in my mouth that makes me want to puke. The world spins around me, but despite the horrible feeling taking control of me, I stand, bracing myself against the glass walls.

When the fog clears, my body quakes with fear, because I know what this is. This is the final battle, one of the few moments I've gleaned from the digiscreens. Whoever survives this part will truly become the king's property.

"Congratulations. You've reached the final challenge. Battle simulation activated. Destroy or be terminated," the computerized voice says.

Chapter Twenty-Four
Contest of Fire

AT LEAST THE COMPUTER is being honest this time.

Glancing through the glass, I see over forty tube-like alcoves similar to mine filled with gas, surrounding a circular space in the center. Only around half of them have an occupant, and I have to clutch my necklace to stop myself from thinking about why they're empty. As I glance around the arena, I realize a majority of the missing teens were from Major Psycho's team.

Large metal debris litters the landscape, giving places for us to hide temporarily once the battle starts. I search through the mist for the one person I've worried about this entire time—Luna. At least if I can grab her, I might conceal us by bending light. I've only done it once or twice. Gabriel thinks I've done it more often without thinking about it, but I can't be sure.

Just as my gaze connects with the girl who is as dear to me as a sister, the computer announces, "Injections."

My eyes widen as I jump back, fighting to prevent the needle from reaching my arm. The world is still swirling from the gas, slowing my response time. I berate myself for not burning the poison out of my blood sooner. I weave and bob, my heart pounding as the robotic arm whirs and slams into the wall beside me.

"You must take your medicine," the computer says.

"That's not medicine," I reply before jumping out of the way. The robotic arm narrowly misses me, grazing my arm and making me wish I had my old uniform on. At least with that cloth, my skin would be protected against this foul contraption.

Using my flames, I heal the bleeding skin while leaping toward the other side. The arm whirls around me, faster than I can follow. But there's one thing that can protect me. My flames consume my body, and I push them near the melting point of metal. As the temperature rises, sweat beads on my skin, then the tension in my muscles subsides as the poison leaves my veins. I've had enough of these drugs, and I will burn this place down before they make me take any more.

There's nothing shielding my skin, because what is left of the dress is burning on the floor. I'm blazing sun right now, which will probably melt the retinas of anyone watching me on their digiscreens.

The robotic arm bubbles as it tries to find a weak point in my flames. It's sweating from the heat, and it gives me an idea. I scoot my foot under the remnants of the horrid dress and kick it upward. The cloth wraps around the floating device, catching it and the poison on fire. It melts faster as I throw a fireball in its direction. It whirls around, forcing me to duck before it smacks into the glass, cracking it.

Fire protection devices kick in, extinguishing my flames. My cheeks heat at the thought of being naked in public until I realize I'm in a tank top and shorts. "How..."

"Dress," the computer says as a new black fire-retardant suit appears from the ceiling.

I don't trust the situation, but I'd rather have the gear for the battle than have nothing protecting me while fighting for my life. Cautiously, I take the suit and put it on as fast as I can.

Just as I'm zipping up the black jacket, a needle pierces my skin, making me sick to my stomach. My eyes roll back as I exhale.

"All contestants must take their medication," the computer says.

"I'm just going to burn it off," I yell at the computer as the empty hanger ascends into the ceiling.

"We have anticipated this eventuality for three of you."

"What is that supposed to mean?" I ask as I let my flames extinguish the poison before it reaches any further.

"White Flames have an advantage," is all it says, giving me nothing useful.

"I already know that," I mutter as I glance at the other alcoves. Through the cracked window, I watch the teens bang against the glass like wild, rabid animals. The only ones not acting crazy are Victoria, Serene, and me—the three White Flames.

"Get ready, graduates. The all-out battle against the Shadow Crystal will begin in thirty seconds," the computer says.

Three White Flames against twenty something drugged-up teens and a mysterious crystal that can kill us instantly. I grind my teeth, knowing this is an impossible situation. It's going to pit us against each other. That's why it's trying to drug us—so that we are out of our mind.

I can heal the others, but I can't take on everyone. Luna's a Yellow Flame. If I can get to her or others like her, they can help me burn the poison out. I'm sure the computer has something else in mind, but I won't worry about it until it happens.

"Triage," I tell myself repeatedly, trying to block out the fact that some are going to die.

"Ten Seconds," the computer says as a giant countdown clock appears over the center of the round battle field, illuminating the crystal.

I jump in place, psyching myself up for the ground I need to cover to get to Luna.

"All who remain standing at the end of the ten-minute battle will receive their diploma."

"Oh goodie, just what I need," I roll my eyes.

"Good luck."

The door opens, releasing us from our glass cages simultaneously. I don't hesitate, running as fast as possible and using my flames to propel me toward Luna. She's all I care about right now. I have to save her.

Someone tackles me, sending me rolling to the ground. They pin me in place, shoving my face against the hard earthen floor. With a surge of adrenaline, I kick back, connecting with my attacker and eliciting a guttural howl from their throat.

Using the distraction, I roll upward, pinning the boy to the ground with my legs. I suck in a breath as Freddy bares his teeth at me, but I ignore him, grasping his neck instead. Despite his resistance, I burn off the poison coursing through his veins. His wild, savage eyes return to normal as his body convulses.

His chest heaves one last time before he stares at me. "That's twice you've saved me."

I back off him, extending my hand to help him up. "I seem to remember you saved me, too."

Freddy accepts my help, then surveys the battle. "We're drugged again?"

"Pretty much."

"We need to burn off the poison in everyone?" he asks.

"Yep. And…"

A burst of light shoots across the battlefield, cutting me off. Just when I think things can't get worse, they do. The illusions from the previous simulations form in clusters around the battlefield. A few drones appear overhead, while a fake Major Psycho tackles a boy on the other side. The gigantic spiders are back, too. The crystal is generating horrific, physical representations of our individual fears—a terrifying army designed to keep us from uniting against it.

"We need to work fast," Freddy says while tearing off a loose piece of metal protruding from the ground. He throws it at a drone and it crashes into a column, but another appears from thin air. "Great, they replicate. Let's get started before it manifests anything else for us to fight."

I nod. "I'll go right, you go left. Prioritize Yellow Flames to help us."

"Got it. And try not to die." Freddy runs off, tackling someone to the ground as he heals them.

Searching the battlefield, I try to find Luna, but between the projections, debris, and the flames, it's difficult to find anyone in the chaos. Weaving through the obstacles, I take off in the direction I last saw her. When I see someone holding a pipe in the air, about ready to kill Olivia, I stop.

I don't think, I just act, colliding with the person, knocking the weapon out of her hands. Before she turns around, I grab her neck, releasing my flames to burn off the poison. Becky screeches until her breath comes out ragged. She's not a Yellow Flame, but one less crazy person on the field is better than nothing.

"Thanks," she says as I roll off her.

Just as I'm about to stand, something smacks me hard across the arm, tipping me into the dirt. Olivia has the pipe now, readying to kill Becky.

With my heart thumping in my chest, I aim my flames toward the metal cylinder, making it too hot for her to hold. She drops it, giving Becky time to scramble away. Olivia chases after her, disappearing behind an enormous metal column before I can help her.

"I'll have to get back to her," I mutter while healing my throbbing arm.

As I weave through the chaos, I stop a few from killing each other, giving me the opportunity to remove the poison. With each person returning to their normal mental state, the battlefield grows less erratic as we help each other. Our plan is working, but I still need to find Luna.

Burning a spider with my flames, I rescue a young boy from becoming its food. Instead of killing it, I box the creature in by melting metal to make a cage on a hunch that if it's still alive, the sinister gemstone won't create another one. I could be wrong, but so far, I haven't seen a new one pop up.

The boy runs off to help his friends, groups of Rylari working together to take out the illusions. I continue my search for Luna, but nearly trip over a dead body. Stephanie's green eyes stare blankly at the ceiling, making me want to vomit.

Leaning against the metal partition wall protruding from the dirty ground, I wipe the sweat from my brow. I knew this was going to be awful before coming in, but dealing with it now, I can't stop the panic that keeps rising inside. I need to reach Luna before someone kills her.

A gleaming piece of metal catches my eyes, and I bend to look at what Stephanie has hidden in her hands—two daggers. I have no clue how she kept them so long, but I take them, sliding them in my belt.

After taking a few small breaths, I jump into the fray, desperately searching for my best friend. A few Yellow Flames surround the tallest teen in our group. It takes several tries before they tackle him to the ground. Even though he fights them off, they keep coming back, using their healing abilities to burn the poison from his blood.

A girl with dark, curly hair streaks by, but I don't get a good look at her before she disappears behind a stone wall. Victoria and Serene run after her. It could be Luna, but I won't know for sure unless I go after her.

Following their trail, I run into the middle section of the battlefield. It's like a maze in here, with walls made of random materials that weave around each other in a haphazard manner. The only thing that really scares me in this place is the crystal sitting on a metal mesh platform. It looms above us, watching us practically kill each other with the indifference of a stone.

Dashing through the labyrinth, I search for Luna, or at least the girl I think is her. I catch a few glimpses through the cracks in the walls, but I still can't get a good look. Increasing my speed, I weave around the barriers, trying to catch up before I lose her again.

The girl screams before falling to the ground at the end of a narrow corridor. Someone is dragging her off. Considering the bright white flames, I can guess who it is. But I don't know why they are trying to hurt Luna.

I run faster to find her but come to a dead end. Spinning around, I look for any clue that will explain where she went. The smooth, cold metal wall yields slightly under my touch, revealing a small, almost invisible indent. When I press it, a door clicks open. With flames at the ready, I jump through.

"There she is," Victoria says as Serene restrains Luna, covering her mouth so she can't talk. "I figured you'd follow your little friend here."

"Victoria, we don't have time for this. That thing—"

"Is controlled by the king," she finishes, smiling while igniting her flames. "Now, if I want the life I deserve, I need to be in his good graces. That means we need to eliminate you, the competition."

"I'm not your competition," I yell, then point to the crystal. "That is your competition."

"Not while the king is in charge, Clarissa. He says—"

"I don't care what the king says," I screech this time. The words are out there for everyone to hear now. For all I know, the king will execute me for just saying such a treasonous thing, but I don't care. I just want my friend back.

"Well, if that doesn't take you out of the competition, I don't know what will."

"Then let her go. Luna has nothing to do with your imaginary competition."

A sinister grin spreads across her face as she ignites her hands with blue flames. My eyes widen. I thought there could only be one Blue Flame in a generation, but then I haven't studied the genetic history of the Rylari. Maybe the stories Luna and Gabriel told me were wrong.

"Why are you doing this? She's done nothing to you." I try inching forward, but Serene places a blade against my friend's neck. "If you want to hurt me, take me out of the competition, kill me, I don't care. But turning on your fellow Rylari will not get you anywhere, Victoria. It will make your people hate you."

I may not know the intricacies of fire wielder culture, but turning on your own people is a universal crime of humanity. It doesn't matter if Victoria's the fabled Blue Flame or not; they won't like her. Not like this.

"And what if I was the Violet Flame?" The fire flickers before it intensifies, changing from blue to purple. "They have to bow to me now, including you. Bow before your queen, Clarissa, and I'll let your friend go."

My mind races, trying to understand what's happening. There's no way Victoria could be a Violet Flame. It's a myth told to children to give them hope or fear, depending on who's telling the story. If she has this power, why am I only finding out about it now? It makes little sense. And from Luna's wide-eyed expression, she's just as confused as me.

The crystal glimmers above, drawing my attention. A tiny ray of light shines on Victoria and Serene. They are an illusion of fear, just like the other creatures I've encountered.

I take a steading breath to calm my racing heart. They have Luna, and even if they are holograms, they can hurt her. I'm not fast enough to save her with weapons or fire.

Placing my hands in the air, I sink to my knees. "I surrender, Victoria."

Luna glares at me. I give her only the slightest nod toward the dark stone above us, hoping she figures out what I'm trying to do.

"That's very smart of you," the illusion says, moving toward me slowly, drawing out the moment. She looms over me like a mountain ready to crush me. "And do you accept your fate, Clarissa?"

I gulp, almost afraid to say the words in case it binds me to a contract like some fairytale. "I accept whatever fate has in store for me." Bending low, I grab the blades in my belt.

"Good. Know that you'll be responsible for your friend's death."

Luna screams. I look up in time to see her convulse, the light in her eyes beginning to fade away.

"Say goodbye to your friend, Clarissa."

My eyes widen as Serene's face morphs into my twin while she consumes Luna's powers. Yellow flames flicker out of my friend's body, rising into the girl that now looks like me.

Swiftly taking my blades out, I stab the creature that looks like Victoria. Her eyes roll back, and she drops quickly. I use my white flames to bolster my aim, then launch my second blade. The creature that used to look like Serene ducks out of the way, releasing Luna. Like a leach, the gemstone continues to drain her life away.

With my heart pounding, I try to run for her, but Victoria jumps on top of me, tackling me to the ground. Her violet flames ignite, scorching my body, but I thrash against her despite the pain.

They're not real, I try to convince myself as I shove against her arm.

"Luna killed my sister. She has to pay," Victoria says through clenched teeth.

"You don't have a sister; you have a brother back home." With one swift turn, I push her off me, then grab the blade from the ground and stab her in the side. The purple flames disappear. "You aren't Victoria at all."

She cries out. I go to stab her again, but someone stops me, twisting it back so I drop the blade. The girl who looks like me pulls my arm further, almost bending it out of socket.

Victoria takes advantage, gripping my neck, squeezing it until I can't breathe. Her eyes darken as her hands tighten, and a beam of light surrounds me. "We need your powers," she says with an eerily deep voice.

I'm frozen, unable to move as the crystal unleashes a searing beam in my direction. My body convulses with pain, and tears pour down my face as I gasp for air. The heat within my body rises as my life essence is drawn from me, then streams toward the crystal like an ember rising in a fire.

I've failed, and now I'm going to die.

Chapter Twenty-Five
Shadow Gem

THERE ARE WORSE THINGS than death.

A burning heat floods my limbs, then a bone-chilling cold sets in as dark spots dance before my eyes. With each agonizing beat of my heart, the dark gemstone sucks the life from me, a slow, relentless drain that leaves me weak and breathless. I've never wanted to die, but the excruciating agony is so intense that I yearn for an end to my suffering. My only regret is that I couldn't save my best friend.

Just when I think I can't handle any more, the aura from the crystal disappears. Unable to stand, I fall to the ground, gasping for air. My chest heaves as the pain subsides.

"Here." Gregory helps me to my feet.

"Thanks," I say as he steadies me. As my powers work to repair the damage, my vision slowly returns, the colors becoming brighter and clearer, each detail snapping into focus.

"We have to stick together." He shrugs.

The Victoria and Serene illusions are gone, but Luna is thrashing on the ground, fighting Ginger and Robert. I rush to her side, with Gregory right behind me.

As adrenaline pumps through me, I attempt to burn the poison out of her, but she continues to throw off anyone who tries to restrain her.

"Hold her still," I say, trying to keep the connection.

"We're trying," Ginger says, then receives a blow to the jaw. She falls backward, releasing Luna's arms.

I pounce on her, pressing her to the ground, and then transfer the last of my energy into her veins. Time hangs heavily, each moment agonizing, until the wildness slowly drains from her bloodshot eyes, leaving behind the warm chocolate brown I know so well.

"Clarissa," she whispers. Her voice releases the last bit of tension I was holding on to.

"You're alright, Luna." I roll off her, and she sits up.

I pull her close in a deep hug, her warmth enveloping me. She had survived whatever treacherous challenges she'd faced, including nearly being drained by those creatures. Now that we are in the final battle for our lives, there is no way I'm going to let her out of my sight.

"Welcome back," Gregory says.

"Good to be back," Luna replies as he helps her to her feet.

Robert stops me from standing, placing a hand on my shoulder.

"You don't have to heal me," I say, remembering Thomas drowning in the lake. I haven't seen him, and I wonder if he is another casualty in this arena. Robert was supposed to save him, but from the downcast eyes, it doesn't look like he succeeded.

"Yes, I do," he says, pointing to the black marks spread across my skin like spiderwebs. I've lost the warmth to my complexion, making me look sickly. "That thing up there just drained most of your energy, and there are still five minutes on the clock."

"Five minutes... really?" It feels like we've been here for months. We have to survive for another five minutes. What horrors are we going to face now?

"If it makes you feel better, it's less than five minutes now."

"Ha. Ha."

"If you'll let me..." Robert holds up his palms with honey-colored light flickering out of them.

I nod. He grasps the side of my neck and arm, filtering radiating warmth through my body. The sharp throbbing pain subsides, and I let out a long, deep breath. The dark veins retreat as my sickly-looking skin returns to its normal healthy tone.

"There, all better," Robert says while helping me to my feet.

"Do you know where the real Victoria and Serene are?" I ask. If we could combine our powers, maybe we could fight off whatever comes next.

"Don't know. We heard Victoria screaming that the crystal duplicated her and Serene. That was the last I saw of them," Gregory answers. "We were on our way to help them when we heard the commotion in here. I'm glad we got here in time."

"Thank you!" Since he saved our lives, I feel I owe him more than just thanks.

"Don't mention it," Robert says, then bumps my shoulder.

"Now we need to survive whatever that thing is going to do next," Ginger says.

"I vote we move away from the deadly crystal and take advantage of our White Flame here to conceal us from all the deadly stuff that's about to happen," Robert says. "That's what Victoria and Serene have been doing this the whole time."

"What about the others?" I ask.

"We'll see what we can do," Gregory replies. "For now, let's get away from that thing."

I grab Luna's hand in a firm grip. There's no way I'm letting her get away from me this time. We weave out of the maze only to find ourselves surrounded by our fears. At least, I assume they are everyone's fears, because Ty looks at me like he's either ready to kill me or marry me, which is basically the same thing in my eyes.

"Where's your dress, sweetheart?" Ty asks.

"I burned it," I reply.

"That's my ideal date," he says, waggling his eyebrows.

"Ew, you had to deal with that?" Luna asks.

"You don't know the half of it," I mutter.

Gabriel and Abby step behind Ty. Abby laughs, brandishing a very fancy wedding ring. Somehow, with his more practical, minimalistic style, I don't think Gabriel would buy a ring that large and clunky for a girl, but Abby would certainly expect one like that.

Luna glances at me. "And you fear Abby being with Gabriel?"

I shrug. "It's been nice not having her around. I guess I just want to keep it that way."

"Hmm." She presses her lips together. "We're going to talk about this one more after we get out of here."

Several more figures surround us, and I can only assume they're holographic representations of the others' fears, because I don't recognize them.

"Four minutes, graduates," the computer announces.

A dark figure coalesces in front of us, with the same beady black eyes I've come to loathe. All of us take a step back as a menacing grin forms on General Prescott's face.

"Time to make you comply," he says before shooting at us with a discharge gun.

I pull Luna down, shielding her behind a rough stone wall. Dust swirls around us, blocking our attackers' position, the only clue coming from the electrical discharges flying past us. It seems the computer is keeping us close to the crystal for some reason. I glance up at the sinister force; just looking at it sends an icy chill through my body. We have to get out of here before the timer runs out.

Letting my flames reach the maximum temperature my necklace will allow, I throw several fireballs in our attacker's direction, then move Luna to a wall closer to Gregory and the others.

"We need to get away from the crystal," I say, keeping my voice low enough so only they can hear me.

"I know, but we're pinned down," Gregory says.

"We need to go that way." I point behind him. "Try one of the other exits."

"Then what?" Robert asks.

"We stay away from the center and slowly take them out. Maybe just hide," I say.

"Well, I agree with Clarissa. Let's try," Ginger announces before throwing flames at the simulated people blocking our path.

I follow her lead, throwing several more fireballs—their fiery trails hissing and cracking—while the others retreat. Light streams through the gaps in the walls as electrical pulses zip toward us, signaling that it's time for Ginger and me to join the rest.

Running as fast as I can, I weave through the maze, searching for a way out. I stay close to Luna, careful to keep myself between her and the electrical discharges chasing us. Dirt mixes with smoke, making it impossible to see anything as we hurry to keep ahead of the attackers.

"Three minute warning."

"Found one," Robert declares. He dashes to the right, and we follow him. Just as he reaches the exit, an electrical discharge hits him, sending him convulsing to the ground.

Ginger screams. I stop, pulling Luna with me as we make a mad dash away from the fake people trying to take us out. My heart twists for Robert, but we don't have time to mourn. With my friends just behind me, we run toward another exit, ducking out of the way of the discharges from our pursuers.

Gregory pulls ahead, skidding to a stop at the exit before waving us forward. We only make it to the next column outside the maze when an electrical current hits Ginger in the arm. She falls, but Gregory picks her up while Luna and I throw our flames at a lookalike Ms. Brown. Both of us have a vendetta against her, so we take out the computer version of her out without hesitation. It's likely futile, though, since she'll probably just reappear.

Together, we dash across the open field toward an alcove. It has a metal roof that might make it easy for me to bend light if we can reach it before the psycho illusions see us. I aimlessly hurl fireballs behind us, hoping to distract our pursuers.

"Let me," Luna says while intensifying her flames, making it difficult for our attackers to see us. "You need to conserve your energy."

I nod, letting her take control of covering our retreat. Having a lifetime to practice her abilities, she has much better aim and takes a few of them out of commission. Instead of heading directly into our hiding spot, we take the long way around the column. Gregory sets Ginger inside while Luna and I make it look like we ran in the other direction before circling back into the hiding place.

I sit at the entrance and close my eyes. Gabriel's soothing voice enters my mind.

"You've done it before," Gabriel whispers in my ear. *"It's why Ty didn't pick you, because he couldn't see you. Just put yourself in the same place mentally, and it will happen again."*

Increasing my heart rate, I will the fake people to not see us. Heat travels through my extremities before enveloping me. Seeing our pursuers run past us makes my fists ball up. The Ty lookalike turns around, even looking directly at me, but doesn't charge our way. Instead, they fan out, looking for clues.

"Two minute warning," the computer says.

I try to keep my heartbeat steady as a new Ms. Brown lookalike walks right in front of me. Her pinstriped dress swishes through the dirt, creating swirls of dust in the air. It fills my nose, and I'm about to sneeze when Luna pinches it. Carefully, I let out my breath, trying to keep myself as steady as possible.

While the Ty lookalike ran forward, Gabriel and Ms. Brown leisurely search our area. Beads of sweat form on my forehead as I continue the ruse. My arms shake from the effort since I only have a few attempts at this under my belt. With each passing second I maintain the charade, the shaking intensifies. If our attackers would just leave, I could drop it for a minute to rest.

"There you are," a sickeningly sweet voice says above me. Abby smiles at me through a small opening I didn't conceal. "Found them," she calls to the others.

"Good," Ms. Brown says as she turns in our direction.

Luna throws flames through the opening as I drop the illusion. The others scramble out of our hiding place, and I follow behind them with Luna at my side. Gabriel is already in front of us, blocking our path. With a wall on one side, Gabriel in front of us, Ms. Brown on our left side, and Abby behind us, there's no place to go.

I raise my hands, and the others follow my lead.

"Move," Gabriel says while waving his gun toward the crystal.

Our wardens guide us toward the maze at the center. As we approach, the hair on my arms raises. At first, I think it's from the chill of being close to the gemstone, but then I feel an undulating current in the air. The black crystal is pulsing, like it's about to release a deadly electrical charge to anyone in its way.

My heart rate increases as I take in my surroundings. Abby has a metal pole in her hands, using it like a shepherd's staff. If I can get it and super heat it, maybe I can take the crystal out.

I hurry to catch up to Gregory, then try to explain my plan without words. At first, he looks at me like I'm insane until Ginger practically knocks him off his feet. She winks at me, letting me know this is my opening.

Luna pushes Abby over, forcing her to drop the bar, while I blast Gabriel and Ms. Brown with a wall of fire.

"Now it works," I mutter as Luna throws me the bar.

Leaving my friends behind, I run into the maze. I know how to get to the crystal, but I have no idea how I'm going to reach it to damage it. Weaving between the haphazard walls, I examine their tops, noticing angular cuts that look like a makeshift stairway.

I run toward a lower wall, but something knocks into me. Ty pins me to the ground, forcing me to drop the pipe. "You will be mine, White Flame." He practically spits the words in my face.

"One minute warning," the computer says. Despite my thrashing, the Ty lookalike keeps me stuck in place.

Just when I'm about to give up, something knocks him off me. Becky extends her hand, lifting me to my feet, while Freddy uses his power to kill the Ty lookalike. The menacing laugh as the creature dies makes my stomach twist.

"Thanks," I say, then pick up the pipe. "I need to get up there."

"Over here." Edgar points before shoving the lifeless body off to the side.

The crystal flares wildly in anticipation of whatever it's about to do.

Edgar and Freddy lift me to the top of the wall, then hand me the pipe. As soon as I'm stable, Becky screams, then a new Ty stabs Freddy in the back. His eyes widen as the light leaves his eyes.

"You can do it, Blue," Freddy says as he sinks to the ground.

Ty tries to jump on the wall, but Edgar fights him, snapping me out of my temporary paralysis. I run up the stairs and jump carefully to the next wall. I set the pipe on the mesh landing before climbing up. Heating the metal with my flame, I practically fly across the platform.

I hold the red-hot pipe above my head, ready to swing it against the icy surface.

"I wouldn't do that if I were you," General Prescott says, while holding a knife to Luna's neck, forcing me to hesitate.

"Now throw it down," he says.

"Don't listen," Victoria yells from the opposite direction, being held by another computer illusion. "Smash it."

"Ten seconds," the computer says as electrical discharges crackle out of the crystal-like lighting, sending a wave of air that knocks me backward.

"Crack it," Ginger yells above the storm brewing.

I know they're right. We're all going to die if I don't crack this thing open. Just as I am about to smash the crystal, a sudden, jarring impact sends the pipe flying from my hands.

With a fierce yell, Gabriel swings the pole, the wind whistling past my ear as I narrowly avoid it. He comes at me again, and I have barely enough time to throw a fire volley at him. It grazes him, and he's completely unfazed.

"Don't touch the crystal," someone yells below.

It's only then I realize that's exactly where this illusion is forcing me to go. Gabriel comes at me with a full swing. Despite the rising panic, I hold my ground until the last second.

When the pole is about to connect with me, I drop to my knees, then roll under the giant crystal, its surface only a few inches above me. Even though I'm careful not to touch it, I feel its weight and malevolence toward me. As Gabriel's double shatters the crystal, I reach the other side, and a tremendous surge of energy is released.

I fly across the platform as electrical currents shoot out from the dark gem. The impact of the guardrail steals my breath as I crash onto the hard metal platform. The crystal emits a high-pitched squeal as it bursts, unleashing its dark energy.

Squeezing my eyes shut, I curl into a ball, then clutch my head. Pain radiates through me in relentless waves of agony, completely immobilizing me. I hope whatever I did worked because I can't take another minute here. The thunder booms around me, each clap resonating in my skull and intensifying the throbbing pain.

I think if you're dying, you're supposed to feel cold. But warmth surrounds me as tears fall down my cheeks. Someone touches me, and I want to throw off whatever is trying to kill me, but I don't have any energy left.

Just let death come for me. I'm ready.

"Clarissa," a familiar voice whispers.

When I open my eyes, I scream as those familiar green eyes stare back at me. Despite the pain, I try to scramble out of Gabriel's grasp, but he keeps me in place.

"It's me, the real me. I promise," Gabriel says quickly.

I glance around and realize it isn't thunder I'm hearing, but applause. We're not on the battlefield anymore, but above ground in the middle of the stadium. Everyone is on their feet cheering as the video screen replays the crystal being smashed. But it isn't Gabriel smashing it; it's me. I blink a few times, not understanding the disconnect between my memories and the camera.

"You're safe," Gabriel says. I'm not sure I can believe him. The last time I thought I was out of the games, I ended up engaged to Ty.

"I survived?" I whisper, not sure if I should hope for reality or not.

He places a blanket around me. "You survived."

The announcer is repeating the names of each person alive, but I can't hear her clearly. Everything swims before my eyes, a disorienting blur of movement and color as my world spins. My gaze darts around the field, a chaotic scene of healers rushing to aid the injured, the air thick with the smells of sweat, blood, and fear. When I was last supposedly out of the simulation, I found myself in another challenge, and I'm half expecting to see a shimmering doorway somewhere.

"Luna," I whisper. I attempt to rise while looking for her, but Gabriel stops me.

He attempts to inject something into me. I try to bat him away, but his grip is too strong; he pins my hands and does it anyway.

The pain melts away instantly, replaced by a tingling warmth, leaving me in blissful relief. After everything they've shoved into me, what's one more medication, especially if it stops this agonizing pain? A deep sigh escapes my lips, my shoulders slumping with relief.

A stretcher carrying an unseen person shrouded in white cloth rattles past, jolting me back to my mission.

"Luna." I struggle against Gabriel with renewed vigor, trying to find my friend on the field. "I have to save her."

"You're out of the simulation, I promise." He tries to soothe me, but it doesn't work.

I shove him back with my weight, then roll over him to escape, but my legs feel like lead, refusing to support my weight. Instead, I crawl on my hands and knees, the rough ground scraping my skin, desperately searching for her curly black tresses amidst a sea of faces.

Gabriel grabs me. I try to kick him, but his grip is like iron, which is strange for a Glyzul. With practiced ease, he pins me to the ground, his hands gentle but firm as he keeps me securely in place without causing pain.

"Luna is safe." He points them out just ahead. "Zane is helping her right now. You saved her and everyone else."

Zane gently helps Luna up, his movements careful as he assesses her for injuries. He calls over a healer to take care of a gash on her neck. Other than the wound from the general's lookalike and appearing a bit disheveled, she seems okay.

I can't believe we survived that horrible battle. With all the illusions, I wasn't sure we were going to make it. Peering at the dark gemstone looming over us, I wonder what twisted deception is going to happen next.

"It can't hurt you," Gabriel whispers, then slowly releases me. "They've erected a force field around it."

Relaxing into my trainer's comforting embrace, I set aside whatever fear the crystal might unleash upon us. My muscles screamed in protest after the electrocution and attack. Even though the blissful medicine Gabriel injected into me is taking effect, I need to rest. There's no way I can fight that thing like this.

"Can you stand and walk?" he asks as he stands.

"Is this the part where you throw me into a volcano?" I ask. My voice is weak, like I've been sick for weeks and finally got it back.

"Huh?"

"You're going to lull me into a false sense of security, only to kill me somehow, like they do in those prehistoric movies where the virgin girl always dies."

A warm, friendly laugh rumbles in his chest. "This isn't a movie, and I promise you that you're out of the simulation. But we need to get you back to my viewing room. I can give you better medical attention there."

"Can we just get this illusion over with?" I ask while trying to hide myself from the cheering crowd under a blanket my trainer brought. Cameras whoosh around us, making me uneasy. "Is this the fear of being in front of an audience?"

He puts his med kit away, then attaches it to his belt. "I'll take that as a no to my earlier question."

Gabriel picks me up, cradling me in his arms, then carries me off the field. The crowd is still cheering as the giant screen replays different moments from the challenges, focusing on the ones where someone died. Next to the dead Rylari, a person's picture appears along with how much they won from their bets. It makes my stomach sick each time another death is shown.

Glancing over Gabriel's shoulder, I watch the others being carted away from the field. Some are walking, others are carried, but too many have white sheets over them. And despite all of this, fireworks explode overhead in celebration. It feels like the real world, but after spending time in the illusion world, I'm not sure I can tell the difference anymore.

Chapter Twenty-Six
New Reality

IT STILL DOESN'T FEEL real.

Once we're inside Gabriel's viewing room, he sets me gently on the couch. Whatever he gave me earlier is working really well, because I don't feel a thing. Which is good because I'm pretty sure I cracked a rib when I hit that metal guardrail.

Gabriel crosses the room, leaving me cold without his body to keep me warm. He presses his hand against a small screen. I can't read what it says from here, but it looks like a call button of some sort. Then he grabs a fuzzy blanket and throws it over me. It's not the same as being near him, but it will work. It's probably better I don't relish being close to him right now, because the last Gabriel lookalike nearly killed me.

The cushions are soft. I relax into them then close my eyes, but I will myself to stay awake. Until I'm sure this isn't like before, I can't let myself fall asleep.

A savory aroma envelops my senses, causing my stomach to groan. I clutch it to stop the ache that's overwhelming me. I want to see what Gabriel is cooking, but moving is a chore. Even though the pain is gone, the exhaustion makes me feel like my body is made from lead.

A few minutes later, a plate of chicken with bacon-wrapped asparagus is set on the table, along with some juice. It's all cut up in bite-sized portions, like I'm a kid.

"Let me help you sit up," Gabriel says, then pulls me up. "You should eat something. It's been days."

I turn away, not really wanting to give into whatever trick this is. "I've been in here for days? It feels like it's been months."

He kneels in front of me, then takes my hands. "I assume you saw some twisted version of me in there?"

Nodding, I meet his gaze. "How much did you see?"

"We can't see the NPCs; those are just in your head, manifested from your fears. Everything else, we can see."

"NPC?" I ask.

"Non-player character. It's an old gaming term they gave to the illusions you see inside."

"Why didn't you tell me it was going to be like that?"

"I tried to tell you it was all fake, but it's difficult to explain until you actually experience it. I prepared you the best I could. But... every year is different. Depending on the people you go in with and those who are controlling the simulations, you'll experience something different." His face darkens as his jaw tightens.

"Something was different this time?"

"Ty made things worse, feeding his team with nightmares weeks before the event. I think it caused more deaths than normal." He rubs his temples, feeling their pain as intensely as if they were his own family.

"How many survived?" I ask, trying to remember how many were on the field before Gabriel carried me in here.

"Besides you, seventeen."

I tip my head back in disbelief. There were over forty kids to start; that's more than half dead. "How is the king going to increase his soldiers at the war front if he keeps killing us?"

A bell rings, cutting off any reply. Gabriel glances at the monitor behind me. "Enter."

Two young women come in, both in matching gray soldier's uniforms, but from the pins glimmering against their shoulders, I determine one is a Glyzul and the other is Rylari. A handler and lesser pair, I assume.

"We're here to heal, primp, and doll your trainee up," the Glyzul woman says, setting her bag near the door. "My name is Melanie Danton, and this is my lesser. She's a brilliant Yellow Flame that can heal things you didn't know were broken."

Her eyes study me with a hollowness that makes me feel naked. "Help her eat something, Gabe, while my lesser heals her wounds. The king wants all the graduates to head through the city."

Gabriel's forehead scrunches. "I thought the parade wasn't until next week."

"The official one is next week. But the king announced he was so excited by this year's batch of recruits that he wants to bolster the morale of the city with a little victory tour of its future heroes."

From the slight frown and squinting eyes, I can tell the whole idea of parading around in public annoys Gabriel. I'm with him on that one; I don't even have the energy to smile right now.

"Oh, come on, Gabe, you're one of the most eligible bachelors out there. There will be women fawning at your feet." Melanie wags her eyebrows. "And after that awful attack out west, it will be good for the people to see the Forbidden leashed to the king's guard. With three White Flames under his control, it might even stamp out any resistance cells thinking of trying to rescue their loved ones."

He glares at her for a moment, like he's almost as offended as I am about her remarks. It's that stare that convinces me that this is the real Gabriel, not his computer-generated evil twin.

"Let's just get this over with," he replies.

Instead of looking like prisoners in armor vehicles, Gabriel guides me into a beautiful convertible blue hovercraft. Apparently, when you graduate, they no longer see the Rylari as too dangerous to have around the population, instead escorting us through the city in style. With the gold bracelet firmly in place, none of us can even extinguish a flame, let alone think of a revolt.

I pick up my long, glittering black skirt, then carefully scoot into the seat. Gabriel enters behind me, wearing his dress uniform with a few more embellishments to his military awards. It's annoying because I did all the work, nearly dying, but he gets the graduation badge.

He squeezes my hand, as if that alone will calm my nerves. Even though I've accepted this as reality, it's still difficult to get the other Gabriel out of my mind. Going through the middle of town with screaming people who hate my kind isn't going to help me get over it, either.

As the vehicle takes off, I adjust the straps on the silky shirt, then smooth my ponytail to make sure everything is in place. The entire country will watch, possibly the whole world, and the last thing I want to do is embarrass myself more than I probably have in the arena.

"You look beautiful," Gabriel says. "Don't worry about this; it's just a drive down the street. Then we can go back to our apartment, where you can sleep until they announce the official assignments."

I crinkle my nose at his last words.

"Went too far, got it. Pretend I said, 'Go back to our apartment, where you can sleep as long as you need.' Better?"

"I guess. It's kind of hard to forget this isn't over yet."

He holds my gaze. "I promise I will do everything in my power to make sure you're safe."

"And what about the others?" Glancing behind us, I point to the cars following us.

He lets out a breath. "I'm only one person. There's no way I can save everyone."

Taking in his words, I rest my head against the back of the seat. He's right. There are only so many strings he can pull and favors to ask for before someone stops him. Should I ask him to pull them for me? Or should I save them for the others? Something in my gut tells me his decisions will revolve around protecting me. He's already done it a few times; what would change his mind now?

Our transport follows behind Victoria's hovercar as we turn out of the driveway onto the street. She sits on top of the seat, waving like a queen to the crowds that gawk at us. We're lined up in order of our scores and who generated the most money. It's not surprising she's first. Considering how many times I nearly fell or messed up, it's shocking to me I came in second.

Ty's bright blond hair glows in the afternoon sun as he eats up the crowd's cheers. I can't imagine him becoming the crown prince or even the king, or maybe I can. The arena was filled with fears, and he was one of mine. Out of all the scenarios I faced, he's the one I really hope never comes true. I will face the prospect of Gabriel and Abby any day if I can just avoid having Ty in my life.

Black banners with a red snake are strung between buildings as confetti falls from above. The shadows of the towering buildings loom over us as our hovercars continue through the parade. The wide streets are congested, with people lined up on either side snapping pictures with their digicameras. Most cheer and wave at Gabriel, and signs with his name are everywhere with congratulatory words for his accomplishments in the arena. I suppose this is another thing I'll have to get used to—living in his shadow. Whatever my accomplishments are, he'll take the credit, getting another gold medal for my work. Too bad it doesn't work the other way around.

As long as we comply with their demands for entertainment and offer our protection, the people love this slavery dynamic the king created. Seeing the people's voracious appetite for this kind of thing makes me believe they'll never change. If we did escape, where could a child of fire go? I'm not sure there's any place for us to hide in this world of hate. If the king needs more of us, the Dunes may not even be safe for long.

The vehicle turns down another street with more adoring fans, many chanting Ty's name. Where I come from, the people are a little less adoring of the general and his son. Seeing the public like this makes me want to show them what he's really like behind that perfect smile and polite wave.

"Ignore him," Gabriel whispers.

I have no clue what he's talking about until I notice the sparks flickering from my fingers. Quickly, I squeeze my hand to get them under control. "Sorry."

"Don't be. Ty's annoying, but giving him attention in any form just fuels his narcissistic tendencies." Gabriel smiles at some girls swooning over him, making me want to gag. He doesn't wave obnoxiously like Ty, instead just staring at the crowds and scanning them like we're in a war zone, occasionally smiling and nodding at people cheering for him.

Thinking of the NPC version of Gabriel, I can't help but wonder who he's seeing. Because there is a measure of truth in every one of those fears I experienced in the arena. I'm afraid of spiders. The toothy fish is definitely scary, and I would fear them if I ever saw one in the wild, but that was not my fear. Drowning was my fear. Ms. Brown's basement is something I've feared since the first time I was locked down there. I don't fear Abby anymore, but I fear having her in my life. Really, if there was any girl in Gabriel's life, it would affect me if he becomes my handler.

"Gabriel, are you seeing anyone?" I rush the question out as fast as I can.

"What?"

"Um…" I breathe deeply, trying to relax my nerves. "If you're seeing anyone and you decide to settle down with them, it would affect my life. If you're my handler, that is. So I think it's only fair I have veto power."

"You want veto power over my love life?"

"Well, don't say it like that."

"I'm just repeating what you said."

"I'm not telling you who to love, just…"

"Who I marry?" He smirks knowingly. I hate it when he does that.

"Look, whoever is in your life will be in mine. I don't want to have a girl in my life that makes my life miserable."

"That makes two of us."

My jaw drops, and I barely know what to say. "What is that supposed to mean?"

"It means I don't want someone in my life that makes me miserable, either."

"Are you insinuating I make your life miserable?"

He shrugs. "You'll only make my life miserable if I give you veto power over my love life."

I take a minute to think about his words, then remember my original question. "So, are you seeing someone?"

He leans toward me, so close I'm suddenly not sure if he's about to kiss me in public. Which would be illegal for so many reasons. My pulse quickens, a rapid rhythm echoing the anxious thoughts swirling in my head about the public's opinion and the king's reaction.

"It's none of your business, Rissa." Then he leans back to search through the crowd.

I'm about to argue with him when something explodes near Ty's hovercraft. It swerves into the crowd as another bomb goes off up ahead.

Gabriel's on top of me in a flash, shielding me from debris. People are screaming and running for their lives. A few more explosions go off, rendering our vehicles useless as the gravity function switches off, and we fall to the ground with a thud.

My trainer keeps me pinned in place until the explosions stop. He sits up, then glances at the sky. I follow his gaze. A giant circle with a dragon flying through it is burning the building directly above of us. As I glance all around us, I realize the emblem is everywhere. The black snake banners are gone, replaced by red ones with a golden dragon.

"What is that?" I ask.

"The old Artijan flag. Rebels use it all the time," Gabriel whispers before jumping into the driver's seat, taking over autonomic controls by busting open the console and splicing the wires. "We have to get you off the street."

"You mean, get you off the street," I correct. "Wouldn't the rebels want to protect me?"

"Maybe," he answers as the magnets come back to life. "It depends on which ones are here. So maybe not."

The hovercraft sprouts wheels, then takes off fast, the velocity shoving me against my seat. I don't think these things are designed to go this fast, but somehow Gabriel bypasses the safeties.

I never in my wildest dreams pictured my rule-following trainer hot-wiring a vehicle and driving recklessly through the streets, weaving between pedestrians like a lunatic. Maybe it's his military training, or perhaps he's a secret car thief.

The sky blazes with electrical discharges, their crackly charges echoing through the city as they arc overhead. I brace myself between the seat in front of me and the door as we make a sharp turn down an alley. The brick apartment building looms over us. Several people jump between the rooftops, but I can't tell which side they belong to from this distance.

The vehicle bursts out onto another street, then comes to a sudden stop, and I collide against the seat in front of me. Gabriel growls under his breath. I peer over the seat to find several dark, hooded figures wearing masks that cover their faces blocking the street. They hold long bows in their hand, a crude weapon considering what the capital can unleash on them. They do nothing but stand there as people rush around them to get away from the bombs. The only thing identifiable is their fiery eyes—they're Rylari.

"What are they waiting for?" I ask, whispering as I clutch the seat. I wish I knew where Luna was. If I did, I'd grab her and run. Not that we'd make it far with these gold bracelets strapped onto us.

Whirring sounds echo off the buildings. Behind us, a group of drones systematically scan the area, unleashing electrical bursts that subdue anyone caught in their path. My lips part, and I suck in a breath.

"They're waiting for those," Gabriel says as he searches our surroundings.

"But they're just shooting everyone."

Gabriel sighs as he backs the hovercar up. "That's how the king handles uprisings: shoot first, ask questions later."

He turns the hovercraft, aiming it for a narrow alleyway. Just as we enter, the archers unleash burning arrows. I don't think any of them miss because the drones explode before falling to the ground. It's so eerily similar to the arena, I just want to find a bunker and hide.

The pounding wings of a cicadacopter draw my attention upward as it passes over the gap between the tall buildings.

"Curfew is being implemented. All citizens must return to their homes immediately. Report all suspicious activity on the neighborhood watch app on your digidevices," the voice from the copter says. "All graduates are to report to the palace at once."

Gabriel turns down another alleyway, weaving between the buildings and streets. People are screaming as military personnel swarm them. Helplessness grips me, my stomach twisting as I witness the king's soldiers' violence against their own people; the scene is brutal, the air thick with fear and the stench of sweat and injury.

My nails dig into the seats as an officer smacks a woman across the face, sending her to the ground as another officer kills another with a point-blank discharge. I don't think either of them is part of the rebels, just spectators in the crowd.

We turn into a driveway that leads to a massive stone wall. Glyzul guards point their weapons at us until they see my trainer.

A solider salutes Gabriel. "Colonel, good to see you. Please proceed to the west hall. The Forbidden will be deposited in their room before the briefing."

"Thanks, Corporal," Gabriel says, then moves the hovercraft through the gates.

Despite the ancient-looking exterior, the interior is a mixture of modern sleek buildings and old school brick buildings, all surrounding a fabricated square lake lined by trees. Water shoots in the air every few seconds, dancing above the lake before falling toward the surface. A tower stands at the end of the water, with two buildings flanking either side of it. It would be peaceful if there weren't weapons firing and screaming behind us.

Gabriel stops the vehicle in front of a two-story modern building, then jumps out of the transport as several people pour out the front doors. Several guards stand at attention on either side, saluting him but shifting when they see me.

My trainer opens the door, then helps me out. "I'm sorry about this." He presses a button, completely cutting me off my powers, leaving me cold. "It's protocol in these situations. I won't be long."

"We have a room for both of you, my lord," a middle-aged woman says. Her dirty blond hair is swept into a braid that wraps into a bun. "I can take your graduate to her room for you. The king is already waiting."

"What about the others?" Gabriel asks, still clutching my hands.

My breath hitches, hoping for good news.

"They're nearby, with no casualties among the graduates. They should enter the palace grounds soon."

"Very good," he replies.

I must look worried because he leans in so only I can hear him. "This isn't a simulation. I promise, I'll be back for you as soon as I meet with the king. Don't do anything stupid while I'm gone."

He doesn't let me respond before taking off toward another building across the courtyard. "Get her comfortable clothing and pajamas. And see to whatever she needs. She's a talented healer, so once she's settled, provide her with the supplies to help the others."

"Yes, my lord." She dips into a curtsy. "Well, come along, miss. I'll get you set up. My name's Mrs. Carson. Just call for me if you need anything while you stay with us."

I follow her into the building. "Could you just let me know when a girl named Luna gets in? She has dark skin, wild curly hair, fifteen-years-old. I just want to make sure she's okay."

Mrs. Carson smiles as she opens the door for me. "You're a sweetheart, looking after your friend. I will pass along your messages and let you know when she's settled."

"Thanks," I say, following her up the large, fancy stairway to the second floor. Plush carpet that appears to be lined with gold motifs adorns the steps that complement the hand carved bannisters.

With its fancy wallpaper and moldings, the second floor looks just like every other room in the house. It feels like I've gone back in time to a simpler era.

"This was part of the old palace, built after the first people emerged from the caves after Dragons Fall. It's always been kept this way to preserve history," she says as we continue to the end of the hall. "Alright, this is you, Clarissa."

I follow her into the room with a canopy bed trimmed with more red and gold. Thankfully, there's no overly large flower decoration in this room.

"I'm going to track down some clothes for you. Take a bath while I'm gone. If you need anything, just ring this bell." She points to the scan pad next to the door. "In case you're thinking about escape, you can't. This building won't let anyone but a Glyzul in or out without an escort."

I hold up my bracelet. "Not like I could make it far, anyway."

"Right. I like to be on the safe side." She leans, then whispers, "I don't like to see any of you hurt."

She shuts the door, leaving me alone.

I collapse on the soft bed, too tired to do anything else. But I haven't found the shimmering door yet, so I might be stuck here for a while, especially since this is my new reality.

Chapter Twenty-Seven
Surrounded by Serpents

I'VE BECOME AN INSOMNIAC.

The nightmares of the arena haunt my sleep. It's been three days, and I can't even close my eyes without seeing the victims' faces. Beatrice, Eric, Thomas, Freddy, and Robert hit the worst because I witnessed their deaths personally. If I don't sleep soon, I might join them.

Despite my exhaustion, I've been able to heal the others. Not with my powers, but with my skills and knowledge. With the recent rebel forces destroying his precious city, the king, in his magnanimous ways, has decided that no Forbidden shall use their powers until our assignments are handed out. Because I'm without my fire in this gilded cage, I'm freezing cold all the time.

A knock at the door draws my attention. "Miss?"

"Enter," I reply. It's not like I can refuse. I'm pretty sure a soldier would barge in if I told them to go away.

Mrs. Carson enters with a maid and several other people behind her, along with a rack of very expensive dresses. After everything that's happened, I'm in no mood to play dress up. I've already done that once in the arena and have no desire to repeat that anytime soon.

What's the point of this ball, anyway? All of us know where we're going; why can't they just tell us now? Maybe it makes everyone feel better to package us in pretty little outfits before condemning us to die.

"Oh! She has a gorgeous complexion," a taller woman says as she pulls me away from the window. She touches my face, pushing my skin around as if I can hide something there. "I'm Dawn, by the way. Gabriel hired me today. I'm here to make you beautiful for the ball."

Leaning back, I pull away from her. "What if I don't want to go?"

She puts her hands on her hips, making her look like a giant clucking chicken. "Unfortunately, Ms. Unruly, attendance is not optional. The Dragon Festival is attended by everyone. Even though the city celebrations are canceled, the one at the palace must go on. It will be televised for the entire country to see, and you are one of the few with the privilege of dining with the king." The designer studies me. "However, that doesn't mean you can't be fashionably late."

Despite my sour mood, my lips twitch.

"There we go, darling. Maybe by the end of this session, we can teach you how to make the best of this situation." Dawn waggles her eyebrows before sashaying toward the clothing rack. Glancing over her shoulder, she adds, "I have a few dresses with hidden pockets. And all the city's elites will be there tonight."

"How…"

"Dawn knows everything." Dawn picks up a dress, then sets it back down. "Well, Dawn knows everything your trainer told her. Though I dabble in the gossip mill when I can, you wouldn't believe half the stories I could tell you. People are nasty."

"Of course," I say, rolling my eyes.

"Oh honey. Making a friend like Lord Gabriel is a good thing in a place like this. There are snakes everywhere." She points to the motif above my bed, then to the ones on the trim molding. "Literally everywhere. They really need to change this decor."

I've been stuck in this room and didn't notice all the snake art surrounding me. Now that she's pointed them out, I can't unsee them. I usually pride myself on being observant, but now I feel strangely detached and unfocused.

"Sorry, I haven't slept in days."

"Dawn understands." She squeezes my shoulders. "Unfortunately, this trauma won't leave you for quite some time. Until then, I have a serum that will help with the puffy, bloodshot eyes."

She's right; I probably won't sleep well for a long time. It's like the time Abby and I had to sleep in a crawl space of a manor house for several days during a sandstorm. Her proximity kept me awake, with the fear that she might harm me. I sigh.

"Where do we start?"

"In the bathroom," Dawn says, handing me some jars with fragrant oils in them.

"I just showered this morning."

She chuckles. "You could have fooled me."

"Fine." I purse my lips as I stomp toward the bathroom. Now that I think about it, I don't think I've taken a shower since getting out of the arena.

The reptilian creatures have found their way onto my dress. My sleeveless red gown has a golden snake coiled around my waist. From the feel, it drapes across my exposed back, too. I don't look like myself anymore, not with the makeup Dawn caked on me, but I suppose that's the point.

Tonight is about showing submission to the king. Presenting the Rylari survivors who will now be forced to do his bidding is just another part of his games. Maybe we don't really ever leave the arena. Maybe it morphs into a treacherous reality that keeps us compliant in a world full of glitter and convenience.

Dawn adds a golden chain around my neck, disguising the necklace I refuse to take off. "There. Now, it looks like it belongs."

She turns me around toward the mirror. I stare at the gold choker as my fingers drift up to touch it. With my dark locks coiled on my head and the corset hugging my curves, I look nothing like the little orphan girl I once was. I feel like an impostor. If it wasn't for the serpent belt, the gold cuff, and the long chain around my arms reminding me of my status as a slave, I'd think I was a duchess or something.

I don't totally hate it. This dress at least covers the important parts plus a little more and gives me enough movement to kick someone if I wanted.

"You look like a princess, darling," she says as she smooths a wrinkle out of the full skirt.

A knock at the door draws my attention.

Mrs. Carson answers the door. "Lord Caldera is here."

"Beautiful, darling." Dawn smiles, then claps her hands at her assistants. "Come on, let's clean up. Cinderella needs to get to the ball."

Wrinkling my nose at the reference, I back away from the mirror. I really don't know how to handle myself in this outfit. The good part is there are several hidden pockets inside the bodice and a few more in the skirt. It makes the thief part of me eager; a little piece of my old self will get to play tonight. I don't know what Dawn was thinking. If the king catches me stealing, he would probably use the Crystal of Death on me during the ball.

When I see Gabriel standing in the doorway, my breath hitches. His disheveled hair is slicked back and his uniform is replaced by a red-trimmed black dress coat with tails. The snake pin of the Glyzul graces his jacket just above his medals. His beard is trimmed close to the skin, defining his jaw.

He smirks with that half smile that probably drives the girls crazy. I hate it when he does that. He extends his arm. "You clean up nice, Rissa."

"You finally figured out how to use a bath." With a light touch, I run my hand across his chest before taking his arm, feeling the warmth radiating from his body. "That's good. At least I won't have to smell that stench all night."

"You've been smelling me?" Gabriel waggles his eyebrows.

I glare at him. He can be so frustrating sometimes. "Can we just get this stupid festival over with?"

"I'm glad to see you're back to your old self," he says as he guides me into the hallway.

"What does that mean?"

"That I hated seeing you sad." He extends his free hand toward me. "And that you're a thief."

Reluctantly, I hand him back his badge. "Apparently, not a good one. Luna wouldn't have gotten caught."

"You're good, Clarissa. I'm pretty sure you could steal a jewel off the king without getting caught." He chuckles as he puts the pin back on his chest. "But you can't hide things from me."

"Don't remind me." My stomach drops thinking about the possibility he won't be announced as my handler tonight.

We make our way toward the exit. The courtyard between the sleek tower and the Rylari compound is decorated with thousands of twinkling lights that reflect in the enormous fountain in the center. Black banners with the red Glyzul snake hang from every lantern.

Dozens of Rylari walk with their handlers toward the main tower, along with the recent graduates. Like me, they wear beautiful, fancy outfits with a snake coiled around their waists. It's such a waste because we already know our fate; we're all going to die in a long-fought war with Thevania. I really can't understand why we have to go through a ceremony.

"Clarissa."

I turn just in time to brace myself. Luna wraps her arms around me. If it weren't for Gabriel steadying me, we'd probably end up in the fountain.

"I'm so glad that you're here."

After Gabriel stabilizes us, I say, "It's not like this is an optional event."

"That hasn't stopped you before."

Zane stands stoically behind her. He acts more like her personal body guard then her trainer. He acknowledges Gabriel with a nod of his head. Other than that, he stays silent, appearing grimmer than ever. It makes me wonder what they discussed in those meetings with the king.

"We better get inside," Gabriel says.

Biting my lip, I glance at the king's tower. It's almost as tall as the nearest skyscraper. Unlike the thick brick walls surrounding the grounds, it's sleek, curving from the bottom into two connected towers at the top. The king's banner hangs between them, marking them as the Artijan seat of power.

Gabriel guides me inside. Besides the Rylari prisoners, hundreds of guests mingle about. Their evening wear is even more glamorous than my own. Like me, every lord and lady wears a snake jewel of some kind.

My trainer acknowledges some of them before we head into the throne room. It's enormous, with black marbled columns holding up the decorative vaulted ceilings. The dome at the end of the long, rectangular room lets the fading sun cascade inside. Off to the side is a group of musicians playing melodic songs for people to dance. Like outside, black banners with a golden crown over a red snake drape from the ceiling. At the end of the marble-floored room is the throne, a menacing gilded chair that sits high above everyone. In it is the snake king himself, watching over his guests with hooded eyes.

"What do you think?" Gabriel asks.

"It's beautiful," Luna replies. "I wonder what it looked like before the king redecorated."

"A lot less black," Gabriel answers.

I scrunch my face. "How would you know?"

"My father worked here." He takes two drinks from a passing server, handing me one. "He has pictures on his digitablet."

If his father worked here before, then he knew the previous king and queen—they were Rylari. People have differing opinions on them. Some think they were outstanding leaders, but others say they didn't do enough. I guess it's impossible to please everyone, but the mixed feelings led to a world ruled with fear and oppression.

I'm about to ask when a blonde girl interrupts, excitedly hugging my trainer like she knows him a little too well. Upon realization that the blonde girl is none other than Abby, my heart leaps into my throat, and I freeze.

"Gabriel, I'm so glad you're here. I've missed you." She takes his hand, then wraps it around her shoulders. "Come on, let's go dance."

My stomach twists until I feel like I'm going to throw up. The scenario in the arena must have come from my subconscious—Abby is grifting Gabriel. And now I have to face one of my worst nightmares in real life. I search my surroundings for a shimmering door.

"Oh, you must be the pet Gabriel mentioned. My name is Abigail." She smiles at me sweetly, like we don't know each other. All I want to do is scream at her. "I know you have some ceremony or something, but I must steal my betrothed away for a minute."

She smirks at me as my eyes widen, my heart thumping loudly in my ears. They disappear into the dancing couples before I can warn him. I clench my fists. Despite the cool weight of the gold bracelet against my skin, a simmering heat builds in my veins, threatening to boil over.

"What's Abby doing here?" Luna asks.

I clutch my stomach as I finish my drink off, handing the empty glass off to a server. "Exactly what Ms. Brown taught her."

"What exactly did Ms. Brown teach her?" Zane asks.

Normally, I would get into so much trouble for ruining one of Ms. Brown's schemes. I've only done it a few times because I was sure it was going to hurt someone, and I gladly took the punishment each time. But I'm the king's property and, technically, Gabriel's for now. Ms. Brown can't control or punish me anymore. "Abby is a grifter."

He grunts. "Makes sense."

"What does?" Luna asks.

"She appeared out of nowhere at every Silver City high society party there was, claiming she was an heiress to some obscure dead lord. Then she attached herself to just about every titled person before clinging to Gabriel." His gaze travels across the dance floor. "Now that she's here at the king's party, she's definitely moving up."

"Should you warn him?" Luna asks.

"Gabriel can handle himself. He's smarter than he looks. But I do have a few people I need to speak with." He nods at Luna, and they leave me alone.

I take another fruity drink from a passing server before moving toward the wall. There's no point in gawking at them. For now, I can distract myself with some good, old-fashioned thievery. After tonight, this might be the last chance I get. I don't exactly want to steal weapons from my fellow soldiers on a battlefield.

Pretending to look at the architecture, I bump into a lady, careful not to spill either of our drinks. That's always important. Spilling drinks is for amateurs or for distractions to gain a bigger prize. Tonight is just for fun. I won't need anything once I'm gone.

"I'm so sorry," I say, pointing at the intricately decorated columns. "The carvings distracted me."

She glances down her nose at me. "I suggest you sit in the corner like a good little pet and wait for your handler."

I watch her saunter off for a moment while I pocket her gemstone bracelet. It wasn't my plan to keep it, but after she was so rude, I'll consider it a fee for having to deal with her. Circling the grand throne room, I pocket several more jewels before Gabriel finds me again.

"How much did you get?" he asks.

"A girl never tells."

Before I can ask where Abby is, a gong draws my attention. The king rises from his chair, quieting the crowd as they surge forward.

"It's time to announce the assignments." A servant hands him a dig-itablet. "Graduates, please make your way to the front."

Gabriel guides me forward. For the first time, he holds the snake chain draping across my arms. From his grip, I can tell he's doing it for the show. He'd never use it otherwise. At least, I don't think he would. Since seeing Abby here claiming she's his fiancée, I'm not sure anymore.

With my head held high and my jaw set, I stand at the base of the dais. There's no point in showing them weakness. Not at this point. Luna stands next to me. If we were allowed, I'd hold her hand.

"Let's began," the king says. "Private Winston."

Ginger steps forward, her trainer right behind her. She's tense, her hands gripping the fabric of her dress.

"You're assigned to Dune patrol."

Her shoulders relax. At least in the Dunes, she's less likely to die. But the downfall is she'll be expected to take down Rylari and hand them over to the king.

The king calls out several more names. All of them go to the front lines. My focus blurs with each name called. It's so cruel to handle our fates like this in front of cameras and an audience in glittering outfits that will just get swapped out with a uniform.

"Lord Caldera."

My breath hitches as I step forward. Gabriel's fingers graze across my back, temporarily distracting me from my fear.

"Palace guard and healer of the Forbidden."

Closing my eyes for a moment, I shake my head. That can't be right. Being part of the palace guard isn't an option. Rylari are always sent to the front lines, or to some faraway place to hunt for others. From the whispers erupting from the crowd behind me, they're just as shocked as I am.

"The Honorable Lord Caldera will continue as your handler."

I glance at him, but he keeps his eyes forward like the trained soldier he is, then guides me back in line as my head swims.

The king announces more assignments. Some are assigned to the Dunes, and I just hope that Luna is one of them, but most are sent to the front lines. Victoria and Serene are assigned to the palace guard like me. The three most powerful girls are staying here, given assignments that aren't typical for a Rylari. It's strange, but I'm sure the king has his reasons.

"Lieutenant Freeman."

My heart plummets as Luna steps forward with Zane. I hold my breath as my hands clutch the fabric of my gown. Time seems to drag on as I wait to hear my friend's fate. Despite myself, I send up silent prayers as if they could change the words written on the digitablet. Her fate is already sealed, and there is nothing I can do about it.

"Front lines."

My eyes widen as my body shakes. Tears well in my eyes. My dearest friend has received a death sentence, and I am powerless to intervene. If we'd been going together, at least I could have protected her. But what can I do from hundreds of miles away?

Tiny sparks flicker from my fingertips and heat overpowers my body. Gabriel pulls me closer, actually using the chain to restrain me, preventing me from doing something stupid. It quells the sparks but not the heat boiling inside. He knows I'd do anything to stop Luna from going to the front lines.

A rising tide of terror overwhelms me, drowning out the king's voice. My complete focus is on Luna, the girl I've known for years. She's only a few feet away, but soon she will be on the other side of the country, fighting a never-ending war for a country who couldn't care less about her wellbeing.

I send up a silent prayer to the beings who landed here so long ago. *Sky People, please help me.*

Chapter Twenty-Eight
Tethered

THIS IS JUST ONE long nightmare that will never end.

My best friend doesn't show any emotion as she steps back into line. Luna is fifteen; she should show all sorts of emotion. Gregory squeezed his eyes shut when the news was broken to him, but the youngest of our group does nothing.

My handler guides me to the center of the floor in an iron grip that is cutting off the circulation in my arm. I guess it's custom that we dance after being forced together, but I can't remember any of the steps. My mind is in too much chaos to dance.

"Clarissa, focus on me," Gabriel whispers into my ear.

I know he's right, but I can't seem to take my eyes off Luna. She follows Zane to the center of the dance floor, then takes his hands. He whispers something that I can't hear, and a second later, a smirk appears on her lips, like she's holding back a laugh. I don't understand what's happening. All I want to do is go talk to her, but Gabriel almost drags me to the other side of the floor.

He gently takes my arms. "You can't go to her now; everyone is watching."

"I don't care. Luna is way more important than some silly dance," I hiss, then try to leave, but his iron grip keeps me in place.

All I can do is glare at him, but he nods toward the throne. I follow his gaze to a pair of dark, narrow eyes staring directly at me. The king has me in his sights, and I exert every ounce of self-control to avoid visibly shuddering.

"When you're in a den of vipers, you don't poke them with a stick," he whispers, his breath tickling my neck. "I promise I'll find a way for you to see her later. For now, we have to play the part."

Focusing on him, I relax into his embrace, placing one arm on his shoulder while he takes my other hand. When his free hand grazes my back, a wave of goosebumps erupts on my skin, and suddenly I'm hyper aware of how close he is to me. I've never really danced with a man before, at least not like this, because I'm usually too busy trying to pickpocket him.

I'm hoping the next melody is a faster number because I barely remember the popular waltz steps. Since Ms. Brown believed I lacked the skills to be a grifter, she didn't see the need to keep up my dance education. Despite my silent pleas, the orchestra doesn't listen, choosing to play a slow waltz.

Gabriel pulls me in tighter, then glides across the floor, making it look like I know what I'm doing. The music and closeness feel entirely different from my lessons. A part of me wants to enjoy this feeling, but I can't stop worrying about my friend.

"I'm sorry about Luna. It's hard thinking that your friend is going to be in danger," he says.

"What would you know of it? You sit here with privilege in this gilded world filled with expensive jewelry and food."

It's like watching storm clouds pass across his eyes when I meet his gaze. "If you don't remember, Zane is one of my closest friends. Since he's Luna's handler, he is being reassigned to the front lines too. So don't think for a second I don't understand what you're going through."

I miss the next step, feeling a little foolish for not thinking about Zane. He might not be my friend, but, like Gabriel, I don't hate him. My dance partner disguises my misstep with a twirl, then gets us back in time with the music.

"I'm sorry." It's lame, but it's the only thing I can think of to say. "Wait. How did Zane get transferred if he was under your leadership?"

"I'll give you one guess." He twirls me around right next to the blond major I've come to loathe.

When he twirls me close, I ask, "How did Ty reassign Zane? You outrank him."

"When we're in the room with the king, he outranks me."

Rage, sadness, grief, helplessness all course through me, if that's even possible. It's so many contradictory emotions welling inside that my body just feels numb. My head is swirling with all the feelings running through me.

"Can't you pull strings to undo it? I mean, you have friends and..." I don't even know exactly what I'm asking, but I suppose it's that I'd rather go in place Luna. "Can't you have them send me instead?"

His lips twitch, but from the wrinkled skin between his eyebrows, I can tell he doesn't like the answer he's about to give me. "The king wants all the White Flames here. I had to pull all my strings to stay here with you. There are no more favors, Clarissa."

"What do you mean?"

"Ty wants to be the only trainer and handler for all the White Flames."

My breath hitches as I think back to the arena. Gabriel told me Ty injected his influence over the illusions we saw. I glance at him over my handler's shoulder, dancing with Victoria. I just don't know how much of that scenario was him and how much that was in my subconscious.

"Do you understand now?"

I nod, too afraid to say anything.

"We have to play it as safe as we can, Rissa. If we don't, Luna and Zane going to war will be the least of our worries."

The song ends, and he bows while I curtsy, then we face the throne and do it again. The king says something, but I hear nothing; my mind can't comprehend what's happening. All I want to do is scream at him, but I can't, not in this crowd. It would just get me locked up. My blood boils with anger, causing an unbearable heat that suffocates me. With all this fabric circling me, I just can't breathe anymore. I need air.

As soon as the king dismisses us, Zane escorts Luna out of the ballroom to an antechamber with the others destined for war. I try to follow, but Gabriel doesn't let me, pulling me back with the chain. My body shakes as I watch her vanish behind the door.

"Not yet," he whispers, keeping me in place while the king rattles on about crushing the rebels or some nonsense.

When Gabriel releases his grip, I hurry toward the first door I spot. It leads to a large balcony, with cool crisp air that soothes my burning skin. Thankfully, the statue-like guards in their funny serpent skin hats don't follow me. But I'm sure my handler will be out here eventually. I think he was calling after me, but I couldn't stop myself.

I grip the railing, turning my knuckles white. My breathing turns frantic as I try to stop the anxiety from consuming me. Luna is going to die, and I have no way to stop it. Removing my necklace and unleashing my blue flames won't cut it against the palace guards and the sheer number of people in the city. I'm only one person. Even if I could get Gabriel's help, that's only two people. Then where would we go?

Not to mention, my skills are still woefully behind the other fire wielders. I'd likely just blow myself up accidentally if I tried to rescue Luna. Maybe that's why they're keeping me here. They think I need more training.

But if that were true, Victoria and Serene wouldn't be stuck here, too. They're more skilled than anyone in that ballroom, they don't need more training to be sent to war. Yet, the king wants us here. Why?

I should have jumped out of the vehicle the other day when I had a chance. That wouldn't have saved Luna, either. I don't know if I'll find another opportunity to escape, not being here in the palace. The worst part is I doubt I'll find an opportunity in time to save my friend before she leaves.

Glancing out at the city skyline, I shake my head as I think about how I ended up here. Abby's presence fills my thoughts as I touch my necklace. If she hadn't stolen it, my life would be different. Maybe Luna wouldn't be here either. Just thinking about that event spikes my anger.

"I'm sorry about your friend," a familiar voice says, but it lacks the sarcasm I've grown used to these past several months.

Victoria wears a sleek red gown with a gold snake wrapping around her waist before circling her neck and hanging down her chest. It's fitted to her shape, and she wears it with a confidence that I don't have.

"Are you truly sorry, Victoria?"

"Maybe not as much as I should be," she admits. She stands next to me, overlooking the city with its twinkling lights. The buildings affected by the attacks are the only ones without light, leaving a black spot in an otherwise beautiful landscape. "But I know how you feel. I thought I was going to lose Serene. And when I realized she was replaced by an NPC and thought she was dead, I didn't know what to do. I lost it in there. You saved the day, and if you hadn't, Serene wouldn't be here now. So, thank you."

"But in the end, most of them are going to die anyway."

"Even if the king never found them, death was always a possibility, Clarissa. Don't be so narrowminded. Everyone knows the risks when taking part in the king's games."

"What does that mean?" I ask. "It's not like we have a choice."

"I forget sometimes you didn't grow up in the Dunes. Food and water are so scarce there that most go without it for days. If you think you were hungry after the arena, imagine going through that every single day. We may endure it better than the Glyzul, but that doesn't mean it doesn't affect us. Someone dies or is taken to come here all the time; we're used to it." She studies me. "Every path in life leads to death. It's just that some keep your stomach filled and the others don't."

The picture she paints is so much worse than Luna ever described, but every person's story is unique. I knew the Dunes was a tough place to live, but is it so bad they'd choose to join the king's guard? "You chose to come here?"

"'Chose' is a strong word." She wrinkles her nose. "Let's call it a necessity that my mother encouraged after my father died. There was no way she could feed me anymore. So, we made arrangements with some Glyzul who are, let's say, sympathetic to our problems. I was supposed to train with Gabriel until you came along."

"Gabriel knew you were volunteering?"

"Not exactly. But like I said, I worked to change my circumstances to something better. I called in a lot of favors with various factions within our community. While it's at least a little better than it was, you changed the plan and the games, Clarissa. And now, everyone's eyes are on you."

"Did you come out here to just kick me while I'm down?"

"No. I came out here to thank you for saving us. If you hadn't smashed the crystal, we probably all would have died," she says, then fully looks at me. Unlike the first time I met her, there isn't malice in her gaze, just someone who seems resigned to do what she must in order to survive. "And to give you a bit of advice."

I'm not sure what kind of wisdom she could impart to me, but she's definitely got me curious.

"Stay focused on your task, for your own sake. If you don't, the snakes will get to you. And I know, because I'm currently tethered to one."

Now I wonder if that's why she's treats me like I'm her enemy. She's stuck with Ty, and he's one of the cruelest trainers here. I saw what he did to her in the cafeteria, and that's probably not to worst of it.

"I'm sorry."

"Don't be. He may use me to do something stupid, but that doesn't mean I won't use him." Her smile actually reaches her sparkling blue eyes. "Don't worry about Luna too much. She can take care of herself far more than you give her credit for."

"How do you know?" I ask.

She leans on the railing. "There's a lot you don't know about our people and your friend. Luna's story is not mine to tell. However, the Rylari have a common enemy, but no one agrees on how to fix our problems. But let's just say, some well-meaning people have chosen a different way of life compared to the rest of us."

"What are you trying to say?"

"We are trained to survive the horrors of this land from our youth." She points to the dark area the rebels attacked, then holds up her golden bracelet. "So that we are powerful, even when we are tethered to vipers."

Victoria leaves without letting me ask more questions.

As I watch her leave, I see Abby practically wrapping herself like a snake around Gabriel. Seeing them like that brings back memories from the arena. I have to clench my fists just to prevent myself from doing something stupid, like smack her across the face. With the king's decision to chain me to Gabriel, I have no choice but to remain at his side. He can force me to clean her toilet if he wants me to. If he marries her, I'll be stuck having her around for life, I just have to be careful that she doesn't fill my handler's head with lies.

Before I act on my dark thoughts, I turn away from them. With all the security in this place and my bracelet leaving me powerless, I wouldn't get away with it. The last thing I need right now is to fight off a bunch of guards in the middle of a ballroom.

Since becoming the king's property, I almost long for Ms. Brown's blackmail. Even though it made me angry, it was so much simpler than what I'm facing now. The twisted complexities of court and doing the king's bidding are much worse than the consequences of Ms. Brown's machinations. Though I have to admit the line between who is worse is fuzzy.

Was my life before discovering my powers so bad?

Sure, I had to do chores, which I hated, but I would scrub the floors any day rather than lose Luna or face this new world I'm living in. Back then, I only had to deal with Abby. I wrap my arms around my waist, desperately trying to soothe the pain welling inside.

When Luna leaves, I'll be all alone. With my archenemy putting the moves on my handler, I'll be more isolated than ever. Tears fall down my cheeks, and I dab them, careful to not smudge the makeup plastered on my face. Tilting my head back, I stare at the stars, sending up a silent prayer to anyone that's listening.

Blowing out a breath, I try to think through my problem. Ideally, I need to sneak us out of here, but where would we go? The Dunes sound horrible. Artijan is at war with Thevania, our closest neighbors. And the other two countries on this continent aren't exactly friendly. Of course, getting to them would be a challenge; the terrain is difficult even for a Rylari. And then, there are these stupid golden bracelets that only a handler or trainer can take off.

As I glance behind me at the glittering jewels dripping from the elite dancing around the ballroom, I smile. One thing that always talks is money. A lesson Ms. Brown taught me from a young age.

Maybe I can smuggle us out of here with a little bribe.

This is the best dress I've ever worn. After one pass through the ballroom, I've filled most of my hidden pockets, leaving only enough room for a few more items. I aim for only the most expensive things that most won't notice missing. The thrill of taking what isn't mine surges through me, a potent cocktail of rebellion and triumph, as if I'd single-handedly toppled the whole system.

Twirling around the room, I take a few more glittering items. If I want to gloat, I could probably nick a tiara, but I doubt I can walk out with it on my head. None of them are small enough to fit inside my dress, either.

Diagnosis: kleptomaniac.

Given Ms. Brown's training, that's probably what's happening. The crazier part is most nobles ignore me—except one. The older man says nothing. He just stares at me, sipping his wine.

At first, I hesitated to steal something in front of him. With his red sash, I know he's a provincial lord. He could easily turn me in, or worse, kill me. All he did was lift his glass that first time, then take another sip. Now it's almost like a game to see if I can get the others past his gaze. I'm successful with a few, but not every piece. If he sees me, his eyes crinkle as a smirk touches his lips.

When I'm done, I circle the room, careful to avoid Gabriel and Abby. I have no interest in seeing what he's up to with her. And if I have to see them kissing, I might just scream. The last thing I need is to draw attention to myself.

I become a wallflower, hugging the dark corner, observing the nobles overstuff their stomachs. Then I take inventory by feeling of each piece hidden in the fabric of my dress.

"Very impressive."

I jump as the older man from earlier stands by me.

He leans in to whisper, "No one but me noticed a thing. And most of them are so drunk, they probably will never notice."

"You did," I point out.

"Only because I was already watching you," he says as he takes another sip from his gilded cup, its contents sloshing around, spilling on the ground.

His words leave me cold, unsure if he's a friend or foe. I should probably assume the latter, but my gut tells me he's a friend even if he might sit on the fence.

"Why were you watching me?" I ask.

"White Flames are rare. You remind me of someone I knew long ago. With the hair, the dress, and everything, it was like seeing a ghost. She wasn't sneaky like you, but you move like her."

"Did she mean anything to you?" I ask, wondering who the mystery woman is.

"She meant a lot to everyone. But she's a ghost now, so it matters very little." He downs the rest of his drink.

"I'm sorry you lost her."

"Most people with half a brain are sorry she's gone," he says while glancing toward the throne. "They probably shouldn't have treated her like they did, or she wouldn't have made the mistake of trusting the wrong people."

"Why didn't you turn me in?" I ask, very aware he could still out me. With pockets full of jewels, I couldn't claim ignorance—maybe insanity—but I doubt it.

He gestures wildly at the snake chain that wraps around my waist. "You've already lost your freedom, and you looked like you were enjoying yourself. Those jewels these people wear are meaningless, anyway." He leans closer. "Plus, they were stolen from the previous king and queen."

I take a step back because what this man says is treasonous. Talking about the previous government is forbidden. The schools skip hundreds of years of government history and pretend Artijan started seventeen years ago. The only reason I know is because Ms. Brown rarely let us go to regular school unless it served her purposes. Instead, we were given access to books, even banned books for education. It's the only reason I know anything about our actual history. Well, that and Luna.

He inverts his cup, hoping for more liquid, but frowns at the emptiness. "Don't look so shocked. I'm old enough to remember what the world was like before all this. And unlike my fellow lords and ladies, I'm not afraid to acknowledge it."

"You must get into trouble a lot."

"While I am loyal to Artijan, I like to speak the truth." He grins, reminding me of someone, but I can't place it. "Plus, books are better companions to their company."

"Are you drunk?" I ask. In all my years in crashing elite parties, I've never heard a noble dare to speak so boldly, unless they were inebriated.

He shakes his head, then shows me his cup. The contents smell like water. "I wish, but I make sure I keep my head clear in places like this."

"Then why do you pretend you're drinking like everyone else?"

"It gets you away from conversations and people you'd prefer to avoid. An act I think you would appreciate."

I smile, because he's right. "I do."

"So tell me. Why did you take all the jewels?"

I bow my head, not sure what to say. Should I say because I'm sad about my friend? Or should I start with the plan to use this to bribe someone to get me and Luna out of here? Both explanations seem ridiculous and could get me in trouble if someone were to overhear.

"You can tell me. I have no plans to turn you in."

Anxiety rushes over me, and I bite my lip. "I don't even know your name. Why should I tell you?"

"My close friends call me Al. And instead of you telling me, how about I guess what your plans are?"

His name almost makes me laugh, because clearly he's hiding something. But he acts like he's an average guy that works at the local mechanic, rather than a lord that his outfit suggests. "Okay, Al."

"You want to bribe someone to get Luna out of here?"

I must look like a fish, my mouth is open so wide. "How did you know?"

"I may like to avoid my fellow aristocrats, but I pride myself on being observant. But I can tell you, anyone who could get your friend out of here won't take items that can be easily traced back to their owner. It may have worked in the town you come from, but it won't work while you're at court. Secrets and untraceable credits are their currency."

Not really believing he would give me an answer, I ask, "Then what would you suggest?"

He takes a deep breath, then rubs the back of his neck. "If I were in your shoes, I'd find someone that lives on the outside of court. Someone I could trust, who is sympathetic to the Forbidden." He shrugs. "Then I'd wait for an opportunity to get outside these walls before I tried to act on the bribe and plan to escape into the wilderness. Of course, you'd need someone to take off those bracelets."

"But that could take forever, and I don't know anyone who would take off these bracelets."

"Patience usually leads to better results, especially if you're on your own. To move quicker, you'll need some friends, but then you risk their lives too. And they could turn you in, or worse, use those bracelets against you."

Before I can reply, he lifts his cup to me in a salute, then saunters back to his table, leaving me alone.

I lean my head against the wall. If I could leave this party, I would, but until Gabriel is done, I'm stuck here. My gaze travels to the couple across the room. Abby's giggling with that fake laugh of hers while practically hanging off my handler. She's using every trick Ms. Brown taught her to distract him, including her outfit.

My breath hitches when I think of my former guardian. Ms. Brown most certainly would take the jewels hidden in my pocket, and she has a man in her network that would make them untraceable.

It's always a slippery slope dealing with her, but it's the best chance I have to get us out of here. Maybe with Luna gone, Zane won't have to go either. I brace myself for the conversation I'm about to have, because I know it's going to cost me. I just hope I can pay the price.

Chapter Twenty-Nine
Unfortunate Alliances

THE WORST PART OF my plan is the view.

Abby keeps touching Gabriel every chance she gets. It's borderline harassment that makes me want to puke. But this is the girl I've known since I was five years old. She's an actress that will do whatever it takes to get her audience's attention. Right now, she practically consumes his entire view with her chest. Of course, with how lifted they are, she's probably distracting the guards on the other side of the room too.

While she's attached to him, I can't talk to her, and she's my only connection to Ms. Brown that technically isn't part of this glittering world. I need a distraction that will pull them apart long enough for me to talk to her away from prying eyes. But I'm not sure how I can do this without raising suspicions from either of them.

"I didn't know he has a girlfriend," Becky says as she follows my gaze. She joins me by my pillar with Ginger on my other side.

"Apparently, Abigail is his fiancée," I say, and a bitterness coats my tongue. Just thinking about my nemesis in that way makes my stomach roll.

Ginger frowns, scrunching her face together. "He can't be engaged to her."

"That's what she called him tonight. They've apparently been seeing each other for some time."

"Definitely never heard of her," Becky says as she adjusts the lace straps on her glittering black gown. "Or seen them together."

I bite my lip, contemplating if I should tell them the truth. Ms. Brown conditioned me so well, I don't want to foil her plans, especially since I need a favor. But there is an equal part of me that doesn't want to see Gabriel hurt. I've told Zane, and Luna already knows who she is. What difference will it make if I tell Becky and Ginger?

"She's a grifter."

Ginger nearly spits her drink out, barely managing not to spill the red punch on her lavender dress. "How do you know?"

"I grew up with her in the same orphanage." Thinking back on all those months of her talking about the provincial lord's son, I didn't even connect it to Gabriel. My subconscious definitely saw all the clues, forming a fear of them being together in the arena. Watching that fear play out in real life hurts so much more than when it was my imagination.

"Does he know?" Becky asks.

"I don't think so."

"You have to tell him," Ginger says, placing her silky gloved hand on my arm. "Even though I know he would never marry her, she could still hurt him."

Confused, I ask, "How do you know he would never marry her?"

"Because he's a... ouch." Ginger rubs her arm while glaring at Becky.

"You need to stop with your gossiping." She rolls her eyes.

"No. Tell me why you don't think he wouldn't marry her."

Becky and Ginger glance at each other, then Becky says, "This Abby wouldn't meet the requirements of his station."

"But she's pretending to be of his station," I argue.

"He's destined to be with someone else," Ginger blurts out, which prompts Becky to smack her arm.

"You mean he's engaged to someone else?" I ask. It's not unheard of for nobles to promise their children in marriage from young ages for political alliances, even if it is archaic.

"Not exactly engaged, but sure, that's a close enough term," Becky supplies.

The thought of Abby wasting all her time on Gabriel almost makes me laugh out loud. It's so ironic that she'd become solely focused on him just to find out that he's unavailable. Thankfully, this bit of information is the opening I need to talk to her. Now I just need to split them apart.

"Do you think the two of you could do me a favor?" I ask as a plan forms.

"As long as it won't get us into too much trouble," Ginger replies.

"I just need you to get them apart so that I can talk to Abby. You can distract them in any way you want that won't get you in trouble."

"Shouldn't you want to talk to your handler to warn him?" Becky asks.

Squeezing the jewels in my pocket, I contemplate how much to tell them. "I want to save Luna, and Abby's the only contact I have to get her out."

"But Gabriel..." Ginger starts but trails off. "Didn't you say she's a grifter? How can you trust her?"

She isn't wrong. I can't trust Abby or, for that matter, Ms. Brown. Either of them will use my situation to their advantage. "It's a risk I have to take because I have to save Luna from the front lines." I discreetly take a bracelet out of my pocket, careful to conceal it from anyone but them. "I have something she'll answer to above all else."

"Wow," Becky says.

Showing this side of me fuels the anxiety rising inside. For some strange reason, I have a strong desire for them to accept me. Stealing is not something I'm proud of, but I did what was necessary to survive. But who would really want someone like me around?

"We really could have used you in the Dunes," Ginger replies as she hands it back. "You would have been the most popular one there."

"Seriously," Becky agrees. "They probably would have made her queen with those mad skills."

My mouth opens and closes, not sure what to say to their reaction. "You have a queen?"

"Not really, but anyone who can do that is revered because it means you can provide," Becky explains.

"And she's a White Flame," Ginger adds.

"Yeah, that too."

Thinking about the things Victoria said earlier, I realize how much I romanticized the living conditions of a place I've never seen. While living in the orphanage, I supposed everywhere seemed better than what I was dealing with. My whole life's felt alien until now, finally finding people who get me.

"Well, if you're certain that's going to help Luna escape, then we'll help you." Becky places her empty glass on a tray as it passes by. "But have you thought of the others?"

I think back to something Gabriel alluded to before. "I'm only one person. There are only so many favors I can call in."

Ginger nibbles on her lips, then whispers, "Maybe the rebels can help."

I scrunch my brow. Thinking of what happened to the town selectmen and seeing the destruction in the city, I wonder if the rebels can be trusted. Gabriel implied they were dangerous as well. Then Victoria alluded to disagreements among the Rylari. Even if they were sympathetic, some may not want to save a girl like Luna. Maybe if I were to get in touch with ones who would be willing to help, I could convince them.

"I wish I could talk to the rebels. At least the ones that might help." I toy with a gemstone bracelet in my pocket. "Maybe they could get her out of this."

"They have other things to worry about," Ginger says.

"What do you mean?" I ask.

"Because of that stunt in the city, there is talk about making the arena biannual. I think that's why the king is assigning more people to Dune sweeps." She points at me. "And you to the palace guard. That's never happened before."

"If he's planning to use their powers to find other fire wielders, keeping three White Flames here makes sense. You're the only flame class that has that ability. If you can, try not to master that ability or you'll endanger everyone." Becky pushes off the column, then stands in front of me. "The king has always been several steps ahead of everyone. Be careful while you're here. He's going to use you for something big. I just don't know what for."

Ginger elbows her. "Don't be such a downer. She's already upset about her friend."

Becky takes Ginger's arm. "Come on, let's go ask the colonel some questions."

I watch the girls walk away, whispering to each other as they head in Abby's direction. They interject themselves between them, and my former housemate's bubbly face twists in contempt. She opens her mouth to say something, but Gabriel nods, then follows Becky and Ginger into the crowd.

Taking advantage of the shock, I dash toward Abby, taking her arm in mine, then guide her out on to the balcony.

"What are you doing?" Abby tries yanking out of my grip, but I hold tight. I slip a small necklace, probably the least valuable, from my pocket and hold it up for her to see. She immediately snatches it from my hand and stops struggling to get away.

"I'm listening," she says while holding the diamonds up to the light.

"I need a favor." To avoid being overheard, I lead her away from the doors.

"From me or Ms. Brown?"

"Both of you."

"You violated your contract. I highly doubt Ms. Brown will help you at all." She pockets the necklace. "As for me, well, it would cost you dearly, because helping you now could draw too much attention."

"It's not for me; it's for Ms. Brown's favorite fire wielder."

"You want to get Luna out of her conscription?"

"It wouldn't be so difficult for a few Rylari to go missing on their way to the front lines. Ms. Brown has done it loads of times." Of course, it's rare for her to move people, and more for high valued items.

"Helping you do this could ruin my chances with Lord Caldera. So I can't help you."

"Then I'll give you some free information that you might find useful. Gabriel is betrothed to someone else."

Her eyes widen in horror, and I have to use all my willpower to keep a straight face. "You're lying."

"I wish I were, but I spent the last several months training with him." It's the truth, which gives weight to what I tell her because anyone connected to him will be in my life. Since I don't know who this mystery woman is, my future could be even worse than if Abby was in it. I don't have all the facts, but a little creative license might sway her; it's not like I'm lying. "It's an arranged marriage. If a wedding was in your plans, you'll need to alter them."

She stomps her feet. "Ms. Brown is going to be so upset. I don't even have a backup."

I take an emerald bracelet from my pocket and extend it toward her crestfallen face. "You don't have to go home empty-handed."

Her breath hitches. "You always were the better thief."

When she tries to grab it, I pull it away. "Do you agree to relay my message?"

"Besides the jewels, what's in it for me?" She laughs. "And for that matter, what's in it for Ms. Brown?"

"For Ms. Brown, she'll have her precious contract fulfilled, just not in the way she planned." Agreeing to honor the contract makes me cringe, but I don't see another option. "I'm going to be a part of the palace guard and will be here at court most of the time. And I'll be connected to the provincial lord's son she was so keen on acquiring. Surely she can figure out how she wants to exploit me from that."

"She's always wanted a palace asset. I guess she would love to have you back." Abby clucks her tongue. "But what about me?"

Like me, my nemesis wants to get away from Ms. Brown, to live a life of luxury, even if it's as Ms. Brown's asset. Most places are better than staying in the orphanage, and I suppose, on some level, I can sympathize with her situation. "I'll help you find a new target to marry."

Her eyes narrow, then she extends her hand. "This will still cost you."

I roll my eyes and start emptying my pockets, but not all of them. I have to keep a few for surviving. "There, happy?"

She eyes the pile of jewels in her hand like a kid about to dive into a cake. "This will more than make up for my failure. You have yourself a deal, Clarissa."

"Good. Get word to me about the plan through the usual channels. And I'll see what I can do."

Abby stuffs the jewels in various pockets and crevices of her enormous pink dress. Then she turns to leave. "You'll hear something by tomorrow."

"Tomorrow," I whisper. It's just a day away.

Sinking onto the bench, I hold my head in my hands, not caring that my makeup is probably smudging. It's horrible relying on a person I probably shouldn't trust, but Abby is all I have. Luna's life is in danger, and I'll do whatever it takes to keep her from the front lines. The stress of it all is getting to me. All I want to do is cry right now, which is completely unlike me. Ms. Brown conditioned me to not show weakness, but I feel so overwhelmed I just can't hold it in anymore.

"Thanks for sending your friends over to rescue me," Gabriel says.

Quickly dabbing the few stray tears away, I sit up. He stands there with a crooked smile, handsome as ever in the moonlight. The last thing I want is for him to see me like this. I suppose he's already seen me at my worst. Even so, the moment he notices my distress, the questions will begin.

"You're welcome. Though I wasn't sure the gesture would be appreciated. You looked perfectly happy speaking with Abby and, um... admiring her dress."

He studies me for a minute with those inquisitive green eyes. "I am not in love with Abby or... the dress. But I'm also not blind. She's desperately trying to marry me, but until I finish my investigation, I can't cut her loose."

"Investigation?" I ask. *What sparked his suspicions of her?*

"When a mystery girl shows up out of nowhere, you investigate. Especially when she claims to be from a noble house that no one has heard of."

"What have you found out?" My stomach twists because I know Gabriel well enough that he doesn't stop until he gets to the truth. Which means he may already know what she was doing. If he does, it could mess up my plans to rescue Luna.

"Until you came along, I had no solid leads."

My heart pounds like a drum. "You went to Ms. Brown's home?"

"Not personally. My men found Abby there scrubbing the floor, then discovered all the illegal acts being committed. My father shut it down months ago."

"Oh, no." I stand, then start pacing across the stone floor. My plan is unraveling, and it's less than an hour old. "But how is Abby here if Ms. Brown is gone?"

"My father didn't arrest any of the orphans working for her. Abby must have found a way to get an invitation. I imagine, as a grifter, getting into places is easy for her."

"But she... and I... and the jewels." I practically gave her everything I had to help me get Luna out. She pretended like everything was the same and I was stupid to trust her again.

"What's wrong?"

I toy with my necklace, trying to decide. Either I trust that Gabriel won't get so upset that he'll abandon me when I tell him the truth, or I keep it to myself and abandon helping Luna.

"Gabriel, I have to tell you something."

"Is it about Abby?"

I nod.

"What is it?"

"Promise you won't get mad at me." I clutch my stomach in the hopes it will stop flipping.

"I can't make that promise, not knowing what you did."

"Okay, but promise you won't get so mad that you'll abandon me to Ty." That's my actual fear, isn't it? Being forced to work with a man like that is one of my worst nightmares. Maybe it's because his attitude is a worse version of Ms. Brown's.

"That is a promise I can make." He stands, then clasps my shoulders. "What happened?"

"I stole a bunch of jewels."

He nods. "That's why there are pockets in your dress. I figured you'd find comfort in that activity."

Pinching the bridge of my nose, I shake my head. My handler is so bizarre. I doubt anyone else here would let me steal from the elite. I'd almost think he was against them; except he works for the king. Of course, there was the other man tonight, who was just as bizarre.

"After talking to a man named Al, I got an idea to use them as a bribe to ask for outside help to free Luna."

"Al?"

"That's what he said his name is. He's a provincial lord. I can point him out."

"I know who Al is; it's just strange hearing you casually talk about him like that." He shakes his head, holding on to me like he's afraid I'm going to bolt. "You want to free Luna..."

"Abby is the only one I could trust to get a message to Ms. Brown. I gave her almost all the jewels to bribe them to help Luna escape."

"Is that all?" he asks, his voice calm, completely the opposite of how I thought he'd react.

"Well, it was all for nothing because Abby won't help me. And now she has nearly everything I stole, and I have no way of getting Luna out. She's going to go off to die, and she's all I have."

Gabriel pulls me into his chest while I sob, brushing my hair lightly. "You're not alone, Rissa. And if you think for a second I'm not trying to stop Zane from going, you clearly don't know me well."

"But you said there were no more strings to pull to save them." I pull away from him.

"That doesn't mean I'm giving up. A colonel recently died because of the incident with the rebels. If I step into his role, then I have to choose my successor."

"You could pick Zane?" Hope flutters in my chest.

"Yes, but it won't stop his deployment, or Luna's, in time. Promotions usually take months."

Gripping the rail for support, I take a deep breath.

He stands next to me. "It's the only plan we have to get them back. There are some things I can do in my position to at least keep them at base camp, but that will require me—well, us—going with them."

My heart flutters. Remembering Al's words, my mind races to come up with a plan. If we can get outside the walls, I can use what's left of these stolen goods to get her away to freedom. "You mean we escort them outside the palace walls to the base camp?"

"The king wants you here, so it will only be for a short time, with no guarantees that it will help them."

I take his hands in mine. "Please try."

"You really shouldn't be so eager to visit the front lines, even if you won't fight. It might make you feel worse when you have to leave Luna there."

"It's better than nothing."

He lets out a breath and squeezes my hands. "I'll see what I can do."

Something possesses me, maybe it's the moonlight, but I hug him, cuddling into his warm embrace. Luna is the only other person I have ever hugged without stealing something from them. Ms. Brown would flog me for not taking anything, but I don't care. He hugs me back, and for some reason, I wish the moment would last a little longer. For the first time in a long time, I feel safe.

Chapter Thirty
Relinquish

I still can't sleep despite the plush mattress.

Light peeks in through the window, reminding me I don't have time to languish in the bed. Despite my lack of sleep, it's time to follow Gabriel's plan, which I'm still not sure about. It's a slow plan that has no guarantee of helping Luna or Zane at all. They could be dead before we bring them home. And there's also a chance for my handler's potential promotion to backfire on him, which would lead to Ty, not Zane, taking over the training center. While it wouldn't affect me or my graduating class directly, it will be a problem for all the future Rylari.

Could I live with myself if Ty hurts them? Let's hope I don't have to find out.

After crawling out of bed, I head toward the shower. Last night is hazy. The only clear moment that's seared into my mind is the king announcing our asignments. And the weird part is my best friend didn't appear devastated by the news; she almost looked thrilled after Zane whispered something to her. I wish I could talk to her alone, but Gabriel said it wasn't possible until after we get on the road.

Once I dry off, I stand in front of the closet door, examining the black uniform that will become my life sentence. I tremble slightly, a mix of fear and excitement filling me as I put it on. It fits my body perfectly, allowing fluid movement while protecting me from the elements, including my own fire. Everyone fears seeing the king's guard, and it's probably, in part, because of the way they dress. The material feels thick like leather, but softer and more flexible, like cotton. How they make them is a total mystery to me.

I tie my long hair back, braiding and twisting it to keep it from tangling, then I study my reflection in the mirror. Just like when I was wearing my ball gown, I barely recognize myself. It seems it doesn't matter how they dress me; none of it feels like me. With my dark uniform and hair, my bright blue eyes and light skin seem to glow like a dragon about to unleash its deadly breath. With a tug, I tighten my belt, then I pick up the ornate flame pin, its intricate details catching the light as I secure it to my lapel: a symbol of my status as a Forbidden.

A knock reverberates from the door. After I strap on my boots, I meet Gabriel out in the hallway. The high collar really brings out his chiseled jaw and perfectly trimmed beard; he's as handsome as ever. I've seen him in his uniform before, but today feels different. We're working together now in a sort of way, with the same goal to help our friends. The nearly identical uniforms and his demeanor toward me foster a sense of equality, conflicting with the message from my bracelet.

"The king granted my request," Gabriel says, then guides me down the hallway. I let out a slow breath, relief washing over me that our major hurdle is behind us. "We have to be ready to leave in two hours to go with the caravan."

"I thought they weren't leaving for a week. What's the rush?"

"The rebels attacked another city last night. The generals are worried they're trying to control the supply chain to the front lines. So they moved up the timeline for our departure."

"I don't blame the rebels," I blurt out without thinking.

He pulls me to a stop before the front doors, dragging me to the corner so no one will overhear us. "Be very careful what you say and do on this mission. We won't be alone."

"I'm sorry. I don't know why I said that."

"Really? Because I do." He taps my gold bracelet. "The rebels are alluring because they spin ideas of freedom, but at what cost? How many people have to die in the chaos? Because I can tell you, it's not just the Glyzul who die in their attacks. The king punishes everyone, even if they have nothing to do with it."

His words remind me of the drones that traveled through the city streets, attacking anyone that got in their way. And because of the rebel's stunt, Becky said the king was talking about making the graduations more frequent. If they hadn't attacked, Luna might have been sent elsewhere.

"You're right, but so are they. We shouldn't be slaves. No one should."

"They may have a noble cause, but that doesn't mean their methods to effect change are doing anyone any good."

"Then what would you suggest?" I ask, not really expecting an answer.

He doesn't miss a beat. "Stealth and information gathering. It would lead to the least amount of casualties."

I stare at him with wide eyes, because those are almost the exact words Victoria used last night. "Have you thought about freeing the Rylari before?"

"The king pays me for my strategy and training skills. I have to think of every scenario, and I always choose the path with the least deaths." Gabriel steps away from me when a group of trainers and lessers comes through the front door. "Come on, we need to make a stop before we line up."

"What stop?" I ask.

"We have to pick up Fireball. I don't travel that far through the wilderness without her."

We exit the building and head down the stairs. A line of people wearing yellow jumpsuits files past us in chains, blocking us from our waiting vehicle.

"This is your fault," a woman shouts.

I suck in a breath when I see Abby in line with the others. Her jewels are gone, and so is her hair, chopped short to the base of her neck. With bags under her eyes, it doesn't look like she slept all night either.

"You framed me." The weight of the chains clangs as Abby lunges with surprising speed, nearly sending the other prisoners sprawling. With a flick of my wrist, I ignite my flames, a searing white barrier hissing and crackling between us, forcing her to halt inches away.

The fire casts strange shadows on her face as she stares, a dawning realization in her eyes that I'm not the same girl who was taken months ago. It's the first time I've deliberately shown her this power, the raw energy thrumming between us like a taut string. With her lips trembling and her eyes wide with terror, she takes a hesitant step back, her hands shaking.

Her gaze shifts to Gabriel, almost pleading for help. For my whole life, I despised this girl, but now I just feel sorry for her. She may have tormented me, but she was just doing what Ms. Brown taught her, longing for someone to truly love her. Maybe if we hadn't been pitted against each other our whole lives, we could have been friends. But now I have my mission, and she'll be in prison.

"There you are, sweetie." Abby plasters on a smile like nothing has changed between her and Gabriel. "Could you please tell the nice men that this is all just a big misunderstanding?"

My handler places his hand on my arm, and I lower the flames. I'm grateful that he allowed me to choose whether to comply.

He steps forward. "Unfortunately, there is mounting evidence that you have stolen a multitude of jewels last night. And there are several eyewitnesses that name you, Abigail Martin, as a grifter."

"So has she." Abby points at me, her voice shrill.

"My lesser and her punishment for participating in Ms. Brown's crimes are none of your concern. However, if you continue with this behavior, my father will be forced to extend your sentence."

Abby sputters, making her look like a fish with the way her mouth opens and closes. With Ms. Brown soon to be behind bars, she doesn't have anyone to help her.

I sigh, hoping I won't regret this. I move in closer so only the three of us can hear me. "She won't need her sentence extended. Abby is just as much a victim as I am."

Gabriel glances at me. "Would you show her mercy?"

"Yes," my voice is wispy.

Abby's intense glare softens only slightly; she's trained like me not to show vulnerability. I know that's about as much of a thank you as I'll get.

"Then I'll message my father and have him lighten the sentencing," Gabriel nods, then waves for the guards to take the prisoners away. We leave my former bully behind and head toward our waiting transport.

Gabriel opens the door for me to enter, but I pause. I glance behind me toward the tree-lined fountain. The king stands there in his jogging clothes, his face as hard as granite. His icy gaze is fixed on me while the guards behind him shift their weight nervously, their weapons glinting in the light. The sheer weight of his presence sends shivers down my spine.

When Gabriel notices, he bows his head, then reminds me to curtsy with a subtle tap on my elbow. Despite my temporary paralysis, I follow his lead while clenching my fists. He's the one sending Luna to war.

"Bring her back in one piece, Lord Caldera," the king says. "If you do, I'll give you that colonelship you asked for."

"Yes, Your Majesty. It should be no trouble at all." He guides me into the transport, then straps his seatbelt on.

As the hovercar takes off, I can't help but watch the man in charge of a nation through the window. His steely gaze follows us until we reach the stone wall that divides his home from the world, then he turns away, continuing his morning jog.

The way he stared at me leaves me unnerved. What is the real motivation behind keeping three White Flames inside the palace grounds? I guess if I'm stationed here, I'll have plenty of time to find out.

When we arrive in our apartment at the barracks, two suitcases and three packs are waiting for us. Someone had already put my uniforms and undergarments inside. It's a strange thing having other people do things for you. I don't know how people live like this.

By the time we take our bags to the transport, several enormous black military trucks are being loaded with supplies and people. I barely get a glimpse of Luna as she practically skips toward hers, as Zane shuffles behind with their bags. He's somber, at least.

"I don't understand why she looks so happy," I say as the other Rylari enter their designated trucks.

"Some people process things differently." Gabriel shrugs, then guides me toward our transport.

"She's going to war. No one should be enthusiastic about that, especially not a fifteen-year-old."

"At least she's not caged," Gabriel says while handing me my pack as the driver loads the rest of our bags. It's extremely light, only having a few toiletries inside. Other than my necklace, I don't have any other possessions.

I'm about to get inside but freeze when I see a giant dog on the other seat. "Really?"

"I told you she's coming with us."

"But I thought she would ride somewhere else. She takes up the whole back seat."

Gabriel points to Fireball. "She's on her side of the car. I promise she'll stay unless I tell her to move."

"Really..." I trail off when I see the pepper-haired general getting into the transport in front of us. Glancing at my handler, I nod toward General Prescott.

Gabriel purses his lips, then urges me inside the waiting vehicle. "I just found out he's joining us on our excursion. With all the rebel activity, he wants to make sure everyone gets to base camp. And apparently, we're going to make a pit stop."

"Where?" After setting my pack on the floor, I buckle my belt.

"The city the rebels attacked, Tsé. General Prescott is going to deploy a new toy on behalf of the king that will weed out any fire wielder it finds, alerting the officials to their whereabouts."

I hold up my wrist with the gold bracelet. "Don't you already monitor our whereabouts?"

"For the Rylari who are caught, yes, but there is an untold number that gets past the bio-dome monitors. This device scans for your unique DNA markers, including your suspected flame intensity."

Thinking about his words, I frown. "Do you think it will detect"—I glance at the window separating us from the driver, then lean in closer—"you know, my unique flames?"

"It's possible, but your necklace might protect you from it. I won't know until we test it."

I sit back in my seat, then stare out the window as we take off for our six-hour journey. "Great."

Six hours later, we're driving through crowded city streets.

Horns blare as all the transports come to a screeching halt on the main road through town. Compared to the capital's skyscrapers and Silver City's wide avenues, Tsé city feels intimate and quiet. Only six stories high, the tallest tower offers a bleak view of the ravaged town with its crumbling top floors; a few streets, intersecting haphazardly, emphasize the extent of the rebels' destruction.

The air hangs heavy with the smell of smoke and ruin. Rubble litters the ground everywhere, forcing the people to weave between the larger pieces blocking their path. The dragon symbol is scorched into every building we pass, letting everyone know who did this. I can say one thing for the rebels: they're not subtle.

A pit forms in the bottom of my stomach the farther we travel into the city. It's like the rebels took out buildings indiscriminately, leaving poor young children and their parents out in the cold. These rebels might just be as bad as the king.

Do they just plan to tear the entire country apart to achieve their goals? Where would that leave us?

"It's weird that a city so small seems to have more cars than the capital," Gabriel says.

People hurry down sidewalks with their supplies like someone is chasing them. Even the panhandlers get up and leave their spots with all their belongings.

The panic on their faces is strange given it's been a few days since the explosions. Seeing the king's guard roll into town is unsurprisingly upsetting, and I understand people would fear another attack and want to stay in a safe place. But by the way they move, it can't just be from a possibility of something happening.

"Gabriel, something is wrong."

As soon as the words are out of my mouth, our hovercar shakes from an explosion up ahead. Fireball jumps to the floor, then sits at Gabriel's feet. Pressing my head to the window, I see a vague outline of a fiery dragon hovering above the street.

"Apparently, the rebels never left," I whisper.

Screams of terror fill the air as the citizens scatter, their feet pounding the ground, fleeing the devastation. From the buildings nearby, people clad in black hoods and masks rappel down, their movements swift and silent as they land near our transports. Their heavy boots thud on the pavement as the group moves toward our transport trucks. This was a setup to get us here.

"They're going for the Rylari," I say, my heart rate escalating as I think about Luna. *Are these the good rebels or the bad ones?*

Gabriel sighs before clutching my hand. "With General Prescott here, obey me, please, even if you don't like my orders. If you put one foot out of place during this mission, he will take you back to the capital. Then you'll have to deal with Ty. Do you understand?"

"As long as you don't force me to hurt Luna, I have no problem with that."

"Luna won't need our help, trust me."

"She's only fifteen years old. Of course she needs help."

"And you're seventeen. She didn't need you to survive the arena or any of the battle simulations. And she didn't need you to survive the Dunes." He squeezes my arm just to emphasize his point. "Let her go, stay on task, and trust she can protect herself."

"But..."

"She's got Zane and more experience using her powers than you do."

Of course he's right, but I can't help feeling protective of her. "I understand."

He nods. "Follow me."

Gabriel practically leaps from the hovercar, then rolls behind a vehicle on the side of the road, using it for cover. I follow him, the golden bracelet automatically humming against my skin as he accesses my powers. I crouch next to him, the heat igniting beneath my skin like a wildfire, flickering at my fingertips.

Behind our caravans, a hooded rebel opens the back door to Luna's transport, then ducks when flames of different intensities roar past him. Electrical pulses shoot through the opening next, as the handlers and their lessers pour out of the transport, adding to the chaos. The rebels fight back with their own flames and weapons, focusing on the leaders. The doors to the other transports following us bang open, unleashing more chaos as the remaining residents of this town flee for their lives.

Flames and laser fire shoot across the street in a dazzling display of light and shadow as the rebels fight the king's guard.

They wouldn't try to get them out unless they were the good rebels, right?

I might be stuck with Gabriel, but if I can get Luna out, I know she'll be safe.

"Don't even think about it," my handler says. "I see the wheels turning in your head, but Prescott is right behind us, watching."

Following his gaze, I see the general lounging near his hovercar, talking with one of his aides. He looks completely unperturbed by the whole situation, watching it all unfold with mild amusement. Then I remember what Gabriel told me a few hours ago.

"What does that new device do if it detects a Rylari?" I ask, my hands suddenly shaky.

His eyes darken. "Do you remember the drones from the capital?"

I nod.

"It could incinerate them if they don't have a gold bracelet on," Gabriel whispers.

As if on cue, several circular metal aircraft fly over the street, creating a deafening roar that echoes off the buildings. A hail of black iridescent laser fire, unlike anything I'd ever seen, erupts from the pursuing drones, forcing the rebels into a chaotic retreat behind the line of hovercars that were abandoned when the battle began. The handlers push their lessers forward to drive the rebels away from the transports while the drones circle behind them, blocking all escape routes.

My heart hammers in my chest, a frantic drum against my ribs, and I'm not sure I can stomach watching more Rylari die.

"Come on." Gabriel pulls me, weaving through the hovercars until we're between them.

"You're brave," Zane says, joining us in our hiding spots with Luna by his side.

"With Prescott here, I have no choice," Gabriel grunts. "What's the situation?"

Zane launches into the tactical plan and orders already given, but I hear nothing he says because I'm solely focused on Luna.

"I'm so glad you got a posting with Gabriel," Luna whispers.

"But you…"

She shakes her head. "I'll be fine. This isn't my first battle."

Someone screams up ahead, and I glance just in time to see a rebel disintegrate into tiny black flecks of dust. It takes only a few seconds for his life to end, and I think I'm about to hurl.

"It's okay." Luna pats me on the back. "He knew what he was signing up for."

Despite the setback, the other rebels circle back to take out two drones. They explode overhead, forcing us to take cover from the fallout.

"Just like the stupid arena," I mutter, brushing off the plastic pieces littering my uniform.

"It's worse," Luna says while pointing to the inky black stuff coating everything. "It looks like dead Shadow Monsters."

Zane frowns. "The king knows not to use Shadow Creature remnants, right?"

Gabriel remains silent, focusing on the middle of the street where the boy was.

"He didn't. Please tell me he didn't," Zane says.

"He did," Gabriel confirms, pointing to the pile of ash that is swirling like a tornado.

A gasp escapes my lips as the dust from the dead rebel contorts, then dissolves into an inky black human form. It liquefies for a moment before reforming into a distorted mirror image.

My jaw drops. *How do you kill something that's already dead?*

Chapter Thirty-One
Meeting Resistance

Time practically stands still.

Forgetting the battle they were just fighting, everyone stares at the fallen rebel come back to life. Black sludge drips from its body, leaving a disgusting trail in its wake. The creature is not human, but it's not really how I imagined a Shadow Monster, either. No matter how creepy it is, I can't stop staring, despite the danger.

When the drones sweep over us again, everyone snaps out of their hazy fear, remembering they were in the middle of combat. The zombie man unleashes black fire that blows up two hover cars, sending the soldiers hiding behind it flying. Its tirade of destruction continues, a deafening roar of violence that scatters everyone, the screams of the injured lost in the cacophony.

"How is the general going to stop it from killing everyone?" Zane asks.

"I have no clue. This is the first test run." Gabriel ushers us to the sidewalk on the opposite side, keeping low to avoid the fire and electrical discharges overhead.

"You've got to be kidding me," Zane says. "Testing unproven technology is..."

"Insane," Luna supplies. "It seems to follow his M.O. This tech is just another fun way for the king to control everyone."

"It doesn't matter right now," I say as the creature plows through more transports, seeking the stunned Rylari hiding from their former friend. "We need to take it out or we're all going to die."

"She's right," Gabriel says, his face contorting into the hardened look of a commander. "Clarissa, unleash your hottest flames on the fuels cell of the nearest transport. Luna, send a wall of fire around her in its general direction."

"But that will..." Luna trails off when Gabriel glares at her. "Right. The creature is more important."

Before I move to comply with his orders, I ask, "Are you sure you want my hottest flame? We're not exactly concealed."

"It's worth the risk in order to kill that thing." He points in the general direction of the rebels. "Get a little closer to them before you do it and keep hidden as long as you can. And stay away from the drones." Squeezing my hand, he takes off my golden bracelet, then says, "I believe in you, Rissa. You got this."

I nod, then follow Luna into position. The battle between the Rylari rebels, the soldiers, and the creature intensifies; crackling electricity and searing flames arc around us. A terrifying roar rips through the air, then an eruption of black flames spreads rapidly, engulfing and consuming anything in its path. The heat is intense, and the screams of the victims are cut short.

"You should hit that large transport there." Luna points toward its vehicle on the opposite side of the street, keeping low to avoid drawing attention. "The fuel tank is big enough to cause a plasma flame."

"Won't that take out the entire block?"

"The rebels already cleared the area. And most of the Rylari can handle the heat of a plasma fire." Luna ignites her yellow flames in her palms.

"How can you be sure?"

She rolls her eyes and shows off a tattoo on her heart. It's the same circular dragon figure I've seen before. "I've worked with them before, and this is a Rylari-loving town. Trust me, they cleared the block."

"You're a, but... you never told me you were part of the rebels."

"Everyone is a member of one faction or another. We can talk about it later. For now, take that thing out." She holds up her flames, ready to let them fly.

Following Gabriel's direction, I take off my necklace, tucking it carefully in my pocket, then let my flames reach their maximum strength. The heat coursing under my skin intensifies, flickering with gleeful delight that it is finally being unleashed. The glow from my hands changes from red to yellow, then climbs up to white, but it stops changing once I reach the heat levels just below blue. Only one fireball is needed, and yet I can't seem to get my fire to cooperate.

The creature reaches for a hovercar, then throws it behind him, crushing the truck that was part of our caravan. It ignites, forcing the Artijan army to scatter, including our handlers. We're alone, and it's so tempting to take Luna and run for the hills, but who knows what that thing will do to everyone if we let it live?

With a deep breath, I stand, focusing on protecting my friends from this creature the king created. I give myself over to the heat, just like

Gabriel taught me, letting the flames consume my arms. When I see Luna's wide eyes, I realize my fire is bright blue. I never told her about this side of me, but I don't get to explain because she's not the only one to notice.

The creature slithers toward us, drawn to my blue flames like a moth to the light. Clapping my hands together, I unleash the wave of blue energy toward the vehicle's fuel cell while Luna sends a wall of bright yellow flames in every direction, blinding everyone around us.

The zombie man ducks out of the way just in time to avoid the heat. The blue energy wave hits the transport, exploding it and sending a shockwave that knocks me off my feet. I land in an alleyway next to Luna as the plasma fire roars above us.

When the flames settle, I sit up, coughing from the acrid smoke billowing from the truck. From my narrow view, I don't see the creature, only twisted, melted metal everywhere.

"Did we get him?" Luna asks.

"You did," a deep voice answers behind us.

I whip around to find a hooded figure with glowing eyes standing there with a flaming lance in one hand. He takes off his hood and mask, revealing his long, braided brown hair. "So the rumors of the Blue Flame are true? You're finally revealing yourself to the world, as the old prophecies said you would."

Clambering to my feet, I ignite my flames, not sure what to do. As a soldier for the king, he's technically my enemy, but he's a Rylari like me. On both sides, though, I've seen horrific events: rebel atrocities, such as the incident with Paltos' town selectman, and the king's use of drones to kill innocent people. It makes me wonder, with a growing unease, who my true enemy actually is.

"Paytah!" Luna jumps to her feet, hugging him. "You weren't supposed to be here."

"The plans changed, little one." He hugs her back. "We can't be here with their new weapon. We need to leave now."

"But the others?" she asks.

"They'll have to leave however they can. This is your ticket out; let's go." Grabbing her wrist, he taps her golden bracelet with a device. It sparks, then he turns, and Luna follows him. I hesitate. All I wanted was to get out of here, but something prevents me from following them. Maybe it's the brutality unleashed that reminds me too much of the arena. Or maybe it's the trauma from my former caretaker. How can I trust these strangers to be different, when all I've seen is the same violence?

"You should come with us. There's much to teach you if you're going to rise to take your place among your people," he says, stepping forward with his hand outstretched. "I won't make you go, but our people have been waiting for you for a long time. You'll be safer with us than in the palace."

"How do you know all this?" I ask.

"The Dragons of Light are everywhere, including the palace. But we can't stay here. It's too dangerous with that machine."

I think about Gabriel's request to not disobey him, but then Al's words come to mind. He'd find someone on the outside the palace walls to trust and wait for an opportunity. Here, a fellow fire wielder offers me freedom beyond the confines of hunting my kind for the king's vicious sports.

"You can trust him, Rissa. I promise," Luna says.

At her urging, I nod, then run behind them through the streets. The battle spills beyond the roads where it began, cascading into smaller skirmishes throughout the city. Overhead, the drones whiz by, taking out everyone they find with their dark laser fire, including innocent Glyzul. It would sicken my stomach more if I wasn't running for my life.

"This way," Paytah says, then runs for the end of the street.

The protective dome shimmers at the city's border. We're at the last building on the street when six drones turn the corner in front of us, then spread out to block our exit. Paytah skids to a stop, and Luna and I bump into him.

"Run," he says. "I'll take care of them."

"You can't take on six of them," Luna argues.

"Blue is our main objective. Get her out of here, now." Paytah swirls his lance, igniting it and creating a circle of red flame as it twirls.

Luna shakes her head before dragging me toward an alleyway while Paytah fends off our pursuers. We've gone down several alleys before she stops to get a breath.

"Luna, what did he mean that I'm 'the main objective'?" I ask, clutching my chest.

"That day we were captured, I was supposed to bring you to Paytah. I told my friends about you and your necklace. They wanted to see if you were Rylari."

"Why would my necklace make you suspect I was a fire wielder?"

"It looks like the jewelry we have in the Dunes. Silver mixed with Sky Crystals dampens our powers. Usually, it makes us invisible to all devices, except for an actual blood test, letting us go through the country without being detected." She peeks around the corner, then quickly conceals herself again.

"So everyone in the Dunes has something with Sky Crystals?" I ask, thinking about the few times I've ever seen those special luminescent crystals.

"We have access to them. But there is a legend that a group of Rylari children went missing seventeen years ago. Each of them was gifted with special jewelry to hide their true identities before being hidden throughout Artijan. That's why I told Paytah about it."

"You think I'm one of those lost children?" I ask.

"I told you before we were picked up, you might be one. They were descendants of some of the most powerful Rylari to have ever existed. With your Blue Flames, I'm pretty sure you're one of them, maybe even a descendant of Ry herself."

Ry, I say her name internally. Glyzul rarely talk of her for fear of the king's wrath, but she is the girl that saved the world. She is the reason we celebrate Dragons Fall every year. Without her, our planet would be dead, and we wouldn't exist. Until Luna spelled it out for me, I never drew the possible connection.

Luna checks the street again. "The people are gone. We'll head out of the barrier and run for the ridge. Then we'll regroup at nightfall." She ducks around the corner and takes off running.

I put my silver necklace back on. I always knew it was a clue to my past, but I never expected it would link me to the fire wielders. Wearing it feels odd, as it hides a part of me, much like those golden bracelets. It could help me find the answers I've always searched for, like the identities of my parents.

Luna's several paces ahead of me, running at top speed. Pushing myself faster, I use my longer stride to catch up. Just as I'm about to reach her, someone grabs me and yanks me into the alleyway.

Gabriel covers my mouth as I struggle against him, then latches the golden bracelet around my wrist, cutting me off from my powers.

Zane peeks around the corner. "We're too late for her."

I scream through his hands, not understanding what they mean.

"The drones are tracking every fire wielder, including those with bracelets," Gabriel whispers. "Any Forbidden caught trying to escape are to be subdued or turned into one of those creatures. Now, are you going to keep fighting me?"

I relax and shake my head. He removes his hand from my mouth just as Luna yelps. Gabriel forces me to stay in place instead of running to her side.

"Why didn't you help her?" I ask.

"Remember when I said if you put even one foot out of line, you'll end up with Ty? You're the priority."

"Why does everyone think I'm so important?"

He squeezes my hand. "You may not believe me, but the other Rylari look up to you as a leader of sorts. Especially after the arena, and now that you used your Blue Flame in front of them, they're looking to you now more than ever."

"I don't want to be their leader."

"Then what do you want?"

"For Luna to be safe. She's all I have." Tears stream down my face.

Worry mars his features as he releases my hands. "She's not all you have, Clarissa. You're not alone anymore."

Zane clasps my shoulder. "Blue, let me handle Luna. She'll be alright, just a little dazed and locked in a cell for a while."

"That's all?" I ask.

"I promise." He guides me to the end of the alleyway, where we find her unconscious on the ground. Bright red liquid drips from her forehead. "She's had worse among the rebels, trust me."

"She's a rebel," I confirm, but saying it leaves me disillusioned. There's still so much I don't know about my people. "How did you know?"

Zane smiles. "She is one of the most wanted rebels in the entire country. I think she's committed a couple dozen felonies before she was caught."

"A fifteen-year-old? Really?"

"A fifteen-year-old girl is just a person who hasn't finished growing yet. They're still just as capable of the same atrocities as the rest of us."

"Let's get her and take her back with the others." Gabriel guides me toward Luna as the drones leave. "We need to set up camp before the sun sets."

Zane sighs. "I was looking forward to staying in a hotel one more time before being stuck at base camp for months."

"Blame the drones." Gabriel helps Zane pick Luna up and sling her over her handler's shoulders. "If they didn't make that thing, Rissa wouldn't have had to blow up half the city."

I follow the boys back to what is left of our transports. Surprisingly, the one Gabriel and I traveled in is fine, and so is the general's hovercar. Dozens of unconscious Rylari lie in the middle of the road, most with golden bracelets and some without, Paytah being among them.

"Good work," General Prescott says as Zane lays Luna with the rest. "Excellent idea, recalibrating the drones, Gabriel. Other than a few that died in the blast, I think we've recaptured everyone, plus a few more."

I glance at my handler with wide eyes. My blood boils thinking that he's the reason we were captured. Balling my hands into tight fists, I will my arms to stay glued to my side. I'm only one person. It doesn't matter that I'm a Blue Flame, I can't take on an entire regiment of highly trained soldiers and psychotic killing machines.

"Only two lessers escaped before we could recalibrate the devices. Most of the rebels made it through, except for a few." Gabriel points to Paytah. "He only showed a red flame when attacking the drones, but he was skilled, taking down five of the six drones attacking him before he finally fell."

General Prescott looms over the body. "A leader, perhaps. Maybe he was the source of the blue flame?"

"We won't know until he wakes up, sir," Gabriel says.

The general swivels around, his eyes locking with mine before they narrow. "Alright, everyone, get these Forbidden locked up, then set up camp outside the city limits. Someone commandeer a few transports for tomorrow. We leave at first light."

Standing there watching the handlers picking up their lessers unsettles me, especially when I see what's left of the reanimated rebel: a mound of goo near the still-burning transport. The rebels failed today. Not only did they fail to get me to safety, they even lost a few of their members. What's worse is their recapture was orchestrated by Gabriel.

Gabriel and Zane say my best friend is a felon, but I don't care about that. Just being a Forbidden is a prison sentence. She's been there for me when I needed someone. It didn't matter that she was younger than me. It's time for me to return the favor. If there is a way to get her out of this, I will.

"Let's go," Gabriel says, guiding me out of the city with Zane right behind us, carrying my friend over his shoulder.

After today, I'm not sure I can trust my handler anymore. I think he'll always side with his precious government. He may be the kindest of the bunch, but he still works for the enemy. I'll have to get the Rylari out of here myself, then hopefully find the rebels before we freeze to death in the wilderness.

Despite the chaos of the day, it takes only a few hours for a miniature city and a perimeter to be established outside Tsé, under the shadow of the rock formation. Those of us unfortunate enough not to be knocked unconscious were forced to construct every tent and temporary shack. And now, I'm not only upset and angry, I have blisters forming on my hands and feet.

I enter the shack designated for me and my handler, then plop on the plush cot they consider a bed. It could be worse; I could be in a tent on the ground. That's where they took the unconscious Rylari, chaining them to several metal posts they had me solder so they couldn't escape. At least I know exactly where Luna is and how to get her out of the chain, even if they put some device to block my abilities.

Gabriel enters the room. The anger I feel fuels the fire raging beneath my skin, so intense that my handler engages my power dampening cuffs to stop me from incinerating our temporary home. I refuse to talk to him; he doesn't deserve my attention. But when his dog jumps on the bed and lies down on my chest to lick my face, I have no choice.

"Ugh. Get her off me." I try to shove her off, but she doesn't budge.

"She knows you're sad, so she's trying to comfort you," he says, then taps the bed near my feet. The dog jumps off me, coiling at my feet. I scramble to sit up, but it's no use; her paws are already on my legs, pinning me gently as her head finds its place on my lap, a furry pillow.

"This is another form of chaining me here." I cross my arms and pout like I'm six years old.

"I'm sorry about Luna," Gabriel says. His voice is so quiet I almost don't hear him.

Choosing not to acknowledge him, I keep my gaze out the window. He is part of the system, the problem that keeps this cycle between the Rylari and Glyzul going on repeat with no end. I don't really want to hear anything he has to say, but I know he's going to say it anyway.

"If I could have saved her from the drone, I would have, but she was too far ahead." He brushes a hand through his hair, moving it out of place. I have to clench my fist not to straighten it. "I already knew General Prescott was coming. And I knew we were being watched. I can't..."

"You can't jeopardize your career," I say, mimicking his mouth with my hand.

"That's not fair..."

I hold up my golden bracelet, showing him my palm. With the cuffs completely cutting my powers off, I can't even heal them. "This isn't fair. Life isn't fair. Good people die at the hands of murderers and get away with it, which isn't fair either. But you know what? I'm tired of them getting away with it. I'm sick of stupid people thinking they're better than everyone else, because you're not. We're all human."

"You're right."

I don't know what I was expecting him to say, but I didn't think he'd agree with me.

"The world is unfair." He leans forward so that I'm forced to look at him. "But there is a cost for trying to change it too rapidly. Today, it cost lives. Do you think it was worth it?"

Tears well in my eyes, and I shake my head.

"There's also a cost for going too slowly. People also die in that scenario." He brushes the tears from my cheeks. "So, we need to move forward with balance. Work with the system to change it from the inside."

"I'm supposed to sit here as a prisoner and wait for people to change their minds like a good little girl?"

"No."

His answers leave me in disbelief.

"But we have to pick our battles and know when it's the right time to fight. Today, the rebels picked the wrong day, and look what it cost them." He hands me a med-kit. "I can do it if you want, but I assume you don't want me anywhere near you."

Once I take it from him, he picks up a bedroll in the corner and rolls it out.

"What are you doing?"

"Getting my bed ready." He places a pillow on the mat.

Heat rises in my cheeks when I realize there's only one bed in this room. I fell asleep next to him once, but that was an accident. This would be on purpose.

He finishes up, then glances at me. "Are you okay?"

My voice squeaks when I try to answer. I clear it. "I'm fine, just, you're sleeping in here. There's only one bed."

"lessers always stay with their handlers in case they're needed in an emergency. You know this."

"Right." My cheeks heat at the thought.

"I'd stay somewhere else, but then they'd ask why I was giving up my bed for you. It will just cause problems for both of us." He stands, then heads for the door. "I'm going to go grab us some food. I assume you're too sore to go to the mess hall?"

With sore fingers, I wiggle them at him. "You assume right."

He presses the button to unleash my flames, and I sigh at the blessed heat coursing through me, soothing the deep ache in my bones.

"I'm sorry I had to do that, too."

I know it wasn't his fault they cut us off from our flames. "You can just make up for it by giving me double portions of whatever you think is good."

He chuckles. "You trust my palate?"

"It's way better than whoever cooks at the barracks."

"Thanks. I'll be back."

Once the door closes, I open the medicine kit. It's not just basic bandages; it contains medications too. Searching through every bottle in its contents, I read each label, looking for one that might help me escape. When I find it, I smile before glancing at the dog. She looks at me with clear amber eyes, pleading with me.

"If you don't tell, I'll give you my leftovers."

She whimpers, then tilts her head.

I roll my eyes, holding up the vial. "I'll give you a quarter of my plate, and I promise I won't give you any of this."

Her ears perk up, and she smiles.

"Well, Fireball. This just might be the start of a wonderful relationship."

Chapter Thirty-Two
Fading Moonlight

I can't wait any longer.

Fireball watches me with curious eyes as I sneak out of our shack, with Gabriel snoring on the floor. I didn't give him a full dose, just enough to knock him out for an hour or two, which is all I need. He will be mad when he wakes up, but hopefully he'll understand. His promotion will fall through, leaving Zane in the middle of a war zone. That will certainly make him furious, and a part of me feels bad for that, but I'm just one person. I can't save everyone. I just hope he doesn't get into too much trouble for me leaving.

He's an enigma to me, like he plays both sides in the hopes it will bring peace. I've heard that no one can be a slave for two masters, and after the year I've had, I can attest to the truthfulness of those words. You have to pick a side, and tonight, I'm choosing to rebel, which makes the man who has helped me through so much my enemy. And I guess that was always the case, but he tore my walls down and made me believe in him.

After breakfast, the Rylari, along with their handlers, will be sent to the front lines, including my dear friend, and I may not get another opportunity to rescue her. With the sky changing colors over the eastern mountains, I know my time to rescue Luna is running short. According to what I overheard my handler say earlier, the rotations are randomized, which will make sneaking across the newly built camp even harder.

The makeshift prison where they stuffed the disobedient Forbidden is on the opposite side of the camp. Keeping to the shadows, I hurry on silent feet. Technically, as a member of the king's guard, my uniform allows me to pass through the camp without question. Unless someone recognizes me or sees my pin, I won't be questioned. But if they do, they'll escort me back to my handler, or worse, directly to the general.

I freeze when I hear rocks crunching. Just before the soldiers catch me, I duck under a transport. Holding my breath, I send up a silent prayer they don't need to enter this particular hovercraft. If they switch it on, I'm toast.

"What's the last report you read?" one soldier asks.

"About the same. No trace of the rebels so far, but they're heading into a ravine that's near impossible to get out of," the other one says.

"That's what I thought. I read somewhere that there is a flame intensity water can't touch. Isn't there a stream in there or something?" the first guy says.

"Not that again. It's just a silly fable."

"Hey. If you want the war to continue with this stalemate, then by all means, you can stay here. I just want to go home and marry my girlfriend. Then grow fat from all her cooking." I hear him pat his belly for emphasis.

"That's a good point. Maybe we should train the animals better."

"If we train them too well, they'll revolt. Better to drown them."

"And if we don't teach them to overcome the water wielders, you won't grow fat."

"True."

I grit my teeth as the guards pass by. It's not the first time I've heard such derogatory terms, but it still grates my nerves. But their report about the rebels being in the ravine is helpful. I just hope we can find them first. At the very least, they could take these bracelets off. Even if the army can track us, at least I don't have to worry about being shocked by passing through a building designed to cage us.

Crawling out of my hiding place, I weave my way through the makeshift buildings, keeping to the shadows. Unlike the bumbling soldiers, I remain silent on my feet. I go unnoticed as I jump behind anything that can hide me from their sight.

Once I reach the other side of camp, I crouch behind a stack of crates. There are several guards surrounding the shack they call a prison. Clearly, they don't trust their own building. Otherwise, they wouldn't need so many.

The Rylari trapped inside will probably have their dampening devices activated. I've noticed that the other handlers keep them that way. Since they can't access their powers until I cut those devices, everyone will rely on me. Unfortunately, I'm probably the least experienced with my flame, and the most noticeable.

I eye the encroaching light from the east as my heart hammers. If the soldiers don't move soon, my plan will fail. I search for anything that would distract the guards but come up short. Besides the mountains the camp is butted up against, we're in the middle of a valley of dry brush.

It would only take a spark to ignite the entire area. But I can't use my flame; it's too distinguishable. Twisting around to the other side, I stare at the dying flames of the night fire in the center of the camp. My lips twitch.

Stretching out my hand, I connect with the campfire. Then I move through the flames, focusing on a single ember. Altering the direction, I create a mini vortex between the cool night air and the heat. It allows the ember to rise and float on the wind.

As the glowing remnant reaches the dry brush, I remove the heat, allowing it to plummet to the ground. It only takes a few seconds before smoke rises. Within minutes, a nice little flame engulfs the area. Someone shouts as the flames grow higher. I may not be as skilled as the other Rylari, but with subtle distractions, I can do more than I realize.

I turn my attention to the prison. The surrounding guards rush to the flames like little bugs to a lamp. I could kill them with the fire, but I won't. It just feels wrong. Although, I don't think the king would see it that way.

With the guards gone, I make my move. I keep low to the ground as I approach the tent. Even though the flames are spreading, it won't take them long to extinguish it. They have fire suppressing mechanisms all over the camp, just in case one of us tries something.

Once I reach the tent, I open the front and smile. Luna looks up at me with wide eyes.

"What are you doing?" she asks.

"Getting you out of here." I pull the device I stole from the guard earlier in the day when he set it up. The heat from my powers surges through me. I send fire through the chains, and they drop with a soft clunk before I move on to the lock.

Taking out my lock pick, I get to work. Despite all the technology in the capital, this is just a standard tumbler. Just like back home, their high-tech stuff doesn't work out in the boonies. That's a bonus for me because, other than frying the thing, I have no clue how to hack that level of security.

"It's just that…" Luna looks at Paytah.

The men yell outside as more join the firefight. Several soldiers rush by the tent, and I hold my breath, waiting with fire at my fingertips for someone to walk inside.

"It's too late. We'll go while we can," Paytah says.

Luna nods. "Hurry then."

It only takes two seconds for the lock to release and the gate to open. "Keep to the shadows and head for the rock formations. There's a ravine just on the back side of camp."

Everyone rushes out, crouching as they leave the confines of the makeshift prison. Shouts echo from around the camp as the fire spreads. It won't be long now before everyone's awake.

"Hurry," I say as the last captive leaves.

Following behind them, I weave around the buildings. If we can make it to the outcrop just outside the camp before they discover we're gone, I know we'll be fine. Our captors won't be able to find us if we disappear into the wilderness.

Once we're far enough from the tent, we pause behind a transport that looks like it was built to haul produce. The soldiers are almost through putting out the fire. If we're going to make it to the outcrop, we need to get out now. I go to pull Luna along, but she shakes her head.

"No. We have to go that way." She points toward the fire, a path that leads to the city.

"Are you crazy? We'll get caught if we go that way."

She bites her lip as she glances at Paytah, waiting for his instructions.

Paytah shrugs. "She's right, little one. We can't go that way now. Let's go past that rock, then we'll loop around."

We crouch as we run across the open space. Once we're far enough away, I sprint. The cool air whips across my face as I pump my arms. With my heart pounding in my ears, I barely hear the alarm ringing behind us.

"Come on." I wave to everyone, not bothering to stop our trajectory. We have to keep moving until we're past that massive rock, no matter what.

The whirring sounds of hovercrafts roaring to life fills my ears. It's at that moment I realize they're going to find our trail. Almost twenty teens and a few rebels running through dry grass are bound to leave a mark. But there's nothing I can do about that now. If I try to burn anything, it will only lead them to us, and we need every minute we can get.

We're almost to the safety of the outcrop when the first bullet whizzes by my head. I almost pause in shock, but Luna pushes me forward. The soldiers never use ammunition on us. They usually opt for the stun guns. As soon as we're behind the first peaks, I let out a breath.

"We can't stop now, little ember," Paytah says.

"I saw a stream on the map that heads further into the hills. If we follow that, I'm sure we can lose them."

He purses his lips. "That would take us too far away."

"We'll we can't stay here either," Luna replies.

"Alright. We head up the stream until we lose them. Then we head south." He rallies the others and heads down the hill.

"Why are you so determined to go the other way?" I ask as we follow the rest of the group.

"It's a long story. Once we're not being chased, I'll explain."

Despite our distance, I can hear the hovercrafts echoing off the rocky cliffs. It won't be long before they find us. Paytah locates the stream quickly, then crosses to the other side, where there isn't a definite path. It will be difficult for the guards to find us in the low light.

Once everyone is on the other side of the stream, we hurry to conceal ourselves within the brush. It's just in time, too, because the guards swarm the outcrop overhead with their electrical discharge guns activated. The electric light swirling around them almost makes them look like aliens ready to invade the planet.

"We can't move forward with this large of a group," Paytah says. "Let's split up."

"How are we going to split up in this narrow ravine?" I ask.

"She has a point," Luna says. "We'll have to keep moving together."

"We better hurry. The sun is almost up, and we'll lose our advantage," someone says.

Paytah grumbles. "Okay. But if we have to run for it, this half moves to the east side of the stream. The rest stays to the west. Having two tracks to follow will divide their energies."

I roll my eyes. Even though he has a point, I don't think it will work. I've worked too closely with Gabriel to know two tracks won't confuse them. They'll hunt us down, no matter the cost, and they have those death drones. But I don't voice my thoughts; there's no point right now.

Concealing ourselves within the brush, we make the slow journey up the stream. Every sound echoes off the rock, amplifying it for everyone in the area to hear. Even though the guards are on the other side of the ravine where the path is, I worry they'll find us.

"Found it," a soldier says.

I don't have to be a genius to know what they found. Without a word, everyone picks up the pace. A hovercar passes by on the other side of the stream, shining a light into the bushes. It forces us to pause, crouching low to the ground.

"I didn't know those would work here," I admit. A gnawing sensation wrecks my stomach, and I'm starting to regret my plan.

"They keep extra mag packs on them. It allows them to go over any terrain to hunt us," Paytah replies.

As soon as the light passes us by, we hurry deeper into the ravine. Based on the flashing lights, more soldiers have joined the search, surrounding us on all sides. They're cornering us.

We run through the bushes and over rocks as fast as we can without being spotted. There's one more outcrop we have to pass before an incline that leads to the top. It will be tricky, especially with the sun rising.

When we pass the next group of boulders, I hear the unmistakable grumbling growl I've come to know so well over the last year. I freeze, knowing what will happen next. Fireball comes loping up to me with teeth bared. My hands go up, knowing better than to do anything else when she's like this.

"Go," I say to Luna.

She hesitates. "You can't stay, Clarissa."

"If Fireball is here, then Gabriel isn't far behind. Your only chance is to leave me."

"They'll kill you." She tries to tug on my arm, but the Shepherd growls louder. Luna wisely steps away from me with a crease in her brow. "What do you know that I don't?"

I close my eyes, resigning myself to my fate. "Just go."

When I hear the soft pads of her feet marching away with the others, I open my eyes only to find Fireball sitting right in front of me. She's almost grinning, like she's happy to see me. That's when I realize who's behind me.

He says nothing, tossing a treat to the dog before turning me around so I have to face him.

His green eyes are marred with red veins, a product of the sleeping aid I slipped into his food. From the hardness in his features, I can tell he's upset, but not as angry as I assumed. He almost looks confused.

I put my hands out for him to cuff me, but he doesn't do it. It's more unnerving when he's like this because I can't figure out what he's thinking.

Tired of waiting for him to do something, I let out a huff. "Will you just get this punishment over?"

"Why'd you stay behind?"

I point at the dog. "Gee, Gabriel I don't know."

He scratches the dog's ears, causing her to moan. "I told you multiple times, Fireball won't hurt you."

"You could have fooled me."

His lips twitch, but they don't turn up like I'm used to. He's definitely upset, but it's mixed with another emotion I can't quite figure out. As the sun peeks over the horizon, I see the sadness filling his gaze as he turns his attention toward the back of the ravine.

"What's wrong?"

He glances behind us, avoiding my eye contact. "Most of them will never make it out of this canyon."

My stomach drops when I see a hovercar with snake insignia flags is barreling toward us.

"I just had to get to you first." He clutches my wrist, turning on my power dampening device. The cold seeps into my bones, pulling the warmth from my body, and I shiver uncontrollably.

"Keep her here, Fireball." He leaps across the stream, then salutes General Prescott when he steps out of the car.

The dog complies by sitting on my feet. When I try to wiggle my toes, she growls. I sigh and resign to obey my furry warden. At least she's keeping me warm.

The general surveys the land with his icy, narrow eyes. "Status."

"We've corralled them at the end of the canyon. They're headed toward the waterfall. There's a small incline they can crawl up," Gabriel says.

Another soldier hands the general binoculars. He glances through them for a moment before handing them back. "Shoot them."

"But..." Gabriel tries to object.

"You have your orders, Colonel." He pulls his gun from his side, but pauses when he sees me. "What is that doing here?"

"She's a White Flame. She can track them," Gabriel answers.

The general grunts. "Right. Bring it with you."

Gabriel glares at me before whistling at Fireball. The dog growls at me, then shoves me forward with her head. I don't resist her, instead taking my place by Gabriel's side. He grabs my arm, ushering me forward to follow the general and his men.

"Do not say a thing," he warns.

I nod. With the general so close, I don't want to disobey him. They have guns with bullets this time, their electrical guns sitting in their holsters. I pray Gabriel is wrong and my friends escape before we reach them. If they don't, I don't know how I'm going to live with myself.

We weave around the stream, and then General Prescott points at me. "Show me their path."

A lump gets stuck in my throat. I haven't practiced this ability. It's easy to track Luna because I already have a connection to her, but I don't know if I can track the others and I definitely don't want to show him where they're going.

He points the gun at me, and I shake. "Fix it Colonel, now."

"It will be alright," Gabriel whispers, then pretends to turn my cuff on. "Sorry, General, I forgot I deactivated her powers."

He's so close, I almost want to step closer to keep warm. "Hold your hand in front of you and walk forward. The rest will follow. Just remain calm."

Gabriel stays by me as I walk forward, guiding me, sometimes taking a longer path than the one I can see they took.

"There," a soldier says, then discharges his weapon.

I hold my ears to protect them from the deafening sounds echoing off the canyon walls. Even though I can't see the Rylari, I can hear their shoes crunching in the brush as they run. More shots ring out as my friends run.

"It might be better if you stun them," Gabriel says over the noise.

"They're deserters," General Prescott says. "The punishment is death."

"True, sir. But it's easier to send energy discharges through the brush. And His Majesty requested reinforcements."

The general grunts before putting his gun away. "Fine. Knock them out. We'll kill the leaders back at camp; the rest will be flogged."

The guards swap their guns for dischargers, then run after them. Gabriel and I follow behind. The furry creature keeping me in line stays beside me, nudging my legs forward every few steps.

Electrical pulses cascade in front of us, illuminating the shadows long enough to get a glimpse of the kids running ahead of us. It doesn't look like the entire group. If they stuck to Paytah's plan, the other half would be on the far side of the stream. Maybe his instincts to split up were right, but I wish I knew where Luna is.

My heart drops when one of them goes down. The group keeps sweeping the entire area with electrical discharges. More cries echo when the Rylari are hit, followed by a thud. With each kid captured, fear wells up in my stomach.

Searching as best I can in the morning light, I try to find Luna's curly bob. We find nothing. Beside me, Gabriel sweeps the area with more discharges. If I wasn't trapped between him and his dog, I'd run in the opposite direction. It might at least distract them long enough for the others to escape, but I'm not given that luxury.

As soon as I think about it, I find Luna in the dwindling group. She's taking the lead up the incline. Before I can register what's happening, a loud bang pierces my ears. Luna drops to her knees. Her body lists to the side before she rolls a little way down the hill. General Prescott's gun emits curls of smoke, the air heavy with the smell of gunpowder.

My body is numb, and I nearly collapse. Gabriel wraps his arm around me, keeping me supported. My sorrow echoes back to me from the surrounding cliffs. Luna is gone, and there is no way to bring her back.

Luna is gone. Her body sits alone on the hill in a growing pool of red blood. I don't know where the rest of the group is because all I can see is my friend. All our special moments we've had for the last few years flash before my eyes. I'll never get to see her again, and it's all my fault. If I hadn't brought her here, she might still be alive.

"Shut that thing up," General Prescott says.

"I'll take her back to camp. She's served her purpose here," Gabriel says, his voice hard.

He tries to pull me away, but I fight him, wanting to get to Luna's body. I have to see her; maybe I can heal her with my powers. I have that gift, and what good is it to have if I can't use it to help my best friend?

"What is wrong with your pet?" he asks.

Gabriel braces me against his chest. "That girl was from the same town."

"Interesting." His gaze slides to Luna like a snake, and I half wonder if he knew it would hurt me. "Get her out of here."

"Yes, General," Gabriel replies.

He picks me up, placing me over his shoulder to carry me back to my gilded cage. While upside down, I watch the soldiers round up the other Rylari they caught. They force them to the ground, then string their hands together behind their back. My only consolation is that they didn't get everyone. In the chaos, several made it to the top of the mountain. And hopefully, Paytah and his group are far away from here.

The road takes us behind the brush, masking the deadly scene. Tears stream down my face as I hang limply over my handler's shoulders. We pass the general's hovercar, reminding me I'm not the one who shot my friend. I'm not entirely responsible for this massacre. Luna is dead because of that maniac with a vendetta. He shot her when he didn't have to.

"Can you walk?" Gabriel asks with labored breaths. He sets me down despite my non-answer.

"Listen, we need to get back to camp as fast as possible to minimize the damage to the lessers. I'll carry you if I have to, but don't make this more difficult than it has to be."

Finding my bearings again, I say, "I have to help her—"

"She's gone, Clarissa. You can't help her now."

"Luna was my only friend. She deserves a decent..." My voice trails off as the image of her falling to ground fills my thoughts.

"I know what it's like to lose a person close to you. It's one of the worst things that can happen to someone." He brushes his messy hair out of his face. "It's worse when it's your fault."

"What do you mean, it's my fault?"

"You broke them out. What did you expect?"

"I expected to set them free."

He shakes his head. "Sweetheart, that would never happen. Not when the general had set a trap for the rebellion."

I'm taken aback, not understanding what he's saying.

"Why do you think we're here, Rissa?" He points to the top of the cliffs where guards stand with remote controls, sending out drones into the ravine. "With the rebels' attack and the general here, patrols are covering this entire area in all directions for several miles. Are you really that naïve?"

"I..." His words pierce my heart.

He steps closer, wiping the tears from my face. "Be glad I can save some of them. And I'm sorry I can't save her. I don't have the power to bring someone back from the dead."

"Why do we have to be slaves to you?" I ask, taking a step back. "That's the real injustice here."

"Because that's how the world works. And for now, we just have to live with it." He whistles to his dog before heading toward camp.

Fireball nudges my legs, forcing me to trudge forward.

I guess this is my life now. Forever at the mercy of Gabriel's whims. But as Luna's last moments play on repeat in my mind, anger stews in my heart. I'll make the general pay for her death if it's the last thing I do with my life. I just need to find someone to help me, because there is no way Gabriel is going to trust me now.

Chapter Thirty-Three
Ascending

Gabriel was right about the king. If one person steps out of line, everyone suffers the consequences. As soon as we arrived at the palace, I was thrown into the dungeons. Regardless of his support or the others' presence in the capital, all the Forbidden across the nation remain imprisoned, permitted out only for manual labor, including me.

Luna's death replays endlessly in my mind as I gaze at the ceiling, my lumpy mattress pressing into all the wrong spots on my back. My stomach twists with guilt, or hunger, or maybe it's both. They don't feed us while we're down here; it's part of our punishment. It could be worse. I could have been flogged like the others at camp who tried to escape.

At least three died during the escape, including Luna. Half of the Rylari were captured and severely punished. General Prescott made me and the other more seasoned lessers watch from chairs in the front row. Their cries of pain still keep me up at night, almost as much as Luna's death. If it wasn't for Gabriel, the general probably would have forced me to administer the punishments.

Light filters through the tiny window at the top of my cell, letting me know another day has passed by. Rolling over, I ignite my finger and burn a mark into the wall. There are twenty in total. That means Luna's been gone for almost a month. She had a family, that much I know, but I never met them. They won't get her body back for a proper funeral, so she'll likely be left in an unmarked grave somewhere. It breaks my heart, but I know I can't focus on those thoughts anymore.

The last I heard, other escapees and rebels were never found, including Gregory and Paytah. Their safe escape is my only hope; otherwise Luna died for nothing.

I throw off the covers and start my workout. I don't remember how many times Ms. Brown threw me in the basement back home, but this room, which barely lets me stretch to my full length between the walls, feels like home.

Starting with sit-ups, I count them off as I think of Luna. Once I got here, I had a private memorial service for her, etching a likeness of her into the wall with my flames. It's not great, but at least it's something to keep me focused.

Someone wails in another room, but I ignore it as I work on my core muscles. The other Rylari have cried the entire time we've been down here, their voices carrying through the thick walls, especially Victoria and Serene. They're not suited to life like this, but in a way, I am. I'm hardened by years of authoritarian rule with harsh punishments from a lady claiming to be my guardian. The others had hard lives too, but they have family that loves them. My family just loved me for what I could do for them.

It makes me thankful to my former guardian, wherever she is. If it wasn't for her, I'd be going out of my mind right now, especially with Luna's death playing on repeat every time I close my eyes. Her strange methods of training me keep me focused in the dark moments, giving a false sense of safety while locked in this cold, damp prison under the palace, when I feel anything but safe.

"Cleaning time," the guard says as he opens the door. I narrowly avoid being hit by the bucket and brush thrown in my direction.

I pick it up and follow him to whatever room I'm cleaning today. It's the only time I'm allowed outside my cell, a brief respite from the stale air and echoing screams. He guides me to a dark room and shoves me through without turning on the lights. I ignite my flames, then search for the switch. When the light comes on, my breath hitches, because it feels like I'm back in Ms. Brown's orphanage, just with fewer flowers.

Taking the bucket and brush, I get on my hands and knees and start scrubbing the tile floor. I hate chores. I really do. But right now, I'll take the physical activity over staring at the ceiling and remembering my friend's bloody body. It doesn't take me long to get into a steady rhythm, moving my way through this ornate receiving room.

After a few minutes, I almost hear that stupid song Ms. Brown would play all day long. Even in the silence of this beautiful place, it invades my mind again, annoyingly talking about a brighter tomorrow. I've heard the tune so much, my brain has become its own disc player. The only problem is it reminds me of my former home and Luna.

After sitting on my heels, I smack my head as if it will shove the intrusive thought out. This activity is supposed to dull my pain, not force me to relive it. I get enough of that in my cell.

Growling in frustration, I recite the anatomy of the human body from memory as I continue with my cleaning. I bump into a table at least a quarter of the way through cleaning. A piece of paper falls in front of me, and a round, gold metal object clangs on the tile floor.

Setting my cleaning brush aside, I grasp the tiny paper and read it. It's blank, but on instinct, I ignite my flames, revealing an iridescent ink.

You in, Blue?

My gaze is firmly glued to the words on the strip of paper. Only the Rylari call me Blue—well, and Zane, but he was only copying them. I pick up the tiny golden pin, turning it over in my hand. It's a golden dragon, its wings spread in flight: a symbol of the rebels. It's just a little different from the coiled one Luna sported.

With my heart pounding in my throat, I consider its meaning. Dragons of light, Paytah called them. It's literally what the term Rylari stands for. Despite their noble cause, Gabriel is right. They cause a lot of destruction, which freezes me with indecision. I glance at the paper again, then flip it over.

We'll be in touch.

The paper bursts into flames, eating away at the message within seconds, leaving only ashes for me to pick up. It's so cryptic. How will they even know if I accept their invitation?

Paytah said they had spies in the palace, so maybe they're watching my reaction. It's unlikely, but clearly they knew I was going to be cleaning in here today. My eyes dart around the room, searching for hidden devices, but I don't see any.

I tuck the pin in my pocket before I continue with my cleaning. If I'm not done within an hour, they'll make me scrub the bathrooms. I'll take the living room floor over cleaning a toilet any day.

The time flies by as I turn the message over in my head multiple times. In some sense, locking me in the prison is good for me. It's given me a lot of time to think. Luna was part of the rebellion, and in the end, it got her killed. It makes me wonder if Gabriel is right, and the rebels need to move slower.

I blow out a breath as I finish, nowhere near the certainty of what I should choose. My path was so clear before: do anything to save Luna. Without her, I feel lost, only able to focus on the task I'm assigned.

After collecting my things, I knock on the door, and the guard escorts me to my cell. I eye him, wondering if he's the one who left the message inside, but it's not like I can ask him. Even if he did, I doubt he'd admit it inside the palace or really anywhere in the middle of his enemy's home without precautions.

He shoves me in my cell, locking the door behind me, leaving me in the prison of my mind. Which is much worse than being confined to this reality. I sit on the floor staring at the burned drawing of Luna, wondering what we would be doing right now if none of this ever happened.

It's a silly thought because my friend kept a lot from me. If what Gabriel and Zane told me was true, the girl who I called a friend took part in multiple insurgencies and never told me. I didn't even know she had a tattoo marking her as a rebel. Was Luna even her real name?

I take the rebel pin out, flipping it over in my hand. Luna would tell me to embrace the rebels and be part of their network. She told me to trust Paytah, and that every Rylari was part of a faction of rebels. She would probably tell me it's worth it to die rather than staying in this situation. But something holds me back from committing to her ideals. My medical training instilled in me a preference for non-violent conflict resolution, maybe that's why I hesitate.

Curling against the cold, damp wall, I lie on my side, wishing Fireball were here to keep me warm. Even with my flames constantly blazing inside me, the temperature in the cell is too cold for a Rylari. The rags they've provided me with barely cover me, making the cold that much worse. If they don't turn up the heat soon, they might lose all of us, but maybe that's the plan.

The pounding of boots outside the door wakes me up from a deep sleep. I don't know when I dozed off, but there's a kink in my neck from the awkward position.

"She's not usually awake yet at this hour, sir," the guard says.

Quickly, I tuck the pin inside my pocket, then pull up the covers from my cot to give me some sort of modesty.

"I understand, Private," Gabriel says, making my heart flutter. I haven't seen him since I was imprisoned, but if he's here, maybe I'll be getting out of here soon.

"She's right in here," the guard says. "And congratulations on your promotion, sir. Quite an accomplishment becoming a Colonel by twenty."

"Colonel?" I whisper as the door opens.

The guard moves out of the way, revealing the green-eyed man with an angular jaw and a scruffy beard that I've become so familiar with over the last year. His cloak billows behind him as he enters, filling up the entire space. He stares at me for a moment before crouching in front of me.

"Since you did such a good job tracking, the king needs us to track some more rebels," he says, then helps me to my feet. I wobble a little, but he steadies me.

We both know that's a lie. I didn't help them track anything. In fact, he had my dampening cuffs turned on. I didn't use my powers, but Gabriel led me through that desert terrain in a weird zig-zag pattern, as if I was using them.

He drapes a cloak over me, enveloping me in a warmth that I haven't known in weeks. I limp out of the cell with pins and needles prickling my feet. It's probably from lack of proper food and sleep deprivation.

My handler stays right behind me, his arm hovering near my back, but never touching me. I don't like to show weakness, and he knows it. Otherwise, he'd probably just pick me up and carry me to my room.

We reach the desk where General Prescott and his son are waiting. Ty's eyes rove over my bare legs, and if I wasn't weak from hunger, I'd punch him with a fire fist. Gabriel steps between us, nodding before we step outside.

I have to shield my eyes, the sun is so bright. While I've been to places throughout the palace, none of my routes involved me going outside.

"Sorry, this is the quickest path to your room."

"My room?" I ask.

"Yes. I figured you'd want to take a shower first before we head into the city."

He guides me across the courtyard, and the needle feeling in my feet subsides with each step, making it easier to walk. His new pip glistens in the morning light.

"So you got your promotion?" I ask.

"Yes, no longer a Lieutenant Colonel. Zane got a promotion too."

My heart sinks, because in the end, Gabriel's way of getting his friend back from war worked. It's frustrating to think if I had just been more patient, I might have my friend here with me.

"It's not your fault, Clarissa." He keeps his distance from me, probably worried about the optics in the daylight.

"That's not what you said at camp."

"You should have listened to me and not tried to escape. My criticism may have come out a little harsher than I intended, but I was upset by the situation and drugged with sleep meds." His eyebrows lift, causing the heat to rise in my cheeks. "But your friend had just died. You were upset, too. In the grand scheme of things, Luna's death wasn't entirely your fault. There were a series of miscalculations that lead to her being killed."

"But I had a hand in it." I can't conceal the bitterness in my voice.

"So what if your mistake contributed to Luna's death? Instead of wallowing in it, learn from it. Move forward and don't make the same mistake again."

I fidget with my hands. "It's easier said than done."

"You're right. It is easier to say the words, but it's doable. I haven't gotten this far in life without hitting bumps in the road. And yes, people have died under my command. Death doesn't get easier, but it can make you more resilient if you let it."

We arrive at my building and proceed to the room that was mine a month ago. The familiar doors come into view, and I sigh when we enter. It's warm compared to my previous accommodation.

"And how do I let it make me more resilient?" I ask, then take off his cloak.

"The past can't hurt you anymore because it's behind you, don't live in it. Stretch forward to the future, but don't live there either. Stay in the present, and trust that everything you do or whatever happens to you is just part of the process of becoming the person you need to be."

"Then I guess I better decide who I want to become." I take my uniform and head for the bathroom. "Or will that be decided for me, too?"

He takes a seat by the window. "You know I won't do that to you."

I stare at him a moment before closing the door. While I doubt he'd intentionally hurt me, I'm uncertain whose side he'd take if pressured by his superiors.

Once I wash away the grime in the warm shower that chases the last chill away, I dry off then stare at myself in the mirror. I've lost a lot of weight in a month. My eyes are sunken in, my face is a little gray, and my collar bone is sticking out a lot more than I'd like. But I'm still me, just a little more hurt than before.

I pull on the uniform and lace up my boots while thinking of Gabriel's words.

What sort of person do I want to be?

After braiding my hair, I stare at the two gold pins on the countertop. One is a flame, the other a dragon. Technically, I'm both. But no one can be a slave for two masters, at least not in their heart.

Picking up the flame pin, I stick it on my lapel, marking me as a Forbidden in the king's army. Then I pick up the dragon pin and recall Luna's rebel tattoo. That was who she was: a person willing to do what it took to win the freedom of the Rylari. Maybe it's because I lived my life as if I was a Glyzul that I hesitated before. What better way is there to honor a lost friend than to pick up their cause?

A smile touches my lips as I secure the pin inside my uniform near my heart, hidden from everyone but me. For the first time, I wonder if tomorrow might just be a little brighter.

Want to know what happens next? Pre-order *Rebels Spark*, Book 2 now! Click here to buy!

Remember that moment when Gabriel met Clarissa in chapter three. Want to read what he was thinking for free? Download your bonus scene here!

Want to know what happens next? Pre-order *Rebels Spark*, Book 2 now!

https://buy.bookfunnel.com/nz6wbztz04

Remember that moment when Gabriel met Clarissa in chapter three. Want to read what he was thinking for free?

https://bookhip.com/VBMRWQM

Grab your Books
- https://www.sarawrightbooks.com/
embercrownbackofbook

Thank You for Reading Rising Ember

https://www.sarawrightbooks.com/e mbercrownbackofbook

Thank you again for being part of this journey.

~Sara Wright

Also by Sara Wright

Dystopian Fantasy Series

The Ember Crown
Dangerous games. Kill or be killed. Can she survive a king's ruthless arena?

Space Fantasy Series:

The Progenitor Chronicles

A secret long held. An insidious plot ready to hatch. Shattered and alone, can this kind-hearted royal rise to become her people's heroine?

Scan to explore all my series!

Acknowledgements

Writing one book is hard enough, but completing an entire series is wild. I've been looking forward to this second series for a longtime. These characters lived in my head for years, and they've slowly reshaped themselves into extraordinary characters that I admire.

I couldn't have published this book without the generous support of my fellow authors, who shared their knowledge and experience of the publishing world. There's still so much to learn, but I'm grateful for the wisdom I've gained.

Thank you to my husband for inspiring this story during one of my worst headaches. Without your help, the fire wielders wouldn't exist.

To everyone on the Wright ARC and street teams, thank you for sharing and supporting all of my books. Your encouragement means the world to me. I'm especially grateful to those who took the time to leave reviews. Without dedicated readers like you, these stories would never have reached as far as they have.

To my beta readers: your feedback was invaluable. This story was rewritten several times before I found the right balance, and your insights helped shape it into what it is now.

A heartfelt thank you to my editor, Angela, my editor. You truly made this story shine. I appreciate your insight and support.

Mom, thank you for feeding my imagination. Your support, both when I was a child and now as an adult, means everything to me. You're the best mom in the world. I love you.

Thank you to Mandi for your many publishing tips and courses. Without your class, I might not have released this book on time.

Thank you to the Best Page Forward team for helping me with the technical side of publishing a book. There are so many moving parts it's difficult to keep track of them.

Last but not least, to my friends and family who read this book—I love you guys. I'm truly grateful for your support.

"Telling a story in a futuristic world gives you this freedom to explore things that bother you in contemporary times."

~ Suzanne Collins

sarawrightbooks.com.

About the author

Sara Wright writes dystopian fantasy set in futuristic, broken kingdoms where courage is tested, hope is dangerous, and survival is never guaranteed. Her stories blend fantasy, sci-fi, and clean romance into high-stakes adventures where characters must rise against oppressive regimes.

From a young age, imagination was her constant companion, sparking vivid visions of distant realms she would one day turn into epic tales. You'll often find her singing along to her favorite music while channeling that creativity onto the page.

When she isn't dismantling corrupt monarchies or unraveling elemental powers, Sara enjoys hiking through real-world vistas and eating delicious allergy-free foods with her husband and their furry companions.

Connect with Sara:

www.sarawrightbooks.com.